She awoke in the [...] she had no idea [...] hot, so hot she was sweating. She sat up and sniffed the musty air. She could smell smoke. She swung her legs out of bed, stood up and groped along the wall, trying to find the light switch. Then she remembered. She fumbled on the floor and found the candle.

No matches. She'd left them downstairs.

She opened the bedroom door. The landing was thick with smoke, hot choking smoke. She couldn't see a thing. She blundered straight into the wall and gave her head a painful crack. She felt her way to the edge of the staircase and began to descend, slowly, blindly. The smoke got thicker. She was coughing. She began to panic. She was so desperate for breath by the time she reached the bottom of the stairs that she flung open the front door and stumbled outside into the rain, gasping in the fresh air. She took a deep breath and went back inside, into the sitting room.

Philip Trewinnard

THE BURNING

GOLLANCZ HORROR

First published in Great Britain 1995
by Victor Gollancz
An imprint of the Cassell Group
Wellington House, 125 Strand, London WC2R 0BB
First Gollancz Horror paperback edition

© Philip Trewinnard 1995

The right of Philip Trewinnard to be identified as author
of this work has been asserted by him in accordance with
the Copyright, Designs and Patents Act, 1988.

A catalogue record for this book is
available from the British Library.

ISBN 0 575 06057 3

Typeset in Great Britain by
CentraCet Ltd, Cambridge
Printed and bound in Great Britain
by Cox & Wyman Ltd, Reading, Berks

*This book is sold subject to the condition that
it shall not, by way of trade or otherwise, be
lent, resold, hired out, or otherwise circulated
without the publisher's prior consent in any
form of binding or cover other than that in which
it is published and without a similar condition
including this condition being imposed on
the subsequent purchaser.*

For Sally, with my love

ETHAN PIERCE

On the southwestern tip of Cornwall, a narrow B road snakes its way around the jagged coastline from St Ives to Land's End. Not far from the hamlet of Zennor, a quiet lane angles off this road and wanders inland as if by accident. It meanders across the West Penwith moors and down through the quiet valley of Nansgever, beneath the shadow of Carn Ewyn – a curious pile of rocks that stands on top of Trevow Hill, the highest point of the Land's End peninsula.

There was once a tin mine here on the lower slopes of the hill. All that remains of it now is a tumbledown Victorian engine house that stands oblivious to the gales and rain, like something that was shattered by artillery in a long-forgotten war, its crumbling walls lapped by an encroaching sea of yellow-flowering gorse and deep green bracken. The miners who worked there built their homes in the Nansgever valley – small cottages with low lintels and scantle-slate roofs and walls a yard thick. They are now the holiday homes of wealthy upcountry folk, prettified with flowery fabrics and suburban stripped pine, left dark and cold all winter long.

The high land is gaunt and rugged, treeless for the most part, bristling with gorse and heather, swept by gales in winter and whole weeks of driving rain. On still days, fog creeps in off the ocean and can shroud the moors in cold and secrecy for days on end. But the Nansgever valley is sheltered, marshy in places and lightly wooded with osier, hawthorn, spindle and guelder rose. There is a shallow stream that babbles around the foot of Trevow Hill and later joins the Red River, which flows down to Mounts Bay at Marazion. A wide track angles off the valley road, and leads past a small cottage, beyond which it narrows sharply, crosses the stream and becomes a mere footpath that zig-zags up the steepest side of Trevow Hill to Carn Ewyn.

This cottage is called 'Crowjy'. It looks quite old – the walls go back to Tudor times, five hundred years or so – but it has not been a cottage for very long. In the 1920s it was a mere hay barn. And the winding valley road from Zennor was no more than a rutted track, barely the width of an ox-cart.

In the early spring of 1926, a courting couple strolled hand in hand along this valley road one Sunday afternoon. The young man was an apprentice carpenter from the nearby hamlet of Towednack. He was twenty years old. His name was Ethan Pierce. His girlfriend was the daughter of a cowman who worked at Trevow farm on the south side of the hill. She was just seventeen. Her name was Annie Carkeet.

It was mid-April. Spring had come early that year and the peninsula was basking in sunshine that weekend. Ethan and Annie walked off the valley road and up the track towards the barn. They stepped inside, into the sweet-smelling half-dark.

Annie would remember how cool it was in the barn when they first lay down – cold even, despite the warmth of Ethan's body and the passion of their kissing. She would remember gooseflesh on her arms and the rough caresses of his strong calloused hands. She would recall the scratching of the hay on her flesh and the sudden stab of pain as Ethan entered her, the faint gasp he emitted, his teeth clenched and eyes screwed tight. And then the full weight of his body on hers, pressing her down into the prickly hay. She would recall no pleasure, just the rhythmic lurching of his pelvis, the stabbing pain inside her, and the abrasive nuzzling of his beard stubble against her cheek. And then his body arching. A sudden cry, like someone startled from sleep. A gasp, and he dropped slowly away from her and sank into the hay at her side.

He reached for her hand, closed his eyes and drifted off to sleep.

She dozed as well.

She was awoken by a woman's voice. It was so close that it sounded as if it was right there in the barn. She sat up in panic, frightened that they might have been discovered. But no one was there. She listened. But she couldn't hear a sound.

Perhaps she'd dreamt it.

She wondered what time it was. She had no idea how long they'd been lying there. It might have been minutes, it could have been an hour. She felt hot – strangely hot, for the barn had been so cool before. She felt her face with the back of her hand. It was dewy with perspiration. She put a hand to her bosom. The coarse linen of her dress was damp and sticking to her flesh. She looked down at Ethan. He was still sleeping, his shirt open to the waist, his trousers unbuttoned, braces lying slack in the hay. His face was running with sweat, his flesh shining like glass.

She stood up without waking him and walked slowly to the barn door and outside into the fresh air. The sun was lower in the west now. It would soon slip down behind the ridge of Carn Ewyn and plunge the track and the barn in deep shadow. A light breeze was blowing, pleasantly cool on her face. She put a hand to her belly and felt the dampness of her loose-fitting dress. She pinched the fabric between finger and thumb and gently eased it to and fro from her body, trying to fan the cooling breeze inside.

On the other side of the track, about fifty yards from the barn and beyond a grove of scrawny trees, was a pond, known locally as Poldu – a common Cornish name that means 'black pool'. Annie strolled along a path through the thick grass and the scrawny trees until she came to the edge of the pool, where she squatted down on her haunches and dipped her hands into the still, dark surface. She splashed water on her face. She closed her eyes with the pleasure of it. She cupped her hands and dipped them in once more, lifting her face to the sun and splashing water down the front of her dress. She winced as it prickled, icy needles down her bosom, and a shiver of delight coursed through her.

As she squatted there, dipping her hands into the water a third time, she sensed someone standing just behind her, watching her. The sensation was so strong that she turned her head and peered from the corner of her eyes. The tip of someone's shadow had appeared just beside her. She was so sure that it was Ethan who had crept up to startle her, that she whirled round with cupped hands and threw the water at his face and burst out giggling.

But there was no one there.

She looked around in surprise.

She called, 'Ethan . . .?'

Absolute silence. Not even a bird song.

'Ethan?' she called again. 'Whear you to?'

But there was no reply.

She flicked the water off her hands and patted them dry on her dress and walked slowly back to the barn, looking around every few seconds, expecting to see Ethan creep out of the bushes. When she reached the barn and stepped back inside, into the cool gloomy interior, she found Ethan still lying in the straw, just as she had left him. He had just woken up. He began to clamber unsteadily to his feet.

'Ethan?' she said. 'You playen tricks on me, you devil?'

His trousers were still unbuttoned, hanging around his thighs. His braces were dangling, his shirt tails loose. He looked as if he were half drunk. He stared at her and said, 'Annie ... ' in such a puzzled tone of voice, as if he was not sure who she was or why they were here.

She could smell something smouldering.

She could not see him clearly, her eyes were still adjusting to the sepia light, but he seemed to stagger to one side, as if he had lost his balance. She thought he was acting the fool. She giggled again. 'What are'ee playen at?'

He put one hand to his forehead and groaned. 'Dear Loord, I'm took claf here, girl. I'm sweaten like a hog.'

The smell of smouldering grew stronger. Curls of smoke began to drift up from his hair. She could hear a faint crackling sound. And then his whole head seemed to burst into flames, as if it were made of straw and someone had tossed a lighted match into it. Annie screamed in shock as Ethan began to hop about in agony, swiping uselessly at the bouquet of flames around his face, as if he were trying to swat away a swarm of bees. And then his whole body caught light. Wreathed in flames from head to toe, he stumbled to the barn door, his blazing legs setting light to the hay as he went. Annie shrank back against the barn wall, struck dumb with horror, as Ethan staggered outside and ran in strangely balletic slow-motion towards the pond, and threw himself belly-first into the coal-black water.

Annie ran screaming down the track to get help. The nearest house was half a mile away. Smoke began to billow from the barn. Farm workers, relaxing on their day of rest, came running from all directions, but the fire was out of control and all they could do was stand back and watch it burn. No one thought to look for Ethan. No one even knew that he was there until Annie came running back along the track, screaming hysterically about the pond. They ran to the pool and found Ethan floating face down on the dark water, absolutely still.

Annie would smell Ethan's burning flesh for the rest of her short life. No one believed her account of what had happened. Doctors pronounced her mentally deranged. Her evidence was not called at the inquest and the coroner recorded a verdict of death by misadventure. Annie was committed to St Thomas's Hospital, Bodmin, an institution for the insane, where she died of tuberculosis in the winter of 1932.

The people of Nansgever mourned her death in a conspiracy of silence and, in the years that followed, seldom talked about the burning of Ethan Pierce among themselves, and never spoke of it to anyone from outside the valley.

The barn remained a ruin for over thirty years. A builder from Redruth bought it in 1959 and built a cottage within the old granite walls. He named it Crowjy because that was how the place was marked on eighteenth-century mining maps. It was a small house, with a gloomy feel inside and prone to damp. Local people kept their distance from the place and no one who came to Crowjy seemed to stay for very long. It changed hands several times throughout the 1960s and remained dark and empty for long periods.

MICKEY THE RINGS

This is an ancient land. The remains of Stone Age settlements lie scattered everywhere across the windy carns. This is a land of legends, a land of giants and piskeys, of ghost ships and mermaids. A land of fading folk-memories handed down from ancient civilizations, forgotten cultures, whose history had mingled with legend, and legend with myth.

A few miles across the moors from Trevow Hill, overlooking a shallow valley near the small town of St Just, stands Carn Kenidjack, which local people called 'the hooting carn', for the wind howls so among the granite rocks. Legend has it that the Devil rides here in the black hours of night, hunting for lost souls.

In the late 1960s, a raggle-taggle band of travellers – hippies, flower people – strayed into this valley and made camp here for the summer. They came in a motley convoy: an old bus in rainbow colours, a pink taxi with daisies on the side, a converted ambulance, a Bedford coach, a mobile junkyard of home-built camper vans. They wore loon pants and tie-dyed vests and beads and little goat bells that dangled round their chests. They smoked hashish and dropped acid and talked about the solstice and the moon, and listened to the Incredible String Band and Captain Beefheart on battery record-players.

Around the world it was a summer of discontent, of war and revolution; of burning children in Vietnam; of burning draft cards in America; of blazing vehicles on the riot-wrecked streets of Paris, Frankfurt and Milan. It was the summer that Soviet tanks rolled into Czechoslovakia, the summer Jan Palach burned himself to death in Wenceslas Square. It was a summer of burning.

Eva was Dutch, from the southern city of Eindhoven. She met the hippie convoy at Stonehenge in Wiltshire, gathered for the summer solstice. She stayed with them when they moved on westwards through Devon into Cornwall. She was still with them when they ground their slow way into St Just and pitched camp in the Kenidjack valley.

Eva was seventeen but told people she was twenty-two. She slept in the pink taxi with the daisies on the side, with a Scots boy called Spyder who had pimples and bad teeth and wore a black pillbox cap and played Donovan songs on a Framus guitar. She wore cheesecloth shirts of cheap Indian cotton, and cut-down jeans, frayed and tight, and strings of multicoloured beads. She kept everything she had in a rucksack that looked too much for her slight frame. Her hair hung soft and straggly, the colour of a fieldmouse.

Life was slow and easy. They bought and stole food in St Just, took bottled milk from doorsteps, caught mackerel off Cape Cornwall and cooked them on an open fire. They lazed naked on the secluded sands at Portherras Cove and played like children in the surf. They bought hashish in St Ives, and Spyder sang songs on the harbour front. Tourists dropped coins in his pillbox cap; old fishermen watched him, their faces dark, crumpled and inscrutable.

Eva was the restless type. She was a wanderer. She took to hitching lifts and walking on the moors and carns. One morning in late September she hitched a ride in a van that set her down at Boscully Farm, miles inland, near Mulfra Hill. She walked a mile or so towards the highest point in view. She was approaching Trevow Hill.

She climbed to the top, onto Carn Ewyn, and rested a while, enjoying the warmth of the sun and the clear view on all sides. She delved down into her bag – a shoulder bag of hessian, coloured with an Aztec design – and brought out an apple and some chocolate she had stolen in St Just. The chocolate had begun to melt in the sun and had left brown smears on the cover of a book of beatnik poems by Gregory Corso. She rolled a spliff and read some verses.

She fell asleep in the sun.

Bad weather stole up on her. The sun fled. The sky turned pewter. A chilly wind blew off the ocean and thunderheads came rolling in from the Western Approaches. Eva awoke. She had no watch, no idea how long she'd slept, no sense of time without the sun. She stood up and felt the first spots of rain. She looked for shelter. She saw woods and the roof of a cottage in the Nansgever valley.

She hurried down the hillside. The rain came slowly at first, in thick heavy drops, cold as florins, splattering on her face and arms. But as she reached the valley, it began to fall harder. The footpath broadened into a wide track past a copse of spindly trees beside a pond. On the other side of the track was a cottage, set back off the track and backing onto woodlands.

She ran to the front door to seek shelter beneath the granite lintel. But she was facing into the wind, and the rain was angling in towards her, coming down harder every minute, running in rivulets down her bare legs and soaking through her skimpy top and Levi cut-offs. The cottage looked abandoned. Some of the windows were boarded over and the grass outside had been allowed to run wild. She tried the front door but it was locked. She made her way round to the back of the house, wading through waist-high grass. Like trying to walk through surf.

The back door had been padlocked but someone had prised the hasp out of the jamb. All she had to do was lift the latch and push the door open. She stepped inside. She was in a gloomy hall passage that ran from the back door to the front. She caught the sour-sweet smell of dry rot. The place had an instant echo of emptiness. Yet someone had been sleeping rough here; there was a ragged old sofa in the living room, a filthy mattress on the floor, upturned beer crates around the stone fireplace and garbage scattered all around – beer cans, cigarette packets and greasy food wrappings.

Upstairs, there were two empty bedrooms and a bathroom that looked as if it had not been used in years.

She was shivering now. She stood at the kitchen window, watching the rain come down. It was getting heavier all the time. She ran outside into the back garden and looked around. There was a lean-to shed built onto the side of the house. She looked inside. Logs and kindling wood were stacked along one wall. She took some of each, went back inside the house and lit a small fire in the living room. She took off her wet top and held it close to the flames until her arms ached and steam began to drift off the thin cotton.

She took cigarette papers from her Aztec bag, a packet of ten Weights cigarettes and her little foil-wrapped ball of hashish. She smoked a joint, gazing into the fire. The logs crackled and spat glowing embers out onto the bare floorboards beyond the stone hearth. Watching fire had a hypnotic effect on her. She could sit like this for hours, mesmerized by the flickering gold light in the early autumn gloom, while the rain drummed down ever harder, ever louder, on the windows.

She was awoken by motorbikes.

She sat up abruptly. She had dozed off in front of the fire, on the mattress. The fire was almost out. She was still naked to the waist but her cotton top was dry now. She pulled it on, got up off the mattress and glanced out of the window. Three large motorbikes had pulled off the track and stopped outside the house. Eva shrank back from the window and ran on tiptoe to the hallway. She heard the engines shudder away to silence and then voices. She crept up the stairs and hid in the smaller bedroom. She heard footsteps approaching the back of the house. The metallic clump of iron-tipped boots on the flagstones. She heard the door being kicked open. It banged hard against the inside wall. She realized she'd left her hessian bag downstairs.

She heard voices, a man saying something about 'smoky in 'ere', and then a woman's voice. The thud of heavy boots moving about downstairs. More talking, indistinct. Then boots approaching, up the staircase. Eva shrank back against the bedroom wall and held her breath.

A dull thud as someone kicked open the bathroom door. And then the main bedroom door.

Now silence.

She could picture him just outside, standing, listening. She could hear her heartbeat. It seemed to echo round the room. Then the latch flew up with a loud clunk and the door swung open.

He stood in the doorway, watching her. He had shoulder-length hair, rain-drenched and glossy black, with sideburns that reached his jawbone. He wore an oil-streaked denim jerkin over a scuffed and time-worn leather jacket, and reflecting sunglasses. His hands were tattooed. There were thick studded leather bands around his wrists and chunky silver rings on his fingers. His ragged jeans were soaked with rain.

He took in the beads in her hair and the little goat bells that dangled from the leather boot-lace round her neck, and observed her long, slender, brown legs. He wiped rain off his face with the sleeve of his leather jacket and took out a packet of Park Drive cigarettes and lit one, slowly, keeping his gaze fixed on her as he did so.

She was trembling. Partly the cold. *Relax. Be cool. Peace and love. Good vibes.* She wished she could see his eyes behind those dark glasses.

'I'm sorry,' she said in a small voice. 'I didn't know people was living here.'

He didn't reply.

'I was walking. I got wet in the rain. I was cold. I came in to get dry.'

He cocked his head slightly to one side. He seemed intrigued by her accent. 'Where you from, darlin'?'

'From Holland.'

''Olland ... ?' He looked fascinated. 'How about that then? A nippie from 'Olland.'

His accent was not easy to understand.

'Whoss yer name? Tulip?' He pronounced it 'tchoolip'.

He sounded like the cockney boy who drove the rainbow bus.

'Eva.'

'Eva?' A grin revealed ferrety tar-brown teeth. 'Little Eva? Do the locomotion, do yer?' He plucked a shred of tobacco from his tongue with oil-black fingers. 'I'm Mickey, i'nt I? Mickey the Rings.' He held out his hands, extending his fingers like talons, and displayed his silverware: plain rings, twisted rings, jewelled rings, skull rings with rubies in the eyes, coiled serpents, a wolf's head.

Eva smiled weakly. *Don't show fear. Just cool vibes. Peace and love.*

'I didn't know you was living here. I think I better go now.'

He stood quite still, blocking the doorway.

'Can't go out in this, darlin'. Catch yer deaf o'cold. Where yer livin'?'

'St Just.'

He screwed up his face as if St Just were on the other side of Europe.

"Kin'ell, babe . . . Can't walk all that way in the pissin' rain. We'll borrow you a jacket, run you home on the bike. Get you back in two shakes of a donkey's.'

He turned away and started back down the stairs. She was frightened of him, this dark weather-beaten man with the mirror glasses and the crooked ferrety smile; too frightened to move.

'Come on, Tchoolip,' he called back to her as he clumped down the stairs. 'We won't eatcher.'

She came out of the tiny bedroom and followed him down to the hallway. Three other bikers were standing in the living room, waiting, watching the doorway in expectation.

As she walked in, Mickey the Rings said, 'This is Eva,' as if he was presenting his new fiancée to his family, 'a nippie. From 'Olland.'

Mickey turned to a stocky-looking man with curly ginger hair and an ugly squashed face, like a pug.

'This is Grivas,' said Mickey. 'As in grivas bodily harm.'

Grivas said, ''Ullo, 'ippie,' and grinned stupidly. Some of his teeth were missing.

Mickey turned to a shorter, swarthy man, tanned and bearded, with a weathered face like a mariner. 'And this is Casso.'

Casso looked at her strangely, as if he had never seen a Dutch girl before.

Mickey turned to the woman. 'Dido? This is Eva. Eva, Dido.'

'I heard,' Dido replied, without expression.

'Eva's from 'Olland,' said Mickey. 'Where the dykes come from.'

Dido had a hard unpleasant stare. Her hair was long and straight, bleached platinum blonde, yellow in patches and dark at the roots. She wore a leather jacket over a grubby-looking T-shirt and pale blue jeans, as tight as a glove, worn through at the knees.

They'd brought in food and drink – fish and chips wrapped in newspaper bundles, and bottles of Newcastle Brown, lying on the floor at Dido's feet. Dido tossed a parcel of fish and chips to him. Mickey unwrapped it and let the newspaper free-fall to the floor.

Eva caught the sharp smell of vinegar. She was ravenous.

'You 'ungry, Tchoolip?' Mickey asked. He kicked a couple of beer crates towards the hearth and threw some more kindling wood on the dying fire. 'Come and park yer bum with Mickey, girl, and get some nice hot chips down yer.'

She sat down on the crate beside him.

He broke off a piece of battered cod with his fingers and said to the others, 'Tchoolip needs a ride. We can give her a ride, can't we, boys?'

'Easy,' murmured Casso.

Somewhere behind her, Eva heard Grivas laugh. A thick coarse gurgle.

They ate hungrily, without speaking. Mickey shared his fish with Eva. She could feel the eyes of the others behind her, watching her. She felt herself drawn closer to Mickey. He seemed to offer the only protection here, seemed to be the one in command. She let him push the hot greasy fish into her mouth with his oil-black fingers.

'Like fish do yer, Tchoolip?' he said.

Eva nodded. She tried not to think of the filth on his fingers.

'You and Dido better get together then.' He turned and grinned at the raggedy sofa. 'You like to get your mouth round a bit of fish now and again, don'tcher, Dido?'

Another moronic gurgle of laughter from Grivas.

Outside, the sky grew darker. Night was coming in. The rain was cascading down. The fire had revived and was blazing fiercely now. It filled the room with a golden glow and projected dancing shadows on the walls. Eva needed to pee. She got up and fumbled her way upstairs in the almost-dark to the bathroom.

Dido broke the silence. She had a sullen voice.

'Whatcher gonna do with her, Mickey?'

He was silent for a while, as if he hadn't heard the question. Then he said, 'Got any acid left?'

A tricksy smile crept over Dido's face. She unzipped a pocket in her leather jacket.

Something glinted in Grivas's unfocused eyes. ''Kin'ell, yeah ... Slip her a tab.'

The Burning

Dido took a small white LSD tablet from a plastic pack that had once held Aspro. She passed it to Mickey. He placed it on a scrap of newspaper on the stone hearth, took a seven-inch flick-knife from his pocket and used the heel of it to crush the tablet into fine powder. He tipped the powder into the bottle of Newcastle Brown that Eva was drinking from and gently swirled the brown ale around.

Eva was fumbling her way back down the stairs.

It was fully dark out now. Eva had lost all sense of time. Was it evening, was it night? There was no light in the room – no electricity in the house – just the light of the fire. She was feeling very peculiar. She had shared her hashish with Mickey and the others. They had smoked several joints and she'd drunk too much of this sweetish brown ale. Her head was turning inside. She let Mickey ease her down onto the mattress. He began to kiss and fondle her. Casso and Dido were lying on the sofa. Grivas was propped up against the wall, popping pills and washing them down with ale. Eva was feeling sick and giddy. As if she was on a boat that was pitching in a gathering swell. She pushed Mickey off and tried to stand up. She fell back and tried again.

'What's the matter, Tchoolip?' He sounded concerned.

'Feel weird,' said Eva. 'Think I'm going to be sick.'

She rose to her feet like a new-born foal, tottering and wobbling. She stumbled through the darkness, upstairs to the bathroom. She perched on the side of the bath. It was moving, bobbing from side to side like a small boat. She was losing her balance. The room tipped slowly backwards and pitched her into the bath-tub. She banged her head on the enamelled iron side as she fell in and cried out for Spyder. Spyder, in his pink taxi, with the daisies on the side. Love and peace, peace and love.

She struggled out of the bath but she was on a ship now in a heaving swell and the whole room pitched suddenly the other way and tossed her forwards onto the floor. She crawled like a baby on all fours towards the door. She reached the top of the staircase but the stairs had become a fast-flowing river, cascading down rapids into dark depths below. She over-balanced and fell forward into the torrent and was washed down with the flood. She tumbled down the staircase and lay screaming at the bottom, crying out for Spyder.

They gathered round her at the foot of the stairs.

Mickey leaned over her. 'You all right, Tchoolip?'

The only light was the flickering glow from the fire in the sitting room. Eva was clutching one knee, rocking from side to side, shrieking with pain.

'Look like her leg's busted,' Casso observed.

'She's on a bummer,' said Dido.

Eva saw trees above her. The trees had been struck by lightning and just a few spiky boughs had survived, jutting stark from the broad dark trunks. The trees bent slowly towards her. She screamed in horror and tried to wriggle away from the moving forest but her body was trapped at the bottom of a rocky pit. The trees were making terrible sounds, slow and deep, like a record played at quarter-speed. The branches reached down and grabbed her, lifted her up and bore her away. She cried out – the pain in her knee. They were moving her towards a place where a huge fire was burning.

They laid her down on her back.

Dido stroked her hair. 'It's just a trip, lovey ... On the magic spaceship.'

'Yeah, gonna love this, Tchoolip,' said Mickey gently. 'Gonna be nice ...' He began to slip her cotton top upwards off her belly and over her breasts.

'Gonna be lovely,' crooned Casso. He had hold of her hands. Grivas had her feet.

Eva struggled uselessly. Her knee was agony and her arms were so weak.

'Relax,' said Dido softly. 'Go with the ride.' She unzipped Eva's cut-offs and wrenched them down off her hips. Grivas was making more gurgling sounds, his throat thick with anticipation.

Mickey pulled the cotton top over her head with a little tinkle of goat bells.

'Gonna love this, Tchoolip,' he said, unbuckling his belt. 'Gonna see shooting stars. Gonna be all psychedelic and that.'

But Eva's eyes were fixed in terror on the fire. Where the logs were burning in the hearth she saw a pyre of burning timber. She could feel its searing heat and hear the fierce crackling of the flames. She was gripped by a sudden fear that they were going to throw her on the fire to burn. She struggled frantically to free herself but they were too strong for her. She felt her legs being wrenched apart and Mickey forcing himself inside her.

She watched in horror as the fire began to spread. The flames crept slowly, inexorably, outwards from the pyre of burning logs, and up the walls to the ceiling. They crept hungrily along the skirting board and across the floor. They spread everywhere around the room, flowing smoothly, like liquid. Flames encircled Eva and the bikers, trapping them in an ever-tightening noose of fire, coming closer, closer. She screamed that the house was burning, burning, burning ... But the bikers pinned her down, like demons in hell, clutching her tighter, crushing her, all around her and inside her, everywhere inside her, choking her, tearing her with the force of their frenzy.

The flames soared and billowed like great sails in a wild wind, a mad fury of vivid reds and golds, leaping from a stormy ocean of swirling fire that would engulf them all at any second. Its rage was loud in her ears, the ferocious roar, the searing heat on her body. And still those demons inside her, the stabbing pains inside her, and the raging fire all around, burning, burning. She was screaming, screaming, louder, louder ...

She could see Dido through the fire, through the frenzied whorls of flame. Her flesh was on fire, her face melting and drooping like candlewax, her arms outstretched, her burning, melting hands reaching out through the furnace, her hands on Eva's body, her burning fingers, caressing her, kneading her flesh.

She could see Mickey's face, clenched in ecstasy, as he hammered into her body. Tongues of fire flickered around him and licked their way up the length of his arms and legs but his body went on slamming into hers, harder, harder, while flames spread up his torso and across his chest, burning brighter as the fat in his flesh caught light and sizzled like bacon while the skin began to melt. With a savage shriek of release he jerked a few last thrusts into her body and then slipped out of her and seemed to fall away from her, backwards, into the inferno which now came crashing over her and swamped her like a huge tumbling wave in a raging red ocean.

Eva curled herself into a ball and screamed and screamed. She clamped her hands across her face but the heat seared her eyeballs. The sickly sweet stench of roasting flesh poured through her nostrils and the fire thundered in her ears like a starving carnivore, rampaging all around, consuming everything, just relentless burning, burning, burning . . .

When she awoke it was daylight. The rain had stopped.

She pushed herself up onto one elbow and looked around. The room was exactly as she remembered it – the plain granite walls, the bare wooden floorboards, the open-beamed ceiling, the raggedy old sofa with its protruding springs, the filthy mattress on the floor where she lay.

The fire in the hearth had died out. She was alone, naked and cold.

There was blood on the mattress. Her body felt stiff and her head ached. She stood up. One knee was painful but she could walk on it. She peered out of the window. The motorbikes were gone. Her clothes were scattered about the floor. She got dressed and limped up the stairs. She went into the bathroom and sat down to pee. She burned inside.

There were bruises all over her legs and her skin was strangely red. It was like a rash that had come up in the night, a sickly, inflamed red rash. It covered her legs, all the way up to her hips. She lifted her cotton top and looked at her belly. She raised it higher, pulled it right up to her shoulders: the rash was everywhere. She looked repulsive. It covered her whole body. She touched her skin. It was painful to touch, as if she'd been lying naked in the sun for too long.

She stepped out of the house into the cool dawn air. The Atlantic front had cleared away to the east and it would be a warm sunny day. She had no idea where she was. She did not go back the way she had come – her knee was too painful to climb the steep hill path to the carn. Instead she walked down the track. Where it broadened out and joined the quiet winding road through the Nansgever valley, she saw a piece of wooden board that had been nailed to a tree. It was hand-painted with no great skill. She read the name: Crowjy.

She walked away along the valley road and began to weep. She would weep like this, off and on, without warning, for many months to come. And she would see Crowjy in the night, sudden visions of the barn-cottage, dark and abandoned in the rain. Sometimes it seemed like a hallucination. Sometimes it was a dream.

Her skin became paper dry, it felt crisp to the touch. It looked crinkly and shiny, like the scarred tissue that grows after third-degree burns. It was painful to touch, it was painful even to move. She felt tight and brittle. She applied creams and oils, and after a few more days the rash faded and the crisp skin began to peel away all over her body. The skin beneath was pale pink. It was tender and quickly began to burn from the smallest exposure to sunlight. She kept in the shade and applied more and more lotions to make her skin soft and supple again.

She went home to Eindhoven. She was examined by a consultant dermatologist. He had never come across a skin condition of this kind before. She would be examined by many different specialists over the years to come. None of them would be able to treat her. Whenever she lay in the sun, the condition would recur; it would even recur if she sat too close to an open fire. For the rest of her life, Eva would have to avoid sunlight and fire.

BRYAN CARHAYS

In the early 1980s an artist called Bryan Carhays came to live at Crowjy. He was not a local man and made no friends in the valley ... Nor seemed to want to. He didn't 'fit'. He didn't even try to fit. He was a drunk, a foul-mouthed drunk, ill-tempered and anti-social. He was not liked or trusted by anyone in the locality. And yet he stayed, far longer than anyone had done before. He enlarged Crowjy by building a glass-roofed extension to the living room – what had originally been the main body of the old barn. This became his painter's studio. He lived alone there, but had a wife somewhere (or so the gossip went) and sluttish-looking 'models' were seen to come and go at all hours – drunks and slatterns that he picked up in the pubs of Penzance and St Ives, wearers of fishnet tights, carriers of disease ... Or so the local gossip went.

He taught for a while at the Falmouth School of Art but was forced to resign over a scandalous liaison with a student. (And that was gossip in the village too.)

Gossip was important in Boskinnow. In a village of just a few hundred inhabitants – and a few dozen more who lived throughout the valley – it was the mortar of social cohesion that held the scattered community together. The rumour mill, the local minimart of gossip, was Treneer's Store in the heart of Boskinnow village. Treneer's was everything to all men: it was butcher, baker and greengrocer, it was hardware store and liquor shop, and it was the only post office for miles around. Treneer's was the nearest thing that Boskinnow had to a village square, where people gathered to pass the time of day, to schmooze and grumble and discuss other people's private business. Mary Treneer, who owned the store, knew everyone for three miles around and practically everything they did.

Bryan Carhays was not welcome in Treneer's. In the early years he was tolerated – though only just – because of the amount of money he spent on liquor there. But after he resigned his teaching post at art school and his financial affairs began to deteriorate (along with his state of health), his custom ceased to be worth the abuse that came with it, and Mary barred him from the shop.

About the only person in the valley who was on speaking terms with Carhays was his GP, Tim Hendra, who lived half a mile away and was his nearest neighbour, bar the widow Roscarrock. Tim knew all the gossip about Bryan Carhays. He didn't like tittle-tattle (being a divorcee, on his own and in his prime, he was the victim of it himself from time to time) but he could hardly avoid it when he had to make so many house calls in the area.

Mary Treneer had appointed herself his principal informant. Sixty-two years old and never married (and there were salty rumours about *her* as well), Mary lived above the shop with her bedridden mother who was in poor health. Barely a week went by without Tim Hendra having to call in on the old lady. One January afternoon, during the mild winter of 1991, they were coming back downstairs from her mother's bedroom, when Mary said to him: 'You've heard about our artist friend, I take it?'

She was talking about Bryan – yet again. She was always complaining about 'our artist friend', about his debauched ways, his wanton women. There seemed to Tim to be a tinge of sourness in her moral indignation, as if she felt she'd missed out on something in life, as if the very thought of those wanton women tapped down into some dark fantasies of her own.

'I haven't heard, no,' he replied, and did his best to look interested. 'What's he been up to this time?'

'The screaming?' Mary feigned surprise. 'You haven't heard about the screaming?'

Tim shook his head. Mary took him into the storeroom at the back of the shop, as if she didn't want this to be overheard by her customers (although he knew she would have spread this gossip half way round the village by now). She folded her pudding arms across her bosom and said: 'Vera Roscarrock was out walken her dog along the lane t'other night. And she heard screams comen down the track from Crowjy.' The widow Roscarrock was Bryan's only near neighbour; a grim, austere woman and deeply religious. 'It's him, of course,' Mary continued. 'Our artist friend. Top of his voice. Screaming his head off.'

Since Bryan lived a good mile out of the village, tucked away up that little track in the Nansgever valley, Tim found it difficult to see why it was of such intense concern to Mary. However . . .

'When was this?' he asked.

'Two nights ago. Scared the wits out of her. You could hear un half way down the valley. So she phoned Kevin Hosken,' (the local policeman) 'and Kevin drives out to barn-cottage to see what all the racket's about. He finds our artist friend on a binge. Raving, he was. Pink elephant time. Kevin says there's nothen he can do. Carhays wasn't breaken any laws so . . .' Mary shrugged. 'The police don't want to know.' She glared at Tim as if it was somehow *his* responsibility.

'He's dangerous,' she went on, without waiting for an answer. 'He's a danger to himself and he's a danger to other people. Something will have to be done, before someone gets hurt.'

'There's not a lot a GP *can* do,' said Tim, 'unless a person is so ill they have to be hospitalized against their will. I can certainly talk to him, try to reason with him. But I can't compel him to undergo treatment if he doesn't want to.'

Bryan had had a serious alcohol problem for as long as Tim had known him. He was drinking himself to an early grave and Tim had told him often enough, but he took no notice. That same evening, after surgery, Tim stopped off at Crowjy to talk to him about the latest complaints – though he had no idea how he was going to broach the subject of the screaming and the raging. Even if Bryan was sufficiently sober to talk sense to, it would probably be a waste of time and breath, but Tim felt he had to keep trying; no one else would bother.

He parked outside the cottage, behind Bryan's estate car. It was just after eight, a cloudy night and mild for January. Tim banged on the door. He could hear a tape or a record playing inside – sixties' rock music by the sound of it. Bryan opened the door. He looked wrecked but greeted Tim ebulliently.

'Hendra!' he roared. 'Come in, old turd, come in.'

'Busy?' Tim stepped inside.

'Of course I'm busy, always busy. But never too busy for a bevvy.'

Bryan shuffled through the sitting room to his studio – an extension built onto the gable-end wall, with a glass-panelled roof which gave the room plenty of northern light. There was no door into the studio, just a six-foot-wide opening in the sitting-room wall and one step down. He ferreted around among old jam jars stuffed with paint brushes and found an unwashed tumbler. He stepped back into the sitting room.

'Guess who,' he said, referring to the ear-splitting rock music. Tim had no idea. 'Cream,' he said, '1967.' And added affably enough: 'No culture, you quacks.'

'How can you bear it so loud?'

'It's *meant* to be loud.' He turned it up even more. 'That's the whole point of it.'

He tipped some wine into the dirty tumbler and passed it to Tim. They sat down in the half-lighted sitting room, either side of the log fire.

This was beyond a GP's call of duty. But there had been a time, in Bryan's better days, when he and Tim used to enjoy a few beers together at the weekend, even a day's fishing.

The tape finished and left the cottage slumped in dark velvet silence.

'Thank God for that,' said Tim.

Bryan looked amused. 'I had Lily law round here the other night . . . Bloody cheek. Kevin Hosken banging on the door.'

'You're upsetting the neighbours.'

'What neighbours? Not a neighbour in sight.'

'Vera Roscarrock, for one.'

'*Neighbour?*' Bryan retorted. 'She lives half a mile away, miserable sow.'

Bryan was forty-eight. He looked sixty-odd. He had wet pink eyes and drooping lower lids, the way some spaniels or basset hounds go in old age, and the loganberry complexion of a derelict wino, although his rusty steel beard concealed much of it. Once a bulky, solid, chunky man, now he was all flab and paunch. His reddish-brown hair was a dirty alloy colour, long and straggly and unkempt.

'We should talk,' said Tim, wondering how to broach this. Bryan's emotions could flip between extremes without warning. You could never be sure whether he was going to break down in tears and say sorry, or throw a glass in your face. 'It's getting out of hand, Bryan,' he ventured.

Bryan thought about that for a minute or so. 'As a matter of fact,' he said, 'it is. But you don't know the half of it.'

'So tell me.'

'You? You're a quack.' He shook his head contemptuously. 'You couldn't get your head round this.'

'Try me.'

Bryan looked fixedly at Tim for a moment, trying to focus. 'Something or someone in this place ...' A duplicitous grin crept across his face, as if this were really just a put-on. 'Is trying to drive me ... out of ... my mind. Trying to tear my brain in pieces.' His head wobbled slightly on top of his heavy rounded shoulders. He smirked at Tim with spiteful eyes. 'You think I'm doolally. Don't you?'

Tim was not surprised by anything Bryan said these days. He was inured to this kind of conversation.

'Why would anyone be trying to drive you out of your mind?' he said neutrally.

'I don't know *why*. I only know she is.'

'She?'

Bryan poured himself some more wine – just half a glass. He only ever poured half measures. The bottle seemed to last longer that way. It was red wine, something cheap and Italian in a litre plastic bottle. It tasted like antifreeze to Tim. He was putting it to his lips without actually tasting it, just to appear sociable.

'My sister comes to me at night,' said Bryan. And pulled at some loose strands of navy blue wool where the cuff of his worn-out submariner's sweater had begun to come adrift. 'You know that?'

'I didn't even know you had a sister,' said Tim.

'Lives up east. Devon way. We don't have much to do with each other. We don't get on.'

He peeled a paper from a packet of Rizla greens and fed some tobacco into it from a pouch of Old Holborn.

'Why does she come to see you,' said Tim, 'if you don't get on?'

'Because she's a bitch. She's evil. She wants to destroy me. She and her.'

'Why do you think she wants to destroy you?' Tim was not at all convinced that this sister even existed.

'She blames me.'

'For what?'

Bryan rolled his cigarette, licked the gummed edge and sealed it. 'Her mother maybe.' A slight pause. 'I don't know, you tell *me*.'

Tim said nothing and waited for Bryan to continue. Or change the subject. Or throw up. Or smash a glass. Or whatever. You never knew with Bryan.

Bryan looked up at the ceiling and squinted at it as if he were trying to descry something very very small up there between the open beams.

'There's something bad here, guy, this place. Some bad shit going down.'

Tim glanced at the ceiling, wondering what he was talking about, a leak from a water pipe or what. 'How do you mean?'

'Outside of anything I've experienced. I see things by the pool.' Bryan pointed towards the pond across the track. 'I smell things too. The night. I hear whispering. Voices. In the house.'

Tim had been a GP for ten years, a casualty registrar before that, and there wasn't much that an alcoholic could say that would surprise him any more. His face must have said it all, because Bryan started laughing.

'You think I'm crackers, don't you? You think, This poor sick tosser's lost the plot. He's out to lunch, dinner and breakfast.'

'I don't think you're mad,' said Tim. 'You want people to *think* you're mad, but you aren't.' He meant that sincerely. Sodden with drink, for sure, but mad, no. Bryan was an exhibitionist. He seemed to enjoy creating negative images, alienating everyone. *Hate me, hate me*, he seemed to say. He was a kamikaze. He was a speeding truck, out of control on mountain bends.

'You see things in the night?' asked Tim.

Bryan flipped open an old Zippo, worked the roller half a dozen times before the flint sparked, and then lit his cigarette.

'You're going to tell me I've got the DTs.'

'You scream at night. You're scaring the hell out of the locals.'

'Yeah?' Bryan looked quite pleased. He cackled with laughter.

'I want to help you,' said Tim. 'But you won't help *me*.'

Bryan snapped the Zippo shut and spat a fragment of tobacco off the tip of his tongue.

'It's not the DTs, guy.'

He took a draw on his cigarette. A silence.

'Nothing lives long round here. No rabbits, no foxes, no badgers, nothing. Come here at daybreak and listen for the birds – silence. Not a sound.'

'You frighten everything away,' said Tim.

For a second it looked as if Bryan's mood was about to turn ugly. But it was just delayed reaction; neurons misfiring in his sodden brain. He began to smile, as if what Tim had said was quite a compliment. He leaned forward in his chair to share a confidence and lowered his voice. 'She comes at night. She has no hair. Her skin is like frost. White as marble.' A sort of twisted leer crawled across his face. 'She's my succubus.' His voice fell almost to a whisper. 'She gives me such a hard-on, guy. Out on the margins. Right out on the borderline.'

He looked so pissed that Tim thought he was going to fall forwards out of the chair.

'What are you talking about?'

'I'm talking about the *real* sensations. Take it to the edge, guy. The edge of beyond. Death and ecstasy. Walk the high wire. You and death, eyeball to eyeball. Feel her breath on your face, fogging up your vision. Not a hair on her head. The skin is so white. Like marble. But soft, like cold silk. Jesus . . .' He raised his eyes to heaven. 'You've never had head like it. She's a whore come hot from hell.' His eyelids half closed and then he looked back at Tim. 'What does she want, Hendra? The God in hell is she trying to do to me?'

'I don't know,' said Tim. 'But go on drinking the way you are and you'll be able to knock on the door and ask her.'

Bryan's expression slowly changed. He studied Tim through those droopy damp eyes with a look of loathing. 'You're full of shit, Hendra.'

Tim pleaded innocent with a small open gesture of the hands. 'I'm trying to *help*, mate.'

Bryan tried to sit upright, pushing his chest out imperiously. 'Don't give me that.' His face became ugly. '*You* need the help, Hendra.' He was beginning to shout now. 'Help yourself. Physician, heal thyself. Get out of here. Go on. Get the hell out!'

He tried to get out of the chair but fell back into it. Tim got up to leave. It always ended this way nowadays. He was secretly relieved; any excuse to go.

'Some other time,' he sighed, and wondered why he bothered.

He turned and walked across the sitting room.

'You're the one needs help, Hendra!' Bryan was bellowing. 'You're some sick tosser, you know that? You're in serious shit, guy! You know that? You'd better just wise up or . . .'

Tim crossed the hall passage, let himself out and pulled the door shut behind him. As he walked back to his car, he heard the sound of Bryan's wine glass shattering on the sitting room wall. It was probably aimed at the window.

As Tim drove away, the night's rages began.

The rages grew worse over the next month or so. Bryan phoned Tim at home, a number of times, usually in the small hours, when he was savagely drunk and making no sense.

Then peace. The rages ceased abruptly. No more phone calls. The days passed and no one in the valley heard or saw anything of him.

One morning in March, the postman told Tim that electricity-board engineers had called at Crowjy to cut off the supply but had found no one at home. They had left a warning notice and were coming back the following day to force entry.

Tim called at the barn-cottage that same evening. He banged on the front door but there was no response. He shouted through the letterbox and listened but there was no reply. He walked round to the back of the house, in through the garden gate and along the paved path that bisected the densely overgrown lawn. He tried the back door. It was unlocked. He stepped inside the house.

'Bryan?' Silence.

He walked along the hall passage to the sitting room. Peered in.

'Bryan?'

Through the sitting room to the arched opening in the end wall which led through to the studio extension. No one there. Back to the hall passage, to the foot of the stairs. Looking up: 'Bryan?'

Starting up the staircase. An unpleasant smell. Getting worse with every step. Now a putrid stench. Into the main bedroom.

Bryan was lying flat on his back on top of the bed. He was naked. His rotting flesh had a faintly violet hue in the fading light of sunset. A plastic freezer bag covered his face and was loosely cinched around his throat.

A uniformed PC arrived in a panda car, took one look and retreated back downstairs to join Tim in the sitting room and wait for the CID to turn up. Half an hour later a Detective-Sergeant Trembath arrived, and his inspector, a middle-aged bruiser called Ron Vincent. Tim knew him – a south London man, formerly with the Metropolitan Police, scarred veteran of a thousand pub brawls and street demos. He had not adjusted very well to rural life.

'Been driving all round the boonies looking for this dump,' he grumbled, clumping up the stairs ahead of Tim and the DS. 'There's roads out here I didn't even know existed.' He walked inside Bryan's bedroom and took one step back again. 'Mother O'Riley . . . He's a bit ripe.'

He re-entered and walked over to the bed. He put a handkerchief over his nose and looked down. 'Know him?' he asked Tim.

'Bryan Carhays. He was one of my patients.'

Vincent looked more closely at the plastic bag. 'Blood anywhere?'

'None visible. But I haven't moved him.'

'How long do you reckon he's been dead?'

'Couldn't possibly say,' said Tim. 'But I haven't seen or heard from him for about ten days.'

'Anyone else live here? Wife, girlfriend?'

'No.'

'So how did you get in?'

'The back door was unlocked.'

'Neighbours call you?'

'No, but I was concerned about him. The postman told me the SWEB engineers turned up this morning to cut off his electricity.'

Car lights were approaching up the track outside. Trembath looked out of the window. 'It's scene-of-crime, guv,' he said, and went downstairs to let the officer in.

'Suffocation, by the look of it,' said Vincent, but seemed to be asking Tim to confirm it.

'That's for the pathologist to say,' Tim replied.

'What do you know about him? Was he ill? Personal problems?'

'He was a chronic alcoholic. He had a lot of drink-related problems.'

'Ever talk about suicide?'

'Not that I recall. But he talked so much rubbish, I stopped listening after a while. He was killing himself with booze, anyway ... I doubt if this had anything to do with suicide.' Tim pointed down to the freezer bag that was enveloping Bryan's head.

'Well, what else would he be trying to do?' Vincent enquired tartly.

'A man who wants to suffocate himself doesn't cut holes in the bag that enable him to breathe,' Tim pointed out.

Vincent took a closer look. There were two small holes close to the nostrils.

The scene-of-crime officer was upstairs with the pathologist. Trembath was looking around in the kitchen. Vincent was in the sitting room with Tim.

'What about next of kin?'

'There's an ex-wife somewhere. But she's long gone.'

'Children?'

'He never mentioned any.'

'Parents?'

'Both dead.'

'He must have *some* family, somewhere.'

'He mentioned a sister. But I've never met her. He said they didn't get on.'

'Know where she lives?'

'Somewhere in Devon, he told me.'

'Helpful,' Vincent grunted.

He stepped down into the studio and stood casting an eye over Bryan's paintings. He was not impressed.

'What do they call this? Hardly abstract, is it.'

'I don't know what you'd call it,' said Tim.

They wandered round the studio, glancing at the canvases – some finished, some partly finished, some barely started, or simply abandoned. Most of Bryan's pictures portrayed the human form, but they had a sort of deformed, tortured quality that Tim found alienating and depressing. For him, Bryan's work was like his life: an unfathomable mess, dark and irrational.

Vincent was looking at a canvas about three feet by four. It was hard to tell whether it was finished or not. The creature it portrayed was female. Her body was sensual, feminine – even graceful – and yet misshapen. As if it were a distorted reflection of her in a fairground hall of mirrors. Her skin was colourless. It had a translucent quality. She had no hair and no eyebrows and there was only flesh where her eye sockets should have been. Her nipples were the same tone as her flesh. And her crotch was smooth, shapeless, hairless, as if she were enveloped in a sheath. She was like a piece of beautifully deformed sculpture.

Tim was remembering the strange things Bryan said, that night in February.

She comes at night. She has no hair. Her skin is like frost. White as marble.

Her mouth was the only part of her that was coloured. Her lips had a lilac tone. They were fleshy and parted, drawn into an O as if she were about to blow soap bubbles. Behind them, small tongues of flame flickered vividly in the black interior, as if a fire were burning in her throat.

A whore come hot from hell . . . My succubus . . .

'What kind of mind does this?' Vincent wondered.

But Tim's concentration was elsewhere.

What does she want, Hendra? The God in hell is she trying to do to me?

SARA

When Gerald left her, people said things like, Oh, he'll come crawling back within a month. To which she used to reply, In his dreams. And then laugh with brassy derision.

He moved back to Exeter. He'd never really wanted to live out in the country, anyway, he liked university life too much, didn't want to stray too far from campus. He'd given it a try for her sake, but he hadn't liked the travelling ... And then there was the cost. (Ah, the cost, Gerald, always the cost. Always one hand in the pocket, counting the coppers.)

The month crawled by but, of course, he didn't crawl back.

A few more months went by, and one by one – sometimes two by two – their friends (mostly *his* friends, now she came to look back on it) stopped calling her, stopped inviting her to supper. The truth was that he'd been having it away with this other postgrad student for six months or more, and Sara had never once suspected. And everyone was thinking: Poor deluded fool.

Now it was history. It felt as if everything and everyone had moved on, except her. Life felt like a train that had dropped her off at a wayside station and left her behind on a deserted platform.

And here she was, stuck out on the middle of Dartmoor, in a cold damp house whose rent she could no longer afford, with toadstools sprouting from the walls and mildew accumulating beneath the carpet.

Then, one morning in March, the telephone rang. It was such an alien sound these days, it made her jump. She was in the sitting room, working at her PC. Outside, the rain was pouring down.

She didn't know why, but she was so sure it was Gerald that she nearly ignored it, let it ring. She had not found a way to forget him, so she had found a way to despise him instead. But it went on ringing and ringing and ringing, so she picked it up and felt that tight feeling in her chest and a dryness in her throat.

But a man said, 'Miss Carhays?'

'Speaking.'

'My name's Detective Inspector Vincent, Hayle police.'

That threw her completely. 'Did you say *Hayle*?'

'You are Miss Sara Carhays?'

'Yes.'

'Do you have a brother, Mr Bryan Carhays? Of Crowjy, Nansgever?'

'Yes.' And, after a brief silence: 'Why, what's happened?'

'I'm afraid,' said Vincent, 'I've got some sad news for you.'

They were in an interview room, facing each other across a table that seesawed every time she picked up her coffee cup and put it down. A Detective Sergeant Trembath was sitting slightly apart and to one side, with his notebook.

Vincent said, 'I'm sorry you weren't informed sooner. His body was only discovered three nights ago. It's taken us a little while to trace you.'

For some reason she would come to wonder about as the days and weeks went by, none of this came as much of a shock to her.

'I suppose it would have done,' she said. It was a miracle they had found her at all. 'We hadn't been in touch for a long time.'

'He'd been dead for about a week, maybe ten days. We can't be very precise.'

'Who found him?'

'His GP. Doctor Hendra.'

'How did he die?'

'Suffocation.' He had already told her that.

'Yes, but what I mean is . . .'

Trembath was watching her, studying her reaction.

'This plastic bag . . .' She didn't know quite what she was trying to say. She was struggling to get a picture of the scene, trying to imagine what had happened. 'How did it . . .?'

'It was sort of scrunched in around the throat,' said Vincent, and gestured with his hands. 'It could have been an accident.

Or he may have taken his own life. Or there may have been a second person involved.'

'You mean he was murdered?'

'I'm merely saying,' Vincent stressed, 'that it's a possibility. We don't have any evidence so far to suggest that. But there'll be an inquest, of course. And the coroner will have to decide.'

'When exactly,' said Trembath, 'was the last time you spoke to your brother?'

'Spoke to him? About three years ago. When my mother died and I rang to tell him.'

'And when did you last see him?' said Trembath.

'Oh, heavens ...' Thinking back. It was hard to remember exactly, one year seemed to merge with another. 'About ten, eleven years ago.'

'What about your mother's funeral?' asked Vincent.

She shook her head. 'He couldn't be bothered to come to his father's funeral either.' Vincent looked curious. 'Bryan and I were estranged. We had a falling out, the way families do sometimes.'

'I suppose, then,' said Vincent, 'it's pointless asking you about his state of mind these last few months. Whether he was depressed, or whether he's shown any suicidal tendencies in the past.'

'Certainly not when *I* knew him,' she replied. 'But I couldn't tell you anything about his recent past. You'd be better off talking to his friends and neighbours, students, fellow teachers, the people who knew him down here.'

'He doesn't seem to have had very many friends,' said Vincent. 'His doctor appears to have known him better than most – Tim Hendra. Do you know him?'

She shook her head. 'I don't know anyone down here any more. I did live in St Ives for a while, after I left school. But I haven't kept in touch with anyone.'

'How about your family?' said Trembath. 'Are there any other brothers or sisters?'

She shook her head. 'Only the two of us. Dad died when I was seventeen. Mum died three years ago. I've got an elderly aunt in New Zealand, Dad's sister. But we never write or anything. I've never even met her.'

'Did your brother have any children?' asked Trembath.

'No.' But then it occurred to her: 'Well, maybe. It's always possible, I suppose. I don't even know if he got married again. I don't even know if he was living with anyone.'

'Apparently not,' said Vincent. 'His executors are looking after his affairs. They know about his ex-wife, but that's all.'

'Executors ... ?' She was amazed that Bryan had even appointed any. It was not the kind of thing he would have bothered about.

'He appointed his solicitors,' said Vincent. 'Boyce and Rundell. In Alverton Street, Penzance.'

'Ah yes, of course ...' She remembered now.

'You've been in touch?'

'No. But they handled the conveyancing when Bryan bought Crowjy.'

'Perhaps you should call them,' Vincent suggested. 'They're going to get in touch with you. Ask for Nigel Roberts.'

She went to see Nigel Roberts at his office in Penzance. He seemed very young to be dealing with this, barely *her* age.

'I was about to write to you when you telephoned,' he said. 'It's about your brother's estate.'

'Crowjy, in other words?' she said, for Bryan didn't own anything else worth a damn. She presumed he was about to ask her to go through all Bryan's possessions and clear everything out ... In which case she was going to say no, because it had nothing to do with her. The executors could do what they wanted with the place.

'Well, that's more or less all it amounts to,' Roberts replied. 'He named you sole beneficiary in his will.'

She smiled in disbelief. 'I very much doubt it. When was this?'

'The will?' Roberts looked at his papers. 'It was drawn up about ten years ago.'

'Oh no ... No, this can't be right. I don't know what he told you, but Bryan and I were estranged. I haven't even spoken to him since our mother died three years ago. This can't be what he intended.'

Roberts seemed slightly taken aback. 'It's the only will I'm aware of,' he said, almost with apology. 'It will have to go through probate, of course, but as things stand he left everything to you. But the house, I would guess, is the only real asset.'

'But I don't want it,' Sara protested. 'It's probably mortgaged to the hilt, anyway, and I can't afford that.'

'Oh no,' Roberts reassured her. 'There's no question of that. The balance of any mortgage will be redeemed by the life insurance policy.'

'Life insurance?' Sara's eyes widened with mock incredulity. '*Bryan?* He loathed that sort of thing – finance, banks, insurance companies. He was an anarchist . . . Or used to be.'

Roberts seemed flummoxed. Evidently he was not accustomed to dealing with reluctant beneficiaries. 'Anarchist or not,' he said with a bemused shrug, 'it was part and parcel of the mortgage agreement. However, there may well be liabilities that I shall have to discharge – bank overdraft perhaps, credit card borrowings, that sort of thing. I don't know what cash assets he may have had. Did he have a building society account, for example?'

'I haven't a clue,' she replied. 'I don't know anything about his affairs.'

'The point I was going to make,' said Roberts, 'is that if there are insufficient cash assets to cover the liabilities, it may be necessary to liquidate some of the capital tied up in the house.'

'If you mean you want to sell it, that's okay by me. I don't want *any*thing from Bryan. And I'm quite sure he never wanted me to have anything. He obviously forgot to change the will, that's all.'

'That's not quite what I meant,' said Roberts. 'This is a bad time to sell property, the middle of a recession, prices have dropped. I don't know what you plan to do, but you may want to consider taking out a small mortgage . . . That would release some capital to cover any charges against Bryan's estate.'

'A mortgage? *Me?*' Sara smiled. 'You've got to be kidding. What sort of liabilities has he got? What sort of debts are we talking about?'

'I can't say until I've looked at his bank statements, credit card account, tax situation, and so on.'

'Look, let's get one thing straight from the start,' said Sara. 'I'm a postgraduate student, in the middle of a thesis for my Ph.D. I'm living on savings and occasional wages from part-time jobs. So forget about a mortgage. I can't even afford my rent just now.'

'Well, let's not worry about that until we know what his financial situation is,' said Roberts. 'Perhaps you'd be kind enough to take a look around the cottage for me, and let me have his bank statements, tax papers, building society passbook, anything you think I might need.'

She drove slowly through Boskinnow village to where the Nansgever valley road turned off. The trees and hedgerows were beginning to bud with early spring. It all seemed so much smaller than she remembered from ten years ago. Strange, when you'd been away so long, how things appeared to have shrunk with the passing of time.

She turned up the track to Crowjy, pulled up on the granite chippings along the front of the cottage and got out of the car. A scruffy silver-grey Toyota estate languished in the shade, dented and rusting. The house looked tired and sorry for itself. Paint was peeling from the window frames and the garden had run wild.

Nigel Roberts had given her a set of keys. Hayle police had a second set. Sara unlocked the front door and went inside. The air smelt stale. There was a scattering of letters on the hall floor. She picked them up and glanced through them: mostly junk mail.

She went into the sitting room. It looked out on both the front and the back of the house. The walls were exposed granite on three sides, but painted white on the garden side for some reason she couldn't guess at. There was a large granite fireplace along that back wall, with a recess on each side for logs.

Bryan had liked his living space – indeed his whole life – uncluttered and unfussy. He had never been a materialistic man, had never liked too many possessions. They weighed him down, he used to say, made him feel trapped. He'd made most of the furniture here himself. She sat in an armchair; pretty basic but not uncomfortable. There was a small television set in one corner ... And the same record turntable that she remembered from the 1970s, hooked up to the same old Leak amplifier, with all his old vinyl LPs and cassette tapes ranged along a shelf of slate that he'd built himself. Mostly fifties and sixties music: blues, R and B, soul, rock, funk.

She walked through to the extension, down a step. This was new to her, his studio. There were low cupboards along one wall, paints and brushes, rags and paraphernalia scattered across the top. Canvases stood against the walls. Dozens of them. None of them looked finished.

Her attention was caught by a painting of a woman. She was naked, an odd shape. She had no hair, no eyes. Her flesh was almost white but her lips were a pinky-violet colour. There was something about it that both attracted and repelled her.

So much unfinished work. So much talent, Bryan, and all thrown away, all wasted.

Why?

She felt a slight wrench inside, the sight of all this; familiar objects, long forgotten.

She walked back through the sitting room to the hall passage and along to the kitchen. It was painted in bright yellow and cornflower blue. A solid pine table occupied the centre of the room. Bryan had built that too by the looks of it. There was some more mail lying on the table. Several bills. Everything had been opened – by the police, she supposed. She noticed a card in bright red from the electricity board: OUR ENGINEERS CALLED TODAY TO TERMINATE THE SUPPLY.

A small Rayburn stove stood in a recess. It looked as if it had not been lit for some time: a patina of rust had formed across the surface of the iron hobs. Bryan had installed an electric hob as well.

Cook's knives along the wall. Fine, heavy knives. He was a good cook. He always said he should have been a chef not a painter.

She went upstairs. The bathroom and the spare bedroom were above the kitchen. The spare bedroom was minute, scarcely large enough for the narrow bed. Bryan had turned it into a junk room, packed with boxes and suitcases.

His bedroom door was closed. She hesitated outside, almost afraid to go in. Afraid of what? She pushed open the door and stood still in the entrance. It was gloomy-dark. The curtains were drawn across the windows, both on the front-facing side and the garden side.

Was it imagination or was it very cold in here?

She stared at the bed. This was where he was, where the doctor found him. Was he sitting or was he lying?

She felt that wrench again, deep down inside; memories and guilt.

The police thought it was suicide, Vincent had made that quite plain.

Why, Bryan? Whatever possessed you?

She closed the door and went slowly back downstairs.

She unlocked the back door and stepped outside into the garden. The grass came up to her knees. She found a lean-to shed in a poor state of repair. The door was almost off its hinges. Inside, she found logs and kindling wood, some garden tools and a heavy old petrol mower that looked crippled by rust. And empty bottles – dozens of them, mostly wine and vodka bottles.

She eased the shed door closed and went back inside the house. There was nothing more she could do here today. Nigel Roberts would have to wait for his bank statements and tax returns. She hesitated on the front door step for a few moments, wondering whether to drive straight home to Devon now or to take a stroll up to the carn and enjoy this last hour or so of daylight. She decided she could use the fresh air to get the damp musty smell of Crowjy out of her nostrils, and set off up the track to where it crossed the stream and began to zig-zag up the side of Trevow Hill.

From the very top she had a clear view of the sea on three sides of the peninsula. To the northeast, across St Ives Bay. To the west, beyond Cape Cornwall. And to the south at Mount's Bay and the island priory of St Michael. There was a farm just below her on the south side of the hill, an enclosure of buildings in a dip on the lower slopes. She wondered what they farmed; she could see no cattle anywhere and this was not the kind of land for growing crops.

She sat on the carn, watching the watery lemon sun sink slowly towards the horizon, reflected like fish scales across the ocean. So many things she had been intending to say to Bryan. So much bad blood to be cleansed, so many knots to untangle. Why hadn't she said something before? Why hadn't she written? That was the problem with sudden death: unfinished business.

The thought of it soured the pleasure of the moment, the peace of the carn, the still evening, the pale colours of the drowning sun. It would be dark before long. She had two and a half hours' driving ahead. She got up, brushed the dirt off her backside and started back down the hill.

When she reached the cottage she stopped only to make sure the front door was securely shut, then climbed into the VW, started up, turned around and drove down to the valley road. She was on the A30 and heading east for Bodmin by dusk.

She'd been driving for about forty minutes when she glanced at the fuel gauge and noticed she was almost out of petrol. She pulled into a filling station in Indian Queens, a sprawling village scattered by the A30 just west of Bodmin Moor. But even as she drew up beside a pump and turned to take her handbag from the empty seat beside her, she knew what she'd done: she'd left her bag behind at Crowjy, on the kitchen table with Bryan's mail.

She thumped the steering wheel and swore softly. Her wallet, chequebook, credit card, driving licence...

She hunted in her jeans pockets for cash and counted her loose change: two pounds sixty-something. Enough for a gallon, enough to get her back to Crowjy.

She got out of the car, pumped in all the four-star she could afford and set off again for the southwest. It was already dark. She was beginning to feel hungry and thirsty. Apart from a cup of coffee in the solicitor's office she hadn't had anything since lunch. Perhaps she would stop off at a pub on the way back, get a sandwich. At this rate she wasn't going to be home before midnight. And now it was coming on to rain.

It was half past nine by the time she pulled up outside Crowjy. She left the lights on and the engine running, got out and ran through drizzling rain to the front door. For one sickening moment she thought she'd left these keys in her handbag as well, but no, they were in her jeans pocket. She opened the door and stepped inside. She pressed the light switch on the hall wall but no lights came on.

She could see a little by the light of the Beetle's headlamps outside – enough to see her way into the sitting room. She tried the lights in there but nothing happened. Turned off at the mains, perhaps. Then she remembered the card from the electricity board: OUR ENGINEERS ARE CALLING TOMORROW TO TERMINATE YOUR SUPPLY.

She felt her way along the hall passage to the kitchen, retrieved her handbag from the table and came back down the hallway to the front door.

As she stepped outside, she wondered why it was suddenly so dark and quiet. And then she realized . . . The car: the lights had gone out and the engine had stopped.

She made her way towards it through the blackness, slipped into the driver's seat and turned the ignition key. Nothing happened. She jiggled the lightswitch: nothing. She tried the wipers and then the horn: still nothing. The electrics were completely dead. She opened the glovebox and rummaged inside. There was a small torch somewhere but she hadn't used it in ages. She pulled everything out of the glovebox and let it drop to the floor. The torch was at the very back. She switched it on. It responded with a wan, dying light.

She went back indoors to call the breakdown service. There was a telephone in the sitting room but she couldn't get a dialling tone. She tapped the button half a dozen times for a line, but in vain.

The torchlight dipped to a tiny glow and then gave out altogether.

Brilliant. Bloody brilliant. No car, no phone, no lights . . .

There was a public callbox in the village, but it was a long walk through the rain. She remembered a small house not very far along the road, in the opposite direction.

She went back outside and hurried down the track. She had nothing waterproof to wear, but it was only drizzling now. She walked along the lane for about ten minutes and came to a small detached house set back from the road. She could see lights on in one of the rooms downstairs. She walked up to the front door. There was no bellpush, so she knocked. Nobody came. She knocked again, a little harder. A dog barked. Then the door opened revealing a dour-looking middle-aged woman in a dimly lit hallway.

'I'm sorry to bother you,' said Sara. 'My car's broken down

just along the road. I wonder if I could use your phone to call the breakdown service?'

The woman looked at her as if she didn't much like what she saw.

'I don't have a phone,' she said.

She was lying, Sara could tell.

'There's a callbox in the village,' the woman added. And pointed back down the road towards Boskinnow. 'Next door to the shop.'

She nodded good night and closed the door without waiting for Sara to reply.

'Thanks a heap,' Sara muttered, hurrying back down the garden path. She looked along the road but couldn't see the lights of any other houses. The rain was coming down harder again. She decided to run back to Crowjy and shelter there until the rain had stopped.

She was wet through by the time she reached the barn-cottage. And so hungry. She retrieved the torch from the sitting room and gave it a shake. It revived just a little. She went looking for the mains switch and the fuse box. She found them at the end of the hall passage. She shone the light on them. The mains switch was *on*. She switched it off, opened the cover of the fuse box and removed one of the fuses: blown.

She shone the torch around, looking for fuse wire. None. Typical Bryan. She went into the kitchen and searched the drawers and the cupboards. No fuse wire. But candles. And matches. Also some tinned food – baked beans, soup, corned beef and a jar of coffee. She lit three candles and placed them around the kitchen. She found a can opener and a saucepan and opened a tin of chicken soup.

Dumb thinking, dearie... How was she going to heat it? The Rayburn wasn't lit and there was no power for the hob. And if there was no power, then the pump would not be working to draw the water from the well. She went to the sink and turned on the cold tap. A miserable trickle of water drizzled out. But it was enough for coffee.

She was beginning to shiver with cold. She found some firelighters in the recess beside the Rayburn, and brought some coal and logs in from the lean-to shed outside. At least she could dry out and keep warm till the rain stopped.

She lit more candles and scattered them around the sitting room, and laid a fire in the big granite hearth. When that was burning brightly, she balanced the pan of chicken soup on top. She took off her jeans and denim jacket, draped them over the back of two upright chairs to dry and sat in front of the fire, wearing only her plaid shirt.

The soup took an age to warm up.

Strange, she had no unpleasant feelings being here, despite all its associations, despite the manner of his dying. She had dreaded coming here, but now she was here there was nothing about the place that felt tainted with death. Hard to believe that this was her house now. There was a twist of irony about that – the whirligig of time. Impossible to believe that this is what he really wanted. But when people took their own lives perhaps they didn't care what happened afterwards to those who were left behind.

Why, Bryan? Why?

She was thinking about that bizarre painting of a woman with no eyes. She got up and padded barefoot into the studio and brought the picture back to the fireside. She sat contemplating it by candlelight. It was difficult to know whether it was finished or not.

There was something sensual about her, but her body was not a natural shape. Perhaps he had not had time to colour her skin. Even her nipples were colourless. There was no hair anywhere on her body. She looked as if she were made of latex and inflated. Or of wax, melting wax. She was both beautiful and ugly; graceful and deformed. Her lips looked mauve in the candlelight. They were open, as if she were sucking through an invisible straw. There was a glimpse of fire inside her mouth, brilliant gold and crimson flames. It was like looking through a peep-hole into a furnace.

She sat drinking the soup and contemplating the picture.

By the time she had finished the soup and heated the water for coffee it was half past ten. It was still pouring with rain outside. Even if she walked to Boskinnow now, and even if there was no more than an hour's wait for the breakdown van, she would still be lucky if she was home before two in the morning.

She took a candle upstairs and looked inside the spare room.

There was a small bed pushed back against the wall, hidden away behind all the boxes and cases. It was not made up but some folded blankets sat piled up on the mattress with two pillows. She found some sheets in a narrow cupboard which housed the hot-water tank beside the bathroom, cleared some space for herself and made up the bed.

Downstairs, the fire had burnt low. She left her jeans and jacket draped over the chairbacks, blew out the candles – saving just one to light her way upstairs – and went to bed.

She awoke in the pitch dark. For a moment or two she had no idea where she was. She was hot – so hot that she was sweating. She sat up and sniffed the musty air. She could smell smoke. She swung her legs out of bed, stood up and groped along the wall, trying to find the light switch. Then she remembered, the fuses had blown. She fumbled on the floor and found the candle.

No matches . . . She'd left them downstairs.

She opened the bedroom door. The landing was thick with smoke, hot choking smoke. She couldn't see a thing. She blundered straight into the wall and gave her head a painful crack. She felt her way to the edge of the staircase and began to descend, slowly, blindly. The smoke got thicker. She was coughing. She began to panic. She was so desperate for breath by the time she reached the bottom of the stairs that she flung open the front door and stumbled outside into the rain, gasping in the fresh air. She took a few deep breaths and then went back inside, into the sitting room.

What the hell was burning? She could see no flames, not even a glow of embers in the fireplace. But it was so *hot* and the smoke was so dense. She remembered her jeans and jacket that she'd left in front of the fire to dry, and fumbled her way towards the fireplace, coughing and spluttering as the filthy smoke began to get into her lungs. She collided with chairs and felt for the jeans and jacket . . . They were still damp and cold. She retreated to the windows and flung them open. No fire flared up; whatever had been burning had burnt itself out. The smoke began to disperse. She lit a candle and looked around the room. Her jeans and jacket were not even scorched.

Perhaps it was simply the wind, blowing smoke back down the chimney?

But the windows were wide open now and she could feel scarcely a breath of wind.

Perhaps there was a blockage in the chimney?

And then she noticed the painting, or what remained of it ... The picture of the woman with no hair, that she'd left propped up against a chair. She'd left it too close to the hearth. The fire must have spat out a burning fragment and set light to the canvas. It had burnt to ashes. There was nothing left of it but some blackened scraps of fabric pinned to the charred rectangle of the wooden stretchers on which it was mounted.

She slept badly for the remainder of the night, awoke again just after dawn, and went downstairs. There was no smell in the room, not even a lingering trace of that acrid smoke.

She looked again at the charred remains of Bryan's painting. The fire had not even scorched the legs of the chair that it was leaning against. It was a miracle that she hadn't burnt the house down.

She remembered feeling hot in the night ... so hot that she was sweating. Yet now, the house felt chilly and damp.

It was a fine clear morning outside. She thought she would try the car one more time before she set off for Boskinnow to telephone the breakdown service. She put the key in and switched on the ignition. The windscreen wipers came on and the starter motor turned vigorously. The engine fired and spewed blue exhaust into the sweet Penwith air.

Later that day she called British Telecom to ask whether they had disconnected the line to Crowjy. The operator checked and said that the line had not been disconnected; she offered to report a fault to the engineers.

The engineers called her back the following day. They had tested the line to Crowjy. There was nothing wrong with it. It was working quite normally.

ASHES

She moved in two weeks after Easter. It was her birthday, 18 April.

She had her first visitor the following morning. She had not long finished breakfast. She was unpacking all her books in the sitting room when a mud-splashed Renault Espace came up the track and pulled up outside. A woman got out. She was tall, not slim but well made. She had honey-blonde hair and wore a calf-length skirt and turquoise blouse.

Sara opened the front door as the woman approached. She had an open friendly expression.

'Hope it's not a bad time. I'm Clare Doriel. We're neighbours, sort of. I live just around the hill at Trevow. We were friends of Bryan.'

She had a fluent, confident voice, Home Counties perhaps, stockbroker belt.

'I'm Sara, his sister.' They shook hands. 'But I guess you know that already.'

'We did hear.' Clare smiled. 'Down the Boskinnow grapevine.'

'Come in.' Sara stepped back. 'Awful mess but . . .'

'Sure I'm not disturbing you?'

'Not in the least.'

A black Labrador was barking in the back of the Espace, pushing his muzzle through the slightly open window.

'Bring him in, if you want,' said Sara. 'It doesn't worry me.'

'No, he's been rolling in something disgusting,' said Clare. 'He smells ghastly.'

She followed Sara into the kitchen.

'Can I get you something? Tea, coffee?'

'Coffee if you're having one. But don't bother if you're not. I just wanted to say hello, didn't mean to intrude.'

Sara filled the kettle.

'Did you know Bryan very well?'

'Just in a neighbourly sort of way.' Clare sat down at the table. 'He used to come for Sunday lunch sometimes. Perhaps he mentioned us?'

'To be honest with you, Bryan and I hadn't been in touch for a long time.' She didn't see any point in hiding the truth. It would come out eventually.

'We guessed something of the kind,' Clare confessed. 'We didn't know he even *had* a sister until quite recently. He never talked about you.'

'No, well...' Sara smiled ambiguously. 'I'm not surprised.'

'Tim Hendra was the only one he told – our local GP.'

'Ah, yes, the police mentioned him.' Sara spooned instant coffee into two mugs. 'They told me that Bryan didn't have many friends down here, is that true?'

'I suppose he didn't.' Clare sounded as if she hadn't really thought about it before. 'He didn't mix much socially – not in recent years, anyway. Became rather reclusive.'

Sara found that hard to imagine, Bryan being reclusive. She remembered him as being just the opposite. He couldn't bear his own company at one time – except when he was working.

They took their mugs of coffee into the sitting room. Her books and papers were still cluttering the floor space in old grocery boxes. And she still had to find room for her record collection, her stereo equipment, her television and videorecorder, personal computer and all its peripherals.

'Excuse all this,' she said. 'I haven't got room for anything until I sort through Bryan's stuff.'

'Moving in is a nightmare, isn't it?' Clare sympathized. 'Nothing works, nothing fits, and all the locals stare at you as if you've got rabies.'

Sara shifted a box of papers off a chair so that Clare could sit down, but she seemed happy to browse through Bryan's record collection.

'It's all been a bit of a shock round here, what's happened,' she said, picking out a vintage John Lee Hooker album. 'You know what country places are like, how rumours spread. There's all kinds of talk in the village about who's moving in here and whether it's been sold.'

'Well, it may have to be – sold, I mean,' Sara replied. 'But I'll be here for a few months at least, while we get Bryan's affairs sorted out and the police finish their enquiries.'

'They don't think that anyone else was involved, do they?'

'Not as far as I know. They haven't kept me very well informed.'

Clare wandered through to Bryan's studio and cast her eyes over Bryan's unfinished paintings. Sara stood in the open archway.

'I don't know what I'm going to do with those. I've destroyed one already, by accident.'

'Really? What happened?'

Sara told her the whole story: the car not starting, no electricity in the house, the phone line dead, walking down the road, getting soaked, the log fire, waking in the night, the house full of smoke.

'Poor you. What a nightmare.' Clare turned to her, appalled. 'Why on earth didn't you come to us?'

Sara laughed. 'Well, I didn't know I had any neighbours. Except that miserable-looking woman down the road.'

'That must have been Vera Roscarrock.' Clare turned up her nose. 'She's a bit of a sourpuss. Her daughter, Lynn, works for me.' She came back into the sitting room. 'So what caused so much smoke? Can't have just been the picture.'

Sara shrugged. 'Something in the chimney, I suppose.' She looked down at the hearth. 'I'll have to get a sweep in to poke around. Is there anyone local?'

'Alan Penberthy. Lives at the head of the valley. Grumpy old bugger but he does a good job. I don't know his number but you'll find him in the *Yellow Pages*.'

Clare noticed a framed photograph hanging on the wall, between the fireplace and the window that overlooked the back garden. It was a photograph of a barn.

'That looks familiar.'

'We're *in* it,' said Sara. 'Or those four walls, at least.'

'Oh, that was *here*?'

'How it was before the First World War.' Sara took the photograph off the wall and handed it to Clare. There were no chimneys then, and no studio extension. A block and tackle protruded from an opening in the hayloft for loading and unloading wagons. Two labourers were standing in front of the barn looking shyly at the camera.

'1911,' said Sara, 'or so it says on the back.'

Clare flipped the picture over. As she placed it back on its hook she noticed a large grey patch across the thinly plastered wall.

'Looks like you've got some damp coming through.'

Sara had not noticed that before. A grey-brown stain, roughly star-shaped, about three feet high and two feet wide.

Clare ran the flat of her hand over it. 'You can buy silicone stuff to paint or spray on the outside. That usually stops it.'

She ran her hand over it a second time.

'Doesn't actually *feel* damp. Feels bone dry.'

'Maybe it's just an old stain that's been painted over,' said Sara.

Clare looked at her hand. It was covered with a white limey dust. She brushed it off and wiped her hands lightly on her skirt.

That night, as they got ready for bed, her husband, Roger, said: 'How's she taking it?'

'She seems okay. I don't think she knows much about it.'

Roger climbed into bed and picked up a Wilbur Smith paperback from his bedside table.

'I think they must have had a rather difficult relationship,' said Clare.

'She's nothing like him, I hope.'

'Not remotely. She seems very pleasant, easy-going. Doesn't even *look* like him. Looks more Welsh than Cornish. Dark eyes. Pale skin. Extremely attractive.'

'Tim's type?'

'Oh, definitely Tim's type.'

Her right hand was feeling very sore. She turned it into the light of her reading lamp.

Roger glanced at her over his glasses.

'Splinter?'

'Feels as if I've burnt it.'

She got into bed and picked up her book. Her hand was beginning to bother her. The burning sensation was spreading all over the palm and across the fingers. She was feeling it in her other hand as well now. She examined them again. The flesh was turning a deep reddish colour, as if she'd been picking raspberries.

By the following morning, several small blisters had begun to appear on both palms and the hands were sensitive to heat – even to moderately warm water.

'How did you do it?' asked Roger at breakfast, as he helped her pin a bandage around the right hand.

'I can't imagine,' said Clare. 'Perhaps I scalded them when I was cooking. But I can't think when.'

Sara telephoned Penberthy, the sweep. He came a few days later, with his hirsute son, their vacuum cleaner, protective sheets and Dickensian-looking brushes; their ex-Navy Transit van, bumper and rear doors alike secured with bailer twine, and Plymouth Argyle FC stickers brightening up the windscreen in lieu of road tax.

She explained about the smoke. Penberthy was a big man, sallow and morose-looking, with heavy stooping shoulders and a belly that rolled over his thick leather belt. He sucked in air through his teeth and nodded, Ez, ez, ez ... Probably a blocked flue, he said. But when his son scrambled up on the roof and pushed the brushes down, they found the flue was clear. There wasn't even very much soot to dispose of.

'This wadden long ago cleaned,' Penberthy concluded. He wasn't too pleased about it. As if he'd been brought out under false pretences. 'Thear edden nothen up thear.'

'Well, what could have caused all that smoke then?' Sara wondered.

'Prob'ly just the wind all arsey-versey,' he said, as if it were too trivial to discuss.

He pointed to the black metal canopy above the hearth that was supposed to funnel the smoke into the flue. 'They bloody things cause more trouble than they're worth and all.'

'So what do I do if it happens again?' said Sara.

'Try smokeless coal,' he said, and wrote her a bill for twenty pounds.

And where do I get smokeless logs, she was going to enquire. But he didn't seem to have a sense of humour.

*

She sat in Bryan's bedroom. She had avoided this room until now. She was still sleeping in the spare room on the narrow divan. She sat on the bed and tried to draw something out of the atmosphere, some vestige of his existence. She felt absolutely nothing. It was just another room. Strange, he had been such a dominant figure in her life for those few years. Now he was nothing. Like a dusty old china god that had fallen off a shelf and smashed.

She looked at her suitcases, lying open on the floor, still full of clothes because she had nowhere else to put them; there was not even a chest of drawers in the spare room. This was silly, she couldn't go on like this. This was *her* home now, however temporary.

Bryan had built a fitted wardrobe across the end wall of the bedroom, with louvred sliding doors. There was something sinister about those angled slats, the darkness behind them. They were like half-closed eyelids, watching her. She got off the bed, walked across the room and slid open the doors.

An unpleasant smell drifted up from a heap of unwashed clothing on the floor: shirts, socks, underwear. Above them, hanging from a length of scaffolding pipe, was a black leather trenchcoat, old and cracked, some baggy moleskin trousers, heavy-duty corduroys, a suede jacket, a shapeless tweed coat, a leather zipper jacket, a set of trawlerman's oilskins and a dark blue suit.

She tried on the old leather trenchcoat. It was double-breasted, with wide lapels and a belt. She looked like something out of the Gestapo. It drowned her. It almost reached her ankles.

She began to empty the wardrobe. Anything that was too good to throw away, she would take to a charity shop. The rest she would take to the council dump.

She looked around. She would have to buy a long mirror; Bryan seemed to have managed with just the small mirror in the bathroom. There was no dressing table, just a small pine table with a single drawer beneath.

She opened the drawer.

There was nothing in it but a sketchpad. She took the pad out and turned the pages. It was full of drawings, all very similar, all variations of the same bizarre theme.

A woman was facing what looked like a stone wall. She was naked in some of the drawings, partly dressed in others, but her clothes were torn and ragged.

In every drawing her arms were raised out and upwards as if in surrender. Her wrists were bound or chained (the sketches varied) to a pair of iron rings set in the wall.

In some drawings, there were criss-cross marks across her back, as if she'd been beaten, the body slumped from exhaustion. In other drawings, the body was upright, the feet apart, the head raised as if in supplication at the altar to some deity.

If they were supposed to be erotic, in some twisted sado-masochistic way, they failed horribly. All that came out of those drawings was despair; screaming, abandoned despair.

That night, she slept in Bryan's large bed. She awoke early – too early, it was still dark out. She tried to get back to sleep but she could not get her mind off those macabre drawings.

What kind of obsession was it that made a man draw the same sick thing so many many times, in so many different ways?

It grew lighter outside. She hated being awake at this hour. It was that in-between time when it was no longer night but not quite day. She got up and went to the bathroom to pee. When she came back into the room, she stood by the window that overlooked the front of the house and parted the curtains. She opened the window a little wider and put her nose into the dawn air.

She could make out the pond across the track, behind the screen of scrawny blackthorn trees. It was difficult to be sure in this blue-grey half-light, but something appeared to be floating on the water.

At first she thought it was just the twilight playing tricks – shadows and ripples on the surface of the pool – it was hard to tell at this angle: her view was partly obscured by trees. She closed her eyes and opened them again. The longer she stared, the more it looked as if something *was* floating there.

Whatever it was, it was hardly moving.

She closed her eyes and opened them again. It was almost sunrise. It was not a trick of the light – there *was* something there, a dark shape on the water.

It looked like a body. Or an animal.

She went downstairs, put on rubber boots and a blue duffel coat, and went outside. She walked across the track and along the narrow path towards the dark pool.

Her boots squeaked and swished through the dew-drenched grass. She came to the edge of the pool. There was nothing there. Nothing floating on the water, not even a twig. The pool was one glossy black plate. Not a ripple on it.

It struck her how silent it was. It was daybreak already but there was no dawn chorus, not one bird song, not a sound. She could not even hear the stream that ran around the foot of the hill.

She picked up a small stone and tossed it into the middle of the pool and watched the ripples radiating out. She looked down at her reflection. Her hair looked much longer than it really was, cascading down from her head like a black waterfall, almost to her waist. Her face was distorted by the ripples. She saw two heads, two faces, side by side.

The rippling subsided, the two heads merged into one and the cascade of hair shrank back to shoulder-length, and she was left gazing at herself in the coal-black varnish of the pond's surface.

The weather turned cold and heavy rains made the house feel damp. She decided to light the Rayburn. To judge from the rust on the hobs it had not been used for some time. It was coal-fired and Bryan was probably too lazy; solid-fuel ranges needed stoking, ashpans needed emptying.

She opened up the front of the stove to look into the furnace chamber. It was full of ashes. Bryan had been burning papers in there. She picked up a poker and pushed the remains through to the ash pan. They looked like old letters, dozens and dozens of them, torn in small pieces and chucked in the fire.

Some of the pieces were not burnt right through. She picked one up and looked at it. She read:

tearing my brain in shreds

It was not letter paper, it was ruled paper, with a margin, the kind of paper students bought in thick A4 pads for study notes. It was Bryan's handwriting, she was quite sure of that.

He had a very recognizable hand – mature, artistic, but difficult to decipher.

She sat at the kitchen table with the ashes scattered over sheets of newspaper, looking for any more half-burnt scraps where the writing was still legible. They seemed to be the pages of some kind of journal. She found odd part-sentences:

destroying me. Which is what she
sucking the very soul
to punish me? Will she go on
out of my mind thinking about her
dreading the nights yet longing for
no return. It is out of Eden.
there. Getting closer every
under Senara.

She retrieved every last scrap from inside the stove and collected every scrap where the writing was still discernible. She ended up with about a hundred pieces, like the pieces of an enormous jigsaw puzzle.

She spread them out in the studio, on one of the worktops, where there was plenty of space. She managed to put together four pieces. They read:

Why does she keep coming? What in the name of God does she want from me?

She encroached gradually, deeper and deeper, into Bryan's living space, moving his things out and replacing them with her own. Most of his personal papers were stored in a cupboard beneath a bookshelf in the sitting room. It was a conjuring trick, Bryan's magic, a way of making things disappear. Every phone bill, tax assessment, water account, rates demand, overdraft letter, magistrates' summons ... They all disappeared into the cupboard and vanished within the winking of an eye. Open sesame, close sesame: problem solved. It was in no kind of order whatsoever, just one higgledy-piggledy mass, ten years deep.

She was going through it all one afternoon, putting aside anything that might be of use to the executors, when a car pulled up outside the house. She glanced out of the window. A sandy-haired man was climbing out of a dark green Rover.

He looked like another solicitor – one of Nigel Roberts's senior partners, perhaps.

As she opened the front door, he said, 'Sara Carhays?' And seemed pretty confident that she was. He was a good-looking man, forties, solid build. 'Tim Hendra.' He offered his hand. 'I was Bryan's GP.'

'Oh, right.' They shook hands. 'Come on in.' She took him into the sitting room. 'Excuse my filing system.' She indicated the piles of papers that were scattered all over the floor.

'Sorry it's taken me a while to stop by, introduce myself,' he said.

'I was going to write to you,' said Sara. 'There are a few things I wanted to ask you. The police haven't told me very much. I don't really know what's going on.'

He sat on the sofa. 'They don't tell me very much either.'

'Inspector Vincent said you knew Bryan quite well.'

'I wouldn't say that exactly. He liked boats, so we did some fishing occasionally. And I took him sailing once but it really wasn't his idea of fun. I didn't even know he had a sister until a month or so before he died. And then I didn't know whether he was really serious.'

'Why not?' She was curious to know what Bryan had said about her.

'To be frank, he'd had a bit too much to drink that night.'

'You probably know that he and I weren't on very good terms.'

'He did mention it.'

She sensed that he was being diplomatic.

'I don't suppose it was terribly flattering,' she said, 'whatever he told you.'

'I don't think he was given much to flattery, anyway,' Tim replied. 'He never seemed very enamoured of the human race.'

'I didn't really get to know him until I left school and came down here to St Ives. We had an odd relationship. The age gap.'

'Yes, I hadn't realized,' said Tim. 'He didn't mention that.'

'We had another sister, Frances. But she died.'

'He never mentioned her.'

'Clare Doriel told me he'd become reclusive. Is that true?'

'He did tend to shut himself up rather, the last few years.'

'But he had his work, didn't he? His teaching?'

In the days when she was living in St Ives, Bryan had been teaching three days a week at art school in Falmouth.

'He gave up teaching,' said Tim, 'some years ago.'

'Gave up?' She was surprised. Bryan had always loved teaching, loved the company of students. He liked their recklessness, their naïve iconoclasm, the way they pushed at frontiers, smashed down barriers, kicked against the system.

'I think he had problems at art school,' said Tim vaguely. 'Personal problems. He wasn't the easiest of men to get on with. And I think he wanted to devote more time to his own painting.'

'Was he depressed at the time he died? The police asked me the same question, but I couldn't tell them anything useful.'

'I don't think one could isolate a thing like depression from his general psychological state,' said Tim. 'He had a drink problem. I don't know if you knew?'

'No, I didn't.'

'To be frank, he was an alcoholic. He had been for some years.'

'I did wonder,' she confessed. 'All those empty bottles outside in the shed.'

'I don't want to distress you, but it does have some bearing on his state of mind at the time of his death.'

'When you say he was an alcoholic, how bad was it?'

'He was drinking several bottles a day. Severe anxiety attacks, tremor, hallucinations. He also had sclerosis of the liver. The pathologist who conducted the post-mortem said it was unlikely he would have lived much longer, anyway.'

'Did Bryan know that?'

'I certainly warned him time and again. But he didn't seem to care.'

'Do you think that's why he did it? Because he knew he didn't have long to live?'

Tim looked uncomfortable. He took his time answering.

'It's not at all clear,' he said gently, 'that he intended to take his own life. It may very well have been an accident.'

This had been on her mind ever since Vincent had first mentioned the word accident.

'How does a plastic bag end up over a man's head by

accident?' she asked, and couldn't help sounding scornful. 'Either he did it to himself or someone did it *to* him. Either way, it's got to have been a deliberate act.'

'It's not that simple, I'm afraid,' said Tim. 'There's the question of intent.'

'Well, why else does a man stick a plastic bag over his head and scrunch it tight around his neck, if he isn't trying to commit suicide?'

Tim was reluctant to answer.

She said, 'Please ... I'm not a child, just tell me. I want to know. I need to understand, I *need* that. We weren't close, but I'm still his sister and I need to know why he did it. Just tell me ... What possible alternative reason can a man have for wrapping his head in a freezer bag?'

Reluctantly, he said, 'For sexual pleasure.'

'For what?' He had to be kidding. 'His *head*? In a freezer bag?'

'They say it enhances orgasm,' he said, and apologized with his hands, as if to say this had nothing to do with him, he was just conveying the information.

Sara looked at him and snorted. 'Oh, *please*! You're telling me Bryan was kinky for freezer bags?'

'You haven't heard of this before?'

'You're serious?'

'In forensic pathology, there's a well-established connection between asphyxiation and sexual arousal.'

'A guy gets a buzz out of suffocating himself?' She shook her head incredulously.

'If you restrict the oxygen supply to the brain – by, say, a plastic bag over the head or a ligature round the neck – it can tend to produce a very strong tumescence and enhance orgasm.'

'Tell me this is a joke.'

'No joke,' said Tim. 'There's a sort of no man's land between consciousness and blacking out which people sometimes try to reach during masturbation. Not surprisingly – where they get hooked on this kind of thing – they sometimes push it too far.'

'I had absolutely no idea ...' She felt stupid now, sounding off the way she had.

'I'm not saying it's a common practice,' said Tim. 'I'm just saying it's something that pathologists do come across from time to time. It seems to be more prevalent amongst fetishists.'

'And that's what you think Bryan was doing when he died?'

'I didn't want to distress you by going into all this. But it will probably have to come out at the inquest. He did hint at it on one occasion. Only I didn't understand what he meant at the time.'

'Why, what did he say?'

'About two months before he died, Vera Roscarrock called the police. Do you know who I mean?'

'The cheerful one down the road?'

'She was complaining about his screaming rages at night. He had the DTs, he was hallucinating. I came to talk to him about it. We sat down in here. He was very drunk but he was coherent. He started talking about sex – which was not unusual for Bryan. And about sensations. He talked about being on the borderline, taking it to the edge. Him and death. Eyeball to eyeball. Death and ecstasy.'

'Death and ecstasy?'

'On the margins, that was another expression he used.'

'What did he mean?'

'He talked about this fantasy figure who came to him at nights. His succubus, he called it.'

'His *what*?'

'No, I wasn't sure what it was either, till I looked it up. A female demon that comes to men at night for sex.'

'Sounds like Bryan's idea of wish-fulfilment.'

'That was pretty much what I was thinking,' Tim confessed. 'It didn't occur to me to think he might have been playing around with asphyxiation. Or that that was what he meant by being on the edge, taking it to the borderline, death and ecstasy.'

'But how can anyone know for sure that that *is* what he was doing?' said Sara.

'We can't,' Tim conceded. 'But the plastic bag had two small puncture holes, approximately where his nostrils were. Which suggests he was trying to limit the amount of oxygen he was breathing in, but not eliminate it completely.'

'And is that what the police think? That Bryan just pushed his luck a little too far?'

'I think so,' Tim replied. 'But they have to investigate every possibility – because the back door was unlocked at the time, that's how *I* got in. But the pathologist found no signs that Bryan had struggled with anyone. And the scene-of-crime officer found no evidence that anyone else was here. But it's up to the coroner to decide these things.'

Sara had seldom given a thought to Bryan in recent years. The split had been too bitter, too total. But she could never for one moment have imagined him ending up the sad, pathetic creature he must have been. She remembered him as ribald, extrovert, subversive; always the centre of attention, holding court like a guru, surrounded by young admirers.

'He started out with so much talent,' she reflected. 'So much promise. He was so full of energy when he first moved down here. I just can't recognize the man you're talking about – reclusive, alcoholic, dead at forty-eight. Where did it all go so wrong?'

Tim contemplated the question. 'I don't really know. He saw himself as a failure. He had a self-destructive streak. It's not uncommon in artistic people. He seemed to want people to despise him. Behind all the boasting and bragging, he was a man of very low self-esteem. But whether he was an alcoholic because he was a failure, or a failure because he was an alcoholic . . .'

Tim shrugged his shoulders.

She stood in the studio after Tim had gone.

The tragedy of it was, Bryan need not have been either – an alcoholic or a failure. He *was* a good painter. He had enormous talent. She never really knew about his self-destructive side. Maybe she was too young to understand him properly. She was so stupid and naïve in those days.

But he was such a bastard. Said such hateful things.

Strange. She hadn't felt much emotion at all since his death. And now she was going to cry. But it didn't seem to matter.

They were so cruel to each other, so vicious. Like dogs fighting. It was all a kind of madness, looking back.

Her eyes flooded and spilled over.

They could have talked it through. They should have. It

didn't have to end this way. How had it all come down to this? Why did people do these things to each other?

She began to clear out the studio. She couldn't leave it the way it was, like some morbid museum to his memory. It would become *her* workroom now. The trestle-table would be her desk. Plenty of light, power sockets for her computer and printer. And all that storage space going to waste – a long line of empty cupboards beneath a waist-high worktop along one wall, and a ceiling-high fitted cupboard, like a giant wardrobe.

Most of his brushes and paints, pencils and charcoal, were scattered untidily over the worktop. She gathered up everything that was worth saving – paints and brushes that might be of some use to some other struggling artist – and put them in a large grocery box with his various inks and powders and palette knives and any other equipment that looked too useful to be dumped. She put the box in the tall cupboard.

There were some more sketchpads in the cupboard. She looked through them, wondering what to do with them. There was so much work here – years of it probably – but none of it looked very interesting. Most of these sketches looked like tentative ideas, as if he was just toying around with new concepts, possibilities.

One pad was full of drawings that reminded her of the painting that she accidentally burned, her first night here, the painting of the strange female creature with no hair.

She looked through the rest of his paintings. There were twenty-three in total, leaning against the studio wall, gathering dust. It was hard to tell which ones were finished and which were not. Bryan was in the habit of losing interest in a picture and coming back to it months later. Some of the canvases looked as if he'd started three or four different pictures on top of one another.

She wondered how much work he'd actually done in recent years. None of these canvases was dated.

There were only two that she found interesting. They were pictures of a young woman. She was naked in both.

In one, she was sitting cross-legged on a bed, peeling an apple with a long thin blade. She was looking down at what she was doing. Her dark hair hung down across her face like closed curtains.

In the other, she was kneeling on a rug in front of an open fire. Her body was wet, as if she had just stepped out of a bath. The fire was not visible, only the flames, reflected in her glistening damp flesh. Her head was tilted back and her hands were drawing her hair back from her forehead. Her neck was long and slender.

She looked quite young, full-bosomed but well-proportioned. It was impossible to tell whether she was pretty or not, her face was not clearly visible in either picture.

In both, she was wearing a thin gold chain round her neck with a serpent-shaped pendant attached.

Maybe the serpent was a symbol: Eve. The apple.

At first glance, it seemed to be a quiet contemplative picture. But then she noticed what the girl was peeling the apple *with* ... It looked like a razor, an old-fashioned straight razor, what they used to call a cut-throat, the kind her father used to shave with.

She looked even more closely and saw a seam of bright scarlet around the apple peel where it was coming away from the fruit. The apple seemed to be bleeding...

But it wasn't the apple that was bleeding, it was the tips of her fingers. She'd cut clean through the top joints of each finger. All four tips, including the nail, had been sliced off and were lying on the bed, between her folded legs, among the apple peel.

Yet there was no sign of pain in the woman's body language. She looked totally relaxed, composed, at peace. Whereas the other picture, by the fireside, suggested sensual feelings, desire, warmth, the prospect of sex – possibly ecstasy, the way her head was tilted back.

But in the dark patch of pubic hair, Sara could see something even darker. Some creepy-crawly lurking in the bush.

A scorpion. A black scorpion.

Was it just his crippled sense of humour?

What kind of bacillus was festering inside his brain?

She listened to the sounds of the house.

Was he laughing?

Was this what he was *dreading the nights yet longing for*?

She spread out all the burnt torn scraps of his journal, or whatever it was, the pieces she had retrieved from the Rayburn, spread them out on the worktop in the studio. She perched on a stool and sifted slowly through them, trying to find edges that matched or part sentences that joined.

By the time she went to bed that night, she had put together six pieces that read:

Once you have known it, you cannot unknow it. Once you have touched her, there is no return. It is out of Eden.

TREVOW

Clare invited her to Trevow for Sunday lunch.

She could have driven but she preferred to walk – through the woods behind Crowjy, across the stream and over the southeast side of Trevow Hill. About a mile.

The farm buildings stood in a slight depression on the lower slopes of the hill. The old barns and dairy sheds formed three sides of the large yard. The farmhouse made up the fourth side. Sara walked through an open gateway into the yard. Bosun, their black Labrador, came trotting over to greet her. Sara crossed to the kitchen door and walked on inside, into a storm porch.

She heard Clare calling, 'Jo?'

'No, it's Sara.'

'Oh, hi. Come on through.'

Sara kicked off her muddy boots and put on the canvas beach shoes she'd brought with her. She walked through the scullery and into a steamy kitchen with a low open-beamed ceiling. Clare was wearing baggy trousers and a man's flannelette shirt that hung loose over her hips. Her hair was bunched back in a pony-tail.

'Did you walk or drive?'

'Walked,' said Sara. 'But the woods are a quagmire.'

Pots of herbs were ranged along the window ledges; children's watercolour paintings on the wall. A large oil-fired range occupied an alcove of its own. Heavy pans hung from an iron rail above. The table was long and narrow and could have seated twenty in comfort. It had been set for seven. Clare opened the oven door and glanced inside. Sara caught the sweet smell of rosemary.

'Plain old Sunday roast, I'm afraid. I got out of the habit of fancy cooking when we moved down here.'

'I was never in the habit,' Sara confessed. 'Bryan was the only cook in our family.'

Clare crossed to a fridge the size of a wardrobe and took out a bottle of Chilean Cabernet.

'We used to have to entertain a lot when we lived in Hampshire, but that was business mostly. Now I don't have to bother, all Roger wants is school dinners. Things like toad-in-the-hole and suet pudding. Eats it till it comes out of his ears. God knows what it's doing to his arteries.'

She looked around for the corkscrew. Sara saw it lying on the table and offered to take the bottle.

'Would you, thanks,' said Clare, handing it to her. 'Hope it's okay. Roger's found this cheap warehouse near Penryn. All bin-ends. He's such a skinflint – anything marked down for clearance, he buys fifty cases regardless. It all fell off the back of a ship in Falmouth docks, I expect.'

Sara trapped the bottle between her thighs and pulled the cork with a soft grunt of effort.

'Ah, a woman with muscles . . .' A male voice.

She looked up and saw a short chunky-looking man coming into the kitchen from the inner hallway.

'I could do with you in the barn, help me shift some granite.' He approached her, offering his hand. 'Roger Doriel.'

He was older than Clare, several inches shorter and on the tubby side. His hair was short and curly, and he had a closely cropped grey-white beard. He was wearing a faded rugby shirt in Cornwall's county colours, black and gold hoops. The fly zip was broken on his jeans and he was powdered liberally with grey-white dust. He took a can of lager from the fridge as a young woman walked in from the hallway, carrying an infant. She smiled at Sara.

Clare said, 'That's Louisa.'

'Hi, Louisa.'

The young woman laughed and said, 'No, not me, I'm Lynn. *This* is Louisa.' And looked down at the infant.

'Lynn lives just along the road from you at Chy Melyn,' said Clare. 'I think you met her mother.'

'Ah, yes, of course,' said Sara.

'When was that?' asked Lynn.

She was striking, quite tall, busty, greenish eyes. Her hair was raven black and hung down over her shoulders. She wore black Levi's and a batwing T-shirt a couple of sizes too large.

'The first night I spent at Crowjy. My car broke down. I knocked on the door and asked if I could use her phone.'

'I bet she loved that,' said Lynn. 'What did she say?'

'Told me she didn't have a phone.'

Lynn let out a screech of laughter. 'She's a mean old cow, she is.'

Clare tutted and said: 'Shh ... your own mother.' But she was laughing too.

'She gets worse and worse,' Lynn went on. She spoke with a strong local accent. 'We've *always* been on the phone,' she said to Sara. 'At least, as long as I can remember. She just doesn't like strangers.'

Outside in the farmyard, piping treble voices heralded the return of children.

'Did you tell her you were Bryan's sister?' asked Roger, and started sharpening the carving knife.

'Don't think I said anything much,' said Sara. 'I gather there was a bit of ill-feeling between them.' She looked at Lynn. 'The doctor said something... What's his name?'

'Tim Hendra?' said Clare.

'Yes. He said they didn't get on very well.'

Three children tramped in through the scullery from the farmyard, arguing noisily, and began to wash their hands at the sink.

'*No one* gets on with my mother,' said Lynn.

'Not a lot of people got on with Bryan either,' Roger added.

'She doesn't like that place, though,' said Lynn, strapping Louisa into a high chair. 'She never has.'

'Percy Hosken told me they had a lot of trouble there at one time,' said Roger.

'Percy's our retired copper,' Clare explained to Sara. She carried a saddle of lamb to the table for Roger to carve. 'He used to be stationed at Hayle. His son Kevin's the local PC nowadays.'

The children came to sit down at the table. Clare introduced them to Sara. Alex, the elder of the two boys, ten years old. And the twins, Ben and Jo, who were eight.

'It was empty for a long time,' said Lynn, 'so Mum told me.'

'What was?' said Alex. He was dark and skinny, with his father's large, intelligent eyes.

'Bryan's cottage,' said Clare.

'How long has it actually been a cottage?' asked Sara.

'Since about 1960,' said Roger, carving off slices of lamb. 'The Mitchells, who used to farm this place, sold off the barn and that patch of land when they were strapped for cash.'

'It wasn't a proper barn, anyway,' said Lynn. 'It was just a ruin, Mum says. Been a ruin ever since she was a girl.'

'But I think there was a dwelling there originally,' said Sara, 'going way back. I found the surveyor's report among Bryan's papers. The well under the kitchen is about five hundred years old.'

'What kind of trouble was Percy talking about?' asked Clare, and lifted a pan of roast potatoes from the oven.

'Oh, just, you know, riff-raff,' said Roger. 'Squatters, hippies, gangbangs, dossers, all that caper.'

'Gangbangs?' said Clare in disbelief. 'How come *I* never heard about it?'

'I don't think you were invited, dear. You were a good convent girl in those days.'

A grunt of derision from Clare.

'Mum wouldn't let me play in Piskey Woods when I was a little girl,' said Lynn, tying on Louisa's bib. 'They caught a flasher there once.'

'What are Piskey Woods?' asked Ben.

He was a quiet thoughtful child. He didn't look like either of his parents, still less like his twin sister. He had dark, sculpted looks. He might have been Spanish or Italian.

'Behind Crowjy,' said Lynn. 'It was where all the courting couples used to go.'

'*Courting?*' echoed Roger, rather in the way that Clare had queried gangbangs. 'Those woods are all marsh and brambles.'

'There are places,' said Lynn, coyly, 'if you know where to look.'

Alex opened a large bottle of Pepsi and poured it too quickly into his glass. It frothed up over the top, swarmed down the sides and all over the table.

Roger said, 'Look what you're doing, fathead. Now get a cloth.'

'What does courting mean?' asked Ben.

'Bonking,' said Jo.

Clare arched an eyebrow and glanced at Sara. 'Her father's child.'

Jo was a robust-looking girl, leggy, strong, fair-haired and fair-skinned, with grey eyes, like her mother.

'Why are they called Piskey Woods?' asked Ben.

'Because they're full of piskeys, stupid,' said Jo.

'You mean I've got fairies at the bottom of my garden?' said Sara.

'You haven't seen them?' Clare replied, amazed. 'In their black steeple hats and smart red coats?'

'The state my grass is in,' said Sara, 'I wouldn't even see them if they came on a double-decker bus.'

They had coffee in the drawing room – an entire wing of the house that looked out on both sides, eastwards down the hill to Boskinnow Downs, and westwards across the farmyard, with the moors beyond. It was dominated by an inglenook fireplace. There were two bulky sofas and unmatching armchairs that looked bruised by the rigours of family life. Books were everywhere, and dishevelled newspapers, Lego, a child's sock, a slice of buttered toast abandoned by the fireplace, glasses half full of one thing or another, left loitering and forgotten.

There seemed to be a cat dozing in every chair.

'Just chuck 'em out of the way,' said Clare, realizing there was practically nowhere to sit that wasn't occupied by a fur bundle. 'They're used to it.'

Sara dispossessed a sleepy tabby of an armchair.

Roger sank back into a sofa and played with Louisa. Bosun, the Labrador, collapsed in front of the cold, empty hearth as contentedly as if a log fire were blazing in the grate.

Sara was staring at a painting on the wall. It looked familiar.

Clare smiled and said, 'I thought you might recognize it.'

'One of Bryan's?' If there was doubt in her voice, it was because he seldom painted anything that didn't have the human form in it.

'He wasn't going to sell it to me,' said Clare. 'He didn't like it. But I made him an offer he couldn't refuse.'

The painting had a surreal quality. It was a picture of the dark pool that lay across the track from Crowjy. But a Stone

Age menhir – a tall finger of granite, a single standing stone – was protruding from the middle of the pool. There was something about the way he'd painted it that suggested a woman's torso, the swell of breasts and, lower down, a hole right through the centre of the stone. The quality of the light suggested dusk and mist in the air.

'He didn't explain what it was supposed to be,' said Clare.

'What's there to explain?' Roger remarked tartly.

'You don't like it?' Sara presumed.

'I think it's crap,' said Roger.

Clare skewered him with a look.

'But then I'm not very artistic,' he added.

That sounded to Sara like a side-swipe at his wife.

'Am I, Loulou?' He stood Louisa on his knee. 'Bit of an old philistine, Poppa.'

'Do *you* paint?' Clare asked, turning to Sara.

'Unfortunately not. I wish I could.'

'So what *do* you do?' enquired Roger.

'I'm writing a thesis. For my Ph.D.'

'Really?' Clare looked impressed. 'A thesis on what?'

'Tudor history. The An Gof rebellion.'

'The *what*?' Roger pulled a face.

'An Gof,' Sara explained, 'was a blacksmith from St Keverne, near the Lizard. He led an armed rebellion against Henry the Seventh in the summer of 1497. To protest against a tax that was levied to fight the Scots who were supporting Perkin Warbeck.'

'Did he win?' said Roger facetiously.

'Nearly. He got to the outskirts of London with an army of fifteen thousand. But Henry defeated him in battle at Blackheath. He was hanged, drawn and quartered, and his head was spiked on London Bridge. His real name was Michael Joseph, but he was known down here as An Gof – Cornish for "the smith".'

'Extraordinary,' said Clare. 'I've never even heard of him.'

'What would have happened,' Lynn wondered, 'if he'd won?'

'How do you mean?' said Sara.

'Well, he couldn't have been king.' Lynn laughed. 'You can't have a blacksmith from St Keverne be king of England.'

'Why not?' said Roger. 'Look at the kings we *have* had. Frogs, Krauts, Dutchmen, child-killers, syphilitics, queers, loonies, bigamists. What's wrong with a Cornish smithie?'

'But how do you write a thesis about something so obscure?' said Clare. 'You must spend half your life in library vaults.'

'It feels like that sometimes,' said Sara. 'But I quite enjoy research.'

Louisa was growing fractious and beginning to grizzle. Roger tried to pacify her but she just grizzled all the more. Lynn took her and bounced her gently up and down and made soothing noises. The grizzling began to subside.

'I think you'd better take her upstairs,' said Clare. 'She probably wants to sleep. She was awake at the crack of dawn.'

Roger drained his cup of coffee and got up to go back to work. 'Come and see the barn before you go,' he said to Sara.

Bosun trotted out after him. Lynn followed on behind, cradling Louisa.

'She's a godsend,' said Clare, when Lynn had gone. 'I don't know what I'd do without her. I'd never get out of the house.' She finished her coffee. 'Fancy a tour?'

Sara got up. Clare led the way out into the hall and through the kitchen.

'Is she at college?' asked Sara.

'No. She left school a couple of years ago. Two GCSEs. There's such chronic unemployment down here, most girls of her age have got no hope of ever working in their lifetime. They're all bored out of their wits. No wonder she doesn't want children of her own.'

They walked through the scullery and the storm porch and out into the farmyard. The screech of an electric drill on metal echoed from the walled barn on Sara's right. They walked towards the dilapidated milking sheds on the far west side of the yard.

'Sorry about Roger's little *faux pas* just now,' said Clare.

'Not a *faux pas*,' said Sara. 'He's entitled to his views. I thought Bryan was very talented, personally.'

'I did too.'

'But he didn't leave much in the studio that I liked.'

'Roger simply didn't get on with Bryan, that's the truth of it.'

'From what the doctor was telling me, nobody did.'

'Well, Roger and Bryan were total opposites. Roger isn't interested in anything artistic – except jazz, he's passionate about that. And he hates socialists – whereas Bryan was virtually a revolutionary. The only thing they had in common was a very short temper. They actually came to blows on one occasion. We never saw much of Bryan after that.'

'What did they fight about?'

'Oh, something infantile,' said Clare, as if it wasn't worth remembering. 'Bryan came to lunch one day and got pissed and told us we were all bourgeois arseholes. Roger lost his temper and there was a bit of shoving and flailing of fists and ... Oh, it was all too ridiculous for words. Like two schoolboys.'

They came to the milking shed and stood in the doorway, peering into the gloomy interior. It was completely unrestored.

'This is going to be the new stable block eventually,' said Clare. 'I want to make a business out of it. Hire out horses. It needs a lot of work doing. It was empty for about twenty years before we bought it.'

'Nobody wanted it?' Sara was amazed. It was a superb location, the sheltered side of the hill, with National Trust land all around. 'I'd have thought it would have been snapped up.'

'Not for farming, no. The last farmer, Tom Mitchell, had an entire dairy herd wiped out by some nasty disease. The place was quarantined for about five years. The farmer went bust and put it on the market. Then the house was squatted for a while, so it was in a ghastly state. We bought it just for holidays at first and did it up bit by bit. Roger loves all that – paddling around in cement and knocking down walls.'

'So how long have you been here?'

'We bought the place about fifteen years ago. But we didn't move in permanently till the twins started school. I wanted to move sooner but we were shackled to Hampshire because of business.'

They started walking along to the adjacent dairy.

'What is Roger's business?'

'It *was* computer software. He built up his own company and invented some fancy data management system. Then the Americans made him an offer he couldn't refuse, so he decided to sell up and devote his life to meaningful things ... like hot-air ballooning and bashing down old walls. But the deal was tied up with complex share options, so the money's coming through in dribs and drabs. Which means the stables have to sit on the back burner till next year.'

They came to the old buttery and creamery.

'This is my tack room,' said Clare.

They went inside. Four saddles were seated on temporary wooden trestles. Bridles and various bits and pieces of tack that were unfamiliar to Sara dangled from hooks. Even after all these years of disuse it had not lost the smell of stale milk.

'Did you have problems with planning permission?'

'Not for these dairy sheds, no. They're only about a hundred years old. The original ones were burned down in a fire in Victorian times. But the Tudor barn was a nightmare. It's Grade Two listed.'

They stepped back out of the creamery and walked along to the stable.

'There was a family called Doriel who used to farm here a long time ago. But we don't know if they were connected with Roger's family or not.'

'It's an unusual name,' said Sara, 'it shouldn't be difficult to find out. If you don't mind digging around the births registers and the parish records.'

'Well, I've done a bit of that. But I only managed to get back to his great-grandpa, who was a captain in the navy and born in Calcutta ... All rather far removed from farming in West Cornwall.'

They peered inside the stable. There were just two stalls: one for Clare's grey hunter, Shilo, and the other for a chestnut mare called Sheba. Sara moved to pat Shilo but he jerked his head out of the way and flared his nostrils.

'Nothing personal,' said Clare. 'He doesn't like strangers. Lynn's the only one he likes, apart from me.'

'Does she ride?'

'Mm. She's quite good. I can trust her to exercise them. Sheba's an old sweetie, anyway. But I wouldn't put anyone on Shilo if they didn't know what they were doing. He's got Arab blood, he's quite a handful when the breeze gets in his ears.'

They went back out into the yard, walked past Roger's

workshop and approached a large enclosed barn on the north side that adjoined the farmhouse at right angles.

'Now this is my favourite,' said Clare. 'This is Tudor. This was the original farmhouse. Built in about 1520. It's what Roger's working on at the moment.'

The entrance was covered by sheets of galvanized iron.

'We can't get in through here, he's putting in a new door.'

Sara tried to peer in through a window but it was opaque with filth.

'The only way in is through the house,' said Clare.

'This part,' she said, as they walked through the hallway, 'is Elizabethan. Built in about 1600. That room was probably the kitchen in those days ...' She stopped and pointed to a room that abutted the Tudor barn. 'And what is now our kitchen was probably their parlour. This hall and the staircase are where they always were.'

'And what about the drawing room?' said Sara. It was a wing of its own, built onto the side of the hall.

'That's much more recent,' said Clare. 'That's Georgian. Probably about the 1750s. They just extended the house southwards, so it closed off the farmyard. And gave them another six bedrooms into the bargain.'

'Rapid family expansion,' Sara remarked. 'Obviously a fertile lot.'

'Well, that's when the Doriels were living here, we think,' said Clare, taking her upstairs. 'Perhaps that's where Roger gets it from. There was a time when I never seemed to stop being pregnant. But I had several miscarriages. Louisa was a miracle.'

'How did Roger feel about her?'

'Being a dad again at fifty?' Clare made a high-pitched sarcastic grunt. 'Thought he was cock of the walk, my dear. Ever so chuffed with himself. Can't think why.'

'Well, he had the easy part.'

'Oh-ho. And how.'

At the upper landing, Clare pointed down a central passageway with a window at the other end, and three rooms on either side. 'Those are the children's rooms, and there's a guest room which Lynn uses if she sleeps over.'

She took Sara into her and Roger's bedroom, in the Elizabethan part of the house. They had a sweeping view of the coarse grazing land across Boskinnow Downs and the curving track that led up to Trevow from the Mulfra road.

Next to their room and sharing a wall with the Tudor barn was the other guest room. It was plain and square, with one small casement window that faced east.

'It looks quite a big house from the outside,' said Clare, 'but this is the only other guest room. And with four kids, and family descending on us all summer long, we get a bit cramped. That's why we're converting the barn.'

Sara looked down at the cider-gold counterpane covering the double bed. The only touch of colour in the room. She shivered, a sudden shudder down the spine.

Clare noticed. 'It's always cold in here,' she said, 'even in summer. Never gets the sun.'

They went back downstairs, across the hallway and into what had once been the Elizabethan kitchen, beneath the guest room.

'The kids used this as a rumpus room until recently,' said Clare.

It was empty now. A jagged opening had been smashed through the wall, some four feet wide.

'This is the only way into the barn at the moment. There will be a proper door here eventually, of course . . .'

Plastic sheeting had been draped across the opening to keep out the dust. Clare moved aside the plastic and stepped into the barn. Sara followed. The barn was just over sixty feet long. They were putting in an upper floor where there had been none before.

'What are you converting it into?' asked Sara.

'A couple of attic-style rooms for the boys,' said Clare. 'And downstairs there'll be an extra bathroom, a playroom for the kids, and a utility room.'

Roger had marked out where the partition walls for the new rooms were to be built, but it was still one large open space, smelling of cement and newly treated timber. A short flight of wooden stairs in the far corner led down into darkness.

'What's that over there?' asked Sara.

'The old cellar.'

They walked over to have a look. There were only a dozen

or so steps down. Clare switched on a makeshift light that Roger had rigged up. 'It's not very big,' she said, as they started down the stairs. 'Roger's going to use it as a wine cellar.'

It was barely six feet high, with an uneven stone floor.

'It was originally covered over completely. There was a trapdoor in the barn floor and that was the only way to get in. We think it was a smuggler's hidey-hole. There's really not much other use for it.'

There was a small door that led out onto the hillside.

'We think that's quite a recent addition. Roger's going to brick it up and just have a small window there.'

'So these stairs are new?' said Sara.

'And what a sweat they were. Roger had to dig out tons of rock to make the slope.'

Sara noticed two large rusty iron rings set into the rocky wall. One on either side of the stairs, at about shoulder height.

'What are these for?' she asked.

'No idea,' said Clare. 'They look as if they've been there a long time, so we thought we'd leave them.'

Sara touched one of the iron rings. It felt cold and harsh. It seemed to stick to her flesh; like touching the frost in a freezer. At that moment she had a prickly feeling, the sense that she had been here before. She took her hand away abruptly, as if she'd been stung.

She remembered the macabre drawings in the sketchpad she found in Bryan's bedroom – the woman lashed by her wrists to two rings in a wall.

She looked up and saw Lynn sitting at the top of the stairs, looking down, watching her. It was a curious kind of stare: like someone sitting by the wayside, contemplating the odd ways of passing strangers.

That night Sara dreamt of the cellar.

She dreamt that she was awoken by a cry that came from somewhere across the moors. It was a strange wailing cry. A cry of distress. It seemed to rise into the sky like a bird of the night, and then fall and rise again and fade away.

In her dream, she got out of bed and looked out of the

window. She saw nothing but a sliver of moon partially obscured behind a black silhouette of treetops.

She heard the cry again. It sounded like nothing she had ever heard before. It was a cry of anguish, of deep inner pain, like the cry of a broken heart, a cry of the most desolate despair. It troubled her.

In her dream, she went outside. A fine drizzle was falling. She walked along a muddy path across the moors. Clouds sat low and heavy, like fog. She was wearing only her nightdress. Her shoes were slipping in the mud. The gorse was scratching her legs.

She came to the farmyard at Trevow. She was confused, looking round. The house was in total darkness. The windows were covered over – shuttered or just boarded up. It made the house look blind and sinister. She entered the barn. Now she could hear whimpering but it was very faint. She lifted a hatch in the floor and began to descend. There were vertical steps, blocks of wood nailed to the wall. Slowly down into the blackness. The whimpering was louder now. It sounded like a child.

She couldn't see a thing. Her hands groped the darkness in search of the child. She felt the wall. She felt the iron rings. She dropped onto her haunches and fumbled in the darkness. She touched the rough stone floor. She touched liquid. It felt warm and slightly oily. She rubbed her fingers together. She smelt blood. She wiped her hands down her nightdress.

At that moment she heard a scream. And woke up.

Clare awoke with a start and lay there for a minute or so, eyes wide open, wondering if it was Louisa.

She had heard a scream.

Not a sound now, just the faint buzz of Roger's snoring.

Had she dreamt it?

She looked at the red glowing figures on the bedside clock. Twenty past three. *Had* she dreamt it? It sounded so real.

She slipped out of bed, opened the door, stepped out onto the dark landing and listened.

Ben sometimes had nightmares.

Now she could hear Bosun downstairs. She switched on the light and went down to the hall. She found him in the barn, in the dark, his nose pressed to the sheets of corrugated iron that had been fixed across the entrance, where a new door was yet to be fitted. His hackles were up. He was growling, almost barking.

She went back into the hall, through the kitchen and scullery, unlocked the door of the storm porch and stood outside and listened. Bosun came with her and trotted across the yard to the main entrance on the east side and stood in the gateway, looking down the hillside.

Probably a fox ...

Then she heard Shilo, her grey hunter. He was snickering and kicking the door of his stall. She walked across the yard to the stable, opened the outer door and put on the light. Shilo put his head over the door of his stall.

'What's all this, then,' she said to him, 'at this time of night?'

He pushed his muzzle into her hand as she reached out to him. She stayed for a while until he calmed down.

When she locked up the stable and started back across the yard, Bosun was still standing in the gateway, growling softly, looking out into the night.

A few days later, Sara was loading the washing machine. She noticed dirty smears down each side of her nightdress, at about hip level. She spread the nightdress out on the kitchen table and examined it more closely. They were fingermarks. It was not dirt, it was blood.

And there was mud all around the hem. Dry, encrusted mud.

TIM HENDRA

May brought the first long spell of dry summer weather. The garden was turning into a small wilderness, indistinguishable from the scrubby woodlands beyond.

Sara tried to coax life into the old Atco petrol mower in the lean-to shed, but it was a lost cause. She saw a postcard in Mary Treneer's shop window, offering gardening services. She phoned the number and got through to Alan Penberthy, the chimney sweep. His stubby bovine son came to Crowjy and said he'd cut the lot for fifty quid. He did the job in three hours. She spent the afternoon raking it up. For his fifty quid he also threw in an inspection of the old Atco but pronounced a sentence of death. She resigned herself to the expense of a new Flymo and a hundred feet of cable.

She didn't know what to do with the Toyota. It was a typical Bryan-car: dinged and scraped and shunted and rolled. There was no tax disc on it. And if there had ever been an MoT certificate she couldn't find it in his magic cupboard full of papers.

She had the puncture repaired and managed to fire up the engine with a jump-start from the Beetle. According to *Parker's* price guide, that model, that year, was worth fifteen hundred in good condition. She advertised it in the *Cornishman* and sold it for a third of that. And Nigel Roberts, Bryan's executor, promptly relieved her of the cheque.

Summer was making the barn-cottage look shabby. Everywhere, the woodwork was sloughing its old skin – several generations of cheap white gloss by the look of it. Bryan had let it go for too long. Ironical, for a man whose whole life was paint and painting.

She organized a routine of sorts, working on her thesis in the mornings and spending her afternoons outside, working on the house and garden.

She started by scraping the loose paint off the sitting room windows. It came away in large papery flakes. She ran her scraper too close to the window panes in places, and nuggets of dry, cracked putty began to fall out.

She was trying to mould fresh putty into the window frames early one evening when Lynn Roscarrock came down the track, on her way home from Trevow. She stood watching. Sara felt self-conscious. There was putty everywhere except where it was supposed to be – all over the window panes, all over her hands, her clothes, even in her hair. She could feel Lynn's critical gaze like needles in her back. They became sharper and sharper the longer she remained silent.

Just when the silence was getting on Sara's nerves, Lynn said, in an accent that was rather broader than her normal one: 'You'm in a braave ole figary thear, my git lover.'

'I take it that's not good?'

Lynn had a certain type of look, a cocky grin that never seemed to be very far away, like a shifty-looking pal lurking on a street corner.

'Enjoy doen that, do'ee?'

'Not much,' Sara confessed.

The girl was making her feel like a nursery kid with Plasticine on her face. She stopped to brush flecks of old paint from the dark fluey hair on her forearms.

Lynn grinned. 'That's how my old gran used to talk.'

She was very self-assured for a nineteen-year-old, trying to cut a pose, standing there with her large round sunglasses and white shorts cut high at the thigh and tight around her backside. She wore a cotton halter, buttercup yellow, pushed out by her large bust like a spinnaker in a strong breeze.

'Can I make a suggestion?'

Without waiting for an answer, she perched her sunglasses high on her lustrous dark hair and took a small ball of putty. She worked it between the palms of her hands and rolled out a long thin worm.

'Where's the knife?'

Sara held out an old palette knife of Bryan's that she'd been using. Lynn laid the putty down in even lengths, pressing it into place and smoothing the bevelled edge. She did it with speed and fluency. Sara was impressed.

'Where did you learn this?'

'My dad. He was a decorator. I used to watch him, help him sometimes.'

When she had finished the entire window frame, she put the knife down on the ledge and wiped her hands on one of Sara's rags.

'There,' she said. 'Easy really.' She stepped back and surveyed the cottage. 'What are you going to do for ladders?'

Sara shrugged. 'Don't know. Hire them, I suppose.'

'Naah ... Waste of money. I'll ask Roger. He's got some light ali ones. We can stick 'em on his pickup and run 'em round.'

'Do you think he'd mind?' Sara knew from Gerald that men were very wary of lending their toys.

'Not if I ask him in my *special* way,' said Lynn. And a tricksy little smile twitched at the corners of her mouth.

Tim Hendra stopped by one sunny afternoon and was startled to see Lynn perched on top of an extension ladder, wearing white overalls and painting the fascia board beneath the eaves. She waved a brush in greeting and droplets of white undercoat fell around him like birdshit.

'Sara's out the back,' she called down.

The front door was open. Tim stepped inside and walked along the narrow hall passage and out through the back door. Sara was painting the rear kitchen window with undercoat.

'What's she doing up that ladder?' he asked.

'Helping me out. I haven't got a head for heights.'

'Is she safe?' He looked concerned.

'Steady as a rock. Or do you mean, should I trust her with a paint brush?'

'Either. Both.'

'She's a dab hand at it,' said Sara. 'And, best of all, she's cheap.'

'How much is she charging?'

'Lunch. And a few Cokes in between.'

She offered him tea but he said no, he was between house calls.

'I only looked in because I've been given a couple of tickets for the Minack next week. I wondered if you'd like to come.'

The Minack was an open-air theatre at Porthcurno, near Land's End. Amateur companies from all over the UK played there. A different play was presented each week throughout the summer.

'What's playing?'

'Shaw. *Saint Joan*. The tickets are for Thursday. It's the only weekday I don't have an evening surgery.'

'I've never actually been to the Minack,' she confessed. 'What happens if it rains?'

'We get wet.'

'I mean *seriously* rains.'

'We get seriously wet.'

Sara noticed that Lynn had come down from the roof and was standing just inside the back door, sipping a Coke, watching them with just a hint of that sly, aggravating grin.

Later, when they were taking a break, sitting outside on the newly mown grass, Lynn said puckishly, 'I think he fancies you.' And toyed with the daisies.

'Who does?'

'Tim Hendra.'

'Don't be daft,' Sara chided her, smiling. 'He's the local doctor.'

'What's that got to do with anything? He's the same as any other man – more so probably, seeing women with their clothes off every day.'

Sara laughed. 'Don't be ridiculous.' (This would be all round Boskinnow by the weekend, she could see it coming.) 'He's simply a neighbour with a spare ticket for the Minack.'

'There's plenty of other women he could have asked.' Lynn's tone was girlish and teasing. 'St Ives is full of 'em.'

'I'm sure it is,' said Sara.

Lynn lit a cigarette, pulled up her T-shirt to expose a firm young belly and lay back in the sun.

'Did you know he was married?'

'Was or is?'

'Don't know. She left ages ago.'

Lynn let her head roll to one side, looked towards the woods and took a long draw on her cigarette.

'Just packed her bags one day and walked out. She was a city woman at heart. Didn't like us yokels.'

Sara said nothing.

'Do you think he's attractive?' said Lynn.

'I haven't really thought about it.' That wasn't strictly true. She had started comparing him with Gerald. 'Hardly know him, do I?'

'You don't have to *know* a man to find him attractive,' said Lynn. 'You just have to look at him.'

'There's more to it than just looks,' said Sara.

'Depends what you're after, doesn't it?' said Lynn, and closed her eyes against the bright sun.

She sounded cool and coquettish, as if she'd heard that line in a movie somewhere.

It was a spectacular setting for a theatre; as if a giant's hand had reached out and scooped a hollow out of the clifftop, and masons had carved terraces from the rockface, steeply banked in crescents around the open stone stage. Behind the stage, the only backdrop was the ocean, two hundred feet below, and, somewhere beyond the horizon, the north coast of Spain.

It was the interval. Sara had brought a Thermos of coffee. Tim had brought cushions for the flat stone seats but they were glad to stand up now and ease their aching backs. The sun was low in the sky and it was quite chilly with the sea breeze. It had been a hot June day but Sara was thankful now that she'd brought a thick sweater.

He asked how the painting was coming along.

'Slowly when I'm on my own,' she confessed. 'Speeds up no end when Lynn puts in a stint. I don't know quite why she bothers.'

'She gets bored, I suppose.'

'She must have friends, surely?'

'But mostly in St Ives, so far as I can make out. She goes in at weekends. A bit of a rough bunch. She's probably the only one with a job. Most of her old classmates are either pregnant or on probation.'

'How do you know?'

'They're registered with us.' He grinned. 'You'd be amazed how much GPs get to know.'

'What happened to her father?'

'He died about six years ago. Just after I moved here. Lynn was very close to him, it hit her very hard.'

'There doesn't seem to be much love lost between her and her mother,' said Sara.

'No, she's a headstrong girl. She was a bit wayward after her dad died. Vera's never really had any control over her.'

The sun sank beneath the horizon as they burned the Maid of Orléans. The sky was a sumptuous mess of gold and purple and copper. The masthead lights of fishing boats bobbed like stars on the darkening sea, and far out to the southeast flashed the clear bright pulse of the Wolf Rock lighthouse.

It was fully dark by the time they climbed back to the car park.

A tight procession of bright red tail-lights crept down the steep hill into Porthcurno and through the valley towards the St Buryan–Land's End road.

'Do you think the Vatican believed she was a witch?' Tim wondered.

Sara laughed. 'Probably. The Catholic Church always was a bad loser.'

'Didn't it occur to them that if she *was* a witch, she'd have had the power to save herself?'

'I doubt it. The Frogs just wanted someone to take the rap. And it was more fun to burn a woman.'

'You don't sound very sorry for her.'

'I'm not really,' Sara confessed. 'I don't feel a lot of sympathy for these crusading types who say God talks to them in their dreams. They just sound like schizoid wackos to me.'

'Did God talk to An Gof the blacksmith in his dreams?'

Sara laughed. 'I don't think so, no. He just had a grouse about his taxes, that's all. But he took it a bit more to heart than the rest of us.'

They came to the junction with the Land's End–St Buryan road. Tim turned right for Penzance.

'Do you know about dreams?' said Sara. 'I mean, *why* we dream.'

'Don't eat cheese at night. That was Granny Hendra's nostrum.'

'I had a peculiar dream a few weeks ago. It was that Sunday, when I had lunch at Trevow.'

'That'll be the garlic in Clare's cooking. She chucks it in by the fistful.'

'You know the barn they're converting? And the little cellar?'

'I had a quick look when Roger and Shane were putting the new stairs in. What about it?'

'I dreamt I woke up and heard someone cry out, somewhere across the moors ... Like someone in despair. I went outside to find out what it was. I walked across the hillside in the dark. I came to Trevow and went down into the cellar. I heard a whimpering sound. I felt around and touched a pool of liquid on the floor. It was blood. And I wiped my fingers down my nightdress. At that moment I heard a woman scream. And I woke up. I mean I *really* woke up. A few days later, I was putting my nightdress in the washing machine. And I found streaks of dried blood down the side. Fingermarks.'

Tim was overtaking another car at that moment and didn't say anything until he was back in lane again.

'So?'

'So where did the bloody fingermarks come from?'

'How should I know? Were you menstruating?'

It was the kind of thing Gerald would have said. But *he* would have said it in company. She gave him what boxers call an old-fashioned look.

He sensed it and said, 'Well, I'm a doctor, what do you expect?'

'No. I was not. And nor had I cut myself.'

Tim pulled out to overtake another car.

'And that wasn't all ... I found dried mud around the hem. How did *that* get there?'

'Magic.'

'I'm serious.'

'Tez they darn piskeys yo.'

'No, seriously ... How do you get mud on the bottom of your nightdress?'

'I wouldn't know, I don't wear one.'

Sara blew him a raspberry and gave up.

'Well, *I* don't know, do I?' Tim protested, good-humouredly. 'Kitchen floors get muddy. People leave muddy boots by the stove to dry. Maybe you trailed your nightdress along the floor when you loaded up the washing machine. Or let it brush against your muddy boots in the hallway.'

'I hadn't thought of that,' she confessed.

'Well, what else are you suggesting? That you walked through the woods and up to Trevow in your sleep?'

'No, not as far as Trevow, but suppose I *did* walk in my sleep? In the garden, say.'

'Well, what if you did? It's not uncommon. Something like half a million people in this country walk in their sleep.'

'But that still doesn't explain where the blood came from.'

'Are you sure it *was* blood?'

'Well, it looked like blood. Smeared down the sides, like a kid wiping jam off its fingers.'

'Do you eat beetroot? Raspberries, blackberries, strawberries, tomatoes? Use red ink, mess with Bryan's paints?'

'In the middle of the night?'

'How do you know those fingermarks got there in the middle of the night? You said you didn't notice them until you loaded the washing machine a few days after the dream.'

He had a point, she had to admit.

'You could have made those marks on your nightdress at any time,' he continued. 'Could even have been that same morning you did the laundry. If you had something reddish on your fingers you'd have marked the nightdress as soon as you picked it up.'

'I hadn't thought of that either,' said Sara. She felt slightly disappointed. 'Now you've burst my balloon. Spoilt the mystery.'

'I have a habit of doing that, I'm afraid,' he said. 'I'm one of life's dull rationalists. All textbook and no imagination, my ex-wife used to say.'

When they got back to Crowjy, she made some hot chocolate and warmed a pan of soup. When she came back into the sitting room she found Tim looking at the books on her shelves.

'Curious tastes you have.'

'Most of those are Bryan's. Not my kind of thing at all.'

He had a strange passion for Westerns, and a not-so-strange

passion for hardboiled thrillers – Loren Estelman, Elmore Leonard, Ross MacDonald.

'I was thinking of giving them to the hospital,' she said.

'I wasn't referring to the paperbacks,' said Tim.

He removed a volume from among Bryan's outsize art books that were arranged along the bottom shelf, quite separate from the pulp fiction. He read from the spine:

'*Lyall's Forensic Criminology.*'

She came closer to see.

'Heavy stuff.' Tim flipped through it. 'What on earth would he want this for?'

'He was a secondhand book freak. I don't think he ever bought a new book in his life.'

Tim put it back on the shelf and came to sit down on the sofa. He picked up his bowl of soup and a slice of toast. She put some jazz on the record player, one of Bryan's well-worn LPs.

'Not a very interesting supper, I'm afraid. Bryan was the culinary whiz in our family. Did he ever cook for you?'

'Christ, no.' Tim laughed. 'We weren't *that* friendly. I don't think he even cooked for himself for the last year or two. Lived on bread and honey.'

'What about his teeth?'

'When your liver's in that condition, you don't really need to worry about your teeth.'

He was looking at the large stain on the wall, between the fireplace and the window.

'You've got some damp coming through there.'

'I don't know what it is. It doesn't *feel* damp. Was it there before, can you remember?'

Tim broke off a corner of toast and dipped it in his soup.

'Can't say I ever noticed it, no. But, then, I wasn't really looking. When you were with Bryan, you tended to keep your eyes on *him*. You never knew quite whether he was going to throw something at you . . . like a chair, or the poker.'

'I'm going to give it a coat of emulsion,' said Sara, looking over the wall. 'See if that does the trick. It might be just an old stain.'

'Could be. Wine, coffee, tea . . . Bryan was given to throwing all kinds of things around when he was on a binge.'

'Perhaps it was intentional. An inspired flash of abstract genius.'

'An unfinished mural, you mean. "Red wine thrown in anger."' Tim smiled, not unkindly. 'It could have been the one last great work that made his name.'

'Wouldn't that be my luck?' said Sara. 'Rolling two coats of Dulux over something that could be worth a million in ten years' time.'

When Tim left, she remained on the doorstep while he started the car and made a three-point turn. As he drove forwards and swung the car round so that it straddled the old cart track, his headlights were on high beam and briefly cast a strong white light across the area of the pond beyond the copse of trees.

At that moment she thought she saw something move beside the pool. She had no clear sight of it, for the car was swinging round and its lights were sweeping across the trees in one moving arc. But something appeared to dart away from the pond's edge, into the shadow of the trees; as if some timid creature, like a deer, had been drinking there and was startled by the glare of white light.

Tim drove down the track to the lane. She watched as his tail-lights disappeared from view and the sound of his car faded away through the bends of the valley.

She looked up at the clear sky, the stars. She made out the Plough, the only one she could recognize. She smelt the air. There was a faintly acrid tang on the breeze. As if something had been burning – timber perhaps, or straw stubble; and not so very far away.

She went back to the sitting room and retrieved the book Tim had found, the book with the strange title, sandwiched between works on De Hooch and Vermeer. It had a faded green cover. She lifted it off the shelf and sat down on the sofa.

On the title page, beneath *Lyall's Forensic Criminology*, and beneath a list of contributing professors, all of whom seemed to be fellows of the royal institutes of almost everything, she read: 'Volume VII. Case studies of religious, cult, and occult sexual deviancy, paranormal-related sexual psychosis and psychosexual criminality.'

She looked through it. It was printed on glossy paper and

illustrated with grainy black and white photographs, many of them pictures of dead or mutilated bodies.

The text was cold and factual, littered with medical terminology.

She came to a photograph that seemed horribly familiar. It was of a dead woman, naked except for a pair of stiletto-heeled shoes, her arms stretched out and up, her wrists lashed to what looked like hooks set into a wooden crossbeam above her head. Her body was slumped – she was almost on her knees – held up only by the ties that lashed her wrists to the hooks in the beam. She was facing a brick wall, so her features were not visible. She had curly blonde hair. Her back was a mess of blood and weals. Sara wondered why the picture seemed familiar. And then she remembered: it was almost identical to those drawings she had found in Bryan's sketchpad in the bedroom.

She sat at the studio worktop, shifting round the burnt remains of his papers. She added some more to the line that she had put together the first time. She made:

Why does she keep coming? What in the name of God does she want from me? She's tearing my brain in shreds, sucking the very soul out of me. I spend my time dreading the nights yet longing for them. It's all I have left. Is she doing this just to punish me? Will she go on for ever? Until what?

'She'? His succubus?

Then why was she punishing him?

Her eyes kept going back to one solitary scrap on which she could just make out the two words: *under Senara*.

It was a woman's name. Senara was the Latin form of a Celtic saint, from whom Zennor, the west-coast village, took its name. She had never come across it before, except in Cornish literature.

The stain on the wall was a mystery. She rolled a coat of white emulsion over it and obliterated it. But a few days later it began to return. It seemed to seep through the paint, as if the damp were working its way back to the surface. By the end of the week it was as bad as before.

And yet there had been no rain. The weather had been hot

and dry for several weeks. It was the damp patch that was never damp.

She asked Roger's advice, and Roger asked Shane.

Shane Pascoe was the jobbing builder who helped him with the barn from time to time. According to Clare he was chewy, fortyish, and unpredictable. He was a surfer, a former national champion, she said. He came and went according to his moods, the weather and the tide tables.

He turned up at Crowjy one morning and studied the stain on the wall. He had the lean, taut physique of a middleweight boxer. His hair was a mixture of grey and blond, tied back in a pony-tail. He had two gold rings in his left ear-lobe, close together.

'What did you paint over it with?' he asked.

'Just ordinary emulsion,' said Sara. 'But the stain came back.'

The stain was keyhole-shaped, fading as it approached the bottom of the wall. It was about five feet in height and half as wide at its widest point. Shane scowled at it and pushed his thumbs into the waistband of his threadbare cut-offs. He looked like a beach bum at an exhibition of abstract art.

'What I'd do,' he decided, 'is strip'n down. Right back to the granite.' He pointed to some tiny hairline cracks that were already appearing in the emulsion that Sara had applied. 'See, someone put a thin layer of plaster on originally. And then painted over'n. Now the old plaster's flaken away from the wall. That's why she's all cracken up. You can see here . . .' He pushed a fingernail into what looked like a small blister on the wall. It cracked open and flecks of paint and plaster drifted down to the floor. He pointed out several more blisters and did the same thing with those.

'I'd strip un back if I was you,' he said. 'It looks a bit odd anyway – one wall white and all the rest plain granite. Just use a paint scraper – should come off easy enough.'

Some of it came off easily – in big crazy-shaped strips, thick as a postcard. But elsewhere she had to scrape and scrape, and work at it with a wire brush.

It took her the entire afternoon and most of the evening. It was hot work. She couldn't believe how hot. At one point, sweat was trickling down from her forehead and into her eyes and making it difficult to see. She began to feel short of breath. She stopped to take a rest. It was growing dark. She opened the windows to let the breeze blow through and slumped down onto the sofa. Her shirt was wet with perspiration, front and back.

'Dear Lord . . .' She lifted the front of her shirt and wiped her face. 'Sweating like a hog here.'

Where had she heard that before?

She had a mental picture of a young man with his trousers loose around his thighs, his braces dangling. He was staggering, as if he were half drunk.

Dear Loord . . . I'm took claf here, girl. I'm sweaten like a hog.

Where *had* she heard it? It seemed long ago, and yet it was so clear in her mind – the image of him, standing there, staggering, the bewilderment in his voice.

A breeze troubled the edges of the curtains.

She could smell hay. A farmer had mown a field upwind somewhere.

She felt peculiar. She closed her eyes. Maybe she'd go to bed, clear up the mess in the morning.

Took claf here, girl.

She smelt vinegar.

Do the locomotion, do yer?

A man plucking a shred of tobacco from his tongue with oil-black fingers.

She thought of tulips.

She came to. Perhaps she had dozed off. She was slumped on the sofa. It was fully dark out now.

She got up and put on the lights. She felt worn out, and shivery, as if she had a bug, a touch of flu coming on. She brushed up the worst of the mess, tipped all the flakes of paint and plaster into a large plastic bucket and left the rest until the morning.

She felt fine again the next day. She looked at the sitting room in broad daylight. Shane was right. The stain had completely disappeared. She had scraped it all away, along with the paint and plaster. There was no sign of any damp there now; nothing but plain dry granite.

After breakfast she settled down in the studio to work on

her thesis. Her hands felt sore. She wondered why. She looked at them. The skin was red and inflamed. She went back to the kitchen and rubbed intensive care lotion into them but that didn't seem to help. The mere act of rubbing her hands together made them even more sore. It got worse as the day wore on. Her hands felt very sensitive when she put them in warm water, or when she shovelled fuel into the Rayburn, or stirred a pan on the hob.

That night they were so painful that she got up at about two o'clock and took some paracetamol. By the following morning, blisters had begun to appear all over the palms and fleshy underside of her fingers. The blisters grew larger during the day and the flesh around them begun to puff up and turn a deeper red, as if she had been cutting up beetroot.

She put a soft dressing over the blisters and bandaged each hand. The throbbing, burning sensation wore off after a day or so, but then the blisters burst and her hands became so painful she could barely flex them without wincing.

She drove into St Ives to Tim's surgery.

He was one of four partners at the practice. They were in an Edwardian house off The Stennack, the approach road into town from Penzance and the west-coast road. The reception area had been a family sitting room once. Tim's consulting room had been a front bedroom.

He was behind an untidy desk, scribbling on someone's medical records. His suit jacket was hanging over the back of his chair. He pushed a curtain of greying sandy hair back off his eyes, but it kept slipping forward again each time.

Sara sat looking down at her bandaged hands. They were lying in her lap, forlorn, palms uppermost, like a pair of dead creatures she had picked up from the hedgerow.

When he had finished scribbling, Tim looked down at them and said: 'Worn your fingers out? Too much An Gof on the computer?'

'I wish,' she said. 'I can't even get started these mornings. I seem to have burnt them somehow.'

He unwound her clumsy bandaging and took off the mucky dressings. He looked at the wet sticky palms. The broken blisters were oozing a thick yellow-grey pus.

'That looks appetizing,' he murmured. 'Painful?' He gently explored the inflamed flesh at the outer edges of her hand.

'It is if you squeeze, yes, but not when they're just resting.'

'They're quite badly infected.' He put the palm of his hand across her brow. 'How do you feel generally?'

'Okay.'

'You look flushed.'

He put a thermometer in her mouth and then took her pulse.

'Taking medication for anything?'

She shook her head.

He took the thermometer from her mouth and studied it. 'A bit on the high side, but nothing too worrying. How did you burn them?'

'I haven't the faintest idea. I don't remember touching anything hot.'

'How about chemicals – paint strippers, household solvents, that kind of thing?'

She thought back. 'I used white spirit to clean the paint-brushes. But that's all. And I stripped the plaster off the sitting-room wall but I didn't use any solvents.'

'Well, it looks a bit messy but I don't think we'll have to chop them off just yet,' Tim concluded. 'We have a practice nurse who'll clean and dress the wounds. And I'm going to put you on a course of antibiotics – which have to be injected, I'm afraid. Burns injuries are very susceptible to sepsis. You'll have to keep both hands clean and dry for the next week or two, to give the blisters a chance to heal.'

One morning, a few days later, Lynn came to Crowjy to do some more house painting. She went into the lean-to shed, where Sara stored the paint and brushes and all the other paraphernalia. She emerged from the shed a moment later and said, '*Yeukh*.'

Sara was outside in the garden, pulling up huge weeds from the flower beds. She was wearing thick leather gardening gloves over her bandaged hands. She looked round at the sound of Lynn's voice.

'*Yeukh* what?'

'Come and look.' Lynn disappeared back inside the shed.

Sara clambered down from the border and walked over to

the shed. Inside, Lynn pointed to an orange-brown mess on the floor. Sara picked up a garden cane and poked the mess. It was sticky and viscous, like molasses; a pool of it, about two feet across, an inch or so deep. Lying on top of it was a semicircle of thick wire. It was the handle of a plastic bucket.

'*Yeukh* indeed,' Sara agreed. The treacly brown goo was all that was left of the plastic bucket. 'I've never seen anything like it. It's become molten.'

'What has?' asked Lynn.

'That was the plastic bucket I used when I stripped the paint and plaster off the sitting-room wall. It's what I put all the debris into.'

'My God. What was in that plaster? No wonder you burnt your hands. What did you do with the debris after?'

'Chucked it out with the rubbish.'

They went outside. The refuse was collected once a week. In between collections, Sara stored her bags of rubbish in an old galvanized coal bunker to keep them away from scavenging foxes. They went to the bunker. Sara opened it and lifted out the three full plastic bags that were sitting there. One of them was bottomless. Its lower half had melted completely away. The garbage slipped clean through it as Sara lifted it out. They looked down at what was left on the floor of the bunker. Some of the refuse had melted into a gluey mess, like the bucket. It smelt putrid – so putrid it turned Sara's stomach.

In the midst of it all, lay the skeletal remains of a rat – or a stoat, or a weasel, or what? It would have taken a zoologist to identify it. Its fur and flesh had completely dissolved as if it had been soaked in acid. All that was left of it was its skeleton and the blackened mush within that had once been its vital organs.

Lynn turned her head away and brought up her breakfast.

Sara saw Tim that weekend. She was out walking on the moors to the west of Carn Ewyn, following a footpath across Nansgever Downs. The footpath brought her to the northern edge of the downs where it joined the end of a tributary off the valley road, a furtive little lane with high hedgerows that branched off near Chy Melyn, where Lynn and her mother lived. The lane wandered along like an aimless schoolchild for a quarter of a mile or so, servicing a couple of cottages and Tim's modern double-fronted bungalow.

It was early evening when she came off the downs and walked along the lane. Tim's car was parked in front of the open garage, with a large sponge on the roof and a green hosepipe lying idly nearby. Declarations of intent.

Tim was in the garden, on one knee in the middle of a flower bed, scooping a dark fibrous mulch around his rose bushes.

'You're doing what *I* should be doing,' she said.

He looked up.

'Don't know why I bother. I never seem to have time to do it properly.'

He came over to the fence and hitched up his gardening trousers, earthy old cavalry twills.

'How are the hands?'

She flexed her fingers. 'Definitely improving.'

'Hendra's magic.' He smiled. 'We'll have you back on the computer in no time.'

He brushed soil off his hands and dabbed at his brow with the sleeve of a raggedy old cricket sweater. He looked at his watch. 'Tempt you to something? Beer? Glass of wine?'

'No thanks. Heaven forbid I should get in the way of honest toil and manure.' She nodded towards the barrowload of mulch.

'I've got to go in, anyway,' said Tim, 'to check that my dinner hasn't boiled dry. Come on.'

She walked in through the garden gate and followed him along the path. She glimpsed a rotary clothes drier festooned with boxer shorts and socks. He took her to the side door, between the house and the garage. Her walking shoes were muddy. He said, 'Don't worry about that,' and indicated the state of the kitchen floor. But she took them off anyway.

He washed his hands at the kitchen sink.

She admired the view from the picture window – across the moors to Zennor Quoit, with a triangular wedge of ocean just visible on the horizon.

'How long have you been here?'

'Seven years this summer.' He dried his hands, crossed to the hob and lifted the lid of a heavy iron casserole. 'Valerie – my ex-wife – didn't want to come. I was at the Royal Free in

Hampstead for ten years before I went into general practice. Val's a London lass. Only came down here for my sake. Said she'd give it a try. But she couldn't wait to leave.'

'I knew someone like that once,' said Sara, thinking unfondly of Gerald; but it was Exeter that he never wanted to leave, not London.

Tim gave the contents of the pot a gentle stir with a wooden spoon. 'Fish chowder. Hendra's patent recipe.'

'It smells good, whatever it is,' she said.

'Stay and join me. There's plenty of it.'

'I've already dragged you away from your gardening, I can't eat your dinner as well.'

'It's hardly dinner,' he said. 'Not much more than soup really.'

He took a bottle of Australian Chardonnay from the fridge.

'I think I might have discovered what burnt my hands,' she said.

And while he was opening the wine she told him about the decomposed bucket and the remains of the rat.

Tim looked concerned. 'What the hell did they plaster that wall with? You should have those scrapings analysed.'

'It's too late now. The dustmen have been.' She grinned and added with dark humour, 'I wonder what happened to the garbage truck?'

He persuaded her to stay and sample the patent chowder. They had supper in the living room. It was a large room with a dining alcove, and probably exactly as Valerie had left it. Curtains of peach velvet, a busy carpet, full of whorls and complicated flourishes, three-piece suite in dusty pink moquette, modern grandmother clock, and cutesy porcelain animals along the bookshelves. He looked so out of place here ... with his yachting magazines strewn everywhere, his fishing tackle scattered across the sideboard, his university rugby photograph on the bookshelf, his golf clubs in the bath.

There were photographs on the bookcase of a petite pretty woman with short blonde hair. She wondered if that was Valerie.

'My daughter, Susie,' said Tim, turning to see what she was

looking at. 'She lives in Florida. Married to an undersea photographer.'

He served the chowder in attractive moss-green bowls.

'Hand-made,' he said, when she remarked on them. 'Local potter. Clare's always badgering me to support the ethnic crafts.'

'Good for her.'

'I'm not sure it's very ethnic – he comes from Liverpool. There are a lot of potters around here. They buy up all the old chapels. Don't know what the attraction is.'

'Bryan nearly bought a chapel,' said Sara. 'Out at Carfury. But I didn't like it much. I preferred this area.'

Tim smiled. 'Did you have any say in the matter?'

'Well, sort of,' she said vaguely. 'There was a time when we were going to share a place. But it didn't work out. Which is probably as well. One of us had to go back to Lezant to look after Mum, anyway.'

'Why? What was wrong with her?'

'She had a stroke. She was living on her own in this squalid little place we rented a few miles out of Launceston. The stroke left her paralysed down one side. Couldn't walk, couldn't feed herself, couldn't even talk properly. I had to be there night and day. They didn't think she'd live very long. I just thought I was moving back in for a month or so at first. It didn't occur to me this was going to go on, year in, year out. That's when I started the Open University course. In the end Mum soldiered on for about five years.'

Tim nodded sympathetically. 'It's very very hard on the single carer,' he said. 'And it's nearly always a woman on her own.' He topped up their wine glasses. 'Who was it who said, "A daughter is a daughter all her life"?'

Sara smiled bleakly. 'I don't know. But they certainly got *that* right.'

'What about Bryan? Wasn't he able to help?'

'He didn't do a thing. He wouldn't even come and see her.'

'Why not?'

'Oh ... I don't know.' She sighed. It all seemed too complicated to try to explain. 'We had a sister, Frances. But she died when she was twelve. I never knew her. She was Mum and Dad's favourite. Bryan always resented that. Mum was devastated when she died. I suppose they could have tried for another child, but she was already in her mid-forties. So they decided to adopt. You probably guessed, Bryan wasn't my natural brother.'

'I did wonder,' Tim confessed. 'The age gap.'

'But then Mum transferred all her affection from Frances to me. Which left Bryan with an even bigger chip on his shoulder. He didn't get on with Dad either. Dad didn't want him to go to art school. He always wanted him to go into business. Which was everything Bryan hated.'

'What did your father do?'

'He had a music store in Plymouth. But he lost it all in the property crash in the mid-seventies. Bryan was really nasty about it. He more or less said, "Serves you right, that's what capitalism does for you." But it was very traumatic for Dad. He had to sell off our house to repay the bank loans. He never really got over it. He died a couple of years later. He was only sixty.'

'Must have been very traumatic for you too,' said Tim.

'I was still at school. Doing A levels. Which I made a terrible mess of. That's one of the reasons I dropped out for a few years and came down here to St Ives. Bummed around for a while. I just wanted to get away from it all.'

'And that's when you were going to move in with Bryan?'

'Well, that was just an idea. But it didn't work out. His marriage had gone down the Swannee. He'd been teaching in East London and he'd moved down here. I'd never really known him when I was a child. He was sixteen years older than I was. So we were like a couple of strangers, finding out about each other. It was fun for a while. But then Mum had her stroke and I had to move back home to look after her. And it all turned nasty. All the old resentment came out in him.'

'About Frances?'

'And they'd had an awful row because he didn't come to Dad's funeral. She never forgave him. I wrote to him when Mum had her stroke but he didn't even reply. And every time I phoned him, he just hung up on me. He didn't come to her funeral either.'

Tim had finished eating. He looked thoughtful. 'Do you think he felt guilty about that?'

'I think he was seriously screwed up about his whole childhood, I don't think it was just that.'

'The reason I say it is that ... One evening, a couple of months before he died, Bryan said you came to see him at night.'

Sara was mystified. '*I* did?'

'"My sister comes to me at night," he said.'

Sara shook her head and smiled. Another of Bryan's drunken fantasies perhaps. 'That's ridiculous, I hadn't seen him for ten years or more.'

'I was surprised because he'd never mentioned you until then. He said you didn't get along together. He said you were evil. And you were trying to destroy him. He said you blamed him.'

'Blamed him for what?'

'He said something about your mother. But it didn't make any sense at the time. Perhaps that's what it was all about — her illness.'

She was remembering one of those burnt scraps she had retrieved from the stove. That had said something about destroying ...

destroying me, which is what she

'I was furious with him over the way he treated Mum, sure,' she agreed. 'We were stony broke and he didn't lift a finger to help. But why did he think I was trying to destroy him?'

'You've got to remember he was a very sick man by this time. I think he needed someone to blame for the hallucinations, for his awful demons. He thought someone was tormenting him, trying to drive him mad.'

That reminded her of another line from those scraps of burnt paper, but she couldn't remember what it was.

She looked at them again when she got home.

Why does she keep coming? What in the name of God does she want from me? She's tearing my brain in shreds, sucking the very soul out of me. I spend my time dreading the nights yet longing for them. It's all I have left. Is she doing this just to punish me? Will she go on for ever? Until what?

She sat perched on her stool in the studio, shifting pieces

around, trying to make sense of some more of it. She managed to put together six more scraps. They read:

Bryan is destroying me. Which is what she wants, she and her. Bryan has infested my mind. A carnivorous angel from the black pool of hell, an eater of souls. Bryan is devouring me.

Bryan is destroying me?

Was he schizoid?

Was it the alcoholism? Did he think of himself as two people? The artist and the drunk? The one being destroyed by the other?

She studied the writing more closely.

Perhaps it was not *Bryan* ... His writing wasn't easy to read but it looked as if there was an e between the b and the r. It looked like *Beryan*.

She looked to see if there were any other burnt scraps where the name appeared. She found:

is Beryan doing?

It was quite clearly 'Beryan'.

She managed to piece together some more of that page. It read:

is Beryan? What is Beryan doing here? The name is in my ears, is in my brain, is driving me out of my skull. Is like hornets in my head. Who is Beryan? Why is she torturing me with

She re-read what she had pieced together previously, but substituting Beryan for *Bryan*. She read:

Beryan is destroying me. Which is what she wants, she and her. Beryan has infested my mind. A carnivorous angel from the black pool of hell, an eater of souls. Beryan is devouring me.

She looked again at the two paintings. They were still propped up, unframed, against the studio wall.

She found something new in them every time she looked.

The glow of an unseen fire reflected in the glistening wet flesh of the girl by the hearth ... It looked almost as if it were not a reflection at all, but as though the flames were coming out of the surface of her skin. As if her flesh were burning.

And there was something peculiar about her nipples. They looked soft and malformed, as if they were beginning to lose their shape. As if they were turning soft in the heat, melting like chocolate.

MIDSUMMER'S EVE

One evening she saw Roger Doriel on Trevow Hill with the twins. They were lugging pieces of old timber from the farmyard and piling them up on the carn. She asked what it was for.

'It's from the barn,' said Roger. 'It's some of the old rotten timber we had to strip out – the floorboards above the cellar.'

'But what are you dumping it here for?' asked Sara.

'It's for bonfire night,' said little Ben.

'But it's only June,' said Sara. 'Aren't you a bit early for Guy Fawkes?'

'Not Guy Fawkes.' Jo giggled. 'It's Midsummer's Eve.'

In ancient times, it was one of the great pagan fire festivals all over Europe, a celebration of the summer solstice with bonfires and dancing. Like many traditions absorbed into Christian culture, it had gradually disappeared into folk history. But the Cornish had held on doggedly to their Midsummer's Eve celebrations until well into the twentieth century. Almost until the time of the First World War there had been fiery street parties in Penzance, and a chain of bonfires on hilltops the length of Cornwall, starting at Chapel Carn Brea near Land's End and zig-zagging eastwards across the peaks of the duchy until the last fire was alight on Kit Hill at the Devon border. Two world wars had practically killed off the tradition, but it had been revived here and there by groups of enthusiasts on a few isolated carns and hilltops.

About sixty people had gathered on Carn Ewyn by sundown this year. Local students had been busy in the evenings, bringing driftwood scavenged from local coves and beaches, and the pile of firewood had grown to some six or seven feet in height. Tim had driven Sara to Trevow and had left his car there. They had walked up the southeast path with Roger,

Lynn, and the children. Clare had stayed behind to look after Louisa. She was preparing supper for everyone for later.

The sun drowned in the west. Fires were already burning on Trencrom Hill to the northeast, and southeast at Castle-an-Dinas. As darkness fell, the students lit the pile on Carn Ewyn.

Lynn appeared out of the darkness at Sara's side. She was smoking a roll-up. Sara caught the sweet fragrant smell.

Lynn offered her a toke. 'Home-grown,' she said.

Sara took it. She hadn't smoked grass in ages. 'Not in your mum's back yard, I take it?'

Lynn laughed. 'She wouldn't notice if I did, it's so full of weeds.' Sara offered it back but Lynn said, 'No, you have it. I'm well stocked.' She took a cheroot tin out of her pocket and opened it. It contained a dozen spliffs, all neatly rolled and waiting.

'See you later,' said Lynn, with a wink. 'I've got some business.'

She walked away into the crowd. Sara glimpsed her melting back into the darkness with two students.

People began to link hands to form a human chain around the fire. Sara joined them. No one knew how this tradition came about. Some scholars thought it was a celebration of the sun, of the heat and light it gave to sustain life on earth. Others believed the bonfire was a symbol of purification, to eradicate disease and scare off evil spirits.

As the fire burned more fiercely, the heat and smoke became too much for some. People began to drop out of the chain. The chain got smaller and ever closer to the flames. Lynn was on the other side of the circle from Sara, with Tim on one side and Roger on the other. She was grinning at Sara across the fire. She looked stoned. Sara felt strange. The heat was starting to get to her. And the circle was moving faster. Lynn and Tim had drawn closer together. They were laughing about something. Lynn turned to look back at Sara with a kind of malicious glee. It was lascivious, it was conspiratorial, a wood demon dancing in her eyes. And the circle moving faster and faster, the heat burning Sara's face, the smoke in her eyes and lungs. She was feeling hot and sick and giddy.

Someone tripped and fell – a lanky student with long hair and a bandeau round his forehead, Apache style. The dancing came to a ragged stop. The fire had begun to collapse, fanned into a fierce orange core of heat by the westerly breeze. Some students started leaping over it – a throwback to the times when people used to swing their children over the flames and drive their cattle through the embers of the fire to protect them from witchcraft.

The human chain broke up as the wind drove clouds of thick wood smoke into people's eyes. Sara saw Lynn back away from the heat with her arm around Tim. The students began throwing on more wood. The fire swallowed it with a ferocious crackling. The flames sprang up again, made frenzied by the west wind. Sparks and red-hot fragments leapt up into the blackness.

A cloud of smoke enveloped Sara. She wheeled round and stumbled away from the fire, pressing the palms of her hands to her eyes. She wished she hadn't smoked that spliff that Lynn had given her. She felt more and more sick, more and more giddy, as if she'd just got off one of those waltzing-whirling funfair rides. She found herself stumbling downhill. It became steeper. She slipped in the mud and landed heavily on her back, and kept sliding, faster and faster, until the ground seemed to drop away from under her, as if she had walked over a cliff edge. She reached out to grab something and felt the sharp needles of gorse. She tumbled down, bouncing off thick clumps of brambles, and falling sideways down the hillside, rolling and slithering, faster and faster down the near vertical slope, bumping and bouncing, groping desperately into the empty blackness for something to break her fall. Then her head hit rock. It felt as if someone had taken a swing at her with a hammer. And she felt her mind freefalling into unconsciousness . . .

There were about twenty people in the kitchen at Trevow, eating baked potatoes.

'I thought Sara was joining us?' Clare said to Tim.

'So did I,' Tim replied. 'I was going to drive her home afterwards and drop Lynn at Chy Melyn.'

Clare glanced at the old Great Western Railway clock on the kitchen wall. It was getting on for eleven fifteen.

'Didn't anybody see her?' Clare wondered, speaking to everyone.

'She was dancing round the bonfire,' said Lynn. 'I didn't see what happened to her after that.'

'You don't think she forgot, do you?' said Clare.

'Well, where would she have gone?' said Roger. 'She wouldn't have walked down to Crowjy in the pitch dark.'

Clare picked up the phone and called the barn-cottage. But there was no reply.

Sara had no idea where she was. She was lying in undergrowth. She could smell damp earth. She could hear some small creature of the night scuttle through the grass close to her face. The inside of her clothes felt wet with perspiration, yet she was quaking with cold.

She remembered falling...

She wondered how long she'd been lying there.

She tried to stand up. Her right ankle was painful. It was hurting like hell. She stood with her weight on her left foot. Now she could see where she was: at the foot of Trevow Hill, near the pond, across the track from Crowjy. But she was on the other side of the pond, where the weeds and nettles grew head high among plants that looked like giant rhubarb.

The sky was clear and the moon was almost full. Black trees sighed in the wind. Shadows shifted, changed their shape. She heard a crackle of twigs somewhere in the darkness. Her heart kicked out with fright. There was someone there... Watching.

She could hear whispers, murmurs in the deep shadows. She listened so hard that she began to imagine sounds. A horse out there somewhere, the soft jingle of its bridle as it shook its head. A heavy exhalation, almost a sigh.

Silence.

Another crackle of brittle twigs in the undergrowth. There *was* someone there. Very close. She could *feel* it. She heard a rustling sound behind her, like a soft footfall coming quickly, suddenly, through the tall damp grass. She turned so quickly she cricked her neck...

But there was no one there. Her heart kicked like a mule.

She looked towards Crowjy, trying to make out the line of the narrow path that led from the pond to the cart track. It seemed darker now. She looked up at the sky. A cloud had swallowed up the moon.

Tricks of the light.

She pushed her way cautiously through the smaller weeds and around the giant 'rhubarb' plants. They were twice her height, primitive sinister-looking things. She came to the edge of the pond. It gleamed like molasses. She looked down and saw her silhouette reflected in the water.

She looked up at the sky behind her. The cloud had moved on, the moon was bright again. She looked at the stars.

She looked back down at the water, at the reflection of her silhouette and saw a second silhouette beside hers.

For just a second she thought it might be Tim, that he'd come down from the carn and sneaked up on her. She turned ...

But there was no one there.

She looked back at the water. The other silhouette had gone. The only reflection was hers.

She was so frightened she couldn't draw breath. She turned and limped along the marshy path towards Crowjy, slithering ankle-deep in the boggy mud and stumbling over rocks. She came to the track and broke into a hopping run for the last few yards to her front door. She felt her jeans pockets in a flutter of panic. *Thank God*, she hadn't lost her keys in the fall.

She let herself in and snapped on the light switch. Nothing happened. She tried the sitting-room lights. Dead.

The damn bloody fuses again ...

She limped down the hall passage to the kitchen and fumbled in the cupboard for candles and matches. She lit a candle and sank onto a chair by the table. She was trembling all over. Her heart had gone wild. She was panting for breath and wet with cold sweat.

Tim dropped Lynn at Chy Melyn first, and then turned the car round and drove back along the valley to see if Sara was still up and about. A light was on in her bedroom, so he drove up the track and pulled up outside the cottage. He saw the bedroom curtains part and Sara's face appear at the window. She gave him a little wave and went away again. He turned off the engine and lights and got out of the car. The hall light came on and the front door opened.

'Where were you?' he said. 'We practically sent out a search party.'

'I'm sorry, I forgot about supper. I had an accident.'

'We thought you'd eloped with Shane Pascoe.' He noticed the scratches and bruises on her face. 'Hey, hey, hey ... What happened?'

'I fell down the hill and had the fright of my life. This bloody ankle's agony. Come on in.'

He stepped inside. She shut the door.

'What have you done to it?' He looked down at her foot.

'I don't know, sprained it or something. It's come up like a football. I'm amazed I didn't kill myself, arse over tit down that sodding hillside. I think I might have cracked a rib as well.'

'All right, well, let's take a look at you.'

'I don't know whether to go to hospital and get it X-rayed.'

She started to walk into the sitting room, but Tim said: 'I think it might be easier upstairs on the bed.' He added, only half joking, 'You need carrying?'

'No, I can manage. I'm just a bit slow.'

'Well, let me go ahead of you, then I can wash my hands while you're hobbling up the stairs.'

He went up to the bathroom. It was warm and dewy and smelt of sweet things from Body Shop. He washed and dried his hands. As he came out she had just reached the top of the stairs. He followed her into her bedroom. She sat down on the side of the bed. She was wearing a white towelling robe. He knelt down to examine her ankle.

'What happened?'

She explained how she got hot and dizzy, dancing round the fire, how the smoke swallowed her up, and how she wandered blindly into the darkness and slithered down the side of the hill.

'I curled myself up to protect my head. And I went bouncing down like a bloody great beach ball. I must have knocked myself out. I've got a bump like an ostrich egg on the back of my head.'

He examined the back of her head. Her hair was matted with blood. She was right, there was a large swelling.

'How did you manage to fall all the way down?'

It puzzled him. It was the steep side of the hill, true, but even so it was hardly a cliff edge.

'I don't know. I didn't have time to stop and think about that.'

'You want me to look at your ribs?'

She untied the robe, eased her arms out of the sleeves and let it drop onto the bed around her waist. Trim grimaced.

'You *have* been in the wars . . .'

She was covered in bruises. All over. He felt gently around her ribs. She shuddered.

'Painful?'

'No. But your hands are cold.'

'I'd like you to go into Penzance tomorrow and get yourself X-rayed. I'll give you a referral note. I think that ankle is just sprained but that crack on the back of the skull should be checked out, to be on the safe side.' He reached behind her and helped her on with the robe. 'I'll strap up the ankle for you and give you a painkiller to get you through the night. Have you got a crêpe bandage?'

'Try the box in the bathroom.'

He went out to the bathroom and found a plastic box with a red cross on the lid, packed with plasters and lint and sundry ointments. He picked out a bandage and went back to the bedroom.

'How do you feel otherwise? Been sick?'

'No. I just feel shaky. I don't think I've ever been so frightened in my life.'

'I'm not surprised . . . A fall like that, in the dark.'

'It wasn't the fall so much, it was afterwards, when I came to I was lying out there by the pool. I saw someone. I nearly had heart failure.'

He began to bandage her ankle. 'You saw someone where?'

'Right at the edge of the pool – that pool across the track. I saw two silhouettes reflected in the water: mine and someone else's.'

'What do you mean?'

She described what she'd seen. He looked sceptical.

'It's true,' she said. 'I know it sounds unbelievable but that's exactly what I saw.'

'Probably just the wind, making ripples across the pool. Double images.'

'There weren't any ripples. The pool was absolutely still. It was like looking at black glass.'

She put her fingers on the loose end of the bandage while he secured it with a safety pin.

'You don't believe me, do you?' she said.

'I believe you if you say so, of course I do. I believe you saw *something* . . . But there's usually a pretty mundane explanation for these things. What's that line in *A Midsummer Night's Dream*? Something like: "how often in the night is a bush mistaken for a bear".'

'You think I'm being neurotic?'

'I don't think that at all,' Tim replied. 'You've had a nasty fall and I'm not surprised you're so shaken up. You should have phoned Clare. I'd have come round as soon as I got back to Trevow.'

'I might have done if I could see what I was doing. But I got back here and all the damn lights were fused again.'

'Beryan used to complain about that. You should get an electrician in to have a look.'

She turned and stared at him. '*Who* did you say?'

'Bryan.'

'No you didn't, you said *Beryan*.'

'Did I?' Tim shrugged. He hadn't noticed. 'Well, I meant Bryan.'

'Then why did you say Beryan?' She looked agitated. 'Where have you heard it before?'

'I don't know.' He couldn't see that it mattered. 'Just a slip of the tongue.'

'Did Bryan ever mention the name to you?'

'Beryan?' He gave it a moment's thought. 'I don't think so, no. Why?'

She took a breath but then shook her head. 'It's just a coincidence, that's all.' Now she seemed to want to play it down. 'Doesn't matter.'

'How do you mean, a coincidence? In what way?'

'Forget it,' she said, 'it's not important.'

But he could tell from her manner that it was.

'I'm sorry,' he said, slightly bewildered, 'but it's nearly half past one in the morning and I'm a bit tired . . . Just a slip of the tongue, that's all.'

'Forget it, *please*,' she said, a querulous note creeping into her voice now. 'It really doesn't matter.'

After he'd gone, she limped downstairs to the studio and looked again at those burnt scraps of journal that she'd pieced together. She read:

Beryan is destroying me. Which is what she wants, she and her. Beryan has infested my mind. A carnivorous angel from the black pool of hell, an eater of souls. Beryan is devouring me.

Before he fell asleep that night, Tim lay in bed wondering what it was that had made Sara so agitated, and what on earth had put the name Beryan into his mind.

LYNN

Her bruises mellowed from deep aubergine to a watery lemon colour, and the scratches on her face began to heal. There was no cracked skull, no broken bones, no lasting damage ... Only rumours, all round the village and the valley. Boskinnow folk had long been accustomed to seeing Bryan with a black eye or a few stitches in his face after some fracas outside the pubs of St Ives or Penzance. Like brother, like sister, the rumours went. The fact that her face looked as if she had been in a cat fight didn't help.

She was in Treneer's Stores one morning, paying her newspaper bill.

'All fit and shipshape again now?' asked Mary Treneer, as she put on her reading glasses and turned the pages of the accounts book.

She was a pink, porky sort of woman, with tightly permed blue-tinted hair and a stub of pencil tucked behind one ear.

'Doctor Hendra's magic touch,' she added.

She laughed and looked up, over the top of her glasses. There was a flinty look in her eyes. She didn't miss a trick. Her spies were everywhere. She knew everything that went on for three miles around.

'You finished all that painting?' she asked, taking Sara's ten-pound note and making change from the till.

'Not quite,' said Sara. 'A bit more to do.'

'You'll be sorry to sell, now you've done all that work on un.'

She was fishing again.

'I'm not sure I'm going to sell. I might stay on for a while. At least till I finish my thesis.'

'Aw ais?' There was curiosity and something darker in Mary's tone.

Sara wondered if she was going to ask what her thesis was about. But her spies had probably told her that already.

As she was leaving the shop, Lynn's mother walked in. Sara had seen Vera at a distance on a number of occasions, but they hadn't spoken since that first night when the electrics failed on the VW and she knocked on Vera's door to ask if she might use the telephone.

'Mrs Roscarrock?'

Vera stopped and looked at Sara, as if she were being accosted by a beggar.

'I'm Sara Carhays. I live at Crowjy. I don't know if you remember me?'

Vera nodded. She had tired, dour-looking features and a sallow complexion. She wore a dull brown pleated skirt, and a tawny cardigan over a faded pink blouse. She was neither fat nor thin but shapeless; her hips, her waist, her bust were hardly distinguishable. Her hair was lank and grey and unstyled, cut to just above the shoulders. She wore the kind of heavy brown shoes that women used to wear in the army.

'Lynn's been helping me paint the cottage,' said Sara, making an effort to be friendly. 'I don't know if she told you?'

'That so?' Vera's voice was toneless. 'She didn't say.'

'She's very good,' Sara added.

'She would be,' Vera replied. 'She was well learned.' She turned away and began to walk on through the shop towards the counter.

'Oh, I forgot to say,' Sara called after her. Vera stopped and turned. 'Please feel free to use my phone at any time.' She smiled amicably. 'I'd hate you to have to traipse all the way to the village in an emergency.'

Vera's face remained set like a gargoyle and Sara walked out.

Vera walked home, back along the valley road, a mile and a half. She had been walking this road, back and forth, for almost fifty years. She used to walk this way to school each day when she was a child. Rain or shine a child walked in those days; no mollycoddling mums in fancy cars to pick them up. And one minute late, you got the strap, good and hard.

She still walked this way every day, to the village and back, and twice that distance to chapel every Sunday. But now the arthritis was tightening its grip, sinking its vicious teeth ever deeper into her joints. She could feel her bones grinding in their sockets. The pain was slowly engraving itself into her face. She could see it in the mirror every night.

She passed Crowjy and refused to look up the track. She had a mouth on her, that woman. Like brother, like sister. These things ran in families.

That evening, at tea, she said to Lynn, 'I saw the Carhays woman today.'

They still had their tea at the rickety gateleg table in the kitchen, the wireless on, the six o'clock news, just as they always used to when Arthur was alive.

'She told me you've been helpen her paint that place.'

'So what?'

'I thought you were worken up Trevow all day for Mrs Doriel?'

'I am.' A truculent note crept into Lynn's voice. 'When Clare doesn't need me I give Sara a hand down barn-cottage. What of it?'

Vera avoided her hard, aggressive gaze. The girl had become surly and insolent of late.

'You should have more sense, girl,' she muttered. 'Haven't you done enough damage already?'

Lynn's face flushed with colour. 'That wasn't anything to do with me, what happened there,' she replied. 'He was a bloody weirdo. He was a pervert.'

'That's an evil place. And I don't like you hangen around there. You know that.'

'You call yourself a Christian,' Lynn said contemptuously, 'and you believe all that bollocks?'

Vera sat very still and gazed down at her food. 'You wouldn't talk like that to me if your father was here.'

'If Dad was here, I wouldn't *have* to. He wouldn't have any of that superstitious crap in this house. You're a bloody hypocrite, you are.'

Lynn got up from the table and walked out of the kitchen.

'And where do you think you're goen?' Vera demanded. 'You haven't finished your tea.'

'I'm taken Jess for a walk,' Lynn retorted, coming back with the leash and calling for her father's old purblind collie. 'She's a dumb crippled bitch like you, but she's better company.'

Vera suppressed her tears until the girl had gone.

She prayed for Lynn. Every night. It was not her fault. She missed her father. She was confused, going through a phase, under the influence of the Doriel family – upcountry people, money to burn, all that smart, educated talk. Upcountry people were taking over everywhere. They were buying up all the cottages, pushing out the local folk who were born and raised here, driven away for lack of work, forced to live in caravan parks and seedy council homes. These upcountry people, they didn't want to live down here, they just wanted to turn people's homes into twee holiday cottages and let them out at extortionate rents for six months of the year. Or use them for a week or two in spring and summer.

So places like Nansgever were dead now from November to March. Local traders were struggling to survive. Village shops were closing everywhere. And even when these holiday-home owners did come down, they didn't buy from local shops like Mary's in Boskinnow. They took their Range Rovers and their Volvos into Penzance and filled them to the gunwales at Safeways. And if they met a farmer on his tractor in the lanes coming home, they had the impertinence to pomp the horn to tell him to shift out of the way. Then they wondered why local people were unfriendly. If this was Wales they'd be burning down these second-home cottages by now.

These were the kind of people Lynn admired and envied. Envy, the key word of the age. Now she was ashamed of her mother, ashamed of her own home, ashamed of where she came from. She didn't even *speak* the way she used to any more. She wanted to talk like those Doriels.

She was a child of her time, Lynn. It was a godless age. People had no spiritual life today, no faith. The young had lost their way in a maze of greed. They had no values, only material desires. I want, I want. It was an age of instant rich, instant happy, instant everything. They were all groping blindly into the wilderness. They had lost touch with the natural forces from which all life sprang and to which all life would eventually return.

A girl like her wouldn't understand about the old Crowjy.

Things had happened in this valley, long ago. Lynn's generation were too clever by half to comprehend. There were pagan ways that had been a long time dying in these remote corners of the land. They were just a fading folk memory now, passed on down the centuries like Chinese whispers.

It had a history, that place. A history of evil. Vera believed in evil. Evil could dwell among stones and mortar, just as it could dwell within the heart of man. Evil could infest a place, just like decay and disease. And evil infested that damp, dark Crowjy.

'I hear you saw Mum in Treneer's yesterday,' said Lynn. They were relaxing after lunch. She was wearing two scraps of fuchsia-pink Lycra. A pair of sunglasses were perched above her forehead. She squeezed sun-screen from a tube and began to massage it into her legs.

Sara was sitting in a rattan garden chair, in shorts and a cotton tank-top, reading the paper. She had sensitive skin and avoided long periods in the sun.

They had almost finished painting the outside of the house. Lynn came almost every day if Clare didn't need her at Trevow. She did some painting in the mornings, while Sara worked in the studio on her thesis. Then they had lunch together, outside in the garden, and Lynn stretched out in the sun. Her lunch breaks had gradually extended to the point where she was spending hours at a time sunbathing in the garden. She even started bringing a bikini with her.

Sara didn't mind. Lynn had painted practically half the house for her, and she wasn't bad company.

'You got her right pissed off,' Lynn continued. She was sitting on a scruffy foldaway lounger she'd found in the lean-to shed. A radio was playing quietly beside her. 'She don't like me comen here. She thinks there's evil here.'

'Evil?' Sara looked up from her paper. 'Why? Because of Bryan?'

'Partly that. But also, Granny used to tell her there's an old stone circle in the woods. And the Druids used to say Black Mass there and call up the Devil and sacrifice babies. Daft things like that.'

Sara smiled incredulously. 'The *Druids*?'

'Yeah. Gran told her all kinds of stupid stories. She went a bit funny in the head towards the end. She was senile, I think.'

'And where is this stone circle supposed to be?'

The few Stone Age circles that still existed in west Cornwall were well known and documented. And the woods were only eighty acres in total.

'Don't know,' said Lynn. 'Lost in the brambles, Gran used to say.'

'And your mother believes that Druids worshipped the Devil?'

Lynn nodded.

'But they were a pagan cult from the Bronze Age,' said Sara, amused. 'They wouldn't have known who or what the Devil was. Satan was a Hebrew-Christian concept.'

Lynn laughed. 'Yeah, but you can't argue with Vera. She believes everything Gran told her. Gran told her everything that goes wrong in life is punishment from God. So she's grateful she's got arthritis, 'cause she thinks the pain is purifying her. Making her more worthy for heaven. She thinks suffering makes you nearer God.'

Sara shook her head. The woman was obviously barking mad.

'Sick, isn't it?' said Lynn.

She tipped some more sun-screen into the palm of her hand and began smoothing it across her bosom.

'Why do you stay there? Why don't you move out on your own?'

'I can't afford it, can I? Not without a full-time job. And I can't get housing benefit. Or a council flat – unless I get pregnant.'

'Doesn't have to be a flat,' said Sara. 'You could get a room somewhere, in someone's house. Or go abroad. See the world. Go to Australia. You don't need a work permit at your age.'

'Not the work permit that's the problem,' Lynn scoffed, 'it's the thousand quid for the air-fare.'

She finished basting herself and lay back on the lounger.

The idea came to her on a hot afternoon, when she was strolling along the valley road west of Chy Melyn, towards Zennor. She was going nowhere, just wandering, bored. Sara was in Penzance with Bryan's executor, something to do with a mortgage.

Maybe the idea had occurred to her before ... Maybe it just gelled at this moment. But it suddenly seemed so obvious: she would move in at Crowjy. Sara had that spare room, and she could use the extra money. They got on well enough. And it was only half the distance to Trevow. It would be perfect. She wouldn't be in Sara's way – she was up at Trevow a lot of the time, and weekends she stayed with Ginnie in St Ives.

She started back home to Chy Melyn, wondering how to broach it with Sara. It would only be temporary, of course. The long-term aim was to get herself permanently inside Trevow. Crowjy would just be a stepping stone along the way. But that might suit Sara too ...

She was walking past a holiday cottage. There were a lot of them in this area. The cottage was set back from the road. There was a driveway leading up to it. On either side of the driveway there was long grass. A tortoiseshell kitten was wandering through the grass like something piskey-mazed. It was tiny; it couldn't have been more than two months old.

Lynn glanced at the cottage. The front door was wide open. Somewhere inside, a deep posh voice was busy being loud and bossy. Two small girls were playing in the garden, squealing and giggling. A Mercedes estate stood in the driveway with an inflatable boat on the roof.

She stooped down and picked up the kitten. It mewed a sort of hello and peered down from her cupped hands at the ground below, wide-eyed with wonder. There was a flea-collar round its neck with a small bell attached, and a metal strip with a telephone number scratched on it.

Lynn walked away down the road with the kitten in her hands. As soon as she was out of sight of the cottage, she slipped the collar off the kitten's neck and tossed it into the hedgerow.

She walked on, past Chy Melyn, to the barn-cottage. Sara had just got back from Penzance. She was taking a bag of shopping from the front of the Beetle.

'I've brought you a present,' said Lynn, opening her cupped hands to reveal the kitten.

Sara caught her breath; such a tiny creature.

'My girlfriend's mog just had a litter. She didn't know what to do with them. She was going to drown them.'

'Isn't she gorgeous?' said Sara, and reached out, utterly enraptured.

Lynn drew closer and together they stroked the furry mewing bundle in her hand.

'Are you going to keep it?' asked Tim.

'Of course I am. She's adorable.'

They were walking through Piskey Woods, looking for mushrooms.

'I was thinking of getting a cat, anyway. Or a dog. Or something.'

'Did Lynn know that?'

'No. She just turned up with it.'

The woods were barely worthy of the name. They covered about eighty acres between the Nansgever valley road and the northeast side of Trevow Hill. The trees that grew here were sinister, stunted things, scrawny and unhandsome. Like a tribe of dark scavengers camped in the valley, seldom seeing sunlight, yet sucking a meagre life from this poor wedge of marsh and granite. They grew to no more than ten or twelve feet high at most. For the greater part, the woods comprised dense thickets of bracken, hawthorn, and blackberry, with rocky clearings here and there, where the granite protruded.

There were two main paths. The shorter of the two kept close to the stream. The other cut a circuitous route with various small outlets to the valley road. It was not as muddy as the other, not often used. It cut a narrow channel through head-high shrubs and bushes and was almost overgrown in places. They were walking along this latter path.

'Have you given her a name?'

'Charlie.'

There wasn't room to walk side by side. Tim was walloping along behind her in his big heavy gumboots. They came to a clearing where too much granite protruded for anything to grow but grass and weeds. They stopped in the middle of the clearing. Sara cocked her head to one side, listening.

'Hear that?'

He listened. All he could hear was a cuckoo, some distance away, probably on the other side of the valley road.

'Faintly. Why?'

'It's unusual to hear birds in these woods. I put bread out in the garden but they never come.'

'Well, they certainly won't now you've got a moggie.'

They started looking for mushrooms in the grass on the fringes of the clearing. Tim had just remembered something that Bryan once said: That nothing lived around Crowjy. No rabbits, foxes, badgers, birds. No dawn chorus, he said.

'Hey ...' Sara's voice cut through his thoughts. 'Look at this ...'

She was kneeling down, almost in the blackberry bushes.

'What is it?' Tim drew closer and squatted down on his haunches. He thought she'd seen a snake. Adders were plentiful this summer.

'It looks like a fallen stone. A menhir.'

She was looking at a massive length of granite, lying on the ground, almost buried beneath the encroaching mass of brambles. At a guess, it was twice her height, possibly more.

'Isn't that extraordinary?' she said.

It didn't look very extraordinary to Tim. It just looked like another old menhir, long since tumbled to the ground. There were a lot of them scattered around Cornwall, single standing stones, thousands of years old. No one really knew what their original purpose was. A lot of them had been pulled out of the ground by farmers and dragged away on tractor chains to be used as gateposts, or broken up for hedging stone.

'What's extraordinary about it?' he asked.

'The hole through the middle.'

The hole was about half-way along the length of the stone.

'Menhirs date from the Neolithic to the early Bronze Age. This stone could be as much as four thousand years old. How did they make such a beautifully sculpted hole through eighteen inches of granite?'

The hole was very smooth, very round, concave, dipping in towards the centre of the stone like a shallow basin, and then narrowing to a diameter of about five inches where it passed right through to the other side. She pushed one hand through the brambles to feel into the 'basin' itself, to run her fingers over the stone, to feel its smoothness.

'You remember the picture in Clare's drawing room?' she said. 'The one she bought from Bryan?'

'Vaguely.'

'It's a painting of the pond across the track from Crowjy. But he painted a menhir sticking up through the water.'

'I didn't really notice,' Tim confessed. Art was not his strong point. And he didn't think much of Bryan's paintings.

'It's got a hole right through the middle. Just like this one. It's very unusual.'

'This is probably where he got the idea from then.'

'Lynn's granny used to tell Vera that there was once a stone circle in these woods. Maybe this had something to do with it. She used to tell dark tales of Druid sacrifices and Satanic rites here.'

'Who did?'

'Lynn's granny. So Vera thinks this place is evil.'

'Vera thinks a *lot* of things are evil,' said Tim. 'Including sex, chocolate, and television after nine o'clock.'

They were in the kitchen at Chy Melyn. It was late on a Saturday afternoon. Lynn was eating toast and honey. She was sitting on a high stool, one leg crossed over the other, peering out of the window at the vapour trail of an aircraft high in the sky.

'I might go to Australia,' she said.

She said it in a distant, dreamy voice, as if it were just one of many options, so difficult to choose.

Her mother was stooping to pick up the plastic laundry basket by the sink. She grimaced with pain as her hips locked, and said nothing.

'Sara's lending me the money for the air-fare.'

Vera eased herself back to the upright position and turned to look at Lynn, her face ploughed with deep creases.

She looks about eighty years old, some days, Lynn was thinking.

'Sara who?' said Vera.

'Carhays, down barn-cottage.'

Vera's expression didn't alter. She merely shook her head as if nothing the girl said could surprise her any more. She went out through the back door carrying the plastic basket, to unpeg the washing on the line in the yard.

Lynn sat finishing her toast and honey. She only said these things to provoke her mother. Vera was afraid, Lynn knew that. She was afraid of the day when her only precious child would pack her bags and go, and Vera would be left all alone in this drab, dark, dog-smelly house. The echoing tick-tock stillness, tea at six and Radio Four, Arthur's empty chair. Growing old, her hip joints frosting up. Creaking along the valley road to cash her pension every Thursday until she could hobble along no more, just sit in the armchair, listen to the tick-tock days drag by. And wait for death to come along and turn out the lights.

Lynn went up to her room, shucked off her scruffy workaday jeans and her T-shirt that smelt of lunch and Clare's kitchen. She looked at her reflection in the long mirror and wondered how something so desirable could have been born out of the womb of something so ugly. Sometimes she tried to imagine her own conception. A few minutes of loveless heaving in the black, perhaps, a squeak of bedsprings, then torpor, night and silence. She couldn't imagine why her father had ever married Vera. She wondered if Vera had ever felt passion in her life.

She put on her black 501s and the clingy silk shirt that Clare and Roger had given her for Christmas. She sat on her bed and rolled some joints and put them in her empty cheroot tin.

As she was leaving, she called to her mother from the hall, 'I'm off to Ginnie's. Might be back tomorrow.'

Vera was staring dolefully at a quiz show on the television. The only glimpse of glamour in her dreary life.

'Or I might hitch a lift to London,' Lynn added jauntily, 'and never come back at all.'

She took her cotton zipper jacket from a peg by the front door and walked out of the house. She started down the road towards Boskinnow. She was in a skittish mood. The breeze had shifted to the northwest and was freshening up. Rain was in the air.

Ginnie was her best friend. They had been at school together. She lived near Crippleseas, on the Penzance–St Ives road, and they went out most weekends, drinking, dancing, whatever.

They caught the evening bus into St Ives and went on a pub crawl down by the harbour. They picked up a couple of emmets called Jigger and Boke. They were from Liverpool, down on holiday, staying in a caravan on Hayle Towans. They kept buying the drinks, vodka-martinis, Bacardi-Cokes, very free with their money were Jigger and Boke.

When the pubs closed Jigger and Boke bought them fish and chips, and drove them back to Cripplesease in their white three-litre Capri with high-powered air horns that played a snatch of 'Colonel Bogey'. Jigger parked off somewhere, dark and quiet, in a field entrance. They ate the fish and chips and smoked a couple of spliffs. Boke and Ginnie tangled on the back seat, giggled and groped and tugged at zips.

Lynn didn't remember much after that. Just fragments.

Jigger all over her, squashing her. His fish-and-vinegar tongue pushing into her mouth. Sound of rain, clatter clatter, peas into an empty pan. Feeling sick. Boke and Ginnie threshing on the back seat. Clatter clatter of the rain. Jigger tugging at her jeans. World spinning. Need air. Music too loud. Shut eyes. Oh, God. Round and round. Open eyes. Jigger tugging. Something ripped. Ginnie and Coke. Doke. Bloke. Rocking the boat. *Yes, yes*, Ginnie gasping, *shit, yes* ... Eyes closing, open eyes. Can't move. Gotta get out, gotta get air, gonna throw up, gotta—

Oh, Jesus ...

Jigger jumping back off her.

'Ugh! Yer filthy bloody cow!'

All down the side of the door.

'Dairty filthy slag!'

His door opening, her door opening, strong hands on her arm, crushing it, heaving her out.

Ginnie moaning, *No, yes, yes* ...

'Gizz'yer jacket, dairty bitch!' Pulling it off her.

Ginnie and Boke, bouncey bouncey, squeak and rattle.

On her back, in the mud. Raining. *Pissing* down. Wiping the door with her jacket, mopping it up. Four Jiggers swimming in her vision. Balled-up jacket thrown in her face. *Eugh*, the stench ... Door bang one. Door bang two. Slither of skidding tyres screaming for grip on a wet road. Boke and Ginnie shouting from the back seat.

And then gone. Blackness.

She lay there in the rain and mud for a while, waiting for them to come back. They didn't. She clambered unsteadily to her feet. Her jeans were round her knees. Her silk shirt and her pants were soaking ... The puddle she'd been lying in. Or maybe she'd wet herself. Maybe both.

She zipped up her jeans. Bastards. Jacket was ruined. She lurched away down the road. There was no moon, not a single star. The night was black as a raven. Where *was* she?

It began to rain a little harder.

Bastards.

Sara was woken by the doorbell. She ignored it the first time but it rang again and more persistently. She put the bedside light on and looked at the clock. Half past one on a Sunday morning. She got out of bed, put on her robe and went downstairs.

At the front door she called out, 'Who's that?'

A plaintive voice replied, 'Smee.'

'Lynn?' Sara opened the door. 'Good grief.'

She looked as if she'd just been fished out of the pond fully clothed. It was bucketing down out there. Lynn stumbled inside.

'Are you hurt?' said Sara.

She looked as if she'd had an accident. She was covered in mud. Her mascara had run and smudged in the rain, as if she had two black eyes.

'Whatever happened to you?'

'Sodding emmets,' Lynn mumbled. 'That's what happened.'

Sara could smell the drink on her.

'Are you pissed?'

'Pissed *off*, I know that,' said Lynn and stumbled sideways. 'Bastards.'

'What happened?' Sara persisted, helping her along to the kitchen, where the Rayburn made it the one warm room in the house. 'What are you doing out in this? And without a coat ...'

Lynn slumped into a chair. She was drenched to the skin. Her hair hung like rats' tails and her fingers were ivory-blue with cold.

'I didn't even *want* the bloody fish 'n' chips. Serve the bastard right. I hope it went all everywhere.'

Her eyelids were drooping. The whites of her eyes were bloodshot. Her teeth were chattering so much she could hardly talk.

'Get those wet things off before you get pneumonia,' said Sara.

She went upstairs and took a large towel from the airing cupboard and a spare robe from her bedroom. She came back down and found Lynn sitting with her muddy shirt unbuttoned, and struggling to pull her jeans down over her feet.

'God, you're in a state . . .'

Sara knelt down and tugged at her jeans. As she did so she felt dizzy. It came over her very suddenly. So dizzy, she thought for one moment that she was going to black out. She heard someone say:

Go with the ride, lovey.

And a tinkle of goat bells.

And: *Gonna love this, Tchoolip. Gonna see shooting stars. Gonna be all psychedelic and that.*

It flashed through her mind like a clip from a movie. She rose slowly to her feet, holding onto the side of the table to steady herself.

Lynn was slumped in the chair like a rag doll, burbling, 'Wish I'd been sick all over him . . . down his trousers . . .'

Sara sank onto a chair. But the faint feeling was already passing. And that strange memory, those words, the goat bells . . .

'Bloody Ginnie . . .' Lynn slurring her words. 'Legs every-bloody-where, the slag, does sod all to help . . .'

Sara shook her head, as if she were shaking confetti out of her hair. The moment had passed . . . the dizziness, the giddiness. She felt quite all right again.

Lynn had kicked her feet free of her trousers and was just sitting there in her bra and pants, quaking with cold. Sara gave her the towel.

'Here, get the rest of your clothes off and rub yourself down. Then put this on.' She pointed to the towelling robe she'd bought down from her bedroom. 'I'll go and run a hot bath, there's plenty of water. Then I'll make up the bed in the spare room. I'm not driving you home at this time of night.'

Lynn put her hands behind her back and fumbled clumsily with the catch of her bra.

'God, you really are in a state,' said Sara, pushed the girl's hands out of the way and undid the clip for her. 'Now come on, pull yourself together.'

Lynn rocked from one buttock to the other and slid her pants down to her ankles.

'Think I'm gonna be sick,' she mumbled.

'Nice,' said Sara. 'Can you make it to the bathroom?'

'Think so.' Lynn got up off the chair.

Sara draped the robe round her. 'Okay, let's go. Up, up . . .' She clapped her hands and pushed Lynn towards the door.

Lynn tottered along the hall passage and stumbled up the stairs. She just made it to the bathroom in time, fell to her knees and erupted.

Sara was standing by with a glass of water. When she'd finished, Lynn took the glass, pale and exhausted, rinsed out her mouth and spat thickly into the bowl. Sara helped her up and took her into the big bedroom and eased her down onto the bed. 'Lie there for a while till I get the other bed made up. Do you want anything?'

Lynn groaned what sounded like a negative and lay back and pulled the robe tightly round herself.

Sara went back downstairs to the kitchen. She was livid but there was no point in arguing about it now. What did the silly girl come *here* for? Had Vera locked her out? She draped the wet clothes over the towel rail along the front of the stove, and mopped up the muddy rainwater that Lynn had tramped all over the floor. Then she went back upstairs to the spare room and made up the bed. When she went into her own room, Lynn was fast asleep, curled up on one side, angled right across the bed.

'Lynn?'

No response. Her breathing sounded soft and regular.

It was infuriating, but there was no point in waking her. Sara pulled the duvet around her. As she did so, she noticed the pendant hanging from a thin gold chain around Lynn's neck. It was a serpent coiled loosely round a stave. She had seen a pendant very like that before. It was just like the pendant hanging from the neck chain in those two paintings downstairs.

She walked quietly out of the bedroom and went down to the studio. She looked at the two pictures. The pendant dangling from the girl's neck chain was very similar: a serpent coiled round a staff, tail at the top, fat blunt head at the bottom.

She went back upstairs. Lynn had not moved. She looked at the pendant again. It was. Identical.

Someone was going to have to start telling this girl where she got off. Perhaps she felt at home in this bed. Perhaps she'd been in it plenty of times before.

But what could she say to Lynn?

Did you pose for Bryan? Did you let him paint you in the nude? Did you go to bed with him? Did you have an affair with him? Was it *you* he was so obsessed with?

She switched off the light, closed the door and went to bed in the spare room.

Lynn stirred and turned over onto her other side. She was not fully awake, or quite asleep, but in no man's land somewhere in between. She knew she'd been sick. She knew she had a headache coming on. And it felt like the middle of the night. Otherwise she felt on the edge of dreams.

She could feel a draught on her bare shoulders from the open window. It carried with it the faintest breath of scent. A soft lemony fragrance.

Slowly she became aware that she was not alone in the bed. Someone was nestling up to her. She made a little *Mmmm* noise of protest and turned over again. Wanna be left alone. Wanna sleep. She felt an arm moving round her, sliding lightly over her hips and round her waist, a hand across her belly. It was cold, the hand, but soothing. The hand began to caress her, soft silky fingers stroking her body. She felt cold naked flesh behind her, pressing itself against her back, her buttocks, a cold leg sliding in between hers, like a snake through the undergrowth.

Another little *Mmm* of protest. 'So *cold* . . .'

But the skin was so smooth. And that lovely lemon fragrance. The hand caressing her, wandering softly across her breasts, fingertips making tiny circles round her nipples. She could hear faint husky sounds coming from her own dry throat and feel her eyes tightening a little. The hand moving down across her belly in slow circular motions. Fingernails combing through her bush and clawing gently lower. She shifted in her half-sleep and felt herself uncurling, opening like a sea anemone. Cold fingertips found their way inside her. She murmured aloud, small noises of pleasure. So tired, just want to sleep ... But don't stop. So silky, so soft, so cold, so good ...

Sara was dreaming that she was lost in Piskey Woods. The path twisted and turned and dipped and forked. It grew narrower and narrower. Blackberry bushes began to encroach and wild briars, sharp as barbed wire. They clawed her flesh. She brushed past fronds of bracken, bejewelled with dew and cuckoo spit. She pushed shrubs and bushes out of her face. They sighed, they whispered all around her. She felt their dampness soaking through to her skin.

She found herself in a large clearing. The grass was tall and wet with dew. Spiders' webs sparkled in the dawn sunlight. She was looking eastwards. The rising sun was bright, like a spotlight. She shielded her eyes with her hand. In the middle of the clearing stood a tall menhir, a spear of granite leaning at a slight angle and silhouetted against the rising sun. She walked up to it and reached out and touched its cold abrasive surface.

There was a hole through the middle. She touched the sides of the hole, they were curved and felt sensuous, like a marble sculpture. She slowly pushed her hand inside it and right through to the other side. It felt smooth and moist and slippery with the morning dew.

She withdrew her hand. It felt wet and warm and sticky. She eased it out of the stone and looked down. Her hand was not wet with dew, it was wet with blood.

She awoke. It was the middle of the night. She heard a sound somewhere – a stifled sound, a human sound, perhaps a gasp of pleasure, perhaps a stab of pain. Then silence.

For a moment or so, she had no idea where she was. Then memory and reality came swimming up from the depths. She was in the small bed in the spare room. And Lynn was next door.

*

Lynn awoke early. It was daylight. It was Sunday morning. She was alone. She had a headache. Her throat was parched. The walls of her lungs felt like Velcro. Memories of the previous night came drifting back to her like a bad smell ... Those two bastards from Liverpool.

And Ginnie ... How did Ginnie get home?

And why was she in Sara's bed?

She began to remember what had happened in the night. Sara cuddling up to her ... How cold she was. And those soft hands all over her. *Jesus* ... Lynn shuddered at the thought.

So where *was* Sara? The other half of the bed was empty and cold.

Lynn looked at the clock. It was ten to seven. Her head hurt.

She got out of bed and put on the robe that Sara had leant her. She smelt that lemony fragrance again. It was on everything that Sara wore. It brought it back to her, the feel of that arm coiling round her like a snake.

She went into the bathroom and sat down to pee. *The bloody cow's a dyke.* The thought of it made her skin crawl. How could she have let her touch her? *Ugh* ... The middle of the night. While she was stoned, pissed, not even properly conscious. That was sick, really sick.

The door of the spare room was closed. Lynn listened, heard nothing, lifted the latch, eased open the door and peeped in. The curtains were drawn, the air smelt stale. Sara was fast asleep in the small narrow bed. Lynn stepped back onto the landing and closed the door.

That was doubly sick, that was creepy, slithering into bed with another woman in the middle of the night, hands all over her, and then slithering back to another bed afterwards.

Lynn shuddered again. She decided she didn't want to be here when Sara woke up. She wanted to go straight home and have a bath, wash the feel of that woman's cold dykey fingers off her. Her mother would be gone by now, creaking her way to chapel, suffering for God.

She padded barefoot down the stairs. She noticed a strange smell. She stopped in the hallway and sniffed the air. She glanced in the sitting room. The curtains were still drawn. It smelt as if someone had been burning something. It was not smoky, but there was a bitter ashen tang in the air. What had Sara been doing?

That woman was seriously weird. Like her loony brother.

She went along the passage and into the kitchen. Charlie the kitten was sitting on the table, washing herself. She made squeaky mewing sounds. Lynn picked her up and held her to her bosom and stroked her, and felt the soft vibrations from her purring body.

Incredible how you could misjudge people. She seemed so *normal*. Maybe Vera was right, and these things ran in families. And to think she was planning to *move in* with this weirdo.

She put Charlie back on the table and felt her clothes. They were draped over the rail in front of the stove. They were still damp. She took off Sara's robe and got dressed. Her silk shirt was filthy with mud. Now she remembered – Sara was undressing her. Wanted her to have a bath. Christ, it all made sense now . . .

She could smell that lemon fragrance on the robe. She picked it up between thumb and fingertip as if it were contaminated and dropped it over the back of a chair. She found a pen and scribbled *Thanks and sorry – one two many drinks!* on the back of a used envelope and left it on the kitchen table.

She squelched along the hall passage in her soggy trainers and stopped in the sitting-room doorway to sniff the air again.

The burning smell had gone. Completely gone.

Lynn opened the front door, glad to be out of this place, and walked away down the track.

Sara slept late that morning. She found Lynn's note on the kitchen table. Hardly a handsome apology but better than none. *Two* many drinks, hah? And two much smoking da funny stuff. And much two much taking people's good nature for granted. She hadn't even bothered to tidy the bed.

She was relieved that Lynn had pushed off at an early hour. Breakfast would have been a decidedly testy affair. She was still livid but she didn't think she could handle a row first thing on Sunday morning.

She lay in the bath and thought about the serpent pendant and the model in those two paintings. It had to be Lynn. She was only nineteen now, so how old was she when she posed for those pictures?

Did Lynn's mother know? Was that why she hated Bryan, why she thought this place was evil? Was Bryan obsessed with the girl?

It was not until she was having breakfast that she remembered that dizzy feeling that came over her as she tugged at Lynn's saturated jeans. Those extraordinary words that went through her mind. She couldn't remember exactly...

Tulip. Shooting stars.

She sat in the studio that morning and played around for a while with the jigsaw puzzle of burnt scraps from Bryan's papers.

She assembled:

I'm on to you. I'm getting there. Getting closer every

And elsewhere, two scraps that made:

womb of stone. Timeless evil.

INQUEST

Tim was going sailing that Sunday but the forecast was bad after Saturday's storms, so he and Sara went walking, across the moors to Mulfra Quoit. She told him about Lynn arriving drunk in the small hours of the morning and falling asleep in her bed. He seemed to find it quite amusing. She couldn't think why.

'I don't think it's the slightest bit funny,' she said.

'I can see that.'

'Well, what would *you* have done?'

'If Lynn had climbed into *my* bed?'

They were walking side by side along parallel tracks. He was watching where he was treading, dodging the marshier patches.

'I'm serious, Tim. I'm bloody angry about it.'

'Why? Forget it. She's probably very embarrassed. I don't think she'll bother you for a while.'

He was trivializing the whole thing, missing the point.

'But I want to know about her and Bryan. I want to have it out with her.'

'I don't think there's anything much to know.'

'The girl in those pictures is wearing the same pendant as Lynn was wearing last night. It's her, I just know it is.'

'Well, what if it is?'

She couldn't believe how calmly he was taking this.

'Tim . . . Bryan killed himself.'

'That's for the coroner to determine.'

'I'm not interested in legalities, I want to understand *why*.'

'We don't know what was in his mind.'

'You think I'm overreacting?'

'I think,' said Tim, picking his words carefully, 'that Lynn is irrelevant.'

'How can you say that? He must have *hated* the girl in those pictures. He painted a *scorpion* crawling out of her bush, you call that normal? He painted her cutting off her fingers with a razor. Her skin is on fire. Her nipples are melting. That is really, really *sick*.'

'Bryan's problem was with women in general,' said Tim patiently. 'Lynn was just the model, she just did it for money, there was nothing personal in it.'

She stopped walking and stared at him. 'How do *you* know?'

'The police have already talked to her about it. They're aware that she modelled for Bryan. She posed for him for several pictures, about two years ago. The scorpion was just a symbol. Because Lynn's star sign is Scorpio.'

Sara was astonished that he could stand there so coolly and reveal this as if it were last week's football results. 'Why wasn't I told?'

'I only found out on Friday. Ron Vincent – the DI at Hayle – called to put me in the picture before the inquest next week.'

'The police put *you* in the picture?' she said incredulously. 'What about *me*? I'm his bloody sister, for Christ's sake!'

She walked on petulantly. It was the fact that people were hiding these things from her that so angered her. It was like stealing. It belonged to her, this knowledge. They'd kept it from her, like parents keep medicines away from small children.

'I'm a witness,' said Tim, trying to reason with her. 'I have to give evidence at the inquest.'

'Bloody police, doctors, lawyers, judges, civil servants! You're always deciding what the rest of us should be *allowed* to know. Screw you, he was my brother, I have a right to know. And you have no right keeping these things from me.'

'No one's keeping anything from you,' Tim protested.

'Then why didn't Vincent talk to me as well?'

'He was going to. But I asked him to let me talk to you first.'

'About Lynn?'

'About the inquest. Because I've had dealings with Ron Vincent before, and he's not the most tactful man in the world.'

She was getting angrier by the moment. What was going on here, what were they cooking up behind her back?

'There was *no* affair,' said Tim. 'Nothing happened between Lynn and Bryan.'

'How do you know? You've only got her word for it.'

'Well, think about it,' he reasoned. 'She was seventeen at the time. She's been sexually active since her early teens, she gets all the men she wants without hopping into bed with a sick, violent, overweight, middle-aged drunk. Just ask yourself, why would a schoolgirl want to have an affair with a deadbeat soak like Bryan?'

She stopped walking again and stared across the moors. 'I suppose,' she conceded quietly. It did seem illogical. But she was still furious.

'I think,' said Tim, 'you're looking for someone to blame for his death. It's understandable. You want reasons. But Bryan was not a reasonable man at the time. He was very sick. It's no one's *fault* what happened.'

They sloshed on along the saturated track.

He was probably right. Who was she to argue? She hadn't even tried to see him for the past ten years. Perhaps that was why she was looking for someone to blame. So that she wouldn't have to feel guilty herself. 'And that's what Vincent was coming to tell me?'

'I think he wanted to warn you,' said Tim, 'that the inquest will probably be front-page news in the local papers ... because of the nature of the evidence. I'm afraid the local hacks descend like vultures at times like this.'

'You mean you've got to give evidence about asphyxiation and orgasms, and all the "eyeball to eyeball with death" stuff?'

'I'm afraid so. The coroner has to decide whether what happened was an accident or intentional. Ron Vincent thought you might prefer not to be there. In fact, I was going to suggest that you might want to go away, have a break.'

'Run away, you mean? Because everyone's going to be pointing at me and whispering when I go into the village for my paper each morning?'

'There may be some hassle from reporters, people ringing you up. It'll only be a few days. There's no evidence that any other person was involved. It really shouldn't take very long.'

'Is there anything else you haven't told me? Anything else I haven't been allowed to know?'

'Sara, look, I understand why you're angry but—'

'You don't understand *any*thing.' She turned abruptly and

started walking back along the track, the way they had just come.

'Sara. No one's hiding anything from you.'

He started after her, but he was on the wetter of the two tracks, and had to struggle to keep up with her, slithering in the mud.

'Just leave me alone, Tim, will you?' She kept on walking. 'Just go away. Please.'

'We just want to make it easier for you, that's all.'

She stopped and challenged him. 'You really want to make it easier for me? Right now?'

'Of course, I do.'

'Then just back off. Give me space. Let me walk home on my own.'

He stood there, deflated, exasperated. 'That's what you really want?'

'That's exactly what I want.'

Tim made a little gesture with his hands to suggest a certain pointlessness in all this.

She walked on.

He followed, but at a distance. Somewhere along the way he took another path and went west around Trevow Hill, across Nansgever Downs, and back to his bungalow the long way round. She was glad; she didn't want him trailing along behind her, like a sulky boy.

The air was brisk and clean after the night's torrential rain. And yet the day felt tired and soiled, like yesterday's laundry.

She felt cheated. Tricked. She'd begun to fabricate a whole scenario around Lynn, around an unrequited passion, the despairing middle-aged artist and the callous, oversexed teenager. They could be so cruel at Lynn's age: they had never failed, they had no idea how hot and fiercely passion could burn, how cold and bitter the ashes were.

It would at least have explained things, given a sort of sad twisted purpose to Bryan's death, lent some kind of warped meaning to it.

She sat in the studio, shifting pieces around, trying to match up more scraps from his papers. It would have made some kind of sense of these writings too. The serpent, the apple, Eve the temptress: *Once you have known it, you cannot unknow it. Once you have touched her, there is no return. It is out of Eden.*

Now she was back to nothing. No one to blame. No one to dump the guilt on. Only herself.

And now she found a piece with the two words 'tiny sister' written on it.

She spent hours looking at every scrap, trying to find more. She added one more piece and that matched the two scraps she had assembled last time. It now read:

Tiny sister. Born in a womb of stone. Timeless evil.

Tiny sister. Timeless evil. Those four words went round and round in her mind, churning her into a tangle of conflicts and emotions. She was a bog of memories, sinking into herself. Guilt tunnelled into her like worms, twitching and turning inside her.

She went into Boskinnow each day to collect her paper from Treneer's and ignored the stares and murmurs. Thursday, she collected her *Cornishman* and *West Briton* as usual and tossed them both into the refuse bin as soon as she got home. She had no idea what they said about the inquest. She had no idea whether the inquest had started or had finished. The telephone rang, every day, over and over, chirping like a tireless cicada. She didn't pick it up. She let the answering machine take everything, and then wiped the tape.

Cars came up the track and stopped: she didn't even look out of the window. There were knocks on the door: she ignored them all. Envelopes dropped through the letterbox: anything that was not a bill, she stuffed in Bryan's magic cupboard, Open sesame, close sesame, vanished.

She went walking in the woods where no one would see her. One afternoon she was walking along the path by the stream and an old woman approached, an old biddy in a black coat, waddling busily along. Sara stepped off the path into a gap in the bushes to let her go by. She said hello, but the old biddy did not so much as glance at her. Not a nod, not a murmur. As if she was determined not to see Sara, as if Sara were invisible.

She sat at her desk each day and looked at a blank computer screen. Her eyes kept wandering from the screen to the two paintings. And she kept crossing to the worktop to ponder the burnt scraps of Bryan's journal. Her eyes kept returning to those same sentences. She found another piece that fitted. Just one more word. It now read:

Tiny sister. Born in a womb of stone. Timeless evil. Firechild.

Tim's face appeared through the half-open studio window one evening and said, 'Have you heard?'

She was sitting at the trestle table, looking at a single paragraph on the computer screen – the day's work thus far. She looked around.

Tim said, 'It's over.'

'And?'

'Open verdict.'

Which was what they had all been expecting. So Bryan's death was now a legalized question mark.

'Am I intruding?' he asked.

She glanced at the one short paragraph on the computer screen and said, 'Not so as you'd notice.'

She got up from the table and walked through the sitting room to let him in.

'Clare's been calling you,' he said. 'All she got is the answering machine. Ron Vincent's been trying to get hold of you too. We all have.'

'I didn't listen. I kept wiping the tape.'

Tim nodded, as if he'd guessed something like that.

Sara sat on the edge of a chair by the empty hearth. 'So what now? I can bury him?'

'Yes.'

She didn't want a funeral. She just wanted it out of the way as quickly and quietly as possible. She would have liked to put him in the magic cupboard, where he got rid of all his problems, open sesame, close sesame, vanished.

'I don't imagine they'll be queuing up to pay their respects.'

'What do "they" matter?' said Tim. 'He was your brother, not theirs.'

'Bryan wouldn't have wanted it, anyway, chapels and flowers. He thought God was dead. He hated funerals. He wanted to be buried at sea, off Tahiti, by pretty Polynesian girls.'

'Didn't want much, did he?'

'And thrown to the sharks from a war canoe.'

'We could throw him to the mackerel off Zennor Head,' Tim suggested. 'And you could wear a *lei*.'

Sara started to laugh. She got the giggles and couldn't stop, and began to cry.

She had the body cremated at Penmount Crematorium outside Truro.

A few days later she got the ashes back, in a cheap bronze-coloured plastic flask.

Tim took her sailing that weekend. She scattered Bryan's remains over the sea off Gwennap Head near Land's End.

'It's not exactly the South Seas,' she said, 'but still.'

'I don't have radar,' Tim said philosophically. 'There are limits.'

She was very quiet in the car, driving home from the marina. It was Saturday, the week before August bank holiday weekend. Clare's brother and family were staying at Trevow. They were having a barbecue that evening, and a few friends had been invited, including Tim and Sara. Sara felt she ought to go. She had to face people some time, she couldn't hide away for ever. When they got back to Crowjy, before she got out of the car, Tim said, 'They won't mind if we don't go. Clare knows we were going out in the boat. If you'd rather be alone tonight?'

'No,' she said. 'I'd rather go. What happened happened. It's over now, it's history.'

She started to open the door to get out and added, 'I might even get the tiniest bit pissed.'

'I think that's allowed,' he said. 'If I remember Clare's brother, you won't be the only one.'

He drove home and took a shower.

He came back to the barn-cottage just after eight o'clock. Sara had bathed and washed her hair. She had swapped her habitual faded denims for black leggings and a baggy purple shirt, loosely cinched with a black suede belt. She had put on mascara and eye-shadow and a dark lipstick. It was the first time he'd seen her wearing make-up. It was a revelation. She noticed the look on his face and said, 'I don't spend my *entire* life looking like a sharecropper, you know. But how many parties do I get invited to?'

'I don't know. But quite a few more after tonight.'

They were in the sitting room. She looked out at the evening sky. 'Am I going to be warm enough? I've got nothing on under this.' She pinched her satin shirt doubtfully. 'What do you think?'

'I'm your GP. I could be struck off for what I'm thinking.'

She gave him an odd little look, that was somewhere between a smile and a grimace. She turned back to look out of the window. He heard a tiny gasp.

He thought he heard her whisper, 'Bastard . . .'

She turned round again. She was crying. She trapped her lower lip between her teeth, mumbled, 'I'm sorry,' and hurried out of the room and ran up the stairs.

Tim watched her, uncomprehending.

She couldn't explain it. She hadn't felt anything very much when they went out in the boat, the open sky, the vast sea, sprinkling what was left of him over the water. It was when she got home that the world closed in on her. Memories or guilt – or were they one? – were waiting for her like a grim governess, tall and dark, lurking in the gloomy interior. She shut the front door and the governess stepped out of the shadows, her eyes harsh and accusing.

Sara lay in the bath, prickling with indignation. She answered back: It wasn't my fault, he was sick, he was a mess.

But the governess wouldn't listen: You're lying and you know it.

She washed her hair. She towelled down. She powdered her body with talc. She sprayed deodorant. She put on the black leggings she'd bought but never worn because Gerald thought they looked silly on a woman her age. Sod it, she had better legs than Lynn and a better bum to go with it. She put on the plum-coloured satin shirt she'd picked up at Oxfam. Could have fitted two of her into it. She tried it without the belt. That made her look pregnant. She wiped the dust off her little plastic box of eye-shadows and brushed some colour onto her eyelids. Mascara. Lipstick. Good strong red, to go with her black hair and her thick eyebrows. Carmine. Harlot-scarlet. Sod it, make a statement. Look at me, you bastards. I couldn't give a toss what you think about Bryan, about me, about all the lurid crap you've been reading in the papers.

Tim arrived. Cambridge blue chinos and baggy cotton sweater. 'A revelation,' he said, as if he'd never noticed her legs before. He kissed her. He smelt pleasantly of cologne or aftershave.

They went into the sitting room. Should she offer him a drink? She was dying for a drink. She wasn't ready to go, to face all the toothy smiles, Nice-to-see-you, to-see-you-nice ... This is Sara (Hi Sara), Sara's brother was the wacko in the papers last week (Oh, hey, right, yes, we read ... Wow ... The plastic-bag freak, edge of beyond, death and ecstasy ... Hysterical ... We couldn't stop laughing).

She was trying not to cry. She was fighting it off, lashing out at the urge, her emotions were two schoolboys scrapping, all flurry and flailing and panic.

She went to the window so that he couldn't see her face. She looked out at the evening sky and wondered aloud if she was going to be warm enough, nothing on under this. Pulling at her thin satin shirt, thinking: You gave me this place for revenge. You wanted me here, you wanted me beating myself up with memories, you're pinning the whole shitting guilt trip on *me* ...

Tim said something about being struck off for what he was thinking, but she wasn't listening.

You can't pin it on me – 'Bastard,' she whispered.

She was losing the fight. The grief, the resentment, the anger was beginning to flow down her face. She turned to Tim, mumbled 'I'm sorry', and ran upstairs. Locked herself in the bathroom. Sat on the loo, stuffed the corner of a towel in her mouth and cried with a fury, cried for herself. *Damn you, damn you, Bryan, for doing this to me.*

She cried till she felt empty. Squeezed out like a sponge. She got up and crept into the bedroom. Looked at herself in the mirror. She saw a gin-soaked tart tossed out of a pub at closing time. She saw a clown. She saw a weedy guy in bad drag. There were sooty patches round her eyes where her eyeshadow had smudged and her mascara had run. Her lipstick was smeared round her mouth like raspberry jam on the face of a child. Her hair was all spikes and tangles.

She turned from the mirror and saw Tim standing in the

bedroom doorway, looking slightly awkward. His body was apologizing for being there.

'I'm sorry,' she said, in a rather empty, wrung-out voice. 'But I don't think I can face it, after all.'

She sat down on the side of the bed. She was hoping he'd go, just leave her alone. But he came and sat down beside her on the bed. She shrank, her knees and shoulders turned inwards, she made herself hunched and narrow, her body language said, Go away. She was a tortoise in its shell, she was a porcupine, prickling to be alone.

'I didn't think it was a great idea,' he said, and put his arm around her.

'I get muddled. In my head. All this thinking, tumbling around, like laundry, tangled up, higgledy-piggledy, everything gets so knotted.'

She felt Tim drawing her closer, like a protective father. She closed her eyes. She felt his lips on the side of her brow, then her cheek. She thought, Just do it. She felt worthless, she felt like something that had crawled out from under a stone. She felt herself stepping out of her body, abandoning it, hating it, Go on take it, have it, do what you want with it, I don't want it.

She angled her face towards Tim and let him kiss her mouth. She kept her eyes shut. She was a stranger to herself. It was all in her imagination. They were capsizing, he was pulling her down onto the bed. His breathing was harsh in her ear, his hands were huge.

He took her like a clumsy boy with a birthday present. He unwrapped her, peeled back the coverings, tugged and pulled, and explored her, squeezed her, pressed her. She didn't help, she didn't resist. She was a rag doll. She was shaken and squashed and bitten and scratched. She smelt burning, she smelt vinegar. She heard the snicker of a horse, she saw a goat bell dangling from the neck of a skinny girl roasting by the fire. She felt a pitchfork in her gut, she cried out, a stab of pain. Her hands on Bryan's arms, her nails in his flesh, the scratch of his beard. She closed her eyes tighter, crushed them shut. Gonna love this, Tchoolip, see shooting stars, psychedelic. She heard him moaning, felt him shoving, thrusting, pushing, harder, harder, go on, Bryan, go on, you bastard, take it, take what you want, Bryan, and leave me in peace . . .

She heard him cry out, felt his body go rigid, his back arch, a quiver of tension. She heard him gasp, sigh, felt him weaken, deflate and fall away in a heap of exhaustion.

She felt as if she'd been mugged up an alley. She felt like a wall on a bombsite that a drunk had just pissed over.

Maybe they dozed off to sleep. Or perhaps there was just a vast aching silence.

She was conscious of him touching her, stroking her, his fingers moving lightly across her flesh. She could feel his eyes on her, thinking, questioning, wondering why she was so cold, so far away.

'I'm sorry,' she murmured. 'It's not you, not your fault.'

Did she call him Bryan? Did she actually *say* it aloud? She couldn't remember. It was all a blur in her memory, a videotape on fast forward.

After a long silence, she said, 'We were lovers, you see. He bought this house for me.'

He said nothing, just lay close to her, touching her with his fingertips.

'I was pregnant.' She closed her eyes. 'I had an abortion. To punish him.'

'I was eighteen. He was thirty-four.'

They were sitting upright in bed, pillows behind their backs.

'We weren't like brother and sister because we'd never grown up together. He was away at art school in Bristol by the time I was adopted. By the time I was starting school he was already married and living in London.

'I came down to St Ives after I failed my A levels. I was very mixed up after Dad died ... the bankruptcy, having to move to a squalid little rented house. Bryan was ... well, he wasn't my real brother but he was still like forbidden fruit, and that was very exciting to me then. It was like an act of rebellion. It was a way of getting back at everyone. He seemed wild and subversive. Kind of Byronic.

'He didn't much like me at first. He still resented me because I was Mum's pet, brought into the family after Frances died. Then we got legless one night on his birthday. I slept with him at his flat. And it all just took off. Like dropping a match in a box of fireworks.

'I don't remember why I ever came here, to the Nansgever valley. But I remember seeing a "for sale" sign at the bottom of the track one day. And I came up here to look at the place. And it just felt like home to me. I don't know why – the woods, the carn, the peacefulness.

'Bryan wasn't keen at first. He wanted to move nearer Falmouth, because of his teaching. Then I got pregnant. We couldn't afford the Falmouth area. So Bryan made an offer for this place.

'But I never did move in. We had terrible rows. And then I discovered he was screwing one of my best friends in St Ives. I was incredibly jealous. I couldn't believe it. I thought he idolized me. He couldn't understand why I was making such a fuss. Then he told me about all the others. He'd been screwing almost *all* my friends. I was a laughing stock. I was the only one who didn't know.

'I knew then I didn't want a baby, I wasn't ready to be a mother. I had the abortion without telling him. But there were complications. They had to cut me open. That's why I've got this bloody great scar.

'He was devastated. I knew he would be. He'd tried for years to have kids with his wife. But he had a low sperm count. When I got pregnant, he was so shocked he thought it must be someone else's. But it wasn't. I was never unfaithful to him. He couldn't believe I'd had an abortion. I knew how much it would hurt him. I gave him the news as a sort of goodbye present. It was the only time I ever saw him really break down and cry like a baby.'

Tim considered it for a while, very still, holding her hand, frowning at her knuckles, as if he were making a difficult diagnosis.

'And that's why you feel – some way – responsible for what happened? For his drinking, his death?'

'He hated me.'

'You don't know that. You didn't see him for ten years.'

'He called me a timeless evil. A womb of stone.'

'That was probably in the heat of the moment.'

'No no no ... this was much more recently.'

*

They walked through to the studio. It was dark now. She switched on the lights.

'It seems to have been a sort of journal he wrote.'

They stood at the worktop near the french windows. He looked down at the mass of small paper scraps.

'I found them in the Rayburn,' said Sara, 'a few months ago. He tore the pages up and burnt them but you can just read the writing on some of these bits. I've managed to join some of them together. This is the one I meant...'

She directed his gaze to *Tiny sister. Born in a womb of stone. Timeless evil. Firechild.*

Tim read it through a couple of times and shook his head. 'What does it mean?'

'I suppose he's referring to my abortion.'

'But what does firechild mean?'

'I don't know.' She shuddered. 'Horrid, isn't it?'

She pointed to the other part-pages she had put together. Tim read:

Why does she keep coming? What in the name of God does she want from me? She's tearing my brain in shreds, sucking the very soul out of me. I spend my time dreading the nights yet longing for them. It's all I have left. Is she doing this just to punish me? Will she go on for ever? Until what?

And:

Beryan is destroying me. Which is what she wants, she and her. Beryan has infested my mind. A carnivorous angel from the black pool of hell, an eater of souls. Beryan is devouring me.

He turned to Sara. 'This must have been what he was talking about to me ... the creature that was trying to drive him mad. Who is Beryan?'

'That's what *he* wants to know,' said Sara.

She pointed to:

is Beryan? What is Beryan doing here? The name is in my ears, is in my brain, is driving me out of my skull. Is like hornets in my head. Who is Beryan? Why is she torturing me with

'Does he mean the creature in his hallucinations?' Tim wondered.

'I don't know,' said Sara. 'But *you* said the name one night.'

'*I* did?'

'On Midsummer's Eve. When you were looking at my ankle

and checking me over after I fell down the hill. You meant to say Bryan, but you said Beryan.'

'Oh, that, yes ...' He remembered now. 'I wondered why you were making so much fuss at the time. It was just a slip of the tongue.'

'Could it have been subconscious? Could Bryan have mentioned the name?'

Tim considered that for a moment but shook his head. 'I'm sure I'd remember a name like that. It's very unusual.'

He looked down at some more scraps she had pieced together: *Once you have known it, you cannot unknow it. Once you have touched her, there is no return. It is out of Eden.*

'Back to his whore from hell,' Tim murmured. 'His hallucinations.'

He read:

I'm on to you. I'm getting there. Getting closer every

'What sort of hallucinations?' said Sara. 'What was he seeing?'

'He never really explained. He was always too drunk. He called her his succubus, he said something like he'd never had head like it. A whore from hell, he called her. A whore come hot from hell.'

It reminded her of a sentence she had put together from the remains of Bryan's journal: *Carnivorous angel. From the black pool of hell.*

She crossed to the tall cupboard that Bryan had built to store his art materials. She took out one of the sketchpads, put it down on the trestle table and cleared a space amidst her thesis notes. 'Did he show you these?'

'He never showed me any of his drawings.'

She began to turn the pages. 'You think this is what he was seeing at nights?'

'I've seen something like this before,' said Tim. 'In one of his paintings. This creature ... No hair on her body, sort of deformed, her eyes sealed over.'

'I remember it. That's the first picture I noticed when I arrived. Did he ever explain it?'

'No, I didn't see it until the night I found him dead. Ron Vincent and I were looking around while the police pathologist was upstairs.' Tim looked up from the sketchpad. 'Did you get rid of it?'

'Sort of. It was the one I burnt – by accident – my first night. Miracle I didn't burn the house down with it. It was a horrible picture. I wouldn't have kept it anyway.'

'You know what I think?' Tim turned back to look at the burnt remains of Bryan's journal – or whatever it was he was writing. 'I think you should burn all this as well. Shove it all back in the stove, where it belongs.'

He put his arms round her.

'But it's all I've got,' she said. 'There's nothing else.'

'What do you mean, all you've got?'

'All I've got to help me understand – why he did it. It's all there is. The only clue as to what was in his mind.'

He rested his head against hers. 'Sara, Sara . . . You can't let yourself think like this.' He rocked her gently from side to side. 'It was a diseased mind, you shouldn't torture yourself with this kind of rubbish.'

'Perhaps.' She pressed her head against his shoulder. 'Perhaps you're right.'

At that moment, she no longer wanted to make decisions. The inquest was over, the cremation was over, Bryan's remains were gone, and she had told Tim everything. She felt an overwhelming sense of relief. She felt like saying to him, Do whatever you think's best.

As they relaxed out of their embrace, Tim said, 'You were going to make some coffee.'

Was she? She didn't remember saying so. But maybe it was a good idea. Or maybe they should just go back to bed. Maybe that was a better idea, but she was not going to be the one to say so. She gave him another hug and then went back through the sitting room and along the hall passage to the kitchen.

Using his hands as brushes, Tim gathered the burnt scraps of Bryan's journal into a heap and swept them onto a folded newspaper. He carried them out to the kitchen.

She looked at the pile of scraps and hesitated.

'Come on,' he encouraged her.

She moved over to the Rayburn and opened the coal hatch. He angled the sides of the newspaper to form a chute and tipped the whole lot into the furnace. She closed the hatch.

'There . . .' He smiled. 'Better now?'

She nodded, but without much conviction.

While they were drinking their coffee, she showed him the photograph that had interested her in *Lyall's Forensic Criminology*: the picture of a woman with her wrists tied to hooks in a wooden beam above her head, and her back flayed.

'He had an obsession with that picture,' she said. 'I found another sketchpad upstairs, full of variations of this same thing.'

'Extraordinary,' said Tim. 'Did he ever show any interest in this kind of thing before, in bondage, sado-masochism?'

'Not so far as I know. But, then, there's so much I never knew.'

Tim turned back to the title page of the book. He read:

Case studies of religious, cult, and occult sexual deviation, paranormal-related sexual psychosis and psychosexual criminality.

He flipped back to the second paragraph.

'You can see now,' she said, 'why I think he hated women.'

'But this isn't a woman,' said Tim.

She looked down at the flayed slumped body, the bubbly blonde hair, the stiletto-heeled shoes.

'How can you tell?'

'The pelvis, for a start.'

Sara could see what he meant; the hips were not much broader than the waist, and she/he had very flat buttocks.

Beneath the photograph was a textual reference: *Plate 58. Page 219*. Tim turned the pages until he came to 219.

'Here we are . . . Adrian Doriel. Forty-two-year-old merchant seaman.'

'Doriel?' said Sara, curious. 'As in Clare and Roger Doriel?'

'Found in the cellar of a terraced house in Plymouth.'

'Any relation, do you think? It's an unusual name. Clare's been looking for Doriels in the West Country. She couldn't find any in the phone book.'

'She certainly won't find *this* poor chap in the phone book,' Tim observed, reading the text. 'He died in 1959. Acute bodily shock.'

*

The following morning, as she was cleaning the studio, she found just one last half-burnt scrap from Bryan's journal lying on the floor in a corner. It was the piece she had wondered about before, with the unusual name: *under Senara*.

She was sorry now that she had let Tim destroy those burnt remains. It felt as if she had won a petty victory but had short-changed herself into the bargain. It was as if Bryan had *wanted* her to find those enigmatic scraps, had wanted to leave her mystified, had been trying to have the last word. But now she had silenced him for ever. Now she would never know what he was trying to say.

ADRIAN DORIEL

She was even more curious now about that photograph of the flayed body in the Plymouth cellar, the man they said was Adrian Doriel.

The following week she was working at the Cornish Studies Library in Redruth, researching her thesis. The library held microfilm copies of Cornish newspapers dating back to the previous century, so she looked through the *Western Morning News* for the month of April 1959, to see if there was any mention of Adrian Doriel's death. She found it reported first in the edition for Tuesday 21 April, and more detailed information about him appeared over subsequent days.

He was a ship's cook, forty-two years old, unemployed and living in a small terraced house in a rundown district near the naval docks – an area that had been badly bombed in the war and was being redeveloped. The house was awaiting demolition. His mother, a widow, came from the village of Tollford on the southern edge of Dartmoor. His father, a naval officer, had died when Adrian was only nine.

Calculating that that would have been in about 1926, Sara looked through the microfilms of various newspapers, to see if there was any mention of his father's death. She found a brief obituary in the *Cornish and Devon Post*:

George Stanley Doriel, Commander R.N. Died 19 April 1926, suddenly at home at Church View, Tollford, aged 38. Son of the late Edwin Foster Doriel, Captain R.N.

At home that night, she took another look at the text in *Lyall's Forensic Criminology*.

According to this, Adrian Doriel was a convicted prostitute with a long criminal record for sexual offences. A nearby resident had heard a lot of screaming during the night of Sunday 19 April and had reported it to the police. Officers had broken into the house the following day and had searched every room, finding the cellar door locked and having to smash their way in. They had found Adrian dead and cold, his back flayed raw.

What intrigued Sara was that Adrian's hands had been tied to a beam above his head and he had, literally, been flogged to death. But the only door was locked ... and locked from the inside. There was no other way in or out, and no other body in the cellar when police broke in.

The crime – according to this book – had never been solved.

It had obviously fascinated Bryan – almost to the point of obsession. He had filled a sketchbook with drawings and variations of it. Sara wondered if he had ever spoken about it to Clare and Roger.

She went out riding with Clare the following day. They took the bridleway across the downs that lay to the north of Carn Ewyn, just a mile or so from the coast, below Zennor and Sperris quoits. It had been miserable weather all week. There had been no rain today but the wind was buffeting across the moors, whipping through the gorse and bracken.

'How are you feeling?' asked Clare. 'Deep down?'

'I don't know,' Sara said truthfully. 'Tim's been around quite a lot. That's been a help. I'm just glad I didn't go to the inquest or read any of the press reports.'

'How about your work, your thesis?'

'I try to do a bit every day. But I keep getting sidetracked – mentally – thinking about Bryan, wondering why, thinking back, trying to understand.'

They came to a field gate. Clare dismounted, handed the reins of her grey hunter to Sara and opened the gate. Sara urged the chestnut mare to walk on, and led Shilo through to the next field. Clare closed the gate and remounted.

'He had some really strange obsessions,' said Sara. 'Did he ever talk to you about them?'

'What kind of obsessions?'

'Sexual, mainly.'

'No. He wasted a lot of energy trying to get me into bed at one time ... But that was before he and Roger had their punch-up. And before I got pregnant with Loulou.'

'Did Bryan ever talk to you about Roger's family?'

'About the Doriels? No. Why?'

Sara was trying to avoid the subject of Adrian and his macabre death in Plymouth.

'I just wondered,' she said casually. 'The barn-cottage was part of Trevow Farm once, so I thought he might have been interested in the history of it.'

'I don't remember him ever mentioning it, no.'

They came to within sight of the tiny church at the hamlet of Towednack. Clare was on the seaward side. She reined in Shilo and sat gazing northwards, where there was a glimpse of ocean between the coastal hills.

'I'm not even sure that Roger's family *were* connected with Trevow,' she said. 'There are none in the county now.'

'How about Devon?'

'Not as far as I know. Why?'

'I came across the name when I was doing some research at Redruth library. In an old newspaper article. A Doriel family living in Tollford, the south side of Dartmoor. But this was back in the 1920s.'

'Really?' said Clare, though only half-heartedly. 'I can't pretend I've looked very hard, but there are none in the phone book anywhere west of Reading. There aren't many of them anywhere. Roger's an only child. And he's got no uncles on the Doriel side.'

'So how did you know there were Doriels at Trevow once upon a time?' said Sara.

'There's a mention of the name in an old book that Bryan picked up at a jumble sale.'

They had tea in the drawing room when they got back to Trevow. Clare found the book squashed away at the end of a shelf. It was a sorry-looking volume. It was coming adrift in several large chunks, and had no covers.

Clare said, 'Keep it, it's quite interesting. It's yours, anyway. Bryan lent it to me and I forgot to give it back.'

She passed the book to Sara. It smelt of old attics and mice. The title page read: *Journeys Through Penwith*.

And beneath that, in scrolled lettering: *The Diaries of the Reverend John Lanarth of St Ives.*

And beneath that a little mimeograph of a gentleman on a

horse moving through idyllic countryside with a glimpse of sea behind him.

'A wow of a title,' Sara observed.

'Isn't it?' Clare laughed. 'He was writing at the end of the eighteenth century, but I think that's an Edwardian reprint. There's no date on it, though.'

'Where does it say about the Doriel family?'

Clare took it back and browsed through a table of contents.

'Here we are ... "Chapter eighteen: starvation and potato blight; corn shortages; murrain and poverty in the Nansgever valley; the state of the Church; widows and parish relief."'

She looked around for a scrap of paper to use as a bookmark.

'It's okay,' said Sara, 'I can find it now I know where to look.'

Clare passed it back to her.

'How far back have you traced Roger's family?'

'Only as far as his great-grandfather,' said Clare. 'He was born in India. I can't get back any further. I suppose I could try the old Navy Lists. He was a captain.'

'The Doriels I read about in Devon were a navy family,' said Sara. 'What was his great-grandfather's name?'

'Edwin.'

Sara could not remember the details of Adrian's father's obituary at that moment.

'Ring any bells?' asked Clare.

The name Edwin did ring a bell but Sara prevaricated. 'I don't think so,' she said vaguely. 'Can't remember offhand.'

As soon as she got back to Crowjy she took another look at the photocopies she'd taken from the microfilms at Redruth library. She glanced again at the obituary of Adrian Doriel's father:

'George Stanley Doriel, Commander R.N. Died 19 April 1926, suddenly at home at Church View, Tollford, aged 38. Son of the late Edwin Foster Doriel, Captain R.N.'

Then the two families *were* related. Quite closely related. Adrian's father would have been Roger's great-uncle.

Tim took her sailing again at the weekend. The wind dropped around late morning and they were becalmed south of Mounts Bay. While they were eating sandwiches for lunch, she told him about Adrian Doriel.

'So what relation was Roger to Adrian?' Tim wondered.

'First cousin once removed.'

'As close as that?' He fumbled with a ham salad roll. It slipped out of his hand into a puddle of sea water. He picked it up and broke off the soggy parts and threw them to the wheeling waiting gulls. 'Roger's father must have known him then.'

'Unless there was a split in the family,' said Sara, 'with one half not talking to the other.'

'Have you told Clare?'

'No. I don't think I will either. It's not the sort of thing anyone would *want* to know.'

'Maybe Roger knows,' said Tim, 'but keeps it quiet.'

'Possibly. I suppose he'd have been a schoolboy in those days.'

'So why do you think *Bryan* was interested? *Lyall's Forensic Criminology* is hardly the kind of book a layman takes home for a good read. You said he made lots of drawings of that photograph.'

'They were very similar, but they weren't exact copies of it.'

'Was he just turned on by that kind of thing and never noticed that the victim was called Doriel?' Tim wondered. 'Or did he notice the name Doriel and get to wondering?'

Sara shrugged. 'We're never going to know, are we?'

She was thinking of those burnt scraps that read:

I'm on to you. I'm getting there. Getting closer every

Closer to what? *Or to whom, Bryan?*

That evening, when they got back to Crowjy, and while they were waiting for a shepherd's pie to bake in the oven, she showed Tim the old book that Bryan had lent to Clare, *Journeys Through Penwith*, the diaries of the Reverend John Lanarth of St Ives.

The chapter that mentioned Nansgever and the Doriel family was dated January 1797. Tim read:

The failure of the potato crop and the high price and scarcity of corn have brought much distress to the people of Penwith this winter.

To worsen the suffering, cattle are dying for lack of feed

or are sick with the murrain. I have witnessed the pitiful sight of oxen in their death throes, blood flowing from mouth and nostrils, their eyes wide with terror and suffering. Not five miles hence, in the Nansgever valley, the Doriel family, yeomen farmers at Trevow for generations, have lost their oxen, goats and every living thing to this disease. Thomas Doriel, who lost a wife and child to the ague, and now his livestock, has sold his home and land to pay his debts, and his sons are gone away to seek such living as they may.

I have heard them call this terrible affliction the Burning Disease, for it so burns the throat and lungs and does afflict man and beast alike. There is fear of this disease throughout the parish and foolish rumours of sorcery and ill-wishing. For in such parts of West Penwith they have little commerce with persons from outside their parish, and for all that they are hard working and careful with their meagre wages, they are an ill-educated and superstitious lot.

There are many poor but worthy souls here that the Church is failing to reach out to and who are drawn in ever larger numbers to the angry preaching of the brothers Wesley.

'Where did Bryan find this?' Tim enquired. He sniffed the book and pulled a face.

'A jumble sale, I think she said. Donkey's years ago. What do you think the burning disease was?'

'It sounds like ergot poisoning.'

'What's that?' She opened the bottle of red wine that he had brought and poured two glasses.

'It comes from a fungus that blights grain. It was quite common in the Middle Ages when people were so poor they'd eat mouldy anything. They used to call it St Anthony's Fire because of the burning sensation in their throat and lungs. It's practically unheard of these days.'

She moved to the sink and started peeling carrots. 'You can feed Charlie if you want to be useful,' she said. 'There's some leftovers in the fridge.'

Tim got up. 'Were they Roger's ancestors then?' he said. 'Those people in John Lanarth's diaries?'

'Clare thinks they might have been. But she can't trace back any further than Edwin Foster Doriel. He was born in Calcutta and she can't find out where *his* father was born.'

'Why not?' Tim scraped the contents of a half-empty can of fishy mush into Charlie's feeding dish. 'If he was British, he would still have had a birth certificate in the UK, surely?'

'Not if he was born before 1837,' said Sara. 'Clare would have to go back to the parish registers. And I don't think she really knows where to start looking.'

Sara had to go to Truro the following week, to the county library, to do further research for her thesis. She finished at four o'clock and had time to walk round to the Royal Cornwall Museum in River Street where some of the old parish records were available on microfilm. Finding names on the microfilm was a time-consuming chore, but there was an international index compiled by the Genealogical Society of Utah. The index covered only baptisms and marriages – no burials – but it was a useful starting point.

The index was on microfiche. There were about forty Doriels listed in Cornwall and a further four in Devon. Most of the Cornish Doriels were in the parish of Towednack – whose boundaries embraced Boskinnow and the Nansgever valley. The last of them, chronologically, were the family of one Thomas Doriel who – according to the list of baptisms at Towednack – had three sons: Kadan, Matthew and John. He also had a daughter, baptized at Towednack. And her name was Senara.

Sara stared at the name and wondered why it was familiar, where she had come across it before.

When she got back to Crowjy, she looked again at that last surviving half-burnt scrap from Bryan's journal.

under Senara.

That was all that was legible.

Clare asked Sara and Tim to lunch that weekend. It was a beautiful September Sunday. They ate outside in the sun. Clare looked at the photocopies that Sara had taken from the microfiches.

'This Thomas,' said Sara, 'is probably the one that the Reverend Lanarth refers to in his diary, driven to penury by cattle disease. But his youngest son, John, seems to have done quite well for himself . . . You see who he married?'

Clare was long sighted and had trouble reading the tiny print without her glasses.

'Alice Lanberris. Mawnan. 23rd July 1795.'

'The Lanberris family were landed gentry,' said Sara.

'Really?' Clare glanced down the table at Roger. 'That should appeal to you, dear. One of the old Trevow Doriels married into the Lanberris family.'

Roger looked blank. 'Why should that appeal to me?'

'Because you'd love to *be* someone.'

'I *am* someone, thank you very much.'

'Like all little men,' Clare had added. But he hadn't heard that.

'Who is – or was – the Lanberris family?' he enquired.

'One of the richest in Cornwall at one time,' said Sara.

'I bet they were chuffed, then,' said Roger, 'one of their girls marrying a farmboy from the boonies.'

They had finished the main course. Bosun was sniffing around, hoping for a few scraps. Tim was topping up glasses. Lynn was sitting beside Louisa's high chair. She hadn't spoken to Sara yet. She was avoiding her eyes. They hadn't seen each other since the night that Lynn turned up wet through and drunk at two o'clock in the morning.

Clare was studying the two photocopies. 'This is all the Doriels, is it? Between 1670 and 1837?'

'I doubt it,' said Sara. 'The Utah index only lists baptisms and marriages. No burials. And there are quite a few gaps. You'd have to go through the parish registers individually to get the burials. But it gives you a rough idea where to start looking.'

'And these ones in Devon, are they related to the Doriels down here, do you think?'

'Very probably,' said Sara. 'You'll see a Kadan Doriel there, baptized at Towednack in 1775. And you'll find a Kadan Doriel married in Devon about thirty years later. Must surely be the same man with a name like that.'

'Do you think there's any way of tying in the India lot? Making some connection with Roger's great-grandfather?'

'It shouldn't be too difficult to research,' said Sara evasively. She had not told Clare about Adrian Doriel and his father at Tollford, the link with Roger's great-grandfather. 'After all, you're only trying to bridge a gap of forty years or so.'

'Why bother doing it at all?' Roger argued, as if it was the biggest bore since plucking chickens. 'What's the point?'

'It's family history, it's their heritage,' said Clare, referring to the children. 'They could be your ancestors. Aren't you even curious?'

'I can honestly put my hand on my heart,' said Roger, teasing lasagne from his teeth with a cocktail stick, 'and say with profound conviction that I couldn't give a toss. They're dead and gone, they're dust and ashes, they're nothing.'

'They're not *nothing*,' Clare replied. 'They're part of the present. Every generation leaves something of itself behind – not just the stones and mortar. It's here, it's all around us, it's in the atmosphere we breathe.'

'Show me,' said Roger. He opened his arms dramatically towards the house. 'Show me one bit of themselves that they've left behind. Point to it.'

'I can't *show* you,' Clare scoffed, 'don't be silly.'

'Well, there you are, then.'

'It's intangible. It's in the spirit of the place.'

'Oh, Christ.' Roger glanced at Tim with a wilting look. 'Marry a Catholic . . .'

'No, I agree with Clare,' said Tim. 'It's natural to want to know about the past. Everyone wants to know where his roots are.'

'I know where my roots are,' Roger retorted. 'They're halfway between Highgate Hill and the Archway roundabout. And a right dump *that* is.'

The children giggled.

'What bloody use are roots?' he continued. 'Roots don't pay school bills. Roots don't feed a wife and four children. And roots don't pay the vet's bills for those bloody horses down there.' He jerked a thumb towards the stables.

'I knew we'd have to get that one in somehow,' Clare murmured to Sara.

*

They walked back to the valley through Piskey Woods.

'Do you think they're happy?' Tim wondered. He sounded curious but not especially interested.

'She seems it,' said Sara. 'Hard to tell . . . Clare's one of those strong optimistic types who never seems to let things get her down.'

'Do you like Roger?'

'Why? Do I give the impression I don't?'

'Slightly.'

'I don't really know him. I hardly ever talk to him. Whenever I go to Trevow he's always busy in the barn or messing about in his workshop.'

'A lot of women find him attractive.'

'Really?' She found that surprising. He was short and cuddly, and he had quite a handsome face. But she found him overbearing. 'He's a bit too dominant for my liking, too much push and shove.'

'Why don't you come to Florida with me?'

Sara had to play that back in her mind.

'Say again?'

'I said, why don't you come to Florida with me?'

'That's what I thought you said.'

He stopped walking in the middle of the path and turned to face her.

'Did I just miss something?' she asked.

'I don't think so. You said Roger was too dominant, too much push and shove. And I said, "Come to Florida."'

'Are you pissed?'

'Not much.' He put his hands on her waist and drew her to him. 'I just felt like saying it.'

'What do I want to go to Florida for?'

'Christmas.'

'You *are* pissed.'

'Out on the nineteenth, back on the twenty-ninth.'

'No way.' She pushed lightly at his chest. 'Go away. Nasty man. Do I know you?'

He turned to walk on and took her hand. 'I'm serious. Winter sunshine, what's wrong with that?'

'I can't afford it, that's what's wrong with it.'

'But I want you to meet Susie.'

'What's that got to do with it?'
'You'll like Susie.'
'Who's Susie?'
'My daughter. And Jeff. He's an underwater photographer.'
'Oh, *that* Susie.'
'So come with me.'
'On my bike?'
'It's not as expensive as you think.'
'You don't know what I think.'
'London–Orlando is one of the bargain flights.'
'You're not a student.'
'I'll sub you.'
'You'll get it back in pennies then,' she scoffed.
'I'm serious.'
'So am I.'

When they got back to Crowjy, he said, 'Come back to my house and I'll show you some photos. It's not what you imagine, it's not all crack addicts and muggings and hamburger joints.'

'I can't, I'm too sleepy, I need my siesta.'
'Well, siesta at my place.'
'I'm not going to Florida, so forget it.'
'I won't mention Florida. Just look at the photos, that's all.'
'Promise you won't mention Florida?'
'I promise. Scout's honour.'

They dozed off in the low wide bed at his bungalow and awoke around five. He got up and made a pot of tea and brought it back to the bedroom. They looked through his photographs.

'As your GP,' he said, stroking the hair out of her face, 'I'm telling you, you need to get away.'

'You promised you wouldn't mention the F-word.'

'And I haven't mentioned the F-word. I just said you need a change of scene. Plenty of fresh fruit juice, and a skyful of vitamin D.'

She sipped a mug of Earl Grey. 'Anyway, I can't.'

'Why not?'

'I haven't got a passport.'

'You're thirty-two and you haven't been abroad?'

'Of course I have. But only on a visitor's passport. You can't use those in the States.'

'Okay, then, get the real thing. It's only September. Plenty of time.'

'It's not that easy.'

'It's extremely easy.'

'I don't have a copy of my birth certificate.'

'Well, send off your five quid to London and get one.'

'It's not quite that simple for adopted people.'

'What has being adopted got to do with anything?'

'Your birth certificate tells you who your real parents were. And I was never told. Because I never wanted to know.'

'Ahhh . . . Of course.' Tim looked contrite. 'I'm sorry. I hadn't thought of that.'

'It's all right, it's not a monster problem. It's just something I never got around to doing. There's a special procedure. It all seemed like too much effort at the time.'

'So do it now,' Tim coaxed her. 'I'll endorse your passport application. And where it says "identifying marks", I'll put "very long and extremely sexy abdominal scar".'

Sara pinched his nose. 'Now you know why I don't wear bikinis.'

'Not even in somewhere beginning with F?'

'You're not going to shut up about this, are you?'

'No.'

'One last time, read my lips: I can't afford to go to Florida.'

'I'm not asking you to.'

'Then what *are* you asking me?'

'I'm asking you to get a passport. That's all. Nothing else.'

'And then what?'

'Leave the rest to me.'

She telephoned St Catherine's House in London, the Register of Births. She was told that adopted people could only obtain a birth certificate through the Registrar-General's sub-office at Southport.

She telephoned Southport. Southport told her that, before the Registrar-General's office would release a copy of her birth certificate, she would have to meet a counsellor. This was for her own good, because she would be discovering for the first time who her natural parents were.

She asked how long all this would take. Not long, they said; a month or two.

THE MOOR

Sara's counsellor was a woman called Jennifer Glanville. She was appointed by the Registrar-General's office. They met in a small interview room loaned for an hour by the social services department of Cornwall County Council in Truro.

'You're probably wondering why this is necessary,' she said, as they sat down.

She was probably old enough to be Sara's mother. She had a soft voice and a plump sympathetic face.

'The policy towards adopted children has changed since 1975,' she explained. 'Before that time, all parties were assured that under normal circumstances the adopted child would never learn the identity of his or her natural parents.'

'Why was that?' asked Sara.

'It was felt it could be very painful to everyone concerned, especially the adopted child. He or she might try to find the natural parents and discover that he/she was never wanted. Or he/she was illegitimate and the father was unknown. Or the natural mother might not have wanted the child then but suddenly decides she wants the child now, with all the complications that could ensue.

'That policy was reversed by a new Adoption Act in 1976. So where a person adopted prior to that Act wants access to his/her birth record, we try to point out the various difficulties that can arise.'

'You mean,' said Sara, 'if I were to try and make contact with my natural parents?'

'Well, sometimes, you see, adopted people have high expectations.'

'But all I want is a birth certificate, nothing more. Just so that I can apply for a passport. I'm not trying to *find* anyone.'

'Yes, quite. But you see . . .' Mrs Glanville smiled but looked pained at the same time. 'Forgive my asking but . . . Do you have a happy relationship with your adoptive parents?'

'Yes. I did. They're both dead now, but they were very loving parents. Why do you ask?'

'So it wouldn't upset you unduly if you were not able to find your natural mother and father?'

'Not in the slightest. I'm not even interested.'

'I only ask because, you see ...' Mrs Glanville hesitated. 'Normally, Southport would inform me in advance of your name at birth, and the name of your natural mother. So that I could give you that information here and now. But ...' It was obvious from the look on her face that she had something difficult to say. 'I'm afraid there is no record of who your natural mother and father were.'

Sara was puzzled. 'But every birth has to be registered. Even if I'm illegitimate, my mother's name must be on my birth record, surely?'

'The record merely states "not known",' said Mrs Glanville gently.

'Well, how did they ... ?' Sara was still bewildered. 'What are you saying? I was abandoned?'

'Not necessarily. There are all kinds of reasons why infants can become separated from their parents. Especially overseas – civil war or some natural disaster, like an earthquake. But I don't know the facts of your case. You would have to obtain those from the agency that handled your adoption. The adoption order was made at Bodmin County Court. You can apply to the court to release the name of the agency, and contact them for further details.'

Sara was confused. 'But none of this invalidates my birth certificate, does it? This doesn't stop me getting a passport, surely?'

'Not at all. If that's all you want, I've brought a form with me. All you have to do is sign it and send it off to the Registrar-General of Births, and you'll get a short-form copy of your birth certificate just like anybody else.'

'Then why would I want to contact Bodmin County Court?' said Sara.

'You would only want to do so,' said Mrs Glanville, 'if you wished to trace the adoption agency to find out when, why and where you were first taken into care.'

She opened her briefcase and took out a thin folder of documents.

'I've brought a form for you to sign if you do decide that you'd like to obtain the information from the county court. But you may feel that you'd rather not delve back into the past.' Her face was knitted with an ambiguous pattern of sympathetic smiles and frowns. 'Knowing can sometimes be worse than not knowing. It's a very personal decision.'

Sara talked it over with Tim that night. He took her out to an Italian bistro in St Ives.

'Have you decided?' he asked.

'No. That's why I'm asking. What would *you* do?'

Tim thought about it. 'I don't think I'd want to know. What's the point?'

'I might not be English. Look at my black hair, my dark eyes. I could be French or Italian or Spanish.'

'Very pale-skinned for Spanish,' said Tim, not taking that very seriously. 'Welsh perhaps. A touch of the Irish, even.'

'Whatever. I could even be Jewish. I'm just curious.'

She was beginning to feel like a character in a novel – as if her whole life to date were mere fiction and her true origins were in an old forgotten book that was out of print.

'I don't know what to advise,' said Tim. 'I think I'd just settle for a birth certificate and leave it at that.' He shrugged. 'But that's easy for me to say.'

It was a sunny October. Summer was an old tart in a fancy skirt, having one last fling, pretending to be spring but fooling no one. The holiday-makers had gone home, the beaches were empty, the blackberries were ripe and the narrow lanes of Penwith were quiet and deserted again.

She went walking on the moors to try to clear her mind, to think this through. She wondered whether she really wanted to know. What did it matter? Roger was right: what was the point of worrying about roots? What could you do with them, anyway? Did they put food in your mouth, pay the bills? It had all happened so long ago. Her earliest memories were of two people she called Dad and Mum and the old rectory at Lezant. None of that had changed. So what *had*?

Her perception of herself; that's what had changed.

In truth, she *had* wondered about her natural parents – ever since her father had told her she was adopted. She was seventeen. It was shortly before he died. She'd imagined various scenarios – perhaps a father who was widowed young and couldn't cope with a baby on his own. Or perhaps an unmarried mother, deserted by the father, confused, unable to face motherhood alone. They were comforting scenarios, forgiving scenarios, in which her mother was never really to blame.

But now she had no perception at all of where she came from. She felt as if she were living in a vacuum, an empty shell. She was a person walking along an endless grey corridor in a vast empty building. She was an echo of feet on miles and miles of polished parquet flooring. *Abandoned*. It was like something out of Dickens. She felt as if she had been disconnected from something, uncoupled and left behind – like the last coach of a train, while everyone else trundled away down the line and out of sight.

She signed the form and mailed it to Bodmin County Court.

They took an age to reply. She received a letter from them in mid-November. Their records showed that her adoption had been arranged through a children's home at Keyes Manor on the south coast of Cornwall.

Keyes Manor was near Seaton, not far from Plymouth and the Devon border – not very far from her childhood home at Lezant. Keyes Manor was still there. It was listed in the phone book. Sara called them. But it had long since closed its doors to orphans. It was now a hotel and restaurant.

She telephoned Jennifer Glanville in Truro and explained what had happened. Mrs Glanville said that when the Keyes Manor children's home had closed down, they had probably passed their files on to the county council. She said she would make enquiries for Sara.

She called back a few days later. Some of the children's files from Keyes Manor were still held by the social services department in Truro. Many more had been destroyed. Social services had a small amount of additional information they could pass on to Sara. But she would have to come to Truro; they were not allowed to send it through the mail.

*

The Burning

Jennifer Glanville was there again, this time with a young woman called Rees who worked for social services. All they had was a standard filing document, two pages stapled together. It was a question–answer list of personal details.

'I'm afraid all we know,' said Miss Rees, 'is that you were first placed in care at Keyes Manor on 3rd May 1961. You stayed briefly with a Reverend Peter Elman of St Layot near Bodmin before that. And then I'm afraid, everything else is marked "not known".'

She passed the two stapled pages to Sara to look at.

Question after question – father's name, address, occupation, date of birth, mother's name, address, occupation, and so on – was marked simply N/K.

On the second page, under NOTES she read:

> *Taken into care, Bodmin police, 18.4.61 (file report q.v.)*
> *Parents/family whereabouts N/K.*
> *Bodmin police liaison: Sgt Coode.*

Beneath it was printed: AGE AT REGISTRATION. Beside it was typed: *2 yrs (est)*.

Sara flipped back to the first page, to where it said DATE OF BIRTH. Beside it was typed: *18.4.59 (Given)*.

'How were they able to find out my date of birth?' she asked.

'I'm afraid that in these cases they have to estimate the child's age,' Jennifer Glanville replied, 'and give an approximate date of birth.'

'You mean, they guessed? I don't really know how old I am?'

'Paediatricians,' said Miss Rees, trying to reassure her, 'are usually fairly accurate at that age.'

'And so my birthday isn't my real birthday?' said Sara. She flipped to the second page again. '18th April ... That's the day I was taken into care.'

'I know it must be painful,' said Miss Glanville softly, walking on eggshells. 'But they have to choose a day somehow.'

'I suppose they do,' said Sara quietly. She was suddenly so dispirited that she didn't know what to say.

At the end of the section headed NOTES, she read:

Psychiatrist's report: (q.v. file).
Paediatrician's report: (q.v. file).

'Where are all these other reports?' she asked. 'You have copies?'

'I'm afraid not,' said Miss Rees. 'That seems to be all we have. A lot of records were probably destroyed when the home closed down.'

'Until recently,' Jennifer Glanville explained, 'they were not obliged to keep records for more than twenty-five years.'

'There's nothing more you can tell me?' said Sara. 'That's all there is? I was found near St Breward on 18th April 1961?'

'I'm so sorry,' Miss Rees sympathized. 'I can Xerox these papers if you'd like a copy.'

But Sara was already holding up a hand to say no. She shook her head emphatically and handed the two pages back across the desk. All she wanted to do was get out of the place and be alone.

She wondered if there would have been anything in the local Bodmin newspaper. She stopped at Redruth on her way home and went into the reference library, where they kept back copies of all the Cornish newspapers on microfilm.

The weekly paper for east Cornwall was the *Cornish Guardian*. She looked up the edition for Thursday 20 April 1961. She worked her way slowly through it but there was no mention of an abandoned child.

She tried the following week's edition. On page nine she found the headline: MYSTERY CHILD AT MOOR BLAZE. She read:

> Police at Bodmin are trying to trace the parents of a little girl who was found abandoned but unharmed near a blazing building on Bodmin moor last week.
>
> She was discovered by John Argall of Lower Garrow Farm, and his son Keith, who set out in their Land Rover to investigate the fire in a derelict shepherd's cottage not far from Brown Willy at about ten o'clock on the night of Tuesday 18th April.
>
> The girl is thought to be about two years old. She has been unable to tell police her name or where her parents live.
>
> Sergeant Derek Coode of Bodmin police told the *Guard-*

ian, 'We do get travelling tinkers on the moors sometimes. But the only access is along the track past Lower Garrow. The Argalls would have seen travellers coming and going.'

Fire engines from Bodmin and Launceston sped to the blaze but were unable to get near the burning building because of its remote situation.

The little girl, who has dark hair and brown eyes, is being cared for by the vicar of St Layot, the Rev. Peter Elman, and his wife, while police enquiries continue. Anyone who thinks they may have seen the child, alone or with other people on the moor, or who has any information that might be of assistance is asked to contact Sergeant Coode at Bodmin police station.

Beneath the article was a picture of Sara, staring blank-faced and wide-eyed at the camera.

She telephoned Bodmin police station that evening. Derek Coode – long retired – had died some years ago. But Keith Argall, they told her, was still farming at Lower Garrow.

There is only one main road across the moor. It runs between Launceston and Bodmin, a distance of some twenty-two miles, curving and dipping and rising over thousands of acres of bare windswept moorland. There are scattered farms whose dairy herds and flocks of hardy sheep keep the moors cropped. The soil is not suitable for crops. Some of the land is marshy and there are small lakes scattered here and there. There is Dozmary Pool, into which Sir Bedivere is reputed to have thrown King Arthur's sword, Excalibur. There is an army firing range that is seldom used these days. And where there were once white conical mountains of china clay waste, these have now been seeded and become green hills on the landscape.

A few miles southwest of Brown Willy, the highest point on the moors, between the villages of St Breward and Blisland, lies Lower Garrow Farm, on the De Lank river. It was from here that John Argall and his son, Keith, set out in their Land Rover on the night of 18 April 1961 and drove along muddy tracks towards the blazing cottage. It was two miles from the nearest public road.

*

Keith Argall was sixty now.

'Father passed on ten years back,' he said, raising his voice over the clatter of the tractor engine as they bumped along the moorland track. 'He'd be tickled pink if he was here now, seeing you again after all these years.'

Sara was perched against the side of the wheel arch. It was cramped and noisy in the cab. She said, 'I was surprised to find you here.'

'Me? I'll be here till I drop dead.' He laughed. 'I've got all daughters. Farming's not for them. One's a physio, another's in computers, and the youngest, she's in local radio up Bristol.'

They lurched and bumped along the track for about three-quarters of a mile, keeping just north of the marshy valley where the De Lank river lay, almost invisible in places.

'I come up here shooting foxes some evenings. I often pass the old ruin and think back, wonder what became of you.'

'I was never very far away,' said Sara. 'I was adopted. We lived on the other side of the moor, near Lezant.'

'Aw ez. Lewannick way?' He chuckled. 'All they years, so close, and you never knew?'

They were approaching the ruined house. It was small and picturesque in its lonely decay. There was no roof, only the remains of the walls, breaking up, falling down, overgrown with ivy. Keith Argall steered the tractor off the track and pulled up. They climbed down.

'A shepherd had this place,' he said. 'He left before the war. I was just a boy. Wasn't ever much of a house to start weth. Enough to drive a man off ees head liven out here.'

Sara looked at the ruin and then at the moors around. He was right. It was so bleak, so isolated. Anyone who abandoned a child out here must have been desperate indeed.

'Where . . .' She could hardly say the words, she felt so desolate inside. 'Where was I? Where did you find me?'

He thought about it and repositioned himself some thirty feet away from the ruin.

'We must've been stood about here, I suppose, Dad and me. Thear wasn't nothen we could do. The place was burnen like fury. The heat was too much, we couldn't get near. It made some braave old roaring noise – the fire, the wind and all. The roof was caven in and flames were leapen up towards the sky.

All Dad and me could do was stand back and watch un burn. We were so hypnotized by the fire, like, we didn't see no one at first. We didn't think to look. And then ... thear you were. A liddel tiny thing. Just stood thear ...'

Neither of them had noticed where she came from. Suddenly she was there, beside the blazing building, bathed in gold by the fire's reflected light; standing so close to it that she looked as if she might catch light herself. She wore a long nightdress, a cream colour. She was not crying. She didn't seem at all afraid. She was just standing, watching them. She looked at them as if they were just ordinary strangers passing, on an ordinary day. Her eyes were large and open very wide. She sucked on the tip of one thumb.

Keith Argall moved closer to the building, until he was about ten feet away.

'You stood about here, looken at us ... Like you wanted to say, Hello, booys, what are'ee doan 'ere an? You had your thumb in your mouth. And I thought, Dear Christ, she'll roast alive if she stands thear. I ran over, picked you up and carried you away, out of the reach of the flames. And you never cried, you never struggled, not a murmur, anything.

'Father went round the back, right round, shouten, holleren out in the fields in case anyone was lying out there injured, in the dark, thinken your mum and dad must be somewhere about. And I'm looken at the flames and thinken, Dear Loord, there's some poor soul trapped in that lot. Fire engines came but 'twas a waste of good diesel, they couldn't get up the track. They just had to let'n burn out. Soon as they could get inside, they searched but thear wasn't anyone in thear.'

Sara walked inside the ruin. He followed her.

'So how did I get here? Someone brought me here and ...' She shuddered at the thought of what she was saying. 'Just left me? In the building? And set fire to it?'

'I can't explain,' said Keith Argall, shaking his head. 'No one would have wanted to live here. Thear wasn't any water, electricity – wasn't even much of a roof on un, to speak of.'

'Couldn't I tell you anything? I must have said *some*thing.'

'We asked you things but you looked at us like we were talken a foreign language ...'

She had stood there blinking in the flashlights, gazing wide-eyed at the faces of the policemen and the firemen. She did not smile, she didn't cry. They asked her what her name was, where Mummy and Daddy were. She just stared back at them as if she couldn't even understand the words.

'We thought you were deaf and dumb at first. The police thought you must be in shock. They didn't know what to make of you at all. You spent that night in Bodmin, with Derek Coode and his wife.'

'But if I was in a nightdress,' said Sara, 'where were my clothes?'

'They didn't find any.' Argall shrugged. 'Police and fire officers went through the ashes next day but they didn't find a thing. No clothes, no belongings of any kind. Nothen thear. Just a burnt-out ruin. They couldn't even work out how the fire started.'

'And you never heard any more about it?'

'We kept in touch for a liddel while. Sergeant Coode kept us posted for the first few months. But then we heard less and less . . .'

She had been looked after by the vicar of St Layot and his wife for the first two weeks. Then she was made a ward of court and placed in the children's home at Keyes Manor. She was not mute and yet she seldom spoke. She was intelligent and yet she seemed to know nothing of her past. She showed no signs of being in emotional or physical distress but she had bad dreams at night and wet her bed. She looked undernourished and had head lice, but was not otherwise dirty or suffering from disease. She had no vaccination marks. But there were scars across her back that looked like welts that had healed, as if she had been beaten at some time. Paediatricians and child psychiatrists questioned her but she couldn't even tell them what her name was or where she came from.

They named her Sara. And she seemed to like it.

Time passed but no parents came forward to report the loss of a child in north or east Cornwall. She never asked for Mummy or Daddy. She didn't even seem to know the words.

'After a year or so we never heard no more,' said Keith Argall. 'But we never forgot you.'

Sara looked around her. So many secrets buried by time in this cold but oddly picturesque ruin.

She walked back outside. Keith Argall followed.

She turned and looked towards the brooding hump of Brown Willy, the highest tor on the moor.

About sixty yards from where they were standing, stood a menhir – a solitary pillar of stone in the middle of a field, about eight feet tall, narrow and pointed. There was a hole through the middle.

'Queer old stone that,' said Keith Argall. 'Never seen another one quite like un.'

Sara had: in the woods behind Crowjy, fallen down and almost lost in the brambles.

It was also like the strange menhir in Bryan's painting that was now hanging in Clare's drawing room at Trevow.

She walked across the field towards it. It was exactly like the one in Piskey Woods – a hole right through the heart of the stone, carved out like a basin, beautifully made, very smooth, very round, narrowing to a hole that was just large enough to put her hand through. She reached out and touched it. She put her hand into the hole and ran her fingers around its surface. She pushed her hand right through to the other side and felt the faintest tingle in her finger tips, like a tiny charge of static from the quartz.

As she drove away from Lower Garrow Farm she noticed a smear of blood on her finger. She stopped the car, took a tissue from her bag and wiped away the blood. She examined her hand for a cut or even a graze. There was not a mark on it.

She remembered the dream that she had on the night when Lynn turned up drunk and fell asleep in her bed. She remembered reaching into the hole in the stone and withdrawing her hand, sticky with blood.

She rejoined the A30, but instead of turning west to go home, she turned east towards Launceston. She drove a few miles further on and turned right, onto the country road that threaded its way towards the hamlet of Lezant. She drove back to the old rectory where she used to live when she was a child – the house her father had had to surrender to the banks when his business went under in the 1970s.

She parked in a field entrance, about a hundred yards from

the house, and sat in the car, staring at the upper storey – all that was visible above the walls and bushes that surrounded it. It was a Victorian house, solid and square, with bay windows and tall chimneys.

She had always told herself she would never do this – come back. What was it inside us that yearned, deep down, to search for the beginning, the spiritual quest, seeking the homeland, the tribe, the mother, the seed, the creation, the source, the Truth? But she was cut loose, cast off. There was no way back. The path had disappeared, been washed away by time.

She wondered if her adopted parents were ever told how she was found. They took the *Cornish Guardian* every week, they would surely have read about the fire on the moor. Did they ever realize that she was that child?

Sara got out of the car. She walked slowly down the lane and past the house. She glanced over the front gate as she passed. The new people had let the garden go. The grass was long and full of weeds. The shrubs and perennials needed dead-heading. She walked a short distance and started back. It was coming on to rain.

It was dusk by the time she got back to Nansgever. She drove through the valley in the fading light. As she turned off the road and started up the track towards Crowjy, she stopped the car. Her heart stopped with it. In the twilight she could see her mother up ahead, standing, staring at the barn-cottage. An old woman in a black coat. She turned her head and looked down the track at Sara. And then hobbled on her way, turning along the path to Piskey Woods,

It was the briefest glimpse. One moment she was visible, crow-black in the dusk. And then she was gone, out of view behind the barn-cottage, and away to the woods.

Sara's heart kick-started and she recalled the old woman she had seen before, walking through the woods, the old biddy in the black coat who had cut her dead, pretended she wasn't there.

She drove on, parked outside the cottage and walked up to where she could see along the footpath to the woods. The old woman had already disappeared.

Sara felt acutely alone at that moment. She felt like a solitary figure on a landscape, carrying a bundle of too many things, which had come unstrapped and was slipping off her back.

She told Tim everything.

He had no idea how to console her. He was sympathetic in his well-meaning way, but he couldn't understand the depth of abandonment she felt. It was too far outside the ambit of his experience. The structures of her life had suddenly collapsed. Her past felt like a barrel of children's bricks tipped up across the playroom floor.

Tim said it was time to rebuild, then. She had the freedom, had the time. Look on it as an opportunity, a chance for personal growth.

She wept and shook her head. Her emotions were spilling everywhere, like a box of buttons knocked off the arm of a chair by a clumsy child. He rocked her like a small daughter in his arms, and stroked her hair and made soothing noises. But this wasn't what she needed.

She didn't know *what* she needed. She kept thinking about what Bryan had written – the womb of stone, the timeless evil. She felt a sense of foreboding trickle through her, cold and clinging, like the incoming tide encroaches up the beach, thin as glass, and curls round the feet of the timid paddler. She felt afraid but had no idea what she was afraid of. She was aware of a black hole in her life. It felt as if it were somewhere in the very middle of her being, dark and deep and hollow. It was like the hole in the stone. Empty and mysterious. Unknown. Forgotten. The black hole seemed to expand inside her and suck her into itself, into its darkness.

That night, when Tim had gone, she lay on her bed, looking through old family photographs. The earliest had been taken when she was three and a half.

She had photocopied the page from the *Cornish Guardian*. That was now the earliest picture she had from her childhood.

DO YOU KNOW THIS CHILD? the caption asked beneath the picture.

She looked at the wide-eyed ragamuffin and tried to imagine herself in her cream-coloured nightdress, standing outside the burning cottage, thumb in mouth.

Was it her mother who left her? Her father? Both? Were they running away? Why were they so desperate? Why couldn't they leave her on a doorstep in a town or village somewhere? Did they want her to die in that burning building?

She got up and looked at herself in the mirror – her almost Indian-black hair, loose to her shoulders, her dark eyes, her skin, ivory-pale where it had not seen the sun. Were they travellers, her parents? Gypsies or tinkers or showmen? Was there another language and culture inside her, long forgotten?

Why could she remember absolutely *nothing*? Was it trapped down there, somewhere, in her subconscious? Did it come out at night, in her dreaming, like some stealthy nocturnal creature?

She took a large plastic bag from the wardrobe and lay down.

She put out the light and eased the bag over her head and down across her face. It felt tight, like a glove. She crumpled the plastic loosely round her throat and breathed in slowly.

THE EDGE

The days grew shorter. The wind shifted to the northeast and turned sharply colder, pushing days of endless drizzle ahead of it.

She tramped through the rain, across the head of the valley and the downs to the north, and came to the small church at the hamlet of Towednack.

She sat inside. It was cold and empty.

God knew the answer to everything, her father used to say when she was little. And there was no voice so small He could not hear it. Everything was possible through prayer.

So tell me. Tell me who I am.

She sat in a pew near the front. Her mind drifted. She lost track of time. Ten minutes went by or perhaps an hour. She was thinking of the stone in the woods, the stone on the moor, the stone in Bryan's painting. She was remembering Midsummer's Eve, standing by that pool and seeing two silhouettes reflected by the moon. She was remembering waking up at dawn and seeing a dark shape floating on the water.

No dawn chorus. Silence.

Something brought her out of her reverie. She was no longer alone. She turned round. At the back of the church, an old woman was kneeling, head bowed, hands clasped in prayer. Sara turned back to face the altar.

After a while she heard the old woman rise to her feet and cross to the door, the door opening and closing. She sat there for a few minutes longer but the old woman had broken the spell, disturbed her peace. Sara got up and walked out.

The old woman was in the graveyard, stooping over a grave, pulling out weeds. Sara stood on a mound of ground beside the church porch, watching her. After a few minutes, the old woman straightened up, felt her back and groaned in pain. Sara remembered her now. She was the old biddy in a black coat that she'd seen outside Crowjy and walking through the woods. She always seemed to be around, waddling along footpaths or disappearing in the twilight.

Sara walked away from the church, back along the track to the lane.

There was only Clare she could talk to now. (Poor Clare, she was everyone's agony aunt; a victim of her own common sense, a talent for listening, and a marriage that everyone envied.)

That afternoon, she took the path through the woods, across the stream and around the side of the hill to Trevow. It looked as if Clare was out. The Espace was not there, but Roger's battered pickup truck was parked alongside the Tudor barn, where a lot of tools and equipment were lying around and a new main entry door was about to be fitted.

But Roger was nowhere to be seen. Or Lynn, or anyone else.

Sara walked on into the house, through the scullery and into the kitchen. There was no one there. She called out but there was no reply. Bosun padded in from the hallway and barked a couple of woofs of greeting. She patted him and walked on through to the hall, glancing into the empty sitting room, and then into what had been the kids' rumpus room. She looked through the hole in the wall, into the barn, called out, but there was no reply.

She walked back to the kitchen, scribbled a brief note on the scrap-pad on the dresser, tore off the page and left it on the kitchen table, trapped by a pepper mill.

She was about to leave, when she heard a noise upstairs. It sounded like laughter. She walked back into the hall as a bedroom door opened somewhere and she heard Roger say: 'It bloody well should be, the amount it's costing.'

She heard more laughter – a woman's laughter, but it was not Clare. Roger walked across the landing, into the bathroom, directly above the kitchen. Something instinctive told her to turn round and go. Clare was not here. It was only Clare she wanted to talk to. But something else, darker than mere curiosity, drew her towards the staircase.

She began to creep up the stairs. She stopped just a few steps from the top landing. She could see, between the banister rails, into the guest room – the cold room next to Clare and Roger's bedroom at the north end of the house. The door was wide open.

She could see a pair of jeans and a bright scarlet sweatshirt draped over the back of the chair beside the bed. And a white brassière dangling, one strap hooked on one of the uprights. She could see a woman's legs and backside lying naked on the bed, on her side.

It was not Clare, it was Lynn.

She could hear Roger in the bathroom, with the door half open, singing an old Beach Boys number, badly out of tune.

She could smell marijuana.

She heard Roger pull the flush, and his footsteps moving across the bathroom floor towards the door. She crept back down the stairs. Roger stepped out onto the landing and walked back to the guest room.

She heard him say something about Clare's parents coming down from Dorset for Christmas. She didn't catch what Lynn said in reply because he closed the bedroom door behind him.

She crept quickly through the kitchen and scullery, out across the yard and back down the hillside to the woods.

Clare arrived home just after half past four, with Alex and the twins and several boxes of groceries. Roger and Alex carried the groceries inside. Lynn was getting the children's tea ready. Clare unzipped her tweed windjammer and noticed Sara's note on the table.

'I see Sara called in,' she said, to no one in particular.

Lynn was at the stove, stirring a pan of baked beans. She turned and looked at Clare with a blank expression.

'Who did?'

'Sara Carhays.'

Roger lowered a grocery box onto the table. 'When?'

'I don't know,' said Clare, 'some time this afternoon. Didn't you see her?'

Roger shook his head. 'In the barn, I suppose.'

Clare turned and looked at Lynn. 'Where were you?'

'Upstairs with Loulou, I expect,' Lynn replied. And continued stirring the pan of beans.

Sara was churning it over in her mind that night. To tell Clare or not to tell?

Perhaps Lynn was trapped in some way, a hostage to her

job. Unemployment was a plague, Roger could sack her at any time, no reason, there were dozens of girls to take her place.

If she *were* to tell, it might wreck the marriage. Louisa was barely two years old, and the twins were only eight.

Maybe ignorance was a blessing, the lesser of the two evils. She never knew about Gerald and his other affair. She never knew that Bryan had been sleeping with all her so-called friends.

Maybe illusion was kinder than reality. Once the illusion was gone, there was no going back.

On the other hand, if she ignored it, looked the other way, she would become a party to it just by keeping silent. She would have to look Clare in the eye and be dishonest every time they met.

Clare looked in the very next morning. She had a lunch date, the Liberal Democrats' women's committee, Penwith district. She arrived in tan leather and tweedy plaid, in terracotta and sienna and rich autumn colours. Rural chic. She spread herself across the sofa.

'Didn't you even *hear* anyone?' she said. It had obviously been on her mind.

'I saw the car wasn't there, so I didn't wait,' Sara replied.

'I think Lynn's playing games when my back's turned, you know.'

Sara thought, She's asking me. And saw the whole nasty can of worms opening up in front of her.

'What do you mean?' she said. 'What kind of games?'

'Computer games.' Clare toyed with the folds of her tweed skirt. 'Alex has got her hooked. She goes up to his room and plays when he's at school. Roger gave him a new 486 PC last Christmas – far too powerful for his needs, total waste. All he does is play Space Invaders on it.'

Sara felt a huge sense of relief, and knew now that she did not have the courage to tell Clare this morning. Perhaps not ever.

Clare dunked a shortbread biscuit into her coffee. 'Did I tell you that we're going to ask her to move in with us, once the barn's finished?'

'Lynn?' said Sara, trying to keep her voice neutral. 'Move into Trevow? No, you didn't say.'

'There'll be bags of space once Alex and Ben have moved into their new attic rooms. And we won't have to bother driving her home at nights. And if we teach her to drive, it'll mean she can do the school run. Which will leave me free during the days to work on the new stable block.'

'Was this your idea?'

'No. Roger suggested it. He felt it would give me more time and freedom to get out and about.'

Sara nodded woodenly. Clare smiled. 'You don't look wildly enthusiastic.'

Sara shrugged. 'None of my business.'

'But?'

Sara felt trapped. Clare was such an open, honest person, it was not easy to look her in the eye and deceive her. 'I just don't think she's very responsible. She drinks too much for a girl of her age. And she smokes a lot of grass. And I think she mixes with a pretty seedy crowd in St Ives.'

'She wouldn't dare smoke at Trevow,' said Clare. 'I told her I'll kick her arse from here to Friday if I catch her. But I didn't realize she drank a lot. She doesn't have the money, for a start. How do you know?'

'She turned up on my doorstep, absolutely legless, about two o'clock one Sunday morning. A few months ago. Stoned and pissed and soaked to the skin. She'd been out with her friend Ginnie, picked up a couple of strangers in the pub and went off in a car with them. God knows what was going on.'

'She never told *me* about this,' said Clare.

'I'm not surprised. She was violently sick and promptly fell asleep in my bed. I had to sleep in the guest room.'

'Bloody cheek. I hope you gave her what-for in the morning?'

'Didn't get the chance. She was up and gone before I was awake.'

'Has she been round since? To apologize?'

Sara shook her head. 'I should think she's too embarrassed.'

'Want me to have a word with her?'

'No, it's okay. I keep reminding myself she *did* paint half the house for me – the top half, at that.'

Clare helped herself to another shortbread. 'Must stop nibbling ... I've got this infernal lunch. Put on ten pounds this summer. I was actually *thin* before I had Alex. You believe that?'

'What's the lunch in aid of?'

'Yet another sub-committee.' Clare sighed. 'To organize the children's Christmas party. We need helpers to dole out the trifle and wipe snotty noses. Fancy volunteering?'

'When is it?'

'The 20th.'

'I might not be here. Tim's trying to persuade me to go to Florida with him. He flies out on the 19th.'

'Oh?' Clare looked pleasantly surprised. 'What do you mean, *trying*? What's to persuade? I'd go like a shot if I were you.'

'Well, I can't really afford it but—'

'Oh, bollocks,' Clare scoffed. 'Don't be such a wet blanket. What do you mean, can't afford it? Shove it on your Access, silly tart, and go have some fun. Give the rest of us something to gossip about.'

'It's my passport that's the main problem,' said Sara. 'I don't know if it's going to arrive in time.'

'Why not? Are they on strike again?'

'No. But I had to get a copy of my birth certificate and it's a bit of a rigmarole for adopted people.'

'I thought they'd changed the law on that years ago.'

'They did. But people who were adopted *before* the law changed have to meet a counsellor and sign forms and apply to the court and . . .' She groaned and shook her head. 'Oh, it's such a business.'

'Why?' said Clare. 'What happens? Tell me.'

Sara told her about the meetings with Jennifer Glanville in Truro, about how she was found on Bodmin Moor, and the fire.

Clare looked horrified. 'You mean your parents just left you? And set the building on fire?'

'No one knows.'

'Jesus . . .' Clare's face contorted. 'It must have been devastating, going back.'

Sara nodded. Although she felt strangely calm about it now, emotionally numb. Aftershock, perhaps.

'It takes a while for it to sink in. Then it gradually dawns on you that you have no idea who you are. You have no identity – no name, no way back, no roots. You don't even know when your birthday really is.'

'But your parents can't have simply *vanished*,' said Clare. 'They must have heard or read in the paper that you were found – safe. They might have tried to get you back but the courts refused custody. The records might have been in the file at the children's home.'

'It's possible, I suppose,' Sara conceded. 'Anything seems possible after this.'

She recounted her meeting with farmer Keith Argall, and the coincidence of the two standing stones, on Bodmin Moor and in Piskey Woods.

'I didn't know there was a stone like that in Piskey Woods,' said Clare, full of curiosity now. 'That's like the stone in Bryan's painting – the painting I've got in the drawing room. Do you remember?'

'Yes, I do,' said Sara. 'I wanted to ask you about it. Did he ever explain it? What it meant?'

'I did ask. But you never got straight answers from Bryan. He said watery places, especially wells and small pools, were holy to the Celts. And the stone in that picture was both man and woman.'

'But why did he paint it rising from the middle of the pool like that?'

'Search me. He used to say we have two eyes – a conscious eye and a subconscious eye. And in his painting he tried to merge the two.'

'What did he mean by a subconscious eye?'

'Roger thought he was talking a load of pretentious bollocks,' said Clare. 'But I think he was simply referring to dreams.'

She remembered that warm summer day when Lynn had suggested borrowing Roger's ladders to paint the barn-cottage.

'Would he mind?'

'Not if I ask him in my special way.'

That coy tricksy smile playing at the corners of her mouth.

What was Lynn after? Who was using whom? Where did this end?

She felt surrounded by betrayal. They had unwittingly roped

her into their scheme of things, made her a dishonest friend, a liar by omission. She felt soiled by it, contaminated by it, now she was part of it, a co-conspirator. She felt cowardly. It saddened her, it pulled her down.

Outside, the world was grey and brown and still, the peninsula lost in mist. It swallowed up the carns, the ancient stones, the menhirs, the quoits. The jagged remains of old mine buildings loomed like ruins on a bombscape. Damp infested everything. At Crowjy the doors and windows began to swell, became reluctant to open. Slugs invaded the kitchen by night, thick as sausages, cold as leeches, drawn by the scent of grapefruit peel and other waste. She skidded on them sometimes in the early gloom of morning. Spiders came in from the cold and damp, nesting behind the Rayburn, cramped clumps of black pipe cleaners, soaking up the warmth. By night the distant fog horn moaned, a sick bull bellyaching to the ocean a few miles across the moors at Pendeen Watch.

It was not walking weather, it was not gardening weather, it was the dreariest time of year. The days were running out of light. Everything around her seemed corrupted. The valley smelt of mould and decay. She was ambushed by depression. Tim was working all hours now. One of his partners had been injured in a car crash so they were one doctor short at the practice, and he was on call more than usual to make up for his ten days' leave at Christmas. Depression crept up and swamped her like a freak tide in the night. It was so sudden, came from nowhere, it caught her off balance, overwhelmed her resistance. It flooded over her, capsized her, engulfed her, pushed her down and down. She tried to get a grip but everything was swept this way and that in the flood. She was no one. She was firechild. She was cut loose, she was a speck of matter floating pointlessly in space.

She smothered her face with the plastic bag, pulled it down over her head like a mask, to hide from the night, and held it tight around her throat. She didn't want the borderline, the edge of beyond. She didn't care where Bryan had searched and touched and found. She wanted oblivion. Over the edge and beyond.

She gripped the plastic to her throat and breathed in deeply, felt it crinkle against her face. Tiny sister. Womb of stone.

Timeless evil. She felt the darkness creeping into her, filling her mouth and nose, swimming through her passages, seeping deeper, deeper.

She was moving through the dark towards the landing at the top of the stairs. She was going down the staircase. She was walking on air, smooth and silent. Along the hall passage, into the kitchen. A woman was lying on the floor, arms raised in surrender, her wrists lashed to the wall.

Sara felt a rage welling inside her. A sudden outpouring of hurt and anger. She took a large knife from a drawer and cut through the rope that bound the wrists. She took the body in her arms and looked at the face. It was *her* face, it was her body. She cuddled the body, it was cold and still. She wrapped her robe around the body. Was it dead? She put her mouth to the lips and blew air into the lungs. She felt the body move, the chest begin to rise and fall. She felt a tremor of a heartbeat. She blew more air into the lungs. The lips became warmer, became soft and moist. She kissed the lips. The lips responded, parted. Their tongues touched. Their bodies drew closer, their embrace grew tighter. Their hands began to caress, to explore, inquisitive, deeper, intimate strangers. They were intertwined, they were coils and tentacles, a nest of serpents, pale as the moon, smooth and shifting, closer and tighter, searching, discovering, nestling through each other's secrets.

The body was sloughing its skin. Flesh was peeling away wherever Sara touched, like strips of latex, stretching and tearing and sticking to her nails and fingers, the hair was falling out in thick handfuls, and the scalp was peeling away beneath. A new face was appearing, a new body, new hair . . .

The new lips were not *her* lips . . . They were damp with slime and tasted of salt. The teeth were stained and the breath smelt ashen. The eyes glowed with a malicious pleasure, they shone like a wood demon in the night.

It was Lynn's face, Lynn's hair, Lynn's body.

Sara cried out in revulsion, snatched up the kitchen knife and brought it slashing down across Lynn's body, a long diagonal that opened her from breast to hip. Lynn was laughing. Sara was raising her hand again. The knife was flashing through the dark, slicing across Lynn's face. She was still laughing but the expression on her face was mutating from derision to confusion. Sara felt an ecstatic surge of energy, of sexual exhilaration as she brought the knife down again in another wild, slashing diagonal. And again ... And again ... Like great paint-strokes with the blade. Carmine stripes, glossy and beautiful, began to blossom across her flesh, molten rubies pouring down her. She felt the jarring of steel on bone as the blade xylophoned across the ribcage and sliced deep into the soft belly flesh and steam and gas and offal bubbled out and—

She awoke.

It was day.

She was cold. She had thrown off her duvet in the night.

Her heart was pumping hard.

She thought about her nightmare. It was so vivid, that infernal bloody grin on Lynn's face, the jarring of steel on bone.

Then it all came back to her ... Last night. The plastic bag, the desire for extinction, the longing for nothing, for total unexistence.

She got up and put on her bathrobe. She looked for the plastic bag. It wasn't there.

She found it downstairs. It was in the studio.

A large kitchen knife was lying in the middle of the studio floor. Bryan's largest and best Sabatier knife, sharp as a razor. She picked it up. It was covered with dry blood.

There was blood all over her hands.

She stared with horror at the two paintings of Lynn. One was lying on the floor, the other was on the worktop. The canvas hung in shreds. Both pictures had been slashed to ribbons.

She lay in the bath, frightened sick. She felt like a half-drunk driver who had staggered away from a car smash in the dark. She felt like a child afraid of monsters lurking in the night.

She remembered the feeling of ecstasy in her dream, the exhilaration as she swiped the blade through Lynn's face.

She had cut her hand on the knife.

She sat on the side of the bath and looked down at her knees. They were grazed. She'd been on the floor in the night.

She looked higher up her legs, the inside thigh. She found red scratches. Like the clawing of fingernails.

A little higher, close to her groin, she found a love bite.

She remembered something that Bryan had written in his journal:

Once you have known it, you cannot unknow it. Once you have touched her there is no return. It is out of Eden.

She felt as if she were standing at the edge of a deep black chasm, looking down.

What if she did this again, this sleepwalking, this frenzied lashing out? What if she did this at Tim's house one night? What if she did this in Florida?

She was afraid to tell him. What could she say? He wouldn't believe her, he'd think she was coming unglued at the seams. She was beginning to wonder if the inquest, the guilt, the stress, the whole thing was starting to tell ... a kind of breakdown.

She had to take control, to get a hold of this, reassert herself, take command, pull herself together, fight back.

She burnt the two paintings – or what was left of them. She burnt them on a bonfire in the garden. And she burnt Bryan's sketchpads too – all those drawings of the strange creature without hair, and the drawings of the woman tied to the wall. It made her feel better, even if it made no difference to anything. It gave her a sense of *doing* something, taking charge, asserting control.

Her passport came. That made her feel better. And now Tim had the airline tickets. Her depression began to lift as the holiday approached. She slept better, there were no more bad dreams, no more crazy experiments with plastic bags. She felt her confidence returning, the pressure lifting. Tim was right, it was what she needed, to get away, away from the fog and the damp, the relentless grey days, away to the sun, different people, new places. Her spirits began to rise. She had sorted something out in her mind, the guilt, the whole Bryan thing, her mixed-up feelings. It was a botch but it would do – all misshapen pieces, like fragments of the family porcelain, dropped and shattered on the kitchen floor, picked up, collected in a box and put away to be glued together at a later date.

She sent out her Christmas cards. She seemed to have fewer and fewer to send with each passing year. Friends drifted away, got married, started families, lost touch.

She got a card from her aunt in New Zealand. (Sara spelt *Sarah*.) 'Come and see us, dear.' Perhaps she would; finish her thesis, sell Crowjy and go a-visiting.

She got a card from Gerald. 'Think of you often.' *I bet*.

Before she left for Florida, she had supper with Clare at Trevow. Roger was out, having a few beers with his pals from the Land's End flying club. Clare and Sara were eating pasta in the kitchen; fettuccine with a sauce of tomatoes, capers, olives and anchovies.

Clare was saying that she would take care of Charlie over Christmas.

Sara was staring at the children's paintings on the kitchen wall.

'What are you looking at?' asked Clare, craning her neck around.

'The picture of the Michelin men.'

'Oh. Ben drew that. They're giants. It's the legend of Carn Ewyn.'

Two fat men were standing on either side of the picture, hurling what looked like a discus from one to the other. There was a bird in flight in the middle of the picture with a hooked beak.

'What's the legend of Carn Ewyn?' said Sara.

'Two giants were standing on opposite hills,' said Clare, 'playing quoits with a granite capstone. And the capstone hit an eagle in the sky and cut off her toes ... or claws, or whatever eagles have on their feet. They landed on top of a hill. The giants cried for a hundred days and the eagle's claws swelled and petrified to rock. And that's them there ...' Clare pointed towards the top of Trevow Hill. 'The Cornish word for claw is *ewyn*. So it's been known as Carn Ewyn ever since.'

She topped up their glasses with Chianti.

'Isn't that enchanting? Ben's very taken with the story. Gone into every gruesome detail.'

'So I see,' said Sara.

Each little claw was lying on top of the hill in its own little puddle of vivid crimson blood.

It put Sara in mind of the picture that Bryan had painted of Lynn, with her fingertips cut off and lying on the bed, between her legs; the picture she had slashed to ribbons.

THE POOL

'I told Sara we'd look after Charlie,' said Clare.

'Charlie who?'

They were in the drawing room. The children were in bed. Roger was slumped in an armchair watching *Newsnight* on BBC2. Clare was surrounded by Christmas lists. There were dozens of them. They would be endlessly revised, integrated, deleted, lost or chucked on the fire between now and the 25th.

'Her cat. While she's in Florida.'

'I'd have thought we had enough of the bloody things already.'

Roger loathed Christmas. It began too early these days and it went on for too long. This year the shops had been echoing to Bing Crosby since early November.

'I was wondering about Lynn,' said Clare, ignoring his last remark.

'What about her?'

'What to give her for Christmas.'

Roger was trying to concentrate on *Newsnight*.

'I was thinking,' she said, 'about driving lessons.'

'For Lynn?' He stared at Clare as if she were mad. 'Do you realize how much driving lessons cost?'

'Just a few to get her started.'

'Six lessons cost about a hundred quid these days. Have you taken total leave of your senses?'

'She'll be much more use to me here when she can drive. She can do the school run for a start, and all the shopping. I'm going to have the stables to look after, *I* won't have the time.'

That snookered him. He turned back to *Newsnight*.

'Unless, of course, *you* want to do the school run and pick up the shopping.'

He remained silent.

'You're the one who suggested she moves in,' Clare argued.

'What's she going to do if she can't drive? Stuck here like cheese at fourpence.'

'I'll teach her,' said Roger. 'Take her out in the afternoons.'

'Not in the Espace, you won't. And you can't teach her in that clapped-out pickup, it's lethal.'

'I'm not spending a hundred quid on the au pair's bloody Christmas present, and that's that.'

'Well, in that case, we'll get shot of Lynn and find a girl who *can* drive.'

He sat scowling at the television.

'Sara doesn't think it's a very good idea her moving in, anyway,' said Clare.

'What's it got to do with her?'

'She thinks Lynn's irresponsible.'

For a moment Roger was speechless.

'None of her bloody business who we employ,' he said indignantly. 'Tell her to piss off, cheeky cow.'

Later, as he was getting undressed for bed, he said, 'What did she mean, irresponsible?'

It was a dark starless night. The pickup was bouncing and lurching slowly along a secluded track that led nowhere – just field access for tractors. Roger pulled up and switched out the lights. He left the engine idling and the heater fan turned to slow. Lynn took off her coat and they cuddled together under a thick travelling rug. The radio was on low; country and western. Willie Nelson.

'Why can't I move in before the barn's finished?' she grumbled. 'You've got two spare rooms.'

'I don't think Clare would wear it,' said Roger. 'There isn't enough for you to do till we start work on the stables.'

'It's taking forever, this bloody barn,' she said despondently. 'Can't you get Shane in, give you a hand, speed it up?'

'Not at fifteen quid an hour I can't.'

'How about I move in over Christmas? Clare will need me then.'

'There won't be any room. We've got her parents coming down from Lyme Regis, and her sister Jenny's coming down from London.'

'Oh, bloody hell,' she whined. 'I haven't got to spend another Christmas with my cow of a mother, have I?'

'We don't want to push it. Clare's already having second thoughts about you moving in.'

It was too dark to see her face but he could sense the change of expression.

'What do you mean, second thoughts?'

'Sara told her it wasn't a good idea.'

He was teasing her but she wasn't in the mood.

'Sara Carhays?' she said, indignation rising. 'Told her *what*?'

'That you're irresponsible. That you drink too much. And smoke too much weed. And are none too choosy who you go to bed with.'

'The bloody nerve . . .' She was stunned. 'Christ, *she*'s a one to talk.'

'Why?' said Roger, interested now. 'Who's getting his leg over there, apart from Hendra?'

'I crashed out there one night. I was pissed, sick as a dog. I fell asleep . . . Next thing I know she's in bed with me. She's all over me, hands everywhere.'

Roger snorted.

'It's not funny.'

'What did you do?'

'Don't remember. I was too stoned. I fell asleep.'

Roger chuckled and slipped his hand under her sweater. 'Well, you can kip down with Clare and me, if that's what you're into,' he said. 'Then you'll have a bed for Christmas, after all.'

'Don't make jokes about it. It was horrible. Makes me feel sick just thinken about it.'

Roger's hands began to move across her, unclipping, unbuckling. He turned her over and smothered her like a bear. The truck began to rock and squeak.

Looking up through the windscreen at the starless sky, Lynn caught a fleeting memory of the citrus fragrance that lingered in Sara's bedroom, on her hair, her pillow, her robe. She remembered that cold silky skin pressing against hers, the caress of those hands, those long, sensitive, probing fingers. She closed her eyes. The pickup shuddered and creaked like an old boat in the hustling December wind.

*

Lynn hated winter. The evenings were long and black and dead. There was nowhere to go, nothing to do. The valley was a morgue. All the emmets had gone back upcountry and would not be back until spring. Their whitewashed cottages sat dark and safe, sealed up tight with multiple locks and hi-tech alarms; small fortresses defending no one against nothing in the middle of nowhere.

The wind whined like a lost dog among the rocks of Carn Ewyn.

The thought of Christmas made it all seem worse. She had taken it for granted that Clare would need her at Trevow this year. But it would be just the two of them at Chy Melyn, after all. As usual. Her mother's miserable scowling face; the scrawny little turkey; the mean little presents, shampoo and tights; the funereal silences or the babble of television.

She hated winter.

She saw Tim Hendra drive by, the day they flew off to America. He drove past very early, to pick her up, drive to Gatwick, fly to the sun. Him and The Bitch.

Trying to screw her job up. Talking to Clare like that, behind her back. She could hardly believe it. Why would she do that? *Her* life was sweet: the eternal student, a free house thanks to Bryan, Tim Hendra on a string, holiday in Florida, not a care in the world. What did she have to go and ruin someone else's life for? Was she so holy? Or was it spite? Did she feel rejected that night?

Or was it something worse? Did she *hear* them that afternoon at Trevow? Was that possible? Was that why she told Clare it wasn't a good idea, her moving in? Did she tell Clare what she heard? They talked a lot those two, went riding together, shopping trips, all that middle-class Lib-Dem womanly stuff. Was Clare watching them now, on to them?

Or was Sara jealous?

Christ. Vindictive bitch. Everything was going fine till she stuck her oar in.

She lay awake at nights, thinking of ways to get back at her.

Ginnie said they had hurricanes in Florida. Whole houses blew away, the swamps flooded the towns, alligators ate people, black folks rioted, gunned down white folks by the hundred.

Happy Christmas, bitch.

Or maybe the plane would go down.

She pictured a milk bottle full of petrol, stuffed with a flaming rag, crashing through the glass roof at Crowjy, plummeting to earth like a burning 747. Total burn-out. All her computer disks, her precious thesis, An Gof, the whole lot. Nothing left but ashes.

She went to Shane Pascoe's house one evening before Christmas. Shane was the jobbing builder who helped Roger with the barn sometimes. He grew marijuana in his back garden and sold it to her for ten pounds an ounce. She then sold some on to Ginnie and her friends for twice the price and recovered her costs.

Shane asked her in. His wife was out at her mother's.

'Want some weed, do'ee?' Shane presumed.

'No, I want something different tonight,' said Lynn. 'What else can you get me?' Shane could lay hands on any kind of drug, or so the rumours went.

'Well, what kind of thing you looken for?' he asked.

'Somethen stronger. Somethen like Angel Dust.'

'Angel Dust?' Shane laughed. 'You know what that is, do'ee?' He laughed again. 'You won't get Angel Dust down here, my flower. Fat chance. You'll have to go up London for that. What you want stuff like that for? Blow your head off, that will.'

'So what *can* you get?'

'You wanna rave, I can get 'ee some Es.'

Lynn pulled a sneering face. 'Ecstasy . . . big deal.'

'Best I can do,' said Shane. 'I en't a dealer, I don't need the hassle.'

'How much for a dozen Es, then?' she said.

'Oh . . . say fifty.'

'*Fifty?*' Lynn pulled another face. 'Come off it, Shane, I don't make that kind of money. That's a rip-off.'

'The going rate,' said Shane, with a shrug.

'What kind of deal you give me for six?'

'All right, I'll give 'ee six for twenty.'

'Oh, come on, Shane, that's not a deal. A deal's a – you know . . . I've only got ten quid.'

'Oh, yeah?' Shane looked interested. And added with a lazy, curious smile: 'So 'zackly what kind of deal is it you've got in mind, then?'

Lynn slotted her hands into the back pockets of her threadbare jeans and tried to look cool.

'Well . . . 'zackly what is it you fancy?' she enquired.

The following day was Christmas Eve. Lynn went up to Trevow to help Clare in the morning. Clare's divorced sister Jenny had arrived from London, all lah-de-dah and Harrods' carrier bags, and their elderly parents had driven down from Dorset. Their mother was fussing about getting to Midnight Mass and driving Roger mad. Clare let Lynn go home after lunch. Lah-de-dah Jenny offered to run her back to Chy Melyn (Roger was working in the barn, even on Christmas Eve, anything to avoid his in-laws) but Lynn said no, she'd rather walk. They got up her nose, Clare's family.

She walked out across the yard. The front of the house was cluttered with cars: the Espace, Jenny's black Merc and her parents' Jaguar. As she weaved her way between the cars she heard a plaintive mewing. She stopped and looked down. Sara's kitten was curled up under the Merc. She looked up at Lynn and mewed again.

'Hello, Charlie,' said Lynn. And in her granny's broad Penwith accent: 'Whad are'ee a'doan of down thear 'en, my robin?'

She sank onto her haunches, put the plastic carrier bag aside and picked up the kitten. Charlie began to throb and purr as Lynn stroked her.

'All that lah-de-dah bollocks getten up your nose too 'en, ezzer? You wanna fly away, see your mum, do'ee?'

A delicious thought entered her mind.

'Well, Charlie my lover, this could be your lucky day . . .'

She nestled Charlie to her bosom with one hand and picked up the bag of presents with the other. Glancing round to check that no one was watching from the windows at the front of the house, she started away down the hillside towards the woods.

At the foot of the hill she crossed the stream, over the rotting railway sleeper, and took the longer of the two paths, the muddy trail that snaked through the heart of the woods.

Charlie clung to her fearfully, as Lynn's heavy rubber boots thumped and sploshed along the marshy track; her claws dug deep into Lynn's coat.

When she was right in the thick of the woods, about forty acres from nowhere, Lynn stopped and put the bag down.

'Time to fly, Charlie,' she crooned. 'Fly away . . .'

She plucked Charlie from her chest and tossed her away into the bushes. Charlie landed with a squeak and sat staring at Lynn, wide-eyed with shock.

Lynn waved goodbye. 'Happy Christmas, Charlie-barley . . .'

She picked up the bag and continued along the path.

Charlie started after her but the marshy pools were too deep. She hopped, slithering, out of the mud, and stood half buried in the long grass and ferns that fronted the dense growth of brambles.

Charlie was missing all night.

On Christmas Day Clare sent the children out to search the dairy sheds, the tack room, the stable and the old piggery. Before it got dark they walked across the hillside, as well, but there was no sight of Charlie.

Roger was in an even filthier mood now. He was not a lover of cats. He was a dog man. Dogs were sensible, they did what they were told. Cats were perverse stupid creatures.

'She'll turn up,' he said irritably, as they undressed for bed on Christmas night. 'Cats do. They wander off. Come back in their own time.'

'She's only a kitten still,' said Clare, tired and equally irritable – but with Roger, not Charlie.

'Well, maybe a fox has got her, then,' said Roger, and took malicious pleasure in saying it. 'Or a stoat, or a buzzard.'

The children went looking for her on the carn, the next day. They asked other people who were out walking, but no one had seen a tortoiseshell kitten.

During tea that afternoon, little Ben said, 'Maybe she's gone back to Crowjy.'

Jo made a sneering noise and said, 'How's she going to find the way, stupid?'

'Follow the path,' said Alex, 'like anyone else.'

Roger glanced at Clare. 'Have you checked?'

'No, I didn't think of it,' Clare confessed. And felt rather stupid.

Ben wrinkled his nose at Jo and said, 'Nyeah ... See ...' And poked out his tongue.

Sara had left a set of keys with Clare. That evening, while everyone was watching television, Clare took Bosun and drove round to the valley in the pickup.

The night was misty. Boskinnow was deserted. The lanes were empty. She drew up outside the barn-cottage, alongside Sara's Beetle, left the motor running and the headlights on, and clambered out. Bosun scrabbled over the driver's seat and jumped out behind her. He scampered eagerly away into the darkness for a sniff and a piddle.

Clare walked up to Sara's front door and let herself in. She fumbled for the light switch but nothing happened. She tried the lights in the sitting room but they weren't working either. Perhaps Sara had switched off at the mains.

She went back out to the pickup, took a torch from the glovebox and returned to the house. There were a few items of mail on the hall floor. She walked along the passage and shone her torch along the wall. The fuse box was near the back door. She opened the small wooden cabinet and shone the light inside. The main switch was *on*.

She tried the kitchen lights. They weren't working either.

Must have blown a fuse.

It was warm in here. Extraordinarily warm. Sara had filled the Rayburn before she left, but she'd been gone a week; it was amazing it was still alight.

She shone the torch at the bottom of the back door. Sara had paid Shane to install a cat flap, so it was possible that Charlie could have got in. Clare walked along the passage to the sitting room and shone her torch around. No Charlie.

It was warm in this room too, uncomfortably warm. Clare unzipped her tweed jacket and walked upstairs. It was like an oven, this place; she wondered if Sara had left an electric radiator on somewhere.

She shone the torch into Sara's room. Two green-yellow dots flashed back at her – Charlie was curled up on the bed, looking perfectly contented.

'*There* you are, little wanderer . . .'

Clare sat on the side of the bed. Charlie stretched her legs and gave herself a little shake and came over to Clare.

'We thought the foxes had got you.' She lifted Charlie into her lap. 'Pussycat chops, for Madam Brush and all her little brushes.'

Charlie purred quietly, sublimely unconcerned.

Clare got up and carried her downstairs.

She stopped by the front door and listened. She could make out a faint whispering sound somewhere. It sounded as if it was coming from the kitchen. A soft rustling sound, as if someone were crinkling tissue paper. Her first thought was that a rat had got in through the cat flap. She walked down the passage, stood in the kitchen doorway and shone the torch around.

The whispering sound was coming from the heavy aluminium kettle that Sara had left at the back of the Rayburn, behind the covered hobs. A feathery plume of steam was curling lazily out of the spout. Clare put Charlie down on the table, moved over to the stove and picked up the kettle. It was hot to touch and almost empty. She lifted it off the stove and left it on the drainer.

Why was it so hot in here? She shone her torch at the oven door. The thermometer was reading almost zero.

She felt the side of the Rayburn. It was barely even warm. She looked inside the furnace. It had burned itself out.

So why was the kettle steaming?

She picked up Charlie and walked back along the passage to the front door.

Why was the whole house so warm, if the Rayburn had burned out? It was a badly insulated house, a shocking place for draughts.

She stepped outside, pulled the door shut, turned the mortice lock and walked back to the pickup. She whistled to Bosun and waited but he did not appear. She shut Charlie inside the cab of the pickup and strolled up the track towards the foot of the hill, shouting for Bosun and flashing the torch across the marshy acres to the right of the track.

She called again and waited. But still there was no sight of him. Exasperated, she trudged along the muddy path towards the pond. God help him if he had jumped in for a dip. It was the kind of thing he would do, he'd jump in water anywhere, he should have been a dolphin not a Labrador. She would make him ride home on the back of the pickup and leave him outside in the yard till he was dry.

'Bosun!'

Silence. Not even the sound of scuffling through the bracken.

'Bosun!' She was getting angry now. 'Come here, stupid dog!'

She waved the beam of the torch across the marshy ground, the brambles, the gorse. She shone it across the water to the other side. She saw him.

It could have been a log, or a black bin liner, floating in the middle of the pond. Not moving. Just breaking the surface of the water.

With a yelp of anguish, Clare dropped the torch in the mud and plunged into the pool, fully clothed. The water was so cold it made her cry out. She couldn't touch the bottom of the pool, she had to swim. She had so many heavy clothes on, it was like swimming in a nightmare where her arms had no strength. She reached the middle of the pool and grasped Bosun's collar. He gave her no help at all. She had to tow him back to the side of the pool. She scrambled out onto the muddy bank and pulled him out after her. He was an incredible weight. A dead weight. Completely still and lifeless.

The vet examined Bosun's dead body. He had not drowned, he had died of cardiac arrest.

'His heart,' the vet explained, 'simply stopped beating.'

'But why?' Clare was so distraught, she just wanted to understand. 'Was he ill?'

'There doesn't seem to have been anything wrong with him,' said the vet. 'It just happens sometimes. It happens to human beings as well. The heart just stops. Like switching off a car engine. It may have been triggered by shock. The coldness of the water, for example. Severe shock can stop an animal's heart, just as it can a human's.'

The children were heartbroken. They buried him beside the Tudor barn.

Roger felt awkward, short of words to comfort Clare. The death of animals did not much move him. He had seen Clare through the deaths of numerous dogs and horses and God knows how many cats. Horses were the worst; she wept buckets, she heaved and gurgled with grief for days on end, lost pounds in salt water.

He suggested that they cancel the New Year's Eve party. But it was a token gesture of sympathy, he knew it was not a serious option. He touched her that night in bed – for the first time in ages – to console her. But she withdrew from him, turned away, hugged her sadness to her bosom like a sickly infant.

He drove round to Crowjy the next morning to see why the lights were not working. He switched off at the mains and checked the fuse box. The fuses on all five circuits had blown. He put new wire in each one and then tested all the lights and power sockets in the house. They were working normally again.

He couldn't understand what Clare meant when she said it was warm in the house the previous night ... *Very* warm, she'd said. But it was so cold in there now, it felt close to freezing, and his hands were turning blue.

There was a strange smell in the place, as well ... a sour tang in the atmosphere as if someone had been there in the night, burning paper or old lumber.

FLESH

Susie was waiting on the concourse at Orlando: petite, cropped blonde hair, large round sunglasses, white shorts and shocking pink halter. She threw herself at Tim as if she hadn't seen him for twenty years. She was speedy and fizzy, strong calves and tennis wrists; wore her cap at a jaunty angle and her Ray-Bans on a black neck-cord.

They cruised north for a couple of hours on Interstate-95, which followed the Atlantic coast from Miami to Canada. It was seventy-two degrees, the sun was high in a clear sky.

Susie and Jeff lived in a sailing and fishing resort, where the marina was the centre of everything. Jeff had a thirty-foot cabin cruiser that he rented out for fishing trips and used for his underwater photography expeditions. He was from South Carolina, lean and blond, tanned a deep tobacco brown, about ten years older than Susie.

They were renting an apartment from a friend of his brother. It was in a condominium built in mock-Spanish colonial style, with arched windows, white stucco walls and orange tiled roofs, built around small courtyards, dripping with bougainvillaea and honeysuckle. There was a large shared pool in what they called the back yard.

That first evening they sat outside, sipping cocktails in the fading warmth of the sun.

'And this is what you call a yard?' said Sara.

Jeff flipped a peanut in the air and caught it in his mouth.

'You don't like?'

Around them lay half an acre of tropical garden, with swaying palms, yucca, araucaria, and oranges ripening on the trees.

'Oh, I like,' said Sara. 'I like very much. I'm just glad I don't have to do the dead-heading round here.'

*

Her bedroom was large and square, overlooking a tiled yard bright with flowering plants in huge terracotta pots.

She was undressing.

Tim tapped lightly on the door.

She said, 'Come in.'

'Midnight swim?' He was wearing a long striped towelling robe.

'You can't be serious?'

'Try me.'

He slipped his arms round her.

'I've eaten too much lobster, I'll sink.'

She untied his robe and nestled up against him.

'I'll rescue you.'

His hands slid down her back to her buttocks.

'*Now* what are you doing?'

'Undressing you.'

'This is sexual harassment. It's a crime in this country.'

'I'm your physician.'

'Then you're being unethical.'

'You can't go swimming in your underwear.'

'Can't we skip the swim and just be unethical?'

'No, we can swim, and then we can be unethical afterwards.'

He took her hand and towed her towards the door.

'Wait wait wait . . . my swimsuit.'

'You're wearing it.'

'I can't go out like *this*.'

'Why not? I am.'

'Not out *there*!'

'It's seventy degrees—'

'But I'll be *seen*.'

'Only by the cicadas.'

He towed her along the carpeted passage.

'But Susie and Jeff—'

'They're in bed. Being unethical.'

She stood at the edge of the pool, arms folded across her chest.

'I don't believe I'm doing this. It's ten past midnight, it's Christmas week, I'm two hundred yards from a lake creeping and crawling with hideous reptiles—'

'Don't move.'

She froze.
'Right behind you.'
'What is it?'
'Alligator.'

She jumped and shattered the still water with a stifled shriek. Tim dived in after her. She resurfaced and looked around the deserted poolside.

'You bastard! I nearly had heart failure.'
'We're in luck, then. I'm a doctor.'
'*Now* what are you trying to do?'
'Give you mouth to mouth.'

She saw a shadowy figure sitting on the balcony of a second-floor apartment, training what looked like a telescope on them.

'Someone is watching,' she murmured.
'I know.'
'Up on the balcony. He's got a telescope.'
'Or a video camera with telephoto lens.'
'You see it?'
'Of course I see it. There's three more out there if you look hard enough.'
'Why didn't you *say* something?'
'Why should I? It's not me they're looking at.'

They got up late. Jeff was already down at the marina.

'Well, you two young things had fun last night,' said Susie, finding them in the kitchen, making breakfast.

'Did we keep you awake?' Sara looked apologetic.

'No. We heard you go *in* the water, but we didn't hear you get out.'

'She didn't dare,' said Tim, 'for the next two hours.'

'I was too embarrassed. We were being watched.'

'Of course you were.' Susie started brewing coffee. 'This place is full of retired lechers. You're now on a VHS which will be passed around the whole condo.'

Sara peeled an orange. 'How am I going to show my face?'

'It's not your face they want to see,' said Tim.

'Why not?' said Sara. 'They've seen everything else.'

They spent the day on Jeff's boat. Susie was everywhere, for'ard and aft, hauling and stowing, she was deckhand and helm and engineer. They went ten miles out. Tim and Jeff did some fishing. Susie and Sara lay on towels and sunbathed.

Susie said, 'You're good for him. You get him going.'

'You make me sound like a laxative.'

'He came out last year and he looked so middle-aged.'

They had lunch around two. Shellfish, cold meats and salad, and canned beer.

Sara had begun to feel the heat of the sun.

Jeff looked at her and said, 'You'd better cover up. Be sore tonight.'

She hadn't brought anything on the boat with her that had legs or sleeves. She tried to stay in the shade without going below decks but it wasn't easy with the boat drifting gently round in wide circles.

Mid-afternoon, her skin was feeling tender. Susie went below and ferreted in lockers and came up with a sun-faded smock. It smelt of diesel, tar and fish guts. But it kept the sun off Sara's arms and upper body.

She felt sick that evening. She was turning the colour of a lobster. She smoothed lotion into her skin but it was painful to the touch. Tim said they'd better stay home the next day or two. The forecast was for a general clouding over anyway.

That night her skin was so sore it was painful even to undress.

Tim said, 'You want to sleep alone tonight?'

She was reluctant to spoil his holiday. 'Would you mind?'

When he touched her to say goodnight, she winced.

'You *have* got it bad,' said Tim sympathetically. 'We'll take a look in the morning. Maybe get you something from the pharmacy.'

She got into bed. She couldn't sleep with the covers over her, it was too uncomfortable. She slept a few hours and then woke up. She felt sick again. She went to the bathroom and threw up. Her skin felt tight. It was burning, like iodine on open wounds. She took two Bufferin tablets and went back to bed. She slept fitfully.

She came to and found Tim standing by the bed. It was a bright sunny day outside. He looked worried.

'How does it feel?'

'Incredibly sore . . .' She tried to sit up.

'Just lie back,' said Tim. 'Let me look.'

She was wearing nothing but a T-shirt. He eased it over her belly.

'I feel tight all over,' she muttered. 'Like a drum skin. Jesus, it burns.'

'Okay,' said Tim softly. 'Try and relax. I'll have a word with Susie. I think we might run you into the local A and E, get you looked at.'

'Oh, not hospital. It's not that bad. Just give me some painkillers or something.'

'Just lie still,' said Tim. 'I'll be back in a minute.'

He walked out of the bedroom and closed the door.

She tried flexing her hand. She held it up and looked at it. It looked vile. She looked up her arm to the shoulder. She pushed herself upright and looked at her legs. They looked repulsive. She swung her legs off the bed and stood up. Even that was painful. It seemed to burn right down to her muscles. She moved to the window, levelled the slats of the Venetian blind to let in the light and slowly eased the T-shirt up over her body and over her head.

She looked in the mirror. What she saw almost made her sick. Her flesh was an inflamed strawberry red, smooth and shiny. But, worse, it looked as if she had been varnished, as if she were covered in translucent plastic film from head to toe.

Tim walked back in at that moment.

'What the hell is it?' she whispered.

He looked as sickened as she felt.

'I don't know,' he confessed. 'I've never seen anything like it before.'

She was admitted to hospital. She was examined by a consultant dermatologist. He had never seen such an extreme reaction to sunlight. Her skin looked like scar tissue, all over her body. Within a day or so, it had changed from a sickly red to a bubblegum pink.

She was kept in hospital for three days and discharged for Christmas. She was crippled with embarrassment. She disgusted herself; she looked like peppermint rock, Cellophane wrapped; she looked like a condom with wrinkles. What *is* it? she kept asking Tim. He looked through her cosmetics. He asked her if she was on any kind of drug, tetracycline or some other antibiotic. *He* was her GP, she said. Where was she going to get antibiotics from that he didn't know about? And the few cosmetics she used, she'd been using for years.

She had to soften her crackling body with calamine lotion. She couldn't make love, it was too painful. She had to keep out of sunlight, stay in all day long. Tim was very patient. Sometimes he stayed home to keep her company, sometimes he went out fishing or sailing with Jeff, and Susie stayed with her.

After a few days, her skin began to lose its plastic appearance. It got softer and more elastic and less tender. She began to peel. By the last evening of their holiday, she looked no worse than the average English holiday-maker flying home from a week in the sun.

It was dark when they arrived back in Nansgever. Tim carried her suitcase indoors and stayed a moment just to see that everything was all right, and then left her to unpack and drove on home.

She opened the mail that Clare had left for her on the table. A few more Christmas cards. She went upstairs, took off her travelling clothes, changed into jeans and sweater, and switched on the electric immersion heater for a bath. Then she came back down to the kitchen and set about lighting a new fire in the Rayburn.

Before she got into bed that night, she massaged calamine lotion into her body, as she had been doing for the past week. Her skin was still peeling but it was no longer sore. She looked at her back in the long mirror. She noticed something strange. It was criss-crossed with marks, slightly red, stripy marks, all over her upper back, as high as her shoulders. They were new. It looked as if she had been lying on something that had left its criss-cross pattern imprinted on her flesh.

That night she woke up at about three o'clock, feeling uncomfortably hot. Her nightdress was damp with perspiration. She threw back the duvet. She wondered if she had left the Rayburn on its highest setting. She had meant to turn the damper to the half-way mark before she went to bed. But even so ... Even on its highest setting it shouldn't have been *this* hot. It had only been alight for six hours.

Now she became aware of a faint odour, drifting up from downstairs. It smelt as if something were cooking, something meaty but slightly sweet, like roast pork.

She switched on the light, got out of bed and went downstairs. It was even warmer in the hallway. She went into the kitchen and looked at the thermometer on the oven door: 300 Fahrenheit – not even moderately hot. She looked at the damper control: she *had* turned it down. And the cooking smell was not as strong in here as it was upstairs.

But then hot air rises, she told herself.

She walked back along the hall passage to the sitting room. It was warmer in here than it was in the kitchen, and that sweetish, roast-meat smell was slightly stronger.

She went back upstairs. The smell was not so noticeable now. She climbed back into bed and put out the light. The smell had almost gone. Strange. She lay awake thinking about it. Perhaps she'd spilled some cat food on the hobs, or there were splashes of dried fat inside the oven, and it had begun to smell as the Rayburn heated up to working temperature.

She drifted back to sleep and slept perfectly for the remainder of the night.

The following morning, when she went downstairs, the sitting room felt cold and damp, and the air smelt sour.

ECSTASY

Lynn wrote in her diary that night: *'The Bitch is back.'*

And looking ridiculous, like she'd been boiled. Skin flaking off her face like the old white paint off the windows at Chy Melyn.

It was the day before New Year's Eve.

Lynn sat in her room that night, crushing each white tablet with the rounded side of a tablespoon, carefully, almost with affection, as if it was a special ritual. She ground all six tablets into fine white powder.

'Had to earn these, bitch,' she crooned aloud. 'On my bended bloody knees.'

She collected all the powder in a tiny brown bottle that had once contained pills for her mother's blood pressure.

She tasted the powder with a moist fingertip. It tasted of nothing.

Triple-X:

X is for Xmas.

X is for exit.

X is for ecstasy.

This was the third year running that Clare and Roger had given a New Year's Eve party at Trevow. Clare was expecting about sixty people but a few had cried off at the last minute. Her nagging parents had gone back to Lyme Regis, and lah-de-dah Jenny with the horse's teeth had made a dawn dash back to the Hurlingham New Year Ball in her black 480 convertible with a Thermos full of gin. So Lynn was staying overnight.

She knew most of the people here tonight. Very few of them were from the village. The Doriels didn't socialize with Boskinnow folk. Most of these people were upcountry types, like Clare and Roger, who had moved southwest and bought up all the nice old houses that locals could no longer afford, and taken over all the committees and the parish councils.

The food was laid out on the refectory table in the kitchen – hot pasties and cottage pie and spiced sausages and baked potatoes and thick vegetable soup. Lynn ferried platter-loads of hot savouries to and fro and topped up wine glasses.

Tim Hendra and The Bitch were stuck together like Siamese twins.

Lynn said, 'You're not drinking, Doctor Hendra.'

Tim shook his head. 'I'm on call.' He fished his pager out of a jacket pocket. 'Aren't I the lucky one?'

'Roger made a special punch for drivers,' she said. 'There's no booze in it.'

'I saw that,' said Tim. And added diplomatically, 'I thought I'd wait for the coffee. Maybe I'll eat something. What do you recommend?'

'Vegetable soup? Cottage pie? Bangers?'

'Maybe some cottage pie,' said Tim.

'You stay there,' said Lynn, 'and I'll bring you some.'

She looked at The Bitch and smiled. (*So, who threw wallpaper stripper in your face, then?*)

'Would you like some pie?' she asked pleasantly.

Sara shook her head. 'Thanks all the same.'

Lynn turned and started to walk away. She heard The Bitch call, 'Oh, Lynn?'

She stopped and turned.

'Maybe . . .' Sara wrinkled her nose, hesitating. 'Maybe some soup. Thank you.'

'Pleasure.'

(*X-cellent choice, skin-face.*
X-quisite soup.
Sheer X-stasy.)

In the kitchen, she spooned a generous helping of cottage pie and carrots onto a warm plate, and ladled out a full bowl of Clare's spicy vegetable broth. She carried them as far as the dresser and set them down a moment and took the tiny brown bottle from her handbag.

When she returned to the drawing room and approached the Siamese twins, Tim looked her up and down and said, 'You're looking very attractive tonight.'

'Thank you,' she said graciously.

She was wearing a jet black Lycra mini-dress, sheer and

shiny, smooth and tight as a latex glove. Fine black tights and high heels. Blueberry lip-gloss and nail lacquer. Long silver spindles dangled from her earlobes – her Christmas present from the children. Tim's eyes were wandering over her hips, probably wondering what she had on underneath.

Not a lot, Doc. But nothing you'll ever see.

'Doesn't she?' he said and turned to The Bitch.

'Very chic,' Sara agreed.

Lynn smiled sweetly. 'Thank you.' (*Kiss my arse.*) 'Did you have a nice time in Florida?'

Tim smiled. A private joke evidently. 'Well, *I* did,' he said. And began to dig up the cottage pie with his fork.

'I think you caught the sun,' she said to The Bitch, in a nice even tone.

Tim's pager started bleeping at twenty minutes to midnight. He used the phone in Roger's study. When he came back Sara was chatting with one of Clare's friends on the local school PTA. They broke off as he approached. Sara looked at him enquiringly.

'Happy next-year,' he said.

'Oh no ...' said Sara sympathetically. 'Where have you got to go?'

'Morvah.'

It was out on the west coast, between St Just and Zennor. He drained his coffee. 'I could be a couple of hours. Don't wait for me.'

He gave her a quick kiss on the lips and eased his way back through the clustered groups of people and into the hall in search of Clare.

The television was on. Big Ben was striking. Champagne corks were popping. Voices were raised in 'Auld Lang Syne'. Everyone was busy exchanging kisses.

Sara was watching Roger and Lynn. She had been keeping an eye on them all evening. But they were very careful, they were strictly master/maid in front of the audience. It was a convincing show – no touching, no whispering, no meaningful glances, scarcely even a smile. When he came to kiss her Happy

New Year, she received a chaste peck on the cheek, no more than a graze of the lips, not a hand on her.

He came beefing up to Sara, said, 'Happy New Year, old thing,' bussed her on each cheek, and moved quickly on, pecking at cheeks, doing the rounds.

Lynn approached to top up Sara's glass of champagne.

Sara was beginning to feel odd. She was incredibly thirsty.

She said, 'No thanks. I might just have some coffee.'

'It's in the kitchen,' said Lynn unhelpfully.

Sara reached out to put down her champagne and almost lost her balance. Lynn put out a hand to steady her.

'You okay?'

'Yes.' Sara nodded and felt far from okay. 'Yes, I'm fine.'

She was beginning to sweat. She was too near the log fire. Too many people were smoking in here. So hot and airless. She began to push her way through to the door. The floor seemed to move beneath her feet. She lurched and touched the wall to keep herself from falling. Her sense of balance was out of sync. *Christ, I can't be drunk.* All she'd had was wine, all evening. People were giving her suspicious glances. She tried to smile confidently and blundered on across the hallway. She went into what had once been the kids' rumpus room, and was now just the empty ante-room that led into the Tudor barn.

It was dark in the barn and empty. The air was clear and fresh. She tried to open the new door that led out into the farmyard but it was mortice-locked. She stood there, breathing in the cold air that came through the gap between the door and the jamb.

God, she was thirsty . . .

She wondered if she could get as far as the kitchen without making a fool of herself. She retraced her steps to the hallway and almost collided with Clare.

'You look a bit wishy-washy,' said Clare. 'All right?'

'I just feel slightly . . .' She couldn't say *pissed*, it was too embarrassing. 'Could I lie down somewhere for a minute?'

'Of course. Come upstairs.'

Clare took her up to the guest room that was next to her and Roger's room. She put the light on. 'Is it warm enough?'

'I'm absolutely baking,' said Sara. 'I'm sure it'll be fine. Just for a few minutes.'

She flopped down on the bed.

'I'm sorry . . . I'm not drunk, it's just . . .'

Clare was beginning to swim in and out of focus.

'I was too near the fire, and all that cigarette smoke . . .'

'I know, it's vile,' said Clare. 'Just lie back, rest a while. Is there anything I can bring you?'

'Just some water. I'd love a big glass of water.'

'Righto.' Clare gave her an uneasy look and went downstairs.

A few minutes later, Lynn came into the room. 'Clare said you wanted some water.'

Sara sat up and propped herself on one elbow. She took the glass. 'Thanks.'

She drank half of it in one long draught. Lynn was watching her with a bemused expression.

'Am I on your bed?' Sara enquired.

'What do you mean?'

'Aren't you sleeping here tonight?'

'The other room. Down by the children.'

'Ah.' Sara drank the rest of the water. She proffered the glass towards Lynn. 'Could I be a nuisance and ask for another?'

'Sure,' said Lynn, without expression. She took the glass and disappeared from the room.

Sara dropped back onto the bed. She closed her eyes. Her throat was so parched . . .

She awoke to find Clare sitting on the bed.

'How do you feel?'

'What time is it?'

'Twenty past one. They've all gone. We're going to hit the hay.'

'I didn't bring my car . . .'

'Don't be silly,' said Clare, 'we wouldn't let you drive even if you had. The bed's made up. All you've got to do is climb into it.'

Sara didn't argue. She was in no fit state.

Clare said, 'It used to be *our* bed. Roger says he actually prefers it. I tell him he can sleep in here then, any time he likes.'

Sara felt like replying: *He does.*

It was the bed that he and Lynn were using that afternoon, when she walked in and caught them unawares.

'I hope she's not going to honk all over the floor,' muttered Roger as he put the light out on his side of the bed.

'I don't think she will. She doesn't feel sick. She says she isn't pissed. She doesn't *sound* pissed.'

'What's wrong with her, then?'

'Maybe it's just the effects of the sunstroke. And the jet-lag. And she didn't have any supper, just a bowl of soup.'

They lay in the darkness without moving or speaking. Clare reached out for his hand but only found his podgy arm.

'Happy New Year, old grouch,' she said, with a hint of affection.

'And you,' he grunted, and turned onto his other side to sleep.

The first thing Sara knew was a terrible pain in her scalp ... Like red-hot needles thrusting up through her skull. Someone had hold of her hair. Someone was dragging her down onto her knees ... She screamed and lashed out with her fists. Someone was hauling her along the ground by her hair ... Hard stony ground. She screamed and screamed and screamed. Sharp stony ground tearing the flesh off her bare feet, her legs, her knees ... Trawling her through the stony filth like a carcase of meat ... A ferocious scorching pain in her scalp, the roots of her hair burning ... Knuckles pressing down into the top of her skull, winding her hair tighter round his fist ...

She was thrown up against a cold stone wall. Her arms were wrenched from their sockets and pinioned, her face, her body, slammed hard against the wet cold granite. A savage jolting pain boring up through her insides, *Oh, God, Jesus* ... Screaming, screaming, screaming, till it began to tear the soft membrane in her throat.

Clare awoke. It felt like the dead of night. Someone was tapping at the door. She switched on her bedside lamp and looked at the clock. It was twenty past three. Roger was dead to the world.

She got out of bed and put on her robe. She went to the door and found Ben standing on the landing in his pyjamas, his eyes puffy and caked with sleep.

'Mummy, she's screaming.'

Clare could hear it now. Downstairs and rather distant, echoing.

Alex looked out of his bedroom, his eyes screwed up against the light.

'What's going on?'

'I don't know,' said Clare.

She looked at the guest room where Sara was sleeping. The door was wide open but the light was not on.

'Just go back to bed, both of you.'

She went downstairs and switched on the hallway light. There was a terrible caterwauling coming from the barn. It was somewhere between screaming and wailing. And the echo of the empty barn made it worse. Clare hurried across the hall, through the old rumpus room and the jagged opening in the wall, into the barn.

She switched on the lights. The screaming was coming from the far corner of the barn, from down below, in the cellar. She ran across the bare expanse of floor to the top of the stairs and looked down. Sara was lying on the concrete, naked, in a semi-foetal position, her hands clasped over her ears, screaming her head off.

Clare ran down the stairs, knelt down and took her in her arms, comforting her, hushing her over and over again until Sara began to quieten down.

Sara took her hands away from her ears and stared at Clare in shocked bewilderment. She was trembling all over, she had no sense of where she was or what had happened. It was cold down there in the cellar, and yet she was bathed in sweat. Her hair was a mess of frenzied tangles.

Clare was cradling her head, rocking her from side to side, stroking her hair, whispering, 'It's okay, it's okay, it's okay . . .'

Lynn appeared at the top of the stairs.

'Go and make sure the kids are back in bed,' said Clare. 'And see that Loulou's all right.'

'What's she doing down there?' said Lynn, and glared at Sara accusingly. 'What's going on?'

'Just look after the children, *please*,' said Clare, more forcefully.

Lynn turned and walked back across the barn. Alex and the twins were gathered at the hole in the wall, wide-eyed with curiosity. Lynn ushered them back into the house.

'Show's over. Back to bed. Chop-chop ...'

Clare draped her robe around Sara and helped her to her feet. They walked slowly back up the steps and across the barn, through the hallway and into the kitchen. Sara dropped weakly into a chair at the table. All she wanted was water.

Clare filled a glass from the tap. Sara drank it all down in three draughts. Roger appeared in the doorway, looking as if he'd just been raised from the dead. Clare gave him a firm glare and a shake of the head to discourage him from asking. He stood and watched Sara with sleep-befuddled eyes and then retreated back upstairs to bed without saying a word.

Sara was sitting with her head in her hands, struggling to remember what happened.

'I was having a dream,' she murmured. 'Someone was pulling my hair. Had my hair twisted round his fist ... Pulling me along. Don't know who he was or where we were going ... My legs were scraping along the ground. It was so *painful* ... God, it hurt. How did I *get* there?' she said hopelessly. 'I just don't remember.' Her face crumpled as she struggled to recall. 'What was I doing there?'

'Shh,' Clare murmured softly, and stroked her hand. 'Just a dream. Just a bad dream.'

Sara awoke late the next morning. She felt as if she had hardly slept at all. Her head ached, her throat felt dry and powdery. She felt dehydrated. She remembered the night; waking in the barn; Clare rocking her to and fro like a small child.

She pushed back the sheet and blankets, swung her legs out of bed and sat upright. She was still wearing the robe that Clare had draped round her in the barn cellar. She pushed her tangled hair back off her face. Her scalp was very tender. She ran her fingers through her hair; it was quite painful where it tugged at the roots. She recalled her nightmare, her hair wrapped around the man's fist like rope, and being dragged along the stony ground.

She pushed herself up off the bed. Her legs felt weak, her muscles ached. She moved slowly to the one small window and drew back the curtain to let in a thin slab of grey eastern light.

She moved to the door. Her bare feet were cold on the uncarpeted wooden floor. She opened the door and looked out, across the landing and along the passage past the children's rooms. It was quiet. Were they all still in bed? She walked along to the landing. Clare and Roger's bedroom door was ajar. The kids' doors were all wide open. She could hear people downstairs. She walked around the back of the landing and into Clare's bathroom. It was enormous, right above the kitchen. She shuffled over to the lavatory, hitched up the robe and sat down.

When she wiped herself, there was blood on the tissue. She tore off another few sheets of tissue and dabbed again. It was discoloured but not with fresh blood. She took off the robe. There was a large blood stain all over the back of it. She sat on the edge of the bath in a mixture of disbelief and rising misery. What was *going on* with her body? How much worse was this going to get?

She put the robe on and crept out of the bathroom, back to the bedroom. She pulled back the top sheet and blankets. There were several large bloodstains. She touched them. They felt dry. She felt between her legs again. She wasn't bleeding now. She looked back at the sheets. There was *hair* everywhere, all over and around the pillow. Not just one or two strands but dozens and dozens – long black hair from her head. What the hell had she *done*? Was she tearing her own hair out by the roots in the night?

She sat down on the side of the bed. She had no strength. She felt so drained but – worse – so dispirited; as if someone were sapping her morale, sucking the willpower out of her, dragging her down, down.

Roger was still in bed, asleep. Lynn was already up and working, shuffling around in jeans and a rugby shirt, clearing up after the party. Alex was watching cartoons on television in the drawing room. Ben was in the kitchen, slurping and crunching his breakfast cereal. The radio was on low. Clare was in her bathrobe, holding a mug of black coffee, resting her backside against the towel rail along the front of the range, her mind miles away in space.

Jo came into the kitchen. 'Mummy? I think she's crying.'

'Who? Loulou?'

'No, Sara.'

Clare went upstairs and listened at the door of the guest room. She couldn't hear a sound. She tapped on the door, opened it a little way and put her head inside. Sara was sitting on the side of the bed, leaning forward, elbows on knees, face in hands. Clare came right into the room and shut the door. She sat on the bed and put her arm round Sara.

'What is it?'

Sara simply shook her head a little.

'What's the matter?'

'I'm so so sorry.' Sara snuffled and gasped in air.

Clare was bewildered. 'What is it?' she said again.

'I'm so so sorry,' was all that Sara could say.

Clare stripped off the bedlinen and took it down to the scullery. As soon as Sara was ready, Clare drove her back to Crowjy.

Sara felt wretched and humiliated. She was still apologizing.

'Don't even *think* about it,' said Clare, trying to buck her up. 'It happens. It's no big deal.'

By the time she got back to Trevow, Roger was showered and dressed. She found him in the guest room, holding a mug of coffee and eating a slice of Marmite toast, and looking down at the bloodstained mattress. 'Was that her?' he said.

'Well, who do you think?'

'What's wrong with that woman?' He sounded as if he was coming to the end of his patience.

Clare was not in the mood. 'There's nothing *wrong* with her,' she replied tartly. 'She bleeds occasionally, like any other woman.'

'I suppose I've got to fork out for a new mattress now. As well as a new dog. Some bloody Christmas *this* has been.'

It was at moments like this that Clare could understand precisely what could drive a woman to whack a meat cleaver into her husband's jugular.

'If you can't find a way to be helpful,' she said, pushing past him to go back downstairs, 'just sod off and play in your new barn.'

SENARA

'How much do you think you had to drink?' said Tim.

'I don't know,' said Sara, 'they kept topping up my glass. Maybe four glasses of wine. Hardly any champagne.'

It was mid-afternoon. She was lying on her bed. Tim was examining her. He'd been out until four that morning but he had been able to sleep late.

'When did you start to feel ill?'

'About midnight.'

'And no bleeding when you got into bed the first time?'

'No.'

'And none since you got up this morning?'

She shook her head. He took her blood pressure.

'When are you next due?'

'Two weeks.'

'Do you have much bleeding in between?'

'Hardly ever.'

'No bleeding like this before?'

'Not that I can remember . . . Nothing like *that*.'

'Any pain?'

'A kind of muscly ache.'

'Whereabouts?'

'Legs. Back.'

'Any cramps in the night?'

She shook her head.

'Any other pains?' He felt around her abdomen, her kidney area, her breasts. 'How did it feel, this giddiness?'

'Sort of . . . Like on a boat. The floor was rolling, pitching. I couldn't get my balance.'

He put on a pair of surgical gloves and took a Cusco speculum from his bag.

'I don't think I was drunk, Tim, I really don't. I know how I am when I've had too much – I get giggly, I feel sick, I can't talk sense. And it creeps up slowly. Anyway, I don't get that pissed on four glasses of wine.'

'Do you feel sore at all, inside?'

'Yes, I do, a bit.'

She raised her knees and spread her legs.

'Any pain or discharge recently?'

'No.'

He inserted the speculum and looked inside her. After a moment or two he said: 'When we last made love, was it painful at all?'

'No. Why?'

'You have a tear.'

'What do you mean, a tear?'

'A wound, a lesion. In the membrane of the anterior wall. That's the part that's at the front, next to the urethra.'

'And that's what caused the bleeding?'

'It would have caused *some* bleeding, certainly. There are a lot of small blood vessels in the tissue. But the natural clotting process would have stopped it after a few minutes.'

'But how did I do it?'

'Some kind of penetration,' said Tim. 'It's the only way it could have happened.'

Tim peeled off the surgical gloves and dropped them into a plastic disposal bag. 'I can refer you to the gynaecologist at West Cornwall if you'd feel happier, but I think it'll heal up like any other lesion.'

Sara was confused. 'I don't understand. What do you mean, some kind of penetration? How many kinds are there?'

'It's nothing to worry about. Over-vigorous sex can cause these injuries. Sometimes an IUD. Vibrators, all kinds of things.'

'What are you implying?' She sat up, indignant, bewildered.

'Hey, calm down,' said Tim. 'I'm not implying anything.' He sat down beside her on the bed and took her hand. 'There are a lot of blood vessels in the tissue beneath the epithelium that lines the vagina. Something as simple as a fingernail could have done it. It could easily have been me, without realizing it. You might have aggravated it somehow. Alcohol dilates the arterioles, and if you drank more than you realized last night it could have triggered the bleeding.'

She didn't find this very convincing. She wondered if he was telling her the truth. But why would he lie to her?

'Can I put something on now?' she said. 'I'm freezing.'

'Of course.'

She got up off the bed and padded over to the dressing table, where her clothes were draped over the back of the chair.

Tim got up and was about to go out to the bathroom to wash his hands when he noticed her back. It was covered with a lattice of criss-cross marks. They were worse than scratches – as if someone had clawed her skin with long fingernails – and the flesh was bruised, almost purple in places.

She sensed him staring. 'What are you looking at?'

'Is your back sore?'

'Yes. Are those marks still there?'

He came over to her and ran his fingers lightly over the flesh.

'I was rolling around on the concrete floor when Clare found me. And I didn't have anything on.'

'Strange,' he murmured. 'It's very tender new skin after the sunburn. But you'd think it would just be grazed if you were rolling around.'

Alone that night, she tried to think what could have caused that tear inside her. Surely she'd have felt it at the moment that it happened?

Then she remembered the dream.

A wall. Someone pushed her against a wall. It was coming back to her now ... She was thrown up against a stone wall. She was dragged by the hair, slammed against the wall and raped. A ferocious jolting pain went spearing through her insides ...

Clare called round to see how she was. Sara was wondering what they thought of her at Trevow.

'I'm sorry if I scared everyone. Especially the children. They must think I'm some kind of monster.'

'Oh, forget it.' Clare flipped a hand, as if it was a non-event. 'They see far worse on TV every day. Kids love a bit of drama in the night.'

'I seem to be a walking disaster area at the moment. I don't know what's wrong with me. I pretty well ruined Tim's Christmas. And then Bosun dying...'

'Poor Bosun,' said Clare with exasperation and affection. 'Dumb dog. He just couldn't resist water. If it were possible to cross a dog with a seal, I think you'd end up with a Bosun.'

'I feel so bad about that,' said Sara. 'If you hadn't had to come looking for Charlie—'

'Oh, *rubbish*.' Clare waved a hand dismissively. 'Not your fault, not anyone's fault. Bosun lived dangerously, anyway. He nearly jumped headlong down an old mine shaft at Bodrifty last year, chasing rabbits. And then he ran under a forty-ton artic and clean out the other side without being hit. He had more lives than a cat.'

It was a cold January day. The wind was whipping in from the northeast. Draughts were slicing through the cottage like cheese wire. Sara was kneeling at the hearth, trying to liven up the fire.

Clare said, 'Have you ever walked in your sleep before?'

'I don't know. I might have done. I'm not really sure.'

She was lying: there was no way she could have slashed those two paintings of Lynn, for a start, without having walked downstairs in her sleep. But she was thinking at this moment of the night that she dreamt of Trevow.

'It was not long after I moved in here,' she said. 'You remember I came to Sunday lunch and you showed me around? I had a dream about the barn that night. I dreamt I was woken by someone crying out, somewhere across the moors. It was raining. I was walking through the mud. I came to Trevow and went into the barn. And down into the cellar. I could hear a sort of whimpering sound, like a child. There was no one there. I touched blood on the cellar floor. I wiped my fingers on my nightdress. At that moment I heard a scream and I woke up. A few days later, I was loading the washing machine and I noticed blood on my nightdress. Like smears, finger smears. I looked more closely. And I found mud around the hem as well, dried mud.'

Clare gave a little shudder. 'Creepy. Do you think you went outside in your sleep? Into the garden perhaps?'

'I don't know. I talked to Tim about it. He said there were lots of ways I could have got dirt on my nightdress. He was right, I didn't think much more about it at the time. But now I've walked in my sleep again ... And down to that barn cellar of all places. It makes me wonder.'

'We had a girl at school who used to sleepwalk,' Clare recalled. 'She climbed out of the dormitory window one night. The nuns thought she was trying to run away. They locked her up in solitary for three days and put her on bread and marge. They're very keen on isolation, nuns. I pointed out to Mother Superior that the poor girl was barefoot in her nightdress and there was a frost that night so she was hardly likely to be doing a bunk. So they put *me* in isolation as well.'

Sara wanted to tell her more. She wanted to describe that awful dream that turned from sexual pleasure to horror, slashing the paintings with the kitchen knife. But she couldn't summon up the courage.

And she wanted to ask Clare about Christmas night, about Bosun, how she found him in the water. She wanted to tell her about that strange experience at dawn last spring, seeing something on the water; about Midsummer's Eve, when she fell down the steep part of the hill and had that frightening experience at the edge of the pool.

She wanted to discuss all these things, but she couldn't. They'd think she was mad. Clare would ring Tim: Poor girl, she's losing her marbles ... The effect of Bryan's death, the inquest, learning the truth about her adoption, the fire on the moor ... Stress, cumulative, one thing on top of another, can't cope.

When she left, Clare paused outside on the front step and said, 'Don't worry. I can guess how you must feel, but everyone understands.'

That more or less confirmed Sara's fears. They were pitying her.

'You had a lousy year,' Clare added. And reached out and gave Sara's arm a gentle squeeze. '1992 can only be better.'

'It's okay,' Sara assured her. 'I'm handling it. I'm coping.'

'I know you are.' Clare squeezed her arm again.

Clare was not at all convinced that Sara was coping. She seemed like a woman who was holding on; like someone in the water, clinging to floating debris after the ship had gone down.

Too much had come too suddenly: Bryan's death, the inquest, and then the discovery that she'd been abandoned on the moor. It had crushed her sense of self-worth. She seemed to be blaming herself, loading herself with guilt.

Clare kept looking at Bryan's painting on the drawing room wall. She kept thinking about that odd coincidence of the holed stone on Bodmin Moor and the holed stone in the woods behind Crowjy. But worst of all, the painting reminded her of Christmas night, of Bosun, floating, just touching the surface of the water.

It troubled her, that picture. It never had until now. She decided to take it down and put it somewhere else – in one of the guest rooms, perhaps – until she could think of somewhere more suitable.

As she reached out to lift the picture off the wall she saw something that she had never noticed before: there was colour in the stone. The stone was granite grey but there were minute traces of red in it. Vivid red. Pin-size dots here and there. And a trace of it – a thin crescent of scarlet – around the hole in the centre of the stone.

How come she'd never noticed that before? It seemed so conspicuous now. It looked as if the hole in the stone was actually bleeding.

Tim was deeply perplexed, though he tried to hide it from Sara. The vaginal tear would have been so painful at the moment of injury, surely, that she would *have* to have been aware of how it happened?

And now those contusions were appearing all over her back ... They were quite bizarre and were getting worse. She stayed the night at his house the following weekend and he massaged her body with calamine lotion. Her sunburnt skin was healing rapidly and she felt no pain at all now. But the marks on her back had swollen into long ridges of purple bruising, like welts – the kind of welts that might be sustained from a whipping or a beating of some kind. He chose not to question her about them, but there was no way that she'd acquired such injuries by rolling around on the barn floor at Trevow.

He made enquiries about her extraordinary sensitivity to

sunlight. He wrote to specialists – both within the area health authority and beyond – and sent a letter to the *Lancet*, the medical journal, describing Sara's condition and asking whether other doctors had encountered anything like it.

The following month, he was contacted by a consultant dermatologist from Eindhoven in The Netherlands, who recalled a case that sounded very similar. He could only speak from memory and from brief clinical notes that he had made at the time for his own reference.

A young woman of seventeen was travelling in England with a convoy of hippies. They camped for the summer near St Just, in Cornwall. She went out walking one day and had to take shelter from the rain. She entered an abandoned house. She had no idea where it was. A bunch of Hell's Angel types also sought shelter there. They smoked hashish and she alleged they drugged her with something – probably LSD. She suffered terrifying hallucinations and was raped. In her hallucinations, she saw the house burning down around her. She saw the Hell's Angels engulfed in flames and felt the heat of the fire herself.

The next day, she woke up with a red rash all over her body. As the day wore on her skin became too painful to touch. By the following day her skin had dried out and had become crisp and translucent, and had begun to look like the scar tissue that grows after severe burns. This condition had gradually worsened over a period of about a week, she said, and then the skin had begun to peel, and fresh tissue had grown in its place in the normal way.

Normal, except in one respect ... The condition tended to recur. It recurred whenever the woman exposed herself to ultraviolet light for prolonged periods, but more strangely, it sometimes recurred if she sat close to an open fire for any length of time.

The alleged rape had happened almost twenty-five years ago, in 1968. She had never reported it to the police and he had no way of confirming that it had ever happened. But he believed that she was telling the truth – as well as she could remember it. Certainly, her symptoms could not be faked. He had seen a recurrence for himself. He had monitored her case for several years but then she had moved away from Eindhoven and he had heard nothing of her for many years.

He referred to her simply as Eva.

March brought clear skies, pastel blue, crisp and cold. Sara went out riding with Clare some mornings and worked on her thesis in the afternoons. Her skin had healed completely and the strange bruises on her back had disappeared. The tear inside her had healed up and she had suffered no more bleeding. Tim seemed pleased with her recovery.

She was starting to feel in control again, as if she had been through an illness and had come out the other side, slightly scarred but a little bit stronger. She began to make plans. Spring was on the way. She would sell Crowjy. It was a bad time for property but she had nothing to lose – she had come to Crowjy with nothing, she could drive away with the best offer she could get and she would be none the poorer.

She was in Penzance one afternoon, buying paint to redecorate the bedrooms and bathroom. She saw Lynn pushing Louisa in her buggy in the Texas Homecare store on Eastern Green. She assumed that Clare must be there as well because Lynn would not have brought Louisa in by bus. Lynn was about twenty yards away, looking along the displays of tiles. Sara started towards her. And then Roger came into view, also looking along the rows of tiles, but from the other direction. Sara stopped and watched. Roger drifted closer to Lynn and when they finally came together, their hands reached out instinctively and linked, like two opposing magnets.

They looked just like a married couple with their firstborn.

Lynn was saying something, pointing to some ceramic tiles. Roger drew even closer to her to take a look. Their hips collided. Her arm slipped round his back, his hand glided down across her buttocks.

Sara felt sad for Louisa and angry for Clare. She should have turned away and left the store and come back later for what she wanted. She meant to. But she stood there, watching, for just a moment too long. For some reason – perhaps a sixth sense – Lynn turned and glanced back over her shoulder. She looked straight at Sara, saw her staring.

Perhaps the anger was visible on her face; Sara made no

attempt to hide it. Then Roger twisted his head around to see what Lynn was looking at.

Sara simply turned and walked away.

They watched her walk out of the store.

'Bugger,' Roger muttered. 'That wasn't so clever.'

'She won't say anything,' said Lynn confidently. 'She hasn't got the bottle.'

Clare and Sara went riding the following day. Sara was wondering how to break it to her. She felt she had to say something. Those two were wandering around like a young couple in the first flush of married bliss. Soon Lynn would be ensconced inside Trevow, like a cuckoo in the nest. And then what? How much further was this going to go?

When they got back to Trevow and unsaddled the horses, Sara said, 'I've got something I need to talk to you about.'

'And I've got something to show you,' Clare replied. 'I took it out of Penzance library a couple of weeks ago, but I've only just finished it.'

They walked across the yard and into the scullery, tugged off their riding boots, and went inside, into the kitchen. Clare made some coffee. Lynn came in and asked if she could get away for a few hours now that they were back. Of course, said Clare. Lynn looked at Sara and said hi. Her eyes were spiky, her smile was sour and brittle. She brought Louisa into the kitchen so that Clare could keep an eye on her. Louisa was wearing smart new tartan trousers and a scarlet jumper.

'Aren't *you* the young lady?' Clare cooed, as she came in, hand in hand with Lynn.

Before she left, Lynn gave Sara another spiky look, like the one before. It seemed to say: Bust this lot up if you dare.

When Lynn had gone, Clare went into the drawing room and came back with the book she was talking about. It was a biography of Sir George Lanberris, whose daughter had married John Doriel of Trevow.

'Does it mention the Doriels?' asked Sara, leafing through it.

'Very briefly. Doesn't tell me much. I've marked the two places with those slips of paper. Borrow it . . . It's not due back for a fortnight.'

Sara drank her coffee. Clare bounced Louisa on her knee.

'What was it you were going to tell me?' Clare asked.

Sara made a pretence of trying hard to remember. 'Completely slipped my mind,' she said eventually. 'I'll think of it later.'

She felt cheap and cowardly as she drove home to Crowjy; as if she had stolen money out of Clare's purse, or had nosed through her private letters.

That evening, she sat by the fire in the sitting room and skim-read the early chapters of the book.

The Lanberris family had made their fortune from the sea, from a mixture of trade and piracy. Sir George Lanberris had been the last in a line of old sea dogs. He had sired nine children, of whom Alice – who married John Doriel – was the youngest.

Sara turned to the first mention of John Doriel. Clare had marked the place with a slip of paper. She read:

> In the autumn of 1794, Alice announced her betrothal to John Doriel, the youngest son of a farmer from Nansgever in West Penwith and not a popular choice.
>
> 'Papa will not speak of it,' her sister Meg wrote to cousin Catherine at Tresillian. 'He has been unapproachable all week. Mama fears he may send Alice to London to put an end to the matter. Poor John, he has done nothing to give offence but he is something coarse of manner. Yet he is handsome, has fine blue eyes and sits well upon a horse.'
>
> Alice, self-willed in all things, and her father's favourite, had her own way. She and John Doriel were married the following summer at Mawnan.

Turning to the second place that Clare had marked, Sara read:

> In March 1797, to compound the family's woes, Alice died giving birth to her first child. She was twenty-two years of age. Her father was inconsolable. He had tolerated rather than approved her marriage to John Doriel of Nansgever, described by Meg as a ne'er-do-well from a family broken by ill-fortune.
>
> 'They are a queer people who dwell on the Penwith

moors,' she wrote to cousin Catherine, 'taciturn and miserly by nature, not like other Cornish. Yet I feel for poor John. He has lost the three women most dear in his life: his child sister, Senara, who died so strangely, his mother but last summer, and now poor darling Alice.'

The family turned their backs on John after Alice's death and he died a pauper at Stokeland in Devon in 1860.

Sara's eyes returned to those four words: *His child sister, Senara* . . .

Senara. That name again. She thought of that last scrap from Bryan's papers that Tim had left on the studio floor: *under Senara.*

She looked back at the book.

'"Child sister, Senara,"' she read aloud, '"who died so strangely."'

The power voltage dropped at that moment. The table lamp beside her dimmed a fraction, and the log fire flared up as if a gust of wind had jumped on it and caught it napping. The flames leapt up, crackled fiercely and fled into the blackness of the chimney for a half-minute or so, before they slowly settled down again.

She sensed a presence in the room. She looked up. She saw someone's shadow on the wall and caught her breath.

But it was not a shadow: it was the damp patch – the damp patch that was never damp, the patch she had scraped off the wall with the paint and plaster. It had come back.

It was in the same place, it was the same shape, the same size. It was identical. She had never thought of it this way before, but looking at it now in the soft amber light, with the flickering glow of the fire, that was exactly what it looked like: someone's shadow on the wall.

That night, she dreamt of it.

She dreamt she was climbing out of bed and standing in front of the long mirror. She was taking off her nightdress and letting it slip to the floor. She was looking at her naked reflection in the glass. Her skin was very pale . . . almost white. It had a beautiful soft sheen. It looked like marble. Her nipples were colourless. She had no eyebrows. She had no hair. Her skull was smooth and sleek. She was moving very slowly towards her reflection. And her reflection was moving slowly towards her. Their faces touched and pressed closer. Their bodies sank into each other. Her reflection felt soft like silk. Her breath was cold, cold as the Arctic . . .

She awoke. The duvet had slipped off the bed. She was naked. She was shivering. It was the middle of the night.

She got up and threw the quilt back on the bed and looked round for her nightdress. It was not there. She tossed the duvet about, but the nightdress was not caught up inside it. She looked under the bed and all around it. Her nightdress had gone.

When she went downstairs the following morning she found the front door open.

She thought she had been burgled in the night. She looked around the sitting room in panic. But nothing was missing – television, VCR, computer, compact discs, all there. She looked in her handbag in the kitchen. Her money was intact, her driving licence, everything that was worth taking.

Her nightdress was nowhere in the house.

She found it outside, on the other side of the track.

It was floating in the middle of the pool.

This was driving her crazy. Did she walk to the pool in the night, along that marshy path? Why weren't her legs muddy? How did her nightdress end up in the middle of the pool? It was about forty feet across, even at the narrowest point.

Those scraps from Bryan's writings . . . She tried to remember what they said. Why, oh, *why* had she let Tim burn those papers? They were all she had left, the only clues.

She drove along the valley road to his house that evening. He was half-way through dinner. She was practically in tears when he opened the door.

'Sara?' He looked worried. 'What is it?'

'I walked in my sleep again last night.' She pushed past him, into the kitchen. 'And I'm seeing this thing in my dreams, that thing in the painting, Bryan's painting, and his drawings.' Words were tumbling out of her, tripping over each other.

'What are you talking about? Here, sit down.'

'That bloody *thing*!'

'Hey, hey, calm down, calm down.'

'That horrid thing with no hair and her white skin, the painting, the thing I burnt my first night . . . You saw it.'

'All right, all right, slow down . . .' He put his hands on her shoulders. 'Just take deep breaths.'

She took a tissue from her jeans pocket and wiped her eyes and her nose.

'I dreamt of this bloody thing,' she said again, 'you know what I mean.'

'Yes, I remember. Sit down. Relax.'

She sat down at the table. And he resumed his meal.

'I dreamt I got out of bed and looked at myself in the mirror. And instead of my reflection I saw *it*, the thing, whatever it is. I walked right up to the mirror and we touched. And it was like . . . we melted into each other. And it was so cold. Freezing. I woke up, and I really *was* cold. The duvet was on the floor and my nightdress was missing. I'd taken it off in my sleep. I searched everywhere for it. I found it this afternoon. It was in the *pool* – that pond across the track. How did it get there? What is it about that bloody pool?'

Tim finished eating and pushed his plate aside. He seemed so calm she could have hit him. She might just as well have told him the tale of Goldilocks and the Three Bears for all the effect it had had. He reached across the table and took her hands in his.

'There are two separate things here,' he said. 'First, you're walking in your sleep. I realize that's a bit scary, but it's not uncommon. It's not a symptom of anything nasty. Second, you're having a recurrent nightmare. This is also very common. It doesn't make it any less distressing—'

'But what is this *thing*, Tim? Why is it doing this to me?'

'It's not doing *anything*,' he said soothingly. 'You're having nightmares about the hallucination that Bryan drew and painted. That's all.'

His complacency was maddening. He sounded so glib.

'You don't believe me, do you?' She glared at him.

'Of course I believe you. But apart from bolting the doors, there's not much you can do about sleepwalking.'

'All right, then. Explain to me how come I smelt meat

cooking in the night when I got back from Florida. That wasn't a dream.'

'I didn't know you *did* smell meat cooking in the night when you got back from Florida,' he replied, unmoved.

'Well, I did.' She recounted the experience.

Tim shrugged.

'Some spillage on the hob, maybe? Fat, cat food, I don't know.'

'Bull*shit*,' she snapped. 'The Rayburn was three hundred Fahrenheit – it would hardly *warm* meat, let alone cook it. Explain the damp patch on the wall. It's come back. Out of nowhere. It's just suddenly there. It hasn't rained for three weeks. And why do my fuses keep blowing?'

'I don't know. There's obviously something very wrong with the wiring. Call SWEB, get them to send an engineer to have a look.' Tim got up to make some coffee. 'I think you're getting it all out of proportion, my love.' He sounded disappointed. 'I thought you'd got over all this, I thought you'd done really well the last few weeks, after the sunburn and that night you got drunk at Clare's party.'

'I was not drunk!' she replied hotly. 'I don't get drunk! That was Bryan, okay?'

'All right, you were just over-tired, you were run down—'

'Christ, you're so patronizing!' She bashed the table with her fist.

'Sara,' he said, getting exasperated, 'what is wrong with you?'

'There's nothing wrong with *me*. There's something wrong with that house. I don't know what, but it got to Bryan and now it's getting to me.' She got up from the table. 'Bryan told you, but you wouldn't listen to him. And now he's dead. And now it's happening to me and you won't listen to me either!'

'Sara!' he protested. 'Please. Sit down, calm down. You're letting this get totally out of hand. If you're not happy there, come and sleep here.'

'You don't get it, do you?' she said, rounding on him. 'You just don't get it.' She raised her voice: 'I'm not looking for a bed, you bonehead. I'm trying to find out what's happening in my home!'

'I've told you what's happening. You're having a nightmare

that recurs. Little Ben Doriel has one up at Trevow about a wild eagle, it's nothing to be ashamed of.'

'Oh, for Christ's sake.' She marched to the door. 'Have I got to be floating in the pool at midnight, like Clare's dog, before you take any notice?'

He moved to the door to try to stop her. 'Sara, don't be silly. Stay here tonight, we'll talk it all through. You'll feel so much better in the morning.'

'I'm not *ill*, Tim! Stop treating me like some neurotic child. Running away from Crowjy isn't going to help. If it got to me at Trevow on New Year's Eve, it can get to me here, it can get to me anywhere.'

She realized even as she was speaking how crazy this sounded.

'What do you mean it got to you?' said Tim, beginning to lose patience. 'Sara, please. You've had a couple of bad dreams. Nothing's *getting* to you – except worry and stress, perhaps.'

'Oh, screw bloody stress,' she retorted. 'I dreamt I was *raped* that night. I was thrown against a wall and raped, and it hurt like hell. And I bled. And you saw the injury. You examined me, *you* saw it! Now don't give me crap about vibrators and fingernails, you tell me how I got that injury. Self-inflicted, is that what you put it down to?'

'Sara, I'm a doctor, I see these kind of things far more often than you think. I don't judge people, I'm just a GP, I'm a repair man—'

'Oh, save it,' she cut in harshly. 'I'm not looking for a repair man, I'm not broken. I was looking for another kind of man, but obviously I knocked on the wrong door. Good night.'

She stomped out and hurried down the path, leaving him framed in the doorway, calling to her, again and again, as if she were a disobedient dog. She jumped in her car and drove home, seething. Damn and to hell with him, patronizing bastard. Why were medics always so bloody smug, so right, so superior? Anything that wasn't in the medical textbooks couldn't possibly exist.

He would telephone her – but in about half an hour, when the little lady had cooled down ... There, there. She yanked the phone plug out of the wall socket.

She drew the curtains and sat by the fire.

What the hell could she do?

Sell up, move. *Well, sure ... And what happens meantime? I walk down the road in my sleep and get hit by a car? I fall in the pool asleep at four o'clock in the morning?*

She opened the book that Clare had lent her, the biography of Sir George Lanberris. She looked again at those four words: *His child sister, Senara* ...

She went into the studio and looked at that sole surviving scrap of burnt paper from Bryan's journal: *under Senara.*

Why would Bryan have been interested in Senara Doriel?

Tim gave her forty minutes or so to cool down and then tried to phone her. It rang and rang. She was not answering. He gave up.

He lay awake thinking about what she had said about the pool ... And things that Bryan used to say. He talked about it just a month or so before he died. Tim was trying to remember what he'd said.

'*Something bad here, guy, this place ...*'

'*See things by the pool ...*'

'*Smell things too. The night ...*'

'*Nothing lives round here, no rabbits, foxes, badgers ... Come here at daybreak and listen for the birds – silence. Not a sound.*'

'*You think: this poor sick tosser's lost the plot ... It's not the DTs, guy.*'

She drove to Truro and sat upstairs in the Royal Cornwall Museum, looking through the parish records. She looked again at the same microfiches that she had photocopied once before for Clare – the International Genealogical Index of baptisms and marriages.

She made notes in longhand.

Thomas Doriel. Married Anne Trevorrow in 1772.

They had three sons: Kadan, Matthew and John. And one daughter, Senara.

Kadan's marriage appeared on a separate microfiche for Devon. He married Jayne Weeks, in the parish of St Melyn in 1807. They had two children: David, baptized in 1810, and Eliza in 1812.

There was no marriage record for his brother Matthew.

The youngest brother, John, married Alice Lanberris at Mawnan on 23 July 1795.

And there was no marriage record for Senara.

There was no way of telling from the microfiche when any of them died – the international index did not include burials. She had to turn to the parish records.

The original records were stored at County Hall, elsewhere in the city, but there were copies here at the museum. She was asked to sign the visitors' book before she could look at the microfilm. The librarian read her signature and remarked: 'A rare old Cornish name.'

Sara smiled. 'Not many of us left.'

'There was someone else called Carhays here a year or two ago. He was looking through the parish records too.'

'Then that was probably my brother, Bryan.'

Sara began to feel as if she was shadowing everything that he had done before.

The librarian opened one of the drawers of a steel filing cabinet and removed the boxed microfilm for Towednack – baptisms and burials only – and handed it to Sara. She threaded the microfilm onto the projection machine and wound through until she came to the year 1780. From here on she turned the spool slowly forward, looking for Senara.

Towednack was a small rural parish. There were seldom more than a dozen baptisms or burials a year, sometimes no more than three or four. She found Senara's baptism in 1779:

Senara, daughter of Thos and Anne Doriel. November 13.

She wound quickly forwards and came to the burials register. She found Senara. She was buried in the year 1794. The register stated simply:

Senara, daughter of Thomas and Anne Doriel. March 26.

And immediately beneath that entry, Sara found:

Beryan, spinster, April 20.

She stared hard at the name, as if she thought she had misread it.

But no. It was Beryan.

And it was under Senara.

She wound the microfilm back to the 1740s and began to look through the baptisms.

She found Beryan's baptism, recorded in the year 1761:
Beryan, base child, parents unknown. February 28.

Tim called at Chy Melyn. It was the middle of the afternoon. No time was a good time for Vera. She opened the front door just a little, just enough for her face to be visible. Her instinctively hostile glare softened slightly when she saw who it was.

'Oh, Doctor,' she said, and opened the door a little wider. 'Is something wrong? You want Lynn?'

'No, it's you I'd like a word with if I may,' Tim replied. 'I hope I'm not interrupting anything?'

A geriatric vacuum cleaner was standing in the hallway and Vera was clutching a yellow duster.

'Nothen that won't keep,' she said, adding pointedly, 'for just a moment.'

Tim found it difficult to know how to approach Vera. Her standard facial expression said something like: I am suffering you in silence. You are an added burden to my already painful life. You are putting me to great inconvenience, but I will spare you a moment, at great cost to myself.

She even looked that way when people simply said good morning.

'I won't keep you very long,' said Tim. 'But it's a rather difficult matter.'

'About Lynn?' She seemed always to be expecting bad news.

'No, nothing to do with Lynn,' said Tim. 'It's about the barn-cottage.'

Her expression changed. She seemed disappointed.

'You'd better come in a moment,' she said reluctantly.

'Thank you.'

Tim stepped inside. She shut the door and took him into the living room. They sat down. Her old dog came sniffing. Tim knew that Vera didn't like visitors. She did not like people to see how she lived – the faded wallpaper, stained with damp and curling off the wall; the ragged carpet, the threadbare patch where her feet rested as she sat watching television at nights; the ceiling that had become the colour of cheese rind, so long since it was painted.

'So, how can I help you?' said Vera.

'Sara Carhays has been having a rather unpleasant time since her brother died, as you're probably aware.'

Vera remained coldly silent.

'She had to endure the inquest,' Tim went on, 'and not many people roundabouts have shown her much sympathy or neighbourliness.'

If Vera felt so much as a twinge of conscience she did not show it.

'People round here,' said Tim, 'seem to have a superstitious fear of the place.'

'No one liked her brother,' Vera replied evasively. 'I don't like to speak ill of the dead, but there was no good in him. He was bad, through and through. Maybe if that demon drink hadn't got to him . . .'

'But leaving Bryan aside, what is it about Crowjy that people don't like?'

She sat with tight lips, her hands pressed together and resting in her lap, that harassed-and-in-pain look on her face again.

'It's an evil place. It always was and it always will be.'

'In what way evil?'

'I don't have anything to do with the place,' said Vera. 'I don't even like talken about it.'

'Would it surprise you to know that Bryan Carhays used to think there was something strange there too?'

'Nothen you say would surprise me about that man.'

'Tell me about the place. What happened there that makes you think it's evil?'

Vera took so long to answer him that he was beginning to think she had clammed up on him and was going to sit there like a statue until he left. But then she said: 'It used to be a barn. It burned down. In 1926. A young man died there. My mother knew him. His name was Ethan. He had a sister, Rebecca, and she was a schoolfriend of my mother's.'

She lapsed into silence again.

'And what happened?' asked Tim.

'Ethan was courting a girl called Annie Carkeet. Annie's father was a cowman at Trevow. They fell asleep in the old Crowjy barn one Sunday afternoon. Annie woke up feeling hot and walked over to the pool. And when she came back to the barn, she saw Ethan catch fire. His hair began to smoke, and then he just burst into flames, she said. He threw himself in the pool and Annie ran for help. He was dead when they pulled him out of the water.'

Tim was highly sceptical of these hand-me-down tales of local tragedy. Fires in hay barns were not uncommon in those days, and stories like this became inflated and distended with endless retelling down the years, gradually elevating the commonplace to the status of myth and legend.

'They put Annie away up Bodmin,' said Vera, 'the mental hospital. She died there – not much older than Lynn is now. Ethan was buried at Towednack. His sister is still alive. You know Rebecca Pierce?'

'She's not my patient,' said Tim, 'but we say hello when we pass.'

'Well, that's her, my mother's schoolfriend.'

A silence, broken only by the sound of Vera's old dog scratching its fleas.

'But she won't talk about him,' Vera said. 'No use you asken her, she won't speak about un.'

'And the barn?'

'That was a ruin for over thirty years. When we were cheldern, we weren't allowed to go near un. I went in there once, for a dare, and my father found out and gave I such a belting. He never told me why. Someone bought the place – a year or two before I was married – and built the cottage. But he didn't stay long. No one did. Bryan Carhays stayed thear longest. And much good it did him.'

Vera sat back in her ragged little television chair and tidied the lap of her dress.

'If you care about that woman,' she said quietly, 'you get her out of that place. That place is bad.' There was no emotion in her voice, she was quite matter-of-fact. 'It's in the stone, it's in the earth it stands on. I don't know how far back it goes, maybe thousands of years. There are stones in those woods. Lost stones. No one knows what they were for. There were old religions, back before Christian times. They were savages, barbaric people. Believed in thunder gods and water gods. There was killing, there were rituals. My grandmother remembered stories *her* grandma told her, and her grandma before that, and right back in time.'

Tim tried to look as if he was taking this seriously. He did not know quite what to say. He had not come here to argue with Vera. He tried to maintain a sympathetic expression, his doctor's look. Vera smiled. It was such a rare occurrence, he saw the mother–daughter likeness. Hard to imagine that this might be Lynn in thirty years' time.

'I know,' she said, 'you think I'm just an ignorant country woman.'

'That's not true,' said Tim. But there was not much conviction in his voice.

'I did feel pity for Bryan Carhays,' she confessed. 'But thear was no use my tellen him. He wouldn't listen to me. People don't listen any more. People don't believe. They've lost touch with their inner voice, their spiritual side. They worship other gods today. People have no faith. They're all blind and groping in the wilderness. Only those who truly believe in the power of the Light can truly believe in the power of Darkness.'

Sara was in the studio, at her computer, putting down everything that she could remember – everything she could remember from Bryan's burnt papers, everything that had happened to her since she had moved in here, her bad dreams, all the facts she could recall about Adrian Doriel's death, and the genealogical dates she had copied for the Doriel family.

She heard a car approaching up the track and glanced out of the window as Tim's Rover pulled up outside, behind her VW. She walked through to the hallway and opened the front door. She was still furious with him for his patronizing attitude the other night. She stood in the open doorway.

He approached her with an open, apologetic gesture. 'May I come in?'

'Is this going to be more of what I had last time?'

'I'm sorry about the other night.' His tone was not wholly contrite. 'But I'm a doctor. I see things from a medical viewpoint. It's not such a bad thing, you know.'

'So what have you come to say? That I'm a hysterical neurotic who should see a therapist?'

'Oh, come on,' Tim appealed, 'cut me a little slack, will you? Just *listen*, occasionally. Cool down and listen. You might learn something.'

She stayed put in the doorway, arms folded. 'I'm listening.'

'I've been talking to Vera Roscarrock about this place. About why she thinks it's evil.'

'Why? You think it's a load of old tosh, so why bother?'

'Because what you said the other night reminded me of one or two things that Bryan said about a month before he died.'

'What kind of things?'

'Well, may I come in? It's kind of draughty out here.'

She stood back to let him in. 'I've already told you why she thinks it's evil,' she said. 'She's got some loony notion invented by her granny about Druids worshipping Satan. Rather like assuming that Romans ate with chopsticks.'

Tim walked into the sitting room. 'Do you know the history of this place?' he asked.

She followed him into the room. 'I know it was built in about 1960, when Trevow Farm went bust and they sold off the land and outbuildings.'

'That barn,' said Tim, sitting on the sofa and pointing to the old photograph on the wall, 'was burnt down in 1926. A young carpenter called Ethan Pierce died in the fire. He and his girlfriend were inside at the time and he burst into flames, according to Vera.'

It sounded ludicrous. 'What do you mean, burst into flames?'

'Exactly that. His hair began to smoulder and he simply caught fire. So he jumped in the pool, Vera said. His girlfriend, Annie, ran for help. But when she got back, he was already dead in the water.'

'Was *she* hurt?'

'Not physically, no. Psychologically perhaps. She died a few years later at St Thomas's, Bodmin. Ethan was buried in Towednack churchyard. His sister, Rebecca, still lives round here. You might have seen her. She must be well into her eighties now.'

'I had no idea about the fire,' said Sara. 'But I don't see the point you're trying to make. You obviously don't *believe* Vera.'

'Oh, I believe there was a fire, if that's what she says,' Tim replied. 'But I obviously don't believe that he caught light spontaneously.'

'But Vera thinks ... ?' She shook her head questioningly. 'What?'

'I don't quite know what she thinks,' Tim confessed. 'She talks about the powers of Darkness, all that sort of claptrap.'

Sara was thinking about her first night here, when she found the house full of smoke and the painting burnt to ashes, and how hot the house could be in the middle of the night.

'So why are you telling me this?' she asked. She wondered whether he simply felt bad about the other night, or was actually coming round to her way of thinking.

Tim looked disappointed. 'I thought you'd be interested.'

'I am. But is this just a sop to my neurosis? To cheer me up, make me think there *might* be something weird in this place, keep the girl happy?'

'Oh, Lord . . .' Tim sighed wearily.

She pushed on. 'Or is this supposed to be a way of saying I'm sorry for being so bloody patronizing the other night?'

'I'm trying to find common ground. Things you said reminded me of things Bryan said. He said there was something bad here – outside anything he'd experienced before.'

'When was this?'

'The last time he and I ever sat together in this house. About a month before he died. He said he saw things by the pool.'

'Why didn't you tell me before?'

'And he said he smelt things in the night. It was only when you told me about the night we got back from Florida that I thought about it.'

She remembered that warm sweet smell of roast meat.

'You see, he was always so terribly drunk,' said Tim. He seemed to be apologizing for not mentioning this before. 'I got used to his wild ramblings, his hallucinations. All that meaningless kind of rubbish you found torn up in the Rayburn.'

'Except it wasn't quite so meaningless as it looked,' she said.

She got up and went into the studio and came back with the one surviving scrap from Bryan's journal. 'You missed one.' She gave it to Tim. 'I found it on the floor.'

Tim looked at it. 'Under Senara?'

'Did he ever mention that name?'

'Not that I remember. What is it? A star?'

'It's a girl's name.'

She picked up the Lanberris biography that Clare had lent

her. She opened it at the second of the two places that Clare had marked and passed it to Tim. 'Read the third paragraph.'

'"His child sister, Senara . . ."' he read aloud.

'She was the daughter of Thomas Doriel,' Sara explained, 'who seems to have been the last Doriel to farm at Trevow. This was at the end of the eighteenth century.'

'And they were connected to Roger's family?'

'We don't know for sure. Clare's interested in finding out, that's why she got this book out of the library.'

'But why would Bryan have been interested? Why would he have been writing in his journal about Senara?'

'Well, that's what *I* wanted to know too. Just as I wanted to know why he was so obsessed with Adrian Doriel's death in Plymouth. All those pictures he drew, the woman tied up and beaten. So I went to Truro and looked up the parish records on microfilm. The librarian recognized my name. She told me that another person called Carhays was looking at the parish records a year or two ago. It could only have been Bryan.'

'Why would he have been looking through the parish records?' Tim looked mystified. 'For what possible reason?'

'Because he was looking for a name. And I think he found it.'

'How do you know?'

'I looked up Senara Doriel in the register of burials. And I found her. She was buried in 1794. And on the same page in the register I found the name Beryan. I'll show you what I copied out.'

She took him into the studio. She sat down at the trestle table, looked at the computer screen and tapped the keyboard to scroll back a couple of pages.

She pointed at the screen. 'There.'

She was pointing to:

Beryan (?)
Baptized: 28 Feb 1761 (base child, parents unknown)
Buried: 20 Apr 1794 (spinster)

'Beryan who?' said Tim.

'That's all it says on the parish records. She was illegitimate.'

'Beryan?' Tim remembered now. 'This is the name you were talking about?'

'The name Bryan kept writing about in his journal. You remember those bits we found? He said Beryan was destroying him. He said the name was like hornets in his head. He called her a carnivorous angel, from the black pool of hell. She was tearing his brain in shreds, sucking the soul out of him. He dreaded the nights and yet he longed for them.'

'Yes, I remember,' said Tim. 'But this is all you know about her?' He pointed to the screen.

'That's all,' said Sara. 'Illegitimate, and died a spinster at the age of thirty-three, less than a month after Senara Doriel at Trevow.'

'But what makes you think that Bryan ever discovered this? How can you know he was looking up this same register and found her?'

'I can't know for sure,' Sara conceded, 'but ... Beryan's burial entry was not only on the same page as Senara Doriel, it was immediately beneath her name.'

Tim looked baffled. 'So?'

'It was "*under Senara*".' She pointed to the half-burnt scrap of paper in Tim's hand.

He looked at it again. 'So you think Bryan was looking through the parish records to find a Beryan? And that's what this means, under Senara?'

He sounded as if he was about to start rubbishing her theory.

'Yes, I do.'

'But why would Bryan have been going to so much trouble to find Beryan in the first place?'

'Well, you read those burnt remains from his journal – or whatever it was. This Beryan thing was coming to him at nights. You say it was a fantasy, a hallucination. But whatever she was, she was driving him crazy. He seems to have been trying to find out who she was, and trying to connect her in some way to the Doriel family. And he seems to have been getting somewhere. Among those burnt remains I found was a line that said something like: "I'm on to you, I'm getting there, getting closer."'

'So then, why would he have tried to destroy his journal?' Tim argued. 'Why would he have torn up the pages and burnt them after all that work, if he was actually getting somewhere?'

Sara shrugged. 'I don't know. That's the frustrating thing.'

Tim looked back at the computer screen.

'So what's the point of all this?'

She felt pushed back on the defensive. 'I want to keep a record of everything that's happened. And everything that happens in the future.'

Tim tapped the page key to scroll forwards and looked at the data she had been entering. Then he turned and wandered pensively back into the sitting room.

'You see, I don't have any easy answers for all this,' he said. 'But I still think that a lot of it was down to Bryan's state of mind. He was paranoid, he thought his hallucinations were persecuting him. And I think you're letting it get out of proportion. It's beginning to obsess you just as it obsessed Bryan. And it's not healthy.'

'Well, I'm sorry, Tim,' she said, following him back into the sitting room, 'but we're obviously not going to agree on this.' He was beginning to aggravate her again – that glib, patronizing tone. 'And, frankly, it's none of your business what I get obsessed with. Or who, or when, or where, or why.'

He turned to her and smiled. 'Here you go again. Always looking for a fight. What's the matter with you? You're not happy here, Sara. It's no good saying you are, you're not. And I'm not happy your being here either. That's all that concerns me. Nothing else. I don't want you to be unhappy.'

She could hardly deny that she was unhappy here. But she still didn't like his Daddy's-in-charge tone of voice.

'That's none of your business either,' she said, and was conscious of how petulant that sounded.

'It *is* my business, I'm making it my business.' He smiled again. 'What is it with you? I always get the feeling I'm getting punished by you for what some other man did to you.'

There was a kind of stand-off developing now that was getting them nowhere. She turned away with an impatient gesture. 'I don't know why I'm bothering with this conversation. You're just getting me more and more uptight.'

'Okay,' said Tim, 'let's try and find something we can agree on. You're not happy here. So there's one obvious remedy: sell the house, move out.'

'Well, we're agreed on that much, at least,' she said.

Tim seemed relieved. 'You'll consider it, then?'

'What's there to consider? I never meant to stay here for ever. It was purely convenient while the executors were winding up Bryan's affairs. But I don't know how long it's going to take to find a buyer, given the state of the market.'

'Well, if it takes very long,' he said, 'and you're really desperate to get out, there are three empty rooms in my house – doing absolutely nothing.'

Sara smiled awkwardly. She did not want to seem ungracious but ... *Your timing is not good, fella.* She put a cheerful face on it, anyway. 'I appreciate the offer, Tim, it's very kind but—'

'I know, I know,' he cut in, and held up a hand to silence her. 'Independence and all that. Don't need to say. But the offer's there, just bear it in mind.'

She walked out to Towednack the next morning; to the small Norman church with the squat tower. She wandered around the graveyard.

She found him.

A plain granite headstone read:

> Ethan John Pierce
> Departed this life
> 18 April 1926
> Aged 20 years
> Dear son of George and Ethel
> Beloved brother of Rebecca

And at the bottom of the stone, in smaller letters:

> Though I walk through the valley
> of the shadow of death.

THE NIGHT

Lynn had no regrets, it had to be done. Things had reached a stage where it was unavoidable. People had to be taught the error of their ways.

It was partly – but only partly – the Valentine card. That was clumsy, he shouldn't have done that. Clare left the card on the kitchen dresser. There was a big brown bear on the front with a honey-pot, and a feeble joke inside about her 'bear essentials'. He'd written inside, '*All my love, darling. Your huggy-bear*'. And red roses had appeared in the drawing room. A great big bunch. Be my Valentine.

So she couldn't help wondering what had happened to the loveless sexless marriage he kept complaining about. *She* didn't get a Valentine card ... Well, not from *him* at any rate. Not even a mention. And Clare said something to her that evening about going to bed early because the poor boy was panting for it. Or words to that effect.

No, it was not the Valentine card *itself*; on its own, that was unimportant. But it had to be viewed in the light of what was happening with the barn ... Or *not* happening, more to the point. It was all taking far too long. It was supposed to have been finished last summer, but the planning people weren't happy. (Grade Two listed, blah-blah.) Then it was supposed to have been ready by autumn. But there were yet more delays, and completion was put back to Christmas. Now it was March and Roger had only just put in the floor upstairs.

So what was going on here? What was he playing at? Was he pissing her around? Did he actually want her to move into Trevow after all? Or was he just stringing her along? It was getting beyond a joke. Something had to be done. This was her *life* he was playing games with. He had promised her things – like a place to live, a way out of Chy Melyn. It was not right to mess around with someone's life this way.

She wondered what he would do if she got pregnant. And

what Clare would do when she found out. She wondered what he would do if he had to choose between them. She began to wonder what would happen if Clare had an accident . . . Came off her horse perhaps, a bit of loose strapping somewhere, some LSD in Shilo's feed one morning. Nothing lethal – a spinal injury would do the trick, a wheelchair job.

So she *had* to take some action, it was only fair, she had to do something, couldn't just stand back and be pissed around. We have to be taught the error of our ways. She needed to be sure, though. Didn't want to do anything impulsive that she might later regret.

She had a gentle go at him, when he took her home one night. They were driving slowly through Boskinnow. It was a filthy night, the rain lashing down.

She said, 'I can't believe how long that barn's taking.'

'It gets dark so early,' he said. 'I work better in daylight.'

They turned left out of the village, onto the valley road.

'Anyway,' he said, 'no rush. Don't need the space yet. No one ever comes to stay with us before Whitsun.'

'Then it wouldn't be a problem if I moved in *now*, would it?'

She said it lightheartedly. But it stymied him. They bumped along the valley road in silence, past the track where The Bitch lived. She glanced at him. A car was coming the other way. In the glare of its lights she saw the irritation on his face.

He said, 'Clare would say there's no point. There won't be enough for you to do, not before Easter.'

'There's tons I could do,' she countered. 'I could help you in the barn, for a start. I could get on with the decorating.'

They were approaching Chy Melyn. Sometimes he would drive on to somewhere dark and quiet, but tonight he pulled up outside and left the engine running.

'I don't think it's a good time to push Clare on this,' he said. He switched off the headlights. The rain was drubbing hard on the roof. 'Besides . . . I don't know what Sara might have said.'

Ah. The Bitch. Of course.

'I think we ought to take it easy,' said Roger. 'We've got to be careful, not push our luck.'

They sat in silence, watching the wiper blades *slap-slop, slap-slop*, like a metronome. Lynn showed no signs of moving. A car came along the road towards them and passed quickly by.

It was Tim Hendra's Rover. She couldn't believe how gutless he was. Just because The Bitch had seen them together. A two-second glance in Texas Homecare, for Christ's sake . . . Pathetic. What had she seen?

'So you're going off the idea, are you?' she said provocatively.

'Heavens, no.' He sounded shocked that she could even think like that. He reached out for her hand. She let him take it. 'I just don't want to rock the boat right now. If Sara *did* say something to Clare, and Clare's watching us, she'd wonder why I was pressing for you to move in when there's not much for you to do – with the kids at school, and the stables put back till autumn. She's not stupid.'

Lynn said nothing. That was all she needed to know. He had failed the test. Gutless bastard. His bottle had gone.

'Hey, come on . . .' Roger clapped a hand over her thigh and shook it, trying to gee her up. 'Don't be so gloomy. I know it's frustrating, all these delays but you'll be in by summer. I promise.'

He'd said that *last* summer.

No, this was getting silly. Beyond a joke. It would drag on for ever at this rate. Something had to be done. Something decisive.

She didn't plan it. It could have been any time, anywhere. She was just waiting for the right opportunity.

It was the middle of March. Diamond-bright days and crushed-glass nights. Beautiful hacking weather, just a breath of frost, and the sun low in a powder blue sky. Clare was out on the moors with Shilo. Roger was working in the barn, on the upper floor, putting in the plasterboard partition walls for the boys' bedroom. The children were at school.

She brought him a mug of tea and a slice of Dundee cake around eleven o'clock. Carried it up to the new upper floor, where the boys' bedrooms were going to be. The radio was on, echoing, quite loud. He took the mug of tea, said, 'Cheers, sweetie.'

She left him stuffing his face with cake. She came back down to the barn floor. There were no stairs as yet. The only way up and down was by a ladder – the upper half of a wooden extension ladder, poking through a large open space in the upper floor. The bottom of the ladder was standing very near the edge of the cellar stairs. It was *too* close, she was thinking, a silly place to put a ladder. Roger should have known better. If the bottom of the ladder were to slip back a few inches when he put weight on it from above, it could slip clean off the top stair and crash to the bottom ... with very nasty consequences. Could break his back, or his neck.

In moving the ladder up to the very edge, she was doing him a favour, really. It was teaching him a lesson in safety. Helping him to learn by his mistakes. If anything, it was a kindness.

She stood in the yard and looked up at the sun and smelt the air.

Tez a purdy awld day, yo, Granny would've said.

She thought she'd put Loulou in her buggy and take her for a walk ... A nice *long* walk. Down the sloping track that curved round the lower slopes of the hill to the Mulfra road, around the bend and far away.

They had walked about half a mile when she thought she heard him scream. But they were quite far away by now. Perhaps it was just a seagull.

Clare found him when she got back from her long hack across the moors. He had dragged himself inch by inch across the floor of the barn to get to the phone. She found him lying on the floor of the kids' old rumpus room, almost unconscious with pain.

By the time Lynn got back to Trevow, the paramedics were stretchering him out to the ambulance in the yard.

'Ooh, look, Loulou,' she said. 'Nice green men, taking Daddy away.'

They took him to the West Cornwall hospital at Penzance. His left thigh bone was fractured. He had plaster of Paris from his groin to his toes. They were keeping him in hospital for a few days.

Lynn was organizing the children's tea when Clare got back from Penzance with the news.

'He's going to be out of action for several months,' said

Clare. 'I hate to be a bore, but I'm the only driver now. Would you be willing to move in here for a while? At least, till Roger's mobile again?'

'What, full time, you mean?' said Lynn.

'We'd pay you more, obviously,' said Clare.

'Well, I expect we can work something out,' said Lynn selflessly. 'Anything to help.'

'I don't know what I'd do without her,' said Clare. 'I know you've got doubts about her, but she's very loyal in a crisis.'

They were out riding on the moors, just a steady trot, though Shilo had the wind in his ears and was straining to canter ahead.

'If there's anything I can do,' said Sara, 'you will say, won't you?'

'Bless you. But I think Lynn can cover most things now she's moved in. I only wish we'd given her those driving lessons before now. But Roger's so bloody mean. Hoist on his own petard this time.'

Sara was thinking how conveniently it was all turning out for Lynn. Now she was in, what was the next part of the plan?

'How's he feeling?' she said.

'In the shittiest mood imaginable. He hates hospitals, he hates being in bed, hates doing nothing, hates using a bedpan, hates the food. But you know what's really bugging him? There's no one he can blame for what happened. It was totally his own fault. He's bloody livid. It's going to be hell when he comes home. He's going to be in plaster till the end of June. He's going to be like a caged bear. Don't fancy a lodger for the summer, do you?'

Sara laughed. 'You or Roger?'

'Me, of course. I wouldn't wish him on anyone.'

'Happy to oblige,' said Sara, 'but I may not be there much longer.'

'Really?'

'I'm putting the house on the market.'

'Oh, well done, good for you.' Clare sounded relieved. 'You're not really happy there.'

'That's what Tim was saying. He thinks my bad dreams and

the sleepwalking could all be stress-related. He might be right, but I think there's something more. I don't know what.'

'I never did like that house,' Clare confessed. 'And I've liked it even less since I lost Bosun. There's something sinister about the place.'

'You think so too?' Sara was surprised to hear her say that – she was such a calm, practical, down-to-earth type.

The horses were just walking now. They had come to within sight of the lane that ran through the hamlet of Amalveor, not far from Towednack. A short fat woman was waddling along the lane. It was the old woman in the black coat that Sara kept seeing. She was an odd, stunted-looking figure, like something out of a painting by Brueghel the Elder.

'Who *is* that?' said Sara. It was beginning to grate on her nerves. The woman was forever appearing and disappearing.

'Where?' Clare turned to look.

'Walking along the road.'

'Oh, her. That's Rebecca, one of the spinster wrinklies of Boskinnow.'

'I keep seeing her. She gave me the fright of my life one evening. She looked like my mother from a distance.'

'She's a funny old dear. Must be eighty if she's a day. She's always in a hurry. I don't know where she goes or what she does.'

'Rebecca who?'

'Pierce.'

'Ah, *that*'s who she is ...' Sara thought about Ethan's tombstone in Towednack churchyard. She wondered if Clare knew about the fire that destroyed the old barn at Crowjy. 'I think she goes to tidy her brother's grave. I saw her in church one afternoon.'

'I didn't know there was a brother,' said Clare. 'Did he die recently?'

'No, I think he was quite young,' Sara replied. And had a mental image at that moment of his body floating in the dark pool.

She was going to tell Clare, but something stopped her. It was too reminiscent of the way Bosun died.

*

It was a month of wild winds.

Sara drove into Hayle on a blustery day, thunder grey, like the ocean. A northwesterly gale was scuttling in off St Ives Bay and sweeping across the deserted towans.

She walked into the offices of Penna, Rowe and Partners, estate agents. A gust of wind barged past her like a fat man in a hurry and blew loose papers off a vacant desk. Sara pushed the door tight shut.

There were two desks, but only one was occupied. The agent was a homely-looking woman, a few years older than Sara. Soon she would be plump, but not quite yet. She wore a calf-length knitted dress in fuchsia-coloured wool that almost matched her nail lacquer. Her head was heavy with cold, her nose was bright and damp and sore. Close by, a fan heater purred and whined.

It had been a bad winter for property sales. She brightened up at the sight of custom.

Sara said, 'I'd like to sell my house.'

The agent hid her feelings well. She might have said, Who wouldn't? Instead, she flashed an instant smile and asked Sara to take a seat.

'You handled the sale before,' said Sara. 'It's a barn-cottage called Crowjy, in the Nansgever valley.'

'How long ago was this?'

'About 1981.'

The agent got up and crossed to a filing cabinet and opened the middle drawer. Her fingers skipped nimbly along a row of suspension files.

'Nothing here, I'm afraid,' she said at length. She had North-Country vowels, Manchester maybe. 'We'll have to come out and take some fresh details.' She closed the drawer and came back to her desk. 'It's been a bit slow, the market, this winter. But it should pick up after Easter. That always gets people out looking.' She dabbed her inflamed nostrils with a soggy tissue. 'And I don't suppose you're in a rush.'

Someone came out to Crowjy a few days later, a man in a tired suit and muddy suede shoes. He walked around the house, muttering and measuring, jotting notes. He suggested they put it on at £64,950 and told her she might have to drop to sixty.

She wondered if that was not a little on the high side, given the state of the market. He talked in mixed metaphors, about flying kites and putting toes in the water. She said she was keen to sell. He talked about giving it a whirl and seeing how the dice crumbled.

The house knew.

It felt betrayed, it conspired in a grey huddle. It went cold on her, resentful. Even the air began to smell sour. Milk curdled, the butter turned rancid. The March winds blew, carved their way inside through the ill-fitting joinery. Curtains trembled, draughts scuttled here and there like vermin. Shadows conferred like hooded figures shifting in the firelight. There were moans and murmurs in the night, the fire hissed and spat like a cat at bay. Logs cracked like a whip. Something festered in the darkness, the fetid stench of treachery and animosity.

She began to sleep fitfully at nights. She threw off the duvet in her sleep and awoke shaking with cold. The darkness creaked and whispered. The fire in the Rayburn burned out in the night. The power failed again. She called Southwestern Electricity.

They sent engineers who inspected the wiring but found nothing wrong. They came back the next day and installed a piece of equipment to measure sudden surges in the current.

Tim was relieved that she had finally put the barn-cottage on the market. She told him she would take the first sensible offer that came along. It seemed to him that she would be glad to be out of the place. She had been sleeping at his house for the past week now, but spending the days at Crowjy, working on her thesis. He was wondering what she would say if he asked her to move in with him.

Perhaps it was too soon? It was so hard to tell with Sara; she was warm and affectionate, but emotionally reticent. There was a cold spot inside her that never seemed to get the sun.

They were lying in bed that Saturday night, quite late, in the dark, just listening to the whipping of the wind outside. And he said, 'I have to go to London for a few days.'

'What for?'

'Consultations, NHS reforms. The government want GPs to become fund holders and shop around for clinical services. I'm representing the southwest area practitioners' committee. Meet the health minister. Tell him what we think of it.'

'Sounds a riot.'

'So liven it up. Come with me.'

'To meet the health minister?'

He tickled her ribs. She squeaked and giggled.

'You know bloody well what I mean.'

She thought about it for a moment. 'When?'

'I go up on Sunday fortnight.'

'I'm tempted. But I should be working, really. I'm miles behind with my thesis.'

'Don't you ever stop thinking about that? Take a break. You haven't got a deadline.'

'Coming from a doctor who works seven days a week,' she retorted, 'and had to do three weeks on call just so he could go to Florida at Christmas ...' She poked him softly in the kidneys.

'Touché,' he conceded.

'Anyway,' she said, snuggling up to him, 'I don't think about it at nights, do I? You've got my attention *half* the time. That's not such a bad deal, is it?'

Her fingernails combed through the hair on his belly.

On an impulse, he said, 'Are you comfortable working at Crowjy?'

There was a silence – a faintly suspicious silence – as if she was trying to work out where the question was leading.

'Well, I've got everything I need. It's not ideal but ... What do you mean?'

'Why don't you try and rent the cottage out until you find a buyer?'

'Then where do *I* go?'

'Move in here. There are three empty bedrooms. You could make one of them into a study. Do anything you want with the other rooms.'

He knew at once that he had said the wrong thing. He could feel her freezing up on him.

'Okay,' he said, after a silence. 'Consider it unsaid.'

Her hand lay like a dead thing on his belly now.

'I'm nearly thirty-three, Tim.'

She left that suspended, like a bridge that gave out half-way across a river.

'So?'

'I left home when I was eighteen because I couldn't handle Dad going bankrupt and then dying. I moved back because my mother needed me. I spent six years looking after a helpless woman day and night. After she died, I moved in with my history tutor at Exeter. I've not long been free of it all. And I'm still enjoying the freedom.'

'Understood. Completely. Forget I said it.'

'I need my space, Tim, I'm sorry. Maybe eventually, given time—'

'Listen, you don't have to explain, I'm not pressing you.'

But she wouldn't let it go; she seemed to resent that it had even been mentioned.

'We're okay the way we are, aren't we?' She gave his hand a half-hearted squeeze. 'Why spoil it?'

'Listen . . .' Tim kissed her on the mouth. 'I never mentioned it. It's erased, forgotten, never happened.'

He brushed it away as if it were a cobweb. But he felt leaden inside, as if she had just told him that this was as good as it would ever get, this and no more. It felt like a warning. He was suddenly curious. He wanted to know things about her past that he'd never thought very much about . . . Her past lovers, her casual flings, her mad moments, the heartbreakers, everything.

She did mention the history man occasionally, but Tim never enquired.

She said good night. They kissed. She turned onto her side. He lay awake, listening to the gale, furious with himself . . . So clumsy, so insensitive. He had no finesse. He was an ox, he was a drunken sailor on a pitching deck, he was a waltzer with two left feet. Valerie used to say that, when it came to sensitivity, he was like a radio that was never quite tuned in to any station.

Sara slept with her back to him. He could feel the distance.

When he woke up, she was gone.

*

She dreamt that someone was calling for her.

She slid soundlessly from bed, frictionless, the stroke of a knife blade through the air, out into the shrieking night.

Along the lane, onto the valley road, borne like a leaf on a stream, past the black windows of Chy Melyn, Vera sleeping, nearer my God to Thee, groaning like an old tree with her pain.

She came to Crowjy. Its arms were open, the doors and windows flung wide, the black wind a drunk gypsy, dancing with the curtains, flinging and tossing them.

She found a poor naked creature, pale and still in the dark. She took her body in her arms and kissed her face. Her hair smelt of smoke; it was dry and crackly, like straw after stubble-burning. Sara took her scissors and cut away the burnt hair, right down to the scalp.

She kissed those lips. She was kissing her own lips.

The two embraced, their mouths touched, their bodies pressed closer, their arms and legs entwined. She crept over Sara like breath on a winter's night, she clung to her flesh like frost, she melted into her, powder-soft, snow-smooth. Sara inhaled her, absorbed her, they were one, body and soul. They were blind and mute, speaking in fingertips, snug in their secrets, softly exploring, drunk with each other's mysteries. They were sighs and murmurs, they were tongues and tremors, long fingers, slender snakes turning inside each other, deeper and deeper inside. They were quivering with sensations, giddy with rapture, reeling and breathless. They were energized, they were charged, they were vibrant with feeling. It crackled from them like static, it glowed from their flesh, it flashed from their eyes.

Now the dull weight of footsteps approaching. The glow of a candle began to invade their secret darkness. A human shape appeared behind the flickering light.

'Sara . . .?' A man's voice.

She knew it, she knew that voice from somewhere.

She sensed danger. She gripped the scissors, held them up like a knife poised to stab.

Open him up like a pie. The hot red juice oozing through the pale crust . . .

'Sara . . .?'

The curtains leapt at the open windows, dervishes dancing in the frantic wind.

Tim lay listening to the wind; a northwesterly raging in off the ocean, scourging the abject moors. Something was making sporadic knocking sounds outside in the garden. A man with a mallet, thumping a tent peg into the ground.

Sara did not come back to bed. He assumed she was in the bathroom.

He couldn't get back to sleep, wondering what it was that had come loose outside and was banging in the wind. He reached out and switched on the bedside lamp. He sat up and looked across the bed. Charlie was lying there, curled up, asleep. That man outside, thumping the tent peg, was getting on his nerves. He got out of bed and pulled on his bathrobe. He walked out into the hallway and switched on the light.

'Sara...?'

Not a sound. The rest of the house was in darkness. Both bathrooms were empty. He walked from room to room.

'Sara...?'

She was nowhere in the house. He switched on the exterior light and went outside, into the garden. It was the front gate that was banging. There was a wire loop that dropped over the gatepost to keep the gate shut but it had come unhitched.

He went back inside.

Where in the name of God was she? It was twenty to four in the morning. He went back to the bedroom: her clothes were still draped over the back of the chair, where she had left them last night.

He pulled on a pair of jeans, a sweater and a windcheater, grabbed a flashlight from the kitchen and went back outside. Her VW was still in the driveway, in front of the garage. It was a dry night but bitterly cold. He walked around the garden, shining the light, and along the road to the end, where it gave out onto Nansgever Downs. He shouted her name and waved the lamp around. She couldn't possibly be out on the moors wearing only her T-shirt, not for long in this force ten. She would collapse from hypothermia.

He ran back to the house, took her car keys from her bag, hurried outside, climbed into the VW and turned the starter. It was sluggish. *Come on, come on* ... At last it fired. He pushed the seat back a few notches, fumbled for the lights and crunched reverse gear. He backed out and drove along the lane to the valley road, past Vera's house, through the zig-zag bends, and up the track to the barn-cottage.

He pulled up close to the front door. It was wide open. But the house was in darkness. He left the car engine running and the headlights on, got out and went indoors. He hit the light-switch just inside the hall. Nothing happened.

He called out: 'Sara ...?'

Silence.

'Sara?'

Now he could see the back door was open too. It was like a wind tunnel in here. He felt his way into the sitting room and tried the wall switch. Nothing. No lights. Bloody fuses again. And now he remembered he'd left the flashlight at home. There was some light spilling into the house from the Beetle's headlamps, but he had to leave the front door open to take advantage of it. He moved along the hall passage and shut the back door.

How the hell did she get *in*? The keys were in her handbag. Or did she have burglars, on top of all her other troubles?

He fumbled his way into the kitchen. With the fuses blowing so frequently, she kept candles in store now. He found them in one of the cupboards. There were matches there too. He lit a candle, but the moment he stepped out into the hall passage the wind pounced and snuffed it out. He closed the front door to keep out the wind, relit the candle and moved slowly through the sitting room and peered inside the studio. Everything looked normal.

He walked back to the hallway and was about to go upstairs when the back door blew in, crashed back against the inside wall. It frightened the life out of him. The wind stormed through and punched out the candle light. He walked along to the back door, shut it again and bolted it fast this time.

He relit the candle yet again. But it was suddenly very quiet ... So quiet he could hear the ticking of the sitting-room clock. He stood still and listened intently. The car ... It was silent. The engine had stopped.

He stood by the front door and looked out. Not only had the

engine stopped but the lights had gone out. He went outside, climbed into the car and tried the starter. Dead. Not even a grunt. He tried the wipers. They were dead too. This was all he needed.

He went back into the house, relit the candle and started slowly up the stairs, shielding the flame with his free hand.

'Sara . . .?'

He stopped when he reached the landing. Her white T-shirt was lying in the bathroom doorway.

'Sara . . .?'

He stepped into the bathroom. By the glow of the candle-light, he could make out something in the washbasin – all over it, on the floor, everywhere . . . He lowered the candle and touched it. It was hair, masses of it, hair everywhere.

At that moment, he sensed something behind him. He spun round. She was standing right there, a few feet away, her eyes wide and burning with anger. Blood trickled down her face.

'Jesus Christ . . .' he whispered.

She was almost bald. She had cut off all her hair.

He just glimpsed the scissors, a flash in the candlelight, as her fist came down towards him in a hard stabbing arc. He put up his arm to protect his face and sidestepped her, shouting, '*Sara! No!*' But the candle blew out as he did so. She was stabbing and punching wildly in the dark, a frenzy of pumping arms and harsh grunting sounds. He pushed out hard with both hands and sent her stumbling backwards. She backed into the side of the bath, the scissors went flying and landed on the floor somewhere. She started shrieking for help and screaming. He pulled her to him and held her tightly, saying over and over, 'It's okay, it's Tim, it's only me, it's okay, sshh . . .'

All the energy had gone out of her. Suddenly, she was like a rag doll in his arms. She was slippery with sweat, trembling and hunting for breath. He eased her out of the bathroom, into the bedroom and sat her down on the bed.

She was mumbling now – 'Where are we?' and 'Have they gone?' – as if she were coming out of an anaesthetic.

'Just lie back . . .' He eased her down. 'We're at Crowjy. Upstairs. There's no one else here, we're all alone, you're okay now . . .'

He wrapped the duvet round her and felt for the torch that

she kept on her bedside table. He switched it on and looked down at her. She was pale and shaking. Her scalp was a terrible mess.

'I was asleep,' she muttered. 'Was dreaming ... Someone coming up the stairs, coming to get us, going to hurt us ...'

She sat up and looked around the room in a sudden flurry of panic. 'What are we doing here? What's happened?'

'You walked in your sleep again,' he said gently. He sat beside her on the bed and put his arms around her. 'But it's all over now. We'll find you some clothes and get you back to my place.'

He was going to have to clean the blood off her face and explain to her – somehow – what she had done. How was he going to tell her? What could possibly have possessed her to do such a thing?

It was not all over. It was not remotely over. It had hardly begun.

THE CYCLE

She woke up. It was daylight. She was at Tim's. It was after eleven. *So late* . . . Then she remembered, it was Sunday.

She felt muzzy-headed. She had slept for too long. She got out of bed and wrapped herself in his robe and went out to the bathroom. She heard him moving about, doing things in the kitchen. She could hear a radio.

Her feet were hurting. So sore. Why were her feet so painful?

She closed the bathroom door, sat down on the lavatory and lifted her feet. They were filthy. They were more than filthy, they had been bleeding . . .

Now it all began to come back to her . . . Crowjy . . . the raging wind . . .

What had happened? What were they doing there?

She felt as if she had been drunk and was trying to piece it all together.

She got up and flushed the loo and moved to the washbasin and turned on the hot tap. She looked in the mirror. She was wearing . . .

This was ludicrous. She was wearing a hat. Her navy blue bobble-hat. Her fisherman's hat. Why did she go to sleep in a hat? Were they at a party last night? Did she get stoned? Did they have to stop at Crowjy to fetch something?

Then she remembered: they were in bed here, listening to that gale, and Tim said he was going to London, come to London he said. And rent out Crowjy, move in here . . .

That's right . . .

And then that extraordinary dream. Holding her. Kissing her. And scissors . . .

She lifted the hat off her head.

'God . . .' she breathed slowly.

She reached up and touched her scalp. It looked as if she had alopecia, tufts here and there, almost bald elsewhere. And she had cut the flesh, cuts and snicks everywhere.

Steam was rising from the running water. She put in the plug and filled the basin. Was this real or was this the nightmare too? She put her hands into the scalding water and held them there until she could take the pain no longer. It was real, the pain was very real.

What is happening? What in the name of Christ is happening?

That fear she felt last night, that was real too, something behind the candlelight, coming to get her . . .

She heard Tim approaching the bathroom door. He hesitated outside.

'Sara?' A pause. And then, with unease, 'You okay?'

He rapped softly with his knuckles. He tried the door handle, but she had turned the lock.

'I'm okay.' It came out as a scarcely audible croak.

'I'm making coffee. When you feel like it.'

She heard him go away.

What do I mean, I'm okay? I'm not remotely okay.

She wiped a hole in the condensation on the mirror and looked again at what was left of her hair. *Why, why, why?*

She remembered the feel of that poor creature's hair . . . It was like fine raffia, the sort in which they packed delicate porcelain or glass.

She looked into her eyes. She felt as if she were trapped, trapped inside a pressure chamber, looking out through two portholes. Everything looked normal from the outside. *But there's something out of control in here, some kind of chaos breaking loose. Someone better do something . . .*

She sank down onto the side of the bath and began to weep.

Was this madness? Was this how it began? Was this how it felt?

She half filled the bath and lay soaking.

She needed to talk, she could not handle this alone. But she couldn't stay here. This offered no sanctuary. She was a danger to Tim. She could have killed him.

There was a psychiatrist her father used to go to, after his business went belly-up and he had a breakdown. His name was Richard McCormack. He had a practice in Plymouth. He was a family friend of sorts, so he knew a little about her, knew she was adopted. Perhaps she could confide in him?

What was she going to do about her hair?

Oh, God, what have I done, what have I done?

She got out of the bath, dried herself off, put on the hat again and crept back to the bedroom to get dressed. Tim was waiting for her in the kitchen. He poured some coffee. She sat down. He put the coffee in front of her and looked at her across the table. The silence seemed to stretch for miles.

'How do you feel?'

'A bit groggy.'

'I gave you a sleeping pill.'

'Did you? I don't remember.'

She spooned sugar into her coffee and stirred it slowly; something to focus her gaze on. Away from Tim.

'We have to talk about this,' he ventured tentatively. 'We have to tackle it, Sara.'

'I don't know how I got there. I had a dream. I told you.'

'But what was the dream?'

'There was a woman on the floor. And her hair was crisp, like raffia. And I felt so sorry for her. So sorry I wanted to cry. And I began to cut it off, her horrible prickly hair.'

She stopped.

'And then what?'

'I don't know, I can't remember.' She was lying.

Tell him the truth, just tell him. You made love to her.

She couldn't.

'I heard footsteps ... Must have been you coming up the stairs. I saw the candlelight. I didn't know who it was, I just felt danger. The voice, I recognized the voice, I remember. But I couldn't think *who* it was.'

'Did you know,' said Tim patiently, 'that you were attacking me? Trying to stab me with the scissors?'

She recalled the terrible fear of this invading presence, but from that point on her memory was like a film that had jumped out of the gate and was just blur and judder and then blackness. 'I don't really remember.'

Tim was wearing his doctor's expression. 'We've got to do something about this, Sara.'

'I'm going to see someone. I've decided. Someone my father knew. A psychiatrist in Plymouth. He was a friend of the family. My father trusted him.'

'What's his name?'

'Richard McCormack.'

'Is he properly qualified? I don't think a mere therapist is—'

'No, no, he's a proper shrink, the real thing. He was very good with my father.'

Tim nodded reluctantly. He looked so grim and concerned.

'All right,' he agreed. 'I was going to suggest someone you should see. But if you'd rather try this man, fair enough.'

She wished he would smile, or at least not stare like that. He had an awful look in his eyes. So accusing.

'You think I'm ill, don't you?' she said. 'You think I'm having a mental breakdown or something.'

He reached across the table for her hand. He took an age to choose his words, like someone tiptoeing barefoot through broken glass.

'I think you've been under intolerable strain. Too many things coming on top of you, too quickly.'

She didn't want him to say that. She wanted him to say, It's not you, you're not ill, of course you're not ill.

'The important thing is,' he said, 'you know there's a problem. You don't need me to tell you. And you're happy to talk to someone about it, someone qualified. That's very positive. That's a good sign.'

He drove her back to Crowjy. While she cleaned up in the bathroom, he mended the fuses.

He got into the VW and turned the key. The engine fired first time.

She cooked a late lunch. But she had no appetite.

They sat by the fire in the sitting room.

'I know this goes against the grain,' he began.

And she knew, intuitively, what he was going to say.

'But I really would be very much happier if you moved in with me for a few days.' Before she could speak, he went on, 'Just a few days, that's all. No pressure. Sleep in your own room if you want, do anything you want, but I'd just rather you were there and not here.'

She took her time replying, but that was simply because she did not want to appear stubborn or ungrateful.

'I don't think so,' she said quietly.

'I'd rather you did.'

'I know you mean well but I definitely have to be on my own for a while, Tim. I need my space.'

'It's your own safety I'm thinking about.'

'I was with you last night,' she reasoned, 'but what good did that do? I got out of your bed and you didn't even wake up. What are you going to do next? Handcuff us together and lock the bedroom door?'

'Sara . . .' He gave her an odd look – as if he was both appealing to her and warning her. 'Don't push me away.'

She didn't much care for that look, or for that tone of voice.

'Please, Tim, don't let's argue about it. I don't want to sleep at your house tonight. I certainly won't move in there. It's only adding to the stress. I can't think, I can't be myself, I feel pressurized. You hang around me, you watch me, you've got that bloody look in your eyes, as if you're about to tell me I've got cancer of the brain or something. You don't trust me – I can't even sit on the loo without you rattling the bloody door. I can't live like that.'

She had not meant to sound abrasive, but she couldn't take the dominating, big-brother manner. Gerald was a little like that. But she had put up with it because she loved him; and look where it had got her.

'I'm sorry,' she said, more quietly. 'I know you care, but you're making it worse by crowding me. I can't bear being crowded.'

'I don't mean to crowd you.' He tried a more emollient tone. 'But just as a friend, as a doctor, I have a *responsibility* for you.'

'Tim, I'm going to see a shrink, all right? Of my own free will. I'm taking care of things, okay? I'm thirty-three years old and I'm responsible for myself. So please – I'm doing what you want, I'm doing the right thing, now in return just *please* give me space.'

He was beginning to look more or less resigned to it.

'If I give you something to help you sleep tonight,' he said, 'will you take it?'

'Yes, I promise,' she said. And meant it.

Tim could not understand her emotional claustrophobia, her fear of getting too close to anyone. He wondered if it had something to do with the psychology of the orphan, a fundamental sense of insecurity. And yet, he thought an abandoned child would have *wanted* to make relationships, would have craved them even, not been afraid of them.

He went to Trevow that evening to talk to Clare. Lynn was upstairs, chivvying the twins to bed. Clare was preparing supper. She invited Tim to join them but he declined. He sat at the kitchen table, admiring the casual fluency with which Clare prepared a meal – as if she just made it all up as she went along.

He asked after Roger, but he was only being polite.

'I really came to talk about Sara,' he confessed. 'She hasn't phoned you, has she?'

'I haven't spoken to her since Thursday. Why?'

'She'll hate me for telling you this, but we had another sleepwalking incident last night.'

Clare showed no great surprise, not after the incident on New Year's Eve. 'Your house or hers?'

'Both. She was sleeping at my house but she disappeared in the middle of the night. I went looking for her and found her back at Crowjy. The doors and windows were wide open, and the lights had fused.'

Clare was at the stove, stirring mushrooms and tomatoes in a large iron frying pan. She turned to face him. 'She walked all that way? In her sleep?'

'She looked as if she was in some kind of trance. Says she was dreaming that I was some awful "thing" coming to get her. But that's not the worst of it.'

Clare waited.

'She attacked me. With a pair of scissors.'

'She did *what*?'

'And . . . She had just cut off all her hair.'

Clare didn't speak. Her face said it all.

'She took the scissors,' said Tim, 'and just hacked off all her hair. It's a terrible mess.'

Clare came to the table and sat down. 'But *why*?'

'All she remembers – or all she *says* she remembers – is dreaming of a woman on the floor, whose hair was sort of crispy and burnt. And in her dream, she cut it all off because she felt sorry for her.'

'Where was this?'

'In the bathroom. Hair all over the sink, the loo, the floor.'

'But in her *sleep*? She cut her hair off in her sleep?'

'It's a miracle she didn't poke her eye out. And mine, come to that. I don't even know how she got *into* the house – her keys were in her handbag in my bedroom.'

Clare looked deeply troubled. 'Does she remember anything?'

'Not about how she got there, no. I find it hard to believe that anyone walks all that way through a force-ten gale in nothing but a T-shirt and doesn't wake up. Her feet were cut to ribbons.'

'What are you saying? You think she wasn't really sleepwalking?'

'She obviously *walked*, she couldn't have taken the car ... But I think there's something wrong with her psychologically. I don't think she's sleepwalking in the conventional sense of the term. She already suspects that she's cracking up. But a part of her denies it – not surprisingly, she's afraid of it. She says no, she's fine, it's just stress, and she's got it in hand, she's on top of the situation, and all I'm doing is making it worse by pressurizing her.'

'It's more than that,' said Clare. 'She thinks there's something strange going on in that house.'

'The only strange things that are going on,' said Tim, 'are going on in her head.'

'You see, that's *just* what upsets her. She thinks that you put her down as neurotic and won't take her seriously.'

'Good Christ,' said Tim, in disbelief. 'Won't take her seriously? I'm worried *sick* about her. But she's difficult to get close to on an emotional level. I'll be quite honest with you, I don't think she's neurotic, I think she's ...' He glanced towards the hallway and dropped his voice a little. 'I don't say this lightly, Clare, but I don't know who else to talk to about it, because she has no other friends. There's only you and me. And she's got no family. I'm seriously worried about her. I'm falling head over heels in love with that woman, and I think she's mentally ill. And it's scaring the hell out of me.'

'But you're her doctor. If anyone can help, surely to God—'

'There's nothing I can do if she doesn't *want* help. A GP has limited powers – unless a patient is so obviously ill that she has to be sectioned under the Mental Health Act. But that's a major step to take. I want her to see a psychiatrist first. She's going to see a man in Plymouth. A friend of the family apparently. Called McCormack. I'm going to check up and make sure he's genuine.'

'Did you suggest it?'

'I didn't need to. She'd already decided. But now, of course, I'm beginning to wonder ... Maybe she's seen McCormack before. Maybe she has a history of psychiatric problems.'

'It would be on her medical records, wouldn't it?'

'Not necessarily. All I have are the records held by her previous GP. There's no mention of any psychiatric referral, but she could have been treated elsewhere – privately or as an NHS outpatient.'

Clare looked as if she found it difficult to believe.

'How long have you been thinking like this?' she said.

'Only lately. Since New Year's Eve – your party, the business in the barn, the bleeding. Until then I put her moods down to her problems with Bryan and her finding out the truth about her childhood. But since then I've begun to wonder about all kinds of things.'

'Such as?'

'The kind of things that Bryan used to tell me. He told me she was evil, that she was trying to destroy him. He said she came to see him at nights.'

'But he was a raging alcoholic. You didn't believe a word *he* said, surely?'

'Not at the time, no. But now I'm beginning to wonder just what he meant. Has she *really* not seen him for ten years?'

'Why would she lie about a thing like that?'

'Did you know they were lovers? Did you know she was pregnant by him? Did you know she had an abortion?'

Clare looked incredulous.

'No, precisely,' said Tim. 'There's more to it than you think.'

'Bryan told you that?'

'No, *she* did. That's what all this guilt thing is about. Afraid she might have turned Bryan into an alcoholic, ruined his life, destroyed his career.'

'Do you think there's any truth in it?'

'Hard to believe. Bryan didn't even mention her till the last month of his life. But I don't know *what* to believe any more.'

Lynn appeared in the kitchen doorway. 'The twins are in bed now,' she said to Clare. 'You need any help?'

'No,' said Clare. 'Supper'll be about half an hour.'

Lynn nodded. 'I'll be in the drawing room if you need me.'

She disappeared across the hallway.

'And then there was that sunburn in Florida,' Tim resumed. 'I wrote to the *Lancet* about it. I had a letter the following month, from a dermatologist in Holland. He treated a similar case, a Dutch girl back in the 1960s. Claimed she was given LSD and raped in an empty house. She had hallucinations. The house was burning down around her. After that, she claims she developed this skin condition which sounded very much like Sara's. And it recurred whenever she sunbathed for too long. The Dutch consultant said it looked as if she was covered in scar tissue ... Which was exactly how Sara looked until it began to peel.'

'But what does that have to do with Sara?'

'The Dutch girl was here in west Cornwall when the alleged rape took place. She was camped near St Just with a convoy of hippies. She had no idea where the empty house was. She was out walking one day and took shelter from the rain.'

'But Sara's skin was burnt in Florida, not at Crowjy.'

Tim had no answer for that. He was as confused as Clare was.

'I talked to Lynn's mother,' he said, nodding in the direction of the doorway. 'Did you know the old barn was burnt down, back in the 1920s?'

'No, I didn't.'

'Rebecca Pierce's brother died from burns in the fire.'

'So that's what Sara meant. She mentioned him the other day.'

'He threw himself in the pond. His girlfriend ran for help but when she came back she found him dead in the water. Her father was a cowman here at Trevow, Vera said.'

'I had no idea,' said Clare. 'I wonder why Sara didn't tell me?'

'She's got an obsession about that pool. She still blames herself for what happened to Bosun.'

'I keep telling her,' said Clare, exasperated, 'it wasn't *anyone's* fault.'

'But, you see, that house is associated with so much guilt in her mind. The sooner she's out of there the better.'

'When is she seeing this psychiatrist.'

'I don't know. As soon as possible, I hope. She won't open up to me. If I ask too many questions, she says I'm crowding her.'

'Do you want me to have a go? See what I can find out?'

'You'll have to be very tactful,' he warned. 'She's going to guess we've been talking.'

She stood looking at herself in the bathroom mirror. She looked ridiculous. She had missed large patches here and there; they looked like clumps of fur, as if they'd been stuck on with glue. In other places she'd snipped away almost to the bare flesh. She didn't know what to do. She could wear her bobble-hat whenever she went out, but even if she rolled it down over the tops of her ears, the back of her head still looked bald. She wasn't sure whether it was better to shave the whole pate smooth, so that it would grow evenly all over, or to keep trimming the thicker patches until the stubby bits had caught up with them.

Tim phoned to see if she'd made an appointment with Richard McCormack. She lied and said yes. She felt as if he was watching her all the time now, as if she was under suspicion or on probation. She looked up Richard McCormack's number in the book and telephoned his practice in Plymouth. His receptionist warned her that he had a busy schedule; he was a visiting psychiatrist at several major hospitals in the southwest, and the earliest that he could see Sara would be the middle of April.

She was feeling shivery that day. She went to bed early. When she got up the following morning she felt feverish. Her body was aching, her ribs felt tender and she had no energy.

Clare came to see her.

'You look a bit pasty,' she said. 'Are you all right?'

'Don't know. Think I'm going down with something. Feel sort of fluey.'

Clare was not surprised. 'It's a bug, it's everywhere. Half the village has gone down with it.'

They went into the sitting room. Sara huddled by the fire.

'Are you cold now?' said Clare.

Sara was wearing thick dancer's leggings over her jeans, a heavy sweater, and her fisherman's hat.

'Just a little. I get the chills. Comes and goes.' She was looking into the fire but she could sense Clare's eyes on her bobble-hat. 'How's Roger?' she asked. Not that she much cared.

'Oh, being perfectly foul, as always. Constipated as hell, because he's too embarrassed to crap in a bedpan. They're sending him home on Friday. Patch 'em up and shove 'em out so quickly these days. Need the beds I suppose. The nurses can't wait to be shot of him.'

There was an uneasy silence.

'I suppose Tim's been talking to you?' said Sara.

Clare nodded.

'About Saturday night?'

'Yes.'

'He thinks I'm coming unglued, doesn't he? Thinks I'm having a breakdown.'

'He's worried about you. Do you blame him?'

Sara didn't answer. Then she said, 'He thinks I'm going crazy, doesn't he?'

'Oh, come on,' said Clare, 'give the man a break. He's in love with you, you scared him out of his wits. You walk through the valley in the middle of the night in bare feet, a howling gale, and try to stab his eyes out.'

'I know it sounds dreadful but—'

'Put yourself in *his* place, reverse the roles. How would *you* feel?'

'I know, it sounds like I'm some kind of psychotic,' Sara pleaded, 'but I'm not, I'm truly not. Look at me, look me in the eye.'

'I'm looking.'

'Do I look crazy? Do I sound crazy? I'm no more crazy than you are.'

'I know you're not.'

'I've never told you this but ... Last spring, soon after I moved in, I found the remains of a sort of book that Bryan was writing. I call it a journal because I don't really know *what* it was. He'd torn up all the pages and burnt them in the Rayburn. But some small scraps were still readable. Tim saw them – ask him, I'm not making this up.'

'It's all right, I believe you.' Clare smiled sympathetically. 'Tim's the sceptic, not me.'

'Tim read them but he threw them all back in the Rayburn and burnt them, because he said I was getting worked up about nothing.'

'Why? What was in this journal?'

'Something was getting to him here. Someone he called Beryan. He kept on and on about her. Said she was driving him mad, said she was devouring him. I've written down as much as I can remember. I've put it all on computer.' She hitched a thumb back towards the studio. 'I'll run you off a copy, you can read it. Tim put it all down to Bryan's drunken binges. Said it was a mixture of fantasy and the DTs. But it was more than that, I know it was. Because I've *found* her, this Beryan woman. In the old Towednack parish records.'

She explained it exactly as she had explained it to Tim, and how the name Beryan appeared under Senara Doriel in the burials register.

'Beryan was driving Bryan out of his mind,' she said. 'It was obvious from the remains of his journal. He wrote things like: "Why does she keep coming? What in God's name does she want from me? Beryan has infested my mind. Her name is like hornets in my head. Why is she torturing me? Is she doing this just to punish me? Will it go on for ever?" Stuff like that, I can't remember exactly.'

'But how was she driving Bryan mad?' Clare looked totally bewildered. 'What did he mean, "Why does she keep coming"?'

'She came to him at nights, he said. He actually described her. He said she had no hair, her skin was very pale and smooth, and she was very cold. He called her his whore from hell. Tim thought it was a mixture of DTs and sexual fantasy.'

'Well, alcoholics do see these ghastly things, don't they?' Clare reasoned.

'He didn't only see it,' said Sara. 'He actually painted it and made drawings of it – dozens of them. And I think I've seen it.

It's come to me as well. At night. Not just once, several times now.'

Clare was almost smiling, as if she thought Sara was taking the mickey.

'I'm not crazy, Clare, believe me.'

'Oh, don't be silly. What do you mean, it comes to you?'

'It's like a dream but ... You know how hard it is to remember dreams in detail? I just have a vague *impression* of this thing. Sometimes I'm dreaming that I'm looking in the mirror and she comes out of the glass towards me. And wraps herself around me. She's all over me. I get a feeling of kind of ... rapture. It's hard to explain. I've never dreamt anything like it before. But it's more than a dream ...'

She indicated the shadowy patch on the wall. 'You see that?'

'I thought you'd cured that,' said Clare. 'I thought you got rid of it when you scraped off the plaster and paint.'

'I did get rid of it. But now it's come back. I discovered it one evening, a few weeks ago. I'd been reading that Lanberris book you lent me. I was thinking about Senara. I fell asleep by the fire. I woke up and saw that and thought it was someone's shadow on the wall. Scared the life out of me. And that same night she came to me again ... this "thing", this creature, whatever you want to call it.'

'You've told Tim all this?'

'And I wish I hadn't bothered. He's got a convenient doctor's answer for the whole thing, you see. It's all in the mind. Anything that Bryan experienced was because he was a chronic alcoholic. And anything that *I* experience is because I'm stressed out and cracking up. But I'm not cracking up, Clare, believe me. I'm quite quite sane.'

'But what you did to your hair ...' said Clare tentatively. 'I don't understand.'

Sara took off the woollen hat. She had shaven her head all over. She ran her hand across the smooth tender flesh.

'She made me do it. In my sleep.'

Clare looked concerned. 'She?'

'This thing,' said Sara. 'This Beryan thing.'

Clare smiled indulgently. 'I see.'

'She's trying to get at me,' said Sara. 'Just like she got to Bryan.'

She could see now that this was a waste of time. Clare was on Tim's side.

That night she sat up late in the studio, working at her computer, looking through the data she was accumulating on Beryan. She had put down on disk all the scraps of writing that she could remember from Bryan's journal, all the dates she had researched, and every strange incident that had happened to her thus far.

Tonight, she was looking through the dates. She noticed a strange coincidence.

Ethan Pierce died on 18 April 1926.

George Doriel (Adrian's father, and Roger's great-grandfather) died the very next day in south Devon, on 19 April 1926.

Adrian Doriel was found dead in a Plymouth cellar, one day and thirty-three years later, on 20 April 1959.

And in 1794, on the same date, 20 April, Beryan was buried at Towednack.

All four had died on or around 18 April.

It was a date that she could hardly forget. April 18 was her birthday. Or, more precisely, the date that she was found on the moor.

That evening, in the drawing room, Clare said to Lynn: 'Did Roger mention we're going to my parents for Easter?'

Lynn shook her head.

'I don't suppose he'll want to go now, with his broken leg. I might cancel it. Or I might just take Alex and the twins. Trouble is, Loulou gets car sick. If I left her here with you and Roger, could you hold the fort for a couple of days?'

'Sure,' said Lynn, and sounded quite willing.

'I could ask Sara to help out if you need an evening off.'

'No, I don't think I need her help,' Lynn replied.

Clare noticed how like Vera she sounded at that moment; the dour offhand manner.

'Have you and Sara fallen out?' she asked.

'I don't see her much these days,' said Lynn, evading the question.

'You used to spend so much time there in the summer. I thought you two got on rather well.'

'Yeah, well . . . winter and that,' said Lynn vaguely.

The television news was on, though neither of them was really watching. They watched a report of a plane crash, somewhere in Nepal.

Clare said, 'Is it anything to do with the night you turned up at her house, pissed?'

Lynn's eyes remained fixed on the television. 'She tell you I crashed out on her bed?' There was a trace of a smirk on her face.

'Yes,' said Clare. 'I don't think she was very amused.'

'I bet she wasn't.' Something sardonic in Lynn's tone of voice. 'Did she also tell you she got in bed *with* me? While I was asleep?'

Clare considered that. 'What are you implying?'

'Well, what do you think?'

Clare was about to press her further, but decided she didn't really want to know.

'I just keep out of her way now,' said Lynn, with a faint air of righteousness.

Clare thought about it later, as she was getting ready for bed. Lynn was not the most truthful person in the world. If she were faced with two versions of a story Clare would have opted for Sara's version any day.

And yet it was an odd thing for Lynn to tell lies about.

That night, Sara dreamt that she was standing in front of a hole-in-the-wall cash machine. She was feeding her plastic bank card into it and pressing in numbers, but the machine kept regurgitating it. Strange messages flashed up on the screen that she did not understand.

She looked at her card and saw that it was not a cash card at all: it was a floppy disk, a data disk from her computer.

She tossed it aside and took another disk and fed that into the cash machine and pressed in numbers. More messages flashed up. She pressed in more numbers. The disk came back. But no money.

She tossed that disk aside and tried another. And another. And another. And so on, until she had run out of disks. But still she had no money. She heard a peal of laughter – thin mocking laughter, a woman's laughter. She turned and saw herself. She was looking at her own reflection in the mirror. The beautiful smooth white scalp. It gleamed like marble. It was *she* who was laughing.

The next morning, she went into the studio to start work and found all her data disks scattered untidily across the trestle table.

It reminded her of her dream.

She switched on the computer and inserted a data disk that contained research notes. It was blank. There was not a single item on it. She put in a second disk: that was blank too.

She remembered her dream very clearly ... Putting each disk into the automated teller machine ... The messages on the screen.

Panic began to flutter inside her.

She tried all her disks in turn. Eighteen of them. Each and every one had been wiped clean. Every item of data had been erased – her doctoral thesis, her back-up disks, her research, everything. All obliterated, permanently.

The enormity of what she'd done was so frightening it left her numb. It seemed impossible: to have come down in the night, in her sleep, and reformatted every single disk. Every file, vanished without trace. She was so shocked she could not even cry. She sat there trembling, staring wide-eyed at the empty screen.

Why? Why, why, *why* was it doing this to her? Why was it persecuting her? Her thesis ... Eighteen months' work ... Wiped out.

She wandered into the other room, desperately trying to think. There *had* to be some way of clawing back the lost files ...

But there was none. There was no way of recovering what no longer existed. She knew well enough the warning message that flashed up on the screen: *Formatting disks erases all data permanently*.

Oh Christ, why why why why *why*?

She dropped onto the sofa and wept tears of desperation.

She looked at the shadow on the wall, the damp patch that was never damp.

'Why?' she screamed. 'Why are you doing this?'

Her words bounced off the cold grey stone.

'Tell me *why*!' She bunched her fists and punched her temples. 'Tell me *why*!'

Wild ideas began to fly around her mind like pinballs. It wasn't her, it was Lynn. Lynn had a key. Of course. Lynn made copies of the house keys at Christmas, the keys that Clare had. Yes, Lynn ... Obviously. She was getting in at night, she was doing *all* these things. It was spite, it was hate because Sara knew ... Knew what was going on, knew what she was plotting with Roger against Clare. They were persecuting her ...

Or it was Vera ... The woman was sick, she was mad, she was a witch, she was ill-wishing her. Of course. She'd been ill-wished ...

I'm not mad ...

'I'm not mad!' she screamed at the house.

She jumped off the sofa, raging at the dark patch on the wall.

'You wanna break me, is that it? Like you broke Bryan? Okay, so let's see you. Hah? Show me what you've got! You want a fight? Okay, you're on.'

She marched into the hall, threw open the door of the closet beneath the stairs and pulled a sledge hammer from the rusting heap of tools that Bryan had left.

'Because I'm not *him* ... I'm not a pisshead alky. I am *me*!' She stumbled back into the sitting room, shouting: 'You will show me respect! You will *not* break me. I broke *him*!'

She took a clumsy swing at the shadowy patch on the wall. The hammer head bounced off the granite, the shock of it coursing down through her arms.

'I broke that bastard in pieces, and I will break *you* in pieces! I will eradicate you!' She swung the hammer once more at the damp patch on the wall. 'I will break you in pieces, I will smash you to dust! You get off my back!' She took another swing, and granite chippings flew off the wall. 'You and all the whores from hell don't break me! I break *you*, you hear me?'

She took a further swing, which bounced so violently off the wall that the hammer shuddered clean out of her hands and crashed to the floor.

'You hear me?' she screamed. 'Just like I broke him! Because I am timeless, you hear me?' (Thumping the wall with her bare fists now.) 'I am timeless, damn your eyes! I am here, I am now. But you are dead and you are *nothing*!'

The strength and the breath were draining out of her. She began to collapse down the wall, like a puppet when the strings go slack.

'You are nothing, you hear me? So get out of my life . . .' Her voice was breaking down now. 'Out of my life and leave me alone . . .'

She began to sob.

'Just leave me alone . . .'

She slumped in a heap on the floor and wept.

'Oh, please . . .'

That night she awoke in bed, bathed in sweat.

The next day, she felt lethargic. She found it hard to concentrate on anything. Cold spells, hot spells, they began to alternate. She kept dropping off to sleep. She had so much to think about and yet her worries seemed distant and obscure. It was like trying to focus on far-off objects through a heat haze or take bearings in a mist. She felt worn out, she felt as if a horse had rolled over her.

Tim came to see her. She said she felt ill. She did not mention the computer disks. He had come to talk about shows and movies, their London trip.

'I'll have to back out,' she said. 'I'm sorry. I don't feel up to going anywhere.'

She would not have gone now, anyway, with the way things were between them. But this was a convenient excuse.

He did not seem to know how to handle this. Their disagreement, that stormy weekend, had either dampened his ardour or bruised his self-confidence, she was not sure which. He was behaving like a man who felt that whatever he said or did would only make matters worse.

He took her temperature. He said it was probably flu. A virulent strain was on the rampage, spreading down from the north. She should stay in, keep warm, wrap up, plenty of fluids.

She didn't argue, but this was more than flu. A soporific feeling was taking her over, a creeping sense of languor, seeping into her like some kind of parasitic vapour, preying on her, slowly sucking the energy out of her. She tried telling herself it was psychosomatic, that Tim was right, that she was run-down, too much stress. But it was hard to kid herself that stress produced these kind of shivers that woke her up at nights. It was not her imagination. She was weakening. Something was taking hold.

She fought back, her will against *it*. She forced herself to get up each day and work, she tried to reassemble her Beryan file. But her illness left her feeling so languid, so sleepy. It was hard to remember – to remember what Bryan had written, to remember dates, names, anything. She looked for her written notes. But she was mislaying things. First they were here, then they were there. There were so many papers she would need to reconstruct her thesis – her An Gof papers, her research, her chapter notes, her old essays. She sorted through them carefully. But still she couldn't find her Beryan notes. They were lost. Had she thrown them away by mistake, or come down in the night and destroyed them, just as she'd destroyed her computer files?

Connections ... Through the fog of her mind she knew there were connections she had to make. Devon and Doriels. Doriels in Devon. She kept that alliteration in her mind, tried to focus on it. She had to get out of this place. She had to get to where the information was, the Devon county records. Kadan Doriel was the one she wanted: the Devon connection. Devon, Doriels: Doriels, Devon. She kept saying it, like a mantra. It gave her purpose, direction.

Tim left for London on the Sunday. The following morning, she set off for Exeter. She couldn't face the drive. It was not much more than two hours, but she didn't trust herself to keep awake at the wheel. She drove as far as Penzance and took the train instead.

She knew the county record office in Castle Street, she knew it well; she had spent a lot of time researching there in bygone days – her Gerald days.

The microfiche index culled from the Devon parish registers showed that Kadan Doriel was married to Jayne Weeks at St Melyn, in south Devon, in 1807. They had two children: David, baptized in 1810, and Eliza in 1812.

But the microfiche index did not show burials. For burials, she had to look through films of the old parish registers. She took out the microfilm for St Melyn and wound quickly through to the burials for the year 1812, when Kadan's second child was baptized. She then wound slowly forwards, looking for the name Doriel.

Her eyes were slowly closing. She was beginning to doze off at the microfilm reader. A voice inside her said: Come back another day, it doesn't really matter, none of this ... You're too tired, it's not important, not your business, Clare's problem not yours, you're really too sleepy, pack up now, get the train home, the warm train, and home to bed ...

The librarian touched her shoulder. Sara came to with a jolt. Did she need help? the librarian asked. No, fine, Sara replied. Just fine.

She was staring right at it: 1827. Three Doriels.

Jayne, David and Eliza. All three of them buried on 21 April 1827.

She looked again. That couldn't be right ... All three buried on the same day?

Concentrate ... So hot in here ... Concentrate ...

Yes, it was quite clear: Jayne, wife of Kadan; David, son of Kadan; Eliza, daughter of Kadan, 21 April.

An accident? Cholera, typhus? What could have taken them all in one day? His wife and children, but not Kadan himself.

She wound on, almost to the end of the register.

She found his name the following year, 7 July 1828.

She wrote all these dates down in her notebook and wound off the microfilm.

There was no marriage on record for Kadan's brother, Matthew, neither in Cornwall nor in Devon. He seemed to have disappeared. Was he the link with India, the forebear of Edwin Foster Doriel, Roger's great-grandfather, and grandfather of Adrian?

Somewhere there *had* to be a link ...

It could not have been John, their youngest brother: according to the biography of Sir George Lanberris, the family had abandoned him after his wife's early death, and he had died at Stokeland in north Devon in 1860.

She turned to the register of deaths and looked up Stokeland. It came under the registration district of Barnstaple. Sara began to look through the index of deaths for 1860.

She found a John Doriel of Stokeland Abbey. Died 26 April.

That same week in April. It kept recurring. Again and again.

Kadan's wife and children on the 21st. Ethan Pierce on the 18th. Beryan buried on the 20th.

Adrian Doriel died some time around then too...

She looked him up in the deaths register for Plymouth, Devonport. She found an Adrian Charles Doriel. Died on 20 April 1959.

She looked up his father. The village of Tollford came under Paignton register district.

George Stanley Doriel. Died 19 April 1926.

Again and again... That same week, same month.

She listed all the April deaths. They occurred in 1794, 1827, 1860, 1926 and 1959. Scattered across two centuries. Completely random intervals. Meaningless.

She calculated from Beryan's death in April 1794. Thirty-three years later Kadan's wife and children died in Devon. Thirty-three years later, Kadan's brother, John, died at Stokeland Abbey.

Sixty-six years later, George Doriel died at Tollford. And the barn caught fire at Crowjy and Ethan Pierce was killed.

And thirty-three years after that, Adrian Doriel died in Plymouth.

Thirty-three. That was another figure that kept recurring.

The years were not so random after all.

When she got back to Crowjy she searched through all her papers yet again. This time she found the handwritten notes that she'd made on her previous visit to Truro. She looked at the dates she had noted down for Beryan. Baptized on 28 February 1761. And buried on 20 April 1794.

She died when she was thirty-three.

Her fever was getting worse, not better; sudden attacks of intense sweating, and then violent shivering. They were occurring ever more frequently, day and night. She started vomiting in the night. Her body gave her no warning. She awoke, sat bolt upright in bed and tasted a rush of bile in her throat. She was sick on the floor before she could even swing her legs out of bed. There was blood in her vomit.

She telephoned Clare. Said, Please come round. Said, We have to talk.

Clare was shocked by Sara's appearance – her yellow-grey pallor and the dark hollows around her eyes. It was midmorning. Sara was still in her nightdress and bathrobe. She seemed surprised to see her.

'I'm sorry,' said Clare. 'Did I get you out of bed?'

'No, no, I've been up . . . quite a while,' Sara replied vaguely. 'I just . . . haven't got around to getting dressed.'

Clare was puzzled. Had she misheard? Did Sara say the afternoon? Or did she get the wrong day?

'May I come in?' she asked.

Sara looked confused. 'Sure.'

They went into the sitting room. There was no fire in the grate. Sara switched on a fan heater and sat close to it.

'You look very thin,' said Clare. 'Are you eating?'

Sara shook her head. 'Not hungry. Can't keep anything down, anyway.' Her clothes looked soiled, as if she'd spilled food down herself but hadn't bothered to wipe it off.

'It's kind of you to look in,' she said. 'I was going to phone you.'

'You did phone me.'

Sara looked blank. 'Did I?'

'Yesterday.'

'I'm sorry.' Sara smiled weakly. 'This bloody bug . . . so totally draining.'

'Can I get you anything?'

'I'd love something to drink – tea, coffee, I don't mind.'

Clare went out to the kitchen. The sink was cluttered with dirty pans and dishes. There was an unfinished meal mouldering on the table, and splashes of spilt food and breadcrumbs. There was dried mud on the floor. Charlie's water bowl was empty and there was mould growing on the food encrusted on her feeding dish.

She made some instant coffee and took it back to the sitting room. Sara had dozed off but woke up as Clare walked in.

'You don't look too wonderful.' Clare handed her the cup. 'Are you all right?'

'Mmm.' Sara smiled with drooping eyelids. 'Half asleep, I think.'

Clare sat down.

'How's Roger?'

'Oh, moaning and groaning as usual. He keeps whingeing about the barn not being finished before next winter. I say to him, "Get Shane Pascoe in." There's not that much left to do and he works twice as fast as Roger. "Oh no," he whines, "it'll cost too much, and I can't keep an eye on him." He bucked up a bit when he realized he wouldn't have to come up to Lyme Regis to see my parents at Easter. He hates going there, so this was a perfect excuse to get out of it.'

'Easter so soon. Seems like yesterday it was Christmas.' Sara looked as if she'd lost the thread of what they were talking about. 'It's funny ... I don't remember Christmas.'

'You're not looking very with it,' said Clare. 'Do you want me to go? So you can sleep?'

'No, no, I'm trying to keep awake, not sleep. I need fresh air but I just can't find the energy.'

'Are you getting out at all?'

'I went to Exeter on Monday. That's why I phoned you. I looked up Kadan Doriel's family in the parish records.'

'You've got flu,' Clare admonished her. 'What on earth did you do a stupid thing like that for? No wonder you're not getting any better.'

'It's hard to explain,' said Sara, struggling to concentrate. 'But there's something I'm not supposed to find out. There's something I'm getting close to ... And *Bryan* was getting close to.'

'Are we back on this Beryan thing we talked about?'

'It's getting worse ... Last week I came down in the night, and I erased all the data off my computer disks. And, apart from a strange dream, I didn't know I was doing it. I've destroyed everything. Including my thesis.'

'What do you mean, *destroyed*?' Clare was so shocked she

didn't know what to say. 'How could you destroy your thesis? Does Tim know about this?'

'To hell with Tim,' Sara replied, but without ill-feeling. 'He doesn't take any notice. Something is trying to stop me finding out about Beryan. But I think I'm on to something ... Something cyclical. And it's to do with the Doriels. The last Doriel who farmed at Trevow, Thomas ... His eldest son Kadan must have moved to Devon after the family lost the farm. He was married in the parish of St Melyn, near Newton Abbot. His wife and children were all buried on the same day, on 21st April. And that week in April keeps on recurring. I've written it down in longhand, in case I wipe the disks again. I'll show you. It's like a kind of cycle. All around the 18th of April.'

She was beginning to sound short of breath. And sweat was breaking out across her face.

'Take it easy,' said Clare, 'slow down, take a break a minute.'

Sara dabbed her brow with a handkerchief.

'But there's one gap. Between 1860 and 1926.'

'What *are* you talking about?'

'If something was happening to the family every thirty-three years, then something should have happened that year – I don't know what, but there must be something in the history somewhere ...'

She was running out of breath and her face was quite wet with perspiration. She looked completely lost and put a hand to her forehead, trying to collect her thoughts. She pointed over her shoulder towards the studio. 'It's in my notes ... I'll show you.'

Her face crumpled.

'What is it?' said Clare.

Sara clutched her belly. 'I'm sorry, I've started getting these attacks of nausea ...'

She got up and shuffled weakly towards the door and up the stairs. Clare heard the bathroom door close. A few minutes later she heard the lavatory flush and then the bathroom door opened. She heard Sara's footsteps on the ceiling above, in her bedroom.

She waited a little while. When Sara did not come down, Clare went upstairs to her bedroom. Sara was lying down with her eyes closed. Clare drew closer and listened. She was asleep.

Clare went back downstairs, washed the dishes that were lying in the sink, and mopped the kitchen floor. Before she left, she went back upstairs. Sara was still sleeping. Some of the colour had returned to her face. Her breathing seemed easy and regular.

She went into the studio and looked at the sheets of scribbled notes that littered the trestle table. They all seemed to be history papers. Perhaps she was trying to reconstruct her thesis. But in the middle of the table, on a single sheet of paper, Sara had scrawled in red, in large bold numerals: *1893?*

1893. Sara was sure there had to be something . . .

She started out for the Cornish Studies Library at Redruth first thing the next morning, to look through microfilms of the old newspapers.

The fever ambushed her, pounced on her out of nowhere, leapt on her like some rabid animal. She could feel her temperature rising over a stretch of several miles. She broke sweat. A headache was coming on. It began to bite harder and harder, a blinding pain behind the forehead. She resisted, she fought back. But the road ahead was starting to shimmer, like a mirage in the desert. Her vision began to swim, the Tarmac became molten, it flowed like a river. She had a burning sensation in her throat. Sweat was rolling down off her brow and trickling into her eyes. She braked and swerved off the carriageway, onto the hard shoulder, and slammed on her brakes. She heard a truck horn blasting hotly somewhere close by. She slumped forward onto the steering wheel and sat there for a while.

She opened the door, to let in some cool air. It was a blustery April day, a keen southeasterly blowing. She clambered out and leaned against the side of the car breathing in deep lungfuls of air. Her underclothes felt wet with sweat. She took out a handkerchief and wiped her face.

She could feel her body cooling down rapidly. Her vision began to clear and the spearing headache began to release its grip. It melted away until it was no more than a dull pain over the eyes. The attack had passed. She felt wrung out, exhausted. Her nose felt swollen and blocked. She put her handkerchief to it and blew. She looked down. The handkerchief was wet with dark blood.

And now the shivers took her. Grabbed her body in its fist and shook her like a sack of skittles, rattled her teeth like dice in a shaker. She sat in the car with the heater blasting.

She battled on to Redruth.

She felt a small glow of satisfaction. One tiny triumph. It was gutless, this thing, a petty thug, a mugger lurking up a dark alley, too scared to show its face.

She left the Beetle in the central car park and walked to the library. She sat upstairs, looking through the microfilm of the 1893 editions of the *Cornishman* and the *West Briton*. Then the *Western Morning News* and the *Cornish Guardian*. But there was no mention of the name Doriel, no obituaries of anyone of that name.

She went back to the microfilm of the *Cornishman* and wound through to the middle of April, and turned slowly forwards for a second time. She stopped looking for the name Doriel and ran her eyes over each and every news item instead.

She found what she was looking for. A very short article hidden away on page seven of the edition for 23 April 1893. Beneath the headline, PIGS DIE IN BLAZE, the *Cornishman* reported:

> A fire caused severe damage to buildings at the farm of Mr Chegwidden on Trevow Hill, Boskinnow Downs, on Saturday night. The fire was first seen by Mrs Chegwidden when she was woken in the early hours of Saturday morning by the barking of the dogs.
>
> Despite the best efforts of Mr Chegwidden and his family to extinguish the flames, the milking sheds, buttery and piggery on the west side of the yard were burned down. Three sows died in the fire and a number of animals suffered injury and were later destroyed by a veterinary surgeon. The cause of the fire is not known.

Sara counted backwards from the date of publication to the night of the fire. If the 23rd was a Thursday then the previous Saturday was the 18th. The fire broke out in the small hours of Saturday, 18 April.

She took a photocopy of the page.

She wanted to copy the article about the death of Adrian Doriel as well, from the *Cornish and Devon Post*. She changed the microfilm and wound quickly through to April 1959. She was turning the reel so quickly that she wound on too far and found herself in the middle of the 8 May edition. She glimpsed the headline: CATTLE VIRUS: NANSGEVER QUARANTINE.

By the time it registered with her, she had already begun to wind back. She stopped and wound slowly forwards until she came to that headline again. She read through the article.

Clare had mentioned this before ... It was why the last farmer had been forced to sell Trevow, and why the farm had been derelict all those years until she and Roger bought it. A large herd of Guernsey cows had been slaughtered after an outbreak of disease. According to this article, the disease had not yet been identified. The cattle were bleeding to death from intestinal haemorrhage. Ministry of Agriculture veterinary officers had placed Trevow Farm under quarantine.

She sat in the studio that night, studying her notes. She felt a mixture of fear and exhilaration. She was getting closer all the time. It was an unending cycle.

Beryan had died in April 1794, aged thirty-three.

Ever since then, something had happened to the Doriel family every thirty-three years. Always around 18 April.

Sara calculated forwards. If the previous cycle date had been around 18 April 1959, then the next one would be this year: 18 April 1992.

It was ten days away. It was Easter weekend.

It was also her birthday.

And she would be thirty-three.

BODY AND SOUL

She lay shivering in bed, hugging the duvet with the hunger of a lover. Her body quaked, her teeth chattered. Fear seeped through her like icy water, trickled everywhere inside her, filled her with cold panic. She felt so helpless. Where could she go from here? She felt like a swimmer in the sea, miles from land and her strength had gone. She felt time closing in, swimming circles round her, ever tighter, like a shark.

She was drifting off to sleep at all hours, day and night. She never heard the telephone, but messages appeared on her answering machine. From the estate agents, from Tim, from Richard McCormack's secretary.

The shrink . . . She had forgotten all about the shrink. Was it this week, her appointment, or next? She looked in her diary. She had not made a note of it. She picked the phone book off the window ledge to look up McCormack's number. It was an old phone book, kept in the kitchen; the newer edition was in the sitting room. A lot of names and numbers had been jotted down on the cover, all in Bryan's handwriting. As she slapped the book down on the kitchen table, she noticed *Stokeland 79641* right in the middle of the cover. Bryan had circled it.

Stokeland. It was so familiar but . . . It was as if a mist had come down inside her head. Why was she looking at this phone book? Who was she trying to call?

She went back into the sitting room and through to the studio and looked through her notes. Stokeland . . .

There it was: Stokeland Abbey. It was where John Doriel had died in 1860.

She looked up the code for Stokeland and dialled the number. It began to ring. What was she going to say? Did you know anyone called Bryan Carhays? It could have been years ago.

A man answered. 'St Eyot's.'

'I'm sorry,' said Sara, 'I was ringing Stokeland Abbey.'

'This *is* Stokeland Abbey,' he replied. 'The Brotherhood of St Eyot.'

'I'm wondering if you could help me,' said Sara. 'I'm enquiring about a man who died at the abbey in 1860. This must sound a strange question but ... Would you have any record of his death? His name was John Doriel.'

'We have an office that deals with public enquiries,' the man replied in a kindly voice. 'But it's only open between two o'clock and four. If you would like to call back later and ask for Brother Stephen ... ?'

She telephoned again just after two. Brother Stephen had been forewarned of her enquiry. He explained that St Eyot's was a religious institution, and anyone who died at the abbey would either have been in holy orders or a novitiate reading to take holy orders. The records showed that there had never been a member of the order by the name of John Doriel. If it was so long ago, it was possible that he might have been what used to be known as a 'penitent' at the abbey, but there was no official register of 'penitents' as such, so it was not possible to check.

'What do you mean by a penitent?' asked Sara.

'They were laymen,' said Brother Stephen, 'who entered St Eyot's to devote themselves to a life of penitence and work within the abbey. Those who had no trade simply laboured on the farm and in the gardens. Few returned to the outside world.'

She was losing track of what he was saying. She was feeling exhausted and confused. She had forgotten why she was speaking to this man. She had forgotten who he was. She could feel her temperature rising. She was breaking sweat. Her head was beginning to ache. Was she speaking to the library, Redruth library? She was sure Redruth had something to do with this ... Was it cattle disease?

'Is this the library?' she asked.

A fierce migraine pain across her head made her gasp.

Brother Stephen paused, completely thrown by her question, 'Is, er, is what the library?' he asked.

She was desperately trying to remember. But this pain behind her forehead ... And the heat in here ...

'I'm sorry,' she murmured, 'I'm not feeling very well.'

'You asked about John Doriel,' said Brother Stephen patiently.

That sounded familiar. She looked down at the notes in her lap. Her vision was beginning to fog over.

Think . . . Concentrate . . .

'He died at the abbey,' she said, 'in 1860. Is there any way I could find out *how* he died? And whether he had relatives who might have been informed?'

'I couldn't possibly say,' said Brother Stephen. 'Deaths were usually recorded in the abbey archives. But they're kept in another part of the building. I could look in the archive for you if you have an exact date. But it would take me a few days. Perhaps you could telephone me next week?'

Why? Why must I phone him? Who is he, this man? The pain was boring through her head like a red-hot skewer. Her face was running with sweat. *Concentrate . . . Think . . .*

'If you could tell me the precise date?' Brother Stephen prompted her gently.

She looked down at her notepad. The words were beginning to swim. She brushed moisture from her eyes with her forefinger.

'1860,' she read. 'April 26th.'

Why am I saying this? What is this date? Why am I talking to this man?

'I'll see if I can find any mention of him,' said Brother Stephen. 'Perhaps you could call me on Monday or Tuesday?'

'Mon or Tues', she scrawled on her notepad. *Call whom?*

'I'm sorry, I've got the flu,' she said. She paused to try to collect her thoughts. 'Who did I . . . ? Who do I call?'

'Just ask for me. Brother Stephen.'

She scribbled that down too. She had already written that name on the page. Why was it there before?

She felt something running out of her nose, down over her lips. A drop of blood fell splat onto her notepad.

'Perhaps I might take a note of your name and number?' he suggested.

'Yes, of course . . .'

What number? A larger gout of blood dripped onto her notepad. *What is my number? Think, for Christ's sake, concentrate . . .*

'Sara Carhays,' she said. She wiped more moisture from her eyes and read the number from the telephone.

'I'll see what I can find out for you,' he replied.

She thanked him, apologized again and put the phone down. She sniffed the blood back into her nose and angled her head back. She put her notepad down on the chair arm, but it fell off and dropped to the floor. She got up to go upstairs to the bathroom but her legs had no strength. She felt dizzy and her feet seemed to sink through the floor as if they were stuck in quicksand. She felt herself falling, folding up like a clay vase sagging and collapsing on the potter's wheel.

When she came to, she was lying on the hall floor. The pain in her head had gone. The feverish spell had passed. Her clothes were damp inside. She went back into the sitting room. The telephone was on the floor; the handset had fallen off. Her notebook was on the floor. She picked it up and looked at the page. There was blood on it.

Who was Brother Stephen?

She looked at herself in the bedroom mirror. Her flesh was the colour of old parchment. It looked obscene, stretched taut across the bony washboard of her ribs. She was scarcely eating. And when she did eat, she felt so sick she couldn't finish whatever it was she had wasted energy preparing. She looked in the kitchen. She was out of bread and milk and cat food. She forced herself to drive into Boskinnow.

There was a queue at the counter in Treneer's. She had not collected her newspapers for several days. Other women stepped out of her way as she walked back through the shop. They gave her unpleasant looks, as if she smelt. Perhaps she did. Perhaps they were staring at the smooth pale flesh below the line of her knitted hat.

Why don't I snatch it off? Look, girls, no dandruff.

Outside, she felt a twinge of nausea. She rested a moment by the side wall of the shop. There were people passing by.

Please God, don't make me sick here, not here. Everyone staring.

She walked along the road towards a patch of waste ground by the derelict chapel, where her car was parked. Her heart was pumping faster. That migraine pain began to skewer through her head again, that twist of barbed wire behind the eyes. Sweat broke out across her face. She felt dizzy and breathless. Her lungs felt glued together, a burning sensation spread down her throat to her lungs.

She was approaching an old woman, the old biddy she had seen so many times before, Rebecca Pierce. The two women stopped and looked at each other. Rebecca had the ruddy weathered complexion of an East European peasant. Her flesh was wrinkled and time-worn, like reptile skin. Yet her eyes were a clear and delicate blue. She reminded Sara of the fish jousters of Newlyn who appeared in old photographs.

Nausea swept over Sara in a rush. She was sick on the ground where she stood. She had eaten so little these past few days but the mere action of vomiting was exhausting. She leaned against the chapel wall and closed her eyes. She was beginning to shiver again.

When she opened her eyes, Rebecca was still staring at her. Sara brushed the vomit off her mouth with a tissue. She felt ashamed. The pain bored deeper into her skull.

'I'm sorry,' she mumbled. 'I'm not well.'

Rebecca said nothing.

'I'll be all right,' said Sara. 'I've got my car. I live just along the valley. Not far.'

'Oh, I know where you live,' Rebecca replied. Her voice cracked like dry twigs. 'I've seen 'ee thear many times.'

The old woman's gaze was hard and accusing. But there was a trace of pity in her eyes as well.

'I've been seeing you thear all my life long, my dear,' she said. 'I was afraid once. But now I'm too old. I just wish to God you'd find peace.'

She walked on, along the village street. Sara stood leaning against the chapel wall, uncomprehending. Faces were watching her, from doorsteps, from cottage windows. They were still watching as she walked slowly back to the car and climbed in.

What did the old woman mean? *Wish to God you'd find peace.*

The silent faces were still watching as she drove away through the village. *All my life long?* Was she senile?

When she got back to Crowjy she found frozen food defrosting on the kitchen table – food she didn't want and had no memory of taking out of the freezer. The next day she found letters waiting to be posted, letters she had no memory of writing. She looked at the addresses: her bank and Bryan's solicitor. She could not remember writing any letters. She opened them. The envelopes were empty.

Small segments of her life were being erased from her mind. Her memory was a film that someone was editing behind her back, snip-snip, scraps on the cutting-room floor. Sometimes it was just a few moments that were lost, sometimes it was an hour or more. She began to confuse mornings with afternoons. Days seemed to be drifting by and merging into one another without distinction. Time was playing tag with her. Time was a scallywag; now she saw him, now she didn't. Time was a three-card trick, time was Spot the Lady. Time shifted before her eyes but she never saw the hands move.

Thoughts flickered through her head. Her mind was like a lamp that was running out of oil.

It was taking her over, taking possession, weakening her, wasting her body, her mind, destroying her, just as it had destroyed Bryan before her.

Once you have known it, you cannot unknow it.
Once you have touched her, there is no return.
It is out of Eden.

Tim was home by Saturday afternoon. He phoned Crowjy but got no reply. He drove along to the barn-cottage. He rang the bell several times but there was no response. He peered through the letterbox. He called inside.

'Sara? It's Tim.'

Silence.

He walked around the side of the house and through the garden to the back door. It was unlocked. He opened it and put his head inside.

'Sara . . .?'

He stepped into the hall passage and closed the door. He looked in the kitchen. Charlie came padding towards him across the table, mewing noisily and hoisting her tail high, rubbing her flanks against his outstretched hand. He looked down at her food tray. It was empty. He wondered when she had last been fed.

It was not warm in here. He touched the side of the Rayburn.

It was cool. He looked inside the furnace; it had almost burnt out.

He walked along the passage, glanced into the sitting room and went upstairs, into Sara's bedroom. She was lying on the bed, on her side, rolled up in the duvet.

The curtains were closed. The room smelt of unwashed linen and stale air. He sat on the side of the bed and put a hand to her brow. She felt cold but damp.

Her eyelids flickered. She made a sleepy murmuring noise.

'Sara, it's Tim.' He took her hand. 'Can you hear me?'

'Mm.'

'Can you speak to me? Are you in pain at all?'

'Mmm.' She shook her head a little.

'I'm going down to get my bag, all right? I'll be back in a minute.'

He hurried downstairs, outside to his car, took his bag from the boot and came back up to her room.

She was lying on her back now, brushing sleep out of her eyes. He washed his hands in the bathroom, put a thermometer under her tongue and felt her pulse.

Her temperature was 102. Her heart rate was 90.

Her blood pressure was high: 140 over 105.

He began to examine her. While he looked in her eyes and probed her glands, she told him about the sudden attacks, the fierce headaches, the fast rises in temperature, the heavy sweating, the chills, the burning sensation in her throat, the nose bleeds, the disorientation, the lapses of memory.

The fever and the rigor he could put down to flu. It was the intermittent nature and the suddenness of the attacks that troubled him – the nose-bleeds, the short, sharp headaches, and the burning sensation in her throat and lungs.

'We'll get a full blood count,' he said, 'and take some samples. I think we're dealing with two separate things. I think you've got flu, but there's something else besides. Either a secondary infection or possibly some kind of poisoning. When was the well water last tested?'

She shook her head and closed her eyes.

'In that case, we'll take a water sample,' he said, 'and get it analysed.'

*

She heard him, she understood him, but she just didn't have the strength to argue. She didn't even have the breath to speak. All she wanted was sleep. Sleep, sweet sleep. Too tired, too drained. It was sucking the life out of her, secretly, insidiously, invading her, filling her, stealing her, devouring her, body and soul . . .

Clare was in Truro that weekend, browsing round the auction rooms. There was to be a large sale of paintings and antique furniture the following week. Today was a public viewing day.

She bought a catalogue. Roger was grumbling about money again – the cost of the barn and the new stable block – but she was looking for something for the drawing room. They had so few paintings and there was a large empty space on the wall now that she had taken down Bryan's picture of the menhir and the dark pond.

She was not much taken with anything here. There were a lot of pictures of sailing ships, of fishing boats and harbours, of stormy seascapes, of dark Victorian wrecks and rain-lashed lighthouses. There were paintings of trams hissing through drizzle in Victorian Camborne, of preacher Bill Bray the Twelveheads miner, of Prussia Cove and Pendennis Point, of Lanhydrock House and Tintagel Head.

And one picture by Bryan.

She found it tucked away in a corner. It was dated 1988. It was a woodland scene. At first glance it appeared sweet and pastoral, a picture for the children's nursery. But on closer inspection it was a nasty surreal wood, a nightmare world of vicious little animals, subtly deformed, sabre-toothed and tiger-clawed. In the middle of the picture was a clearing. And in the centre of the clearing was a standing stone, rather like the holed menhir in the painting she had bought from Bryan. The stone was upright. It was solid stone at the base, but as it rose up, it metamorphosed from stone into human flesh and merged into the body of a woman. By the time it reached her chest, it was entirely woman . . . Or some *sort* of woman.

She was like the creature Sara had described. Her face dominated the picture, pale and expressionless. She had no hair. Not even eyebrows. Her lips were beautifully detailed but a pale lilac colour. She had arms, slender arms that reached down, her hands pressed flat to her body on either side of her groin, where the hole in the stone lay.

She had no fingertips. The stumps of her fingers were bleeding. The blood was trickling down the granite.

But it was the face that was so striking. It was Sara's face.

Clare looked up the lot number in the catalogue and read: *Bryan Carhays. 'Beryan.'*

Ferocious head pains hit her without warning, stabbed her through the temple, hot as bullets, sniper fire out of nowhere. They were so painful they made her sick. And when she was sick she brought up more blood. The blood made her throat burn, the burning made her sweat, and the sweating made her cold. Her feet were ice cold sometimes, she lost all feeling in her toes and the tips of her fingers.

Days and nights they were all one now, a stream of time pocked with blanks and holes and darknesses. She heard voices in the wind that whined through the cracks in the doors and the windows. When the fever had hold of her, her mind was a swamp, it was jungle and steam and confusion. There were times when she was lucid and would pick up the phone to call Clare or Tim, but then the light would go out in her mind, as if someone threw a switch or blew the fuses, and she forgot whom she was calling or why. Her thoughts collided and stalled, like traffic in gridlock on the streets of an alien city.

She was forgetting things that were second nature to her; she was forgetting to bath, forgetting to brush her teeth. Food was turning bad in the fridge and beginning to smell but she no longer noticed. Soiled laundry was piling up. When the washing machine was full she forgot to switch it on. Trickles of dried vomit accumulated on her nightdress where she was sick down herself. There were bloodstains on her sheets.

She was beginning to hallucinate. She was downstairs, feeling dizzy, her mind was out of focus, as if part of her were somewhere else. She stopped in the sitting-room doorway and stared, bewildered.

A young man was clambering unsteadily to his feet. His trousers were unbuttoned, hanging round his thighs. His braces were dangling, his shirt tails loose. He looked as if he were drunk. He looked at her, framed in the doorway, and said, 'Annie . . . ?' in such a puzzled tone of voice. She could smell something smouldering. He staggered to one side, as if he had lost his balance.

'Dear Loord, I'm took claf here, girl. I'm sweaten like a hog.'

Curls of smoke began to drift up from his hair. She could hear a faint crackling sound, like the burning of straw.

A skinny-looking girl with mousy hair sat by the hearth. She wore nothing but a pair of cut-down jeans. She was holding a sleeveless cheesecloth blouse close to the fire; steam was curling off it. Beside the girl was a shoulder-bag of wool or hessian in an Aztec design. She had beads in her hair and little goat bells hanging from a long leather necklace.

At that moment, the floor she stood on melted away beneath her feet and she sank into oblivion.

Then she was in bed and it was night. She heard motorbikes outside, approaching up the track. She looked out of the window but there was nothing there.

The next day she could not remember whether she had really heard them or had only dreamt them. The real and the surreal were slowly merging, so that she was no longer sure what was actually happening in her life and what was merely in her mind.

Tim kept coming to see her. He said soothing things. She tried to talk, the words got jumbled, her thoughts got twisted, he shushed her, wouldn't let her talk, took her temperature and her blood pressure. Every morning, every evening, he came and went, swam around in her vision, like a face under water.

She had things to tell him, urgent desperate things, trapped in her head like shadows, she was struggling with them, had to tell him, had to warn him, still time . . .

But Tim shushing her, smiling. Must rest. Shush and more shush. Lie still, just a fever, doing fine.

So hot, so cold, so tired, so sleepy. The spirit inside her saying, Let him go, we don't need him, we have each other. So soothing, so soft, so cold. Replicating inside her, like a retrovirus, invading her cells, swarming and spawning, massing and merging. Body and soul.

*

Tim had helped himself to her front-door key so that he could let himself in. He was visiting her twice a day. She was getting worse each time he saw her. By Sunday evening her temperature was hovering around the 104 mark. Her blood pressure was 130 over 115.

He called the West Cornwall hospital at Penzance to see whether they had a bed for her. They were full to overflowing with influenza patients, particularly the elderly, many dangerously ill. They said they'd get back to him in the morning.

By the morning she was conscious but slipping away into a shallow sleep every few moments. She was mumbling, not very coherently, and in obvious distress. He called West Cornwall. They said they would take her on Tuesday. He called the Royal Cornwall hospital at Truro. They had no beds. Their intensive care unit was full and they were referring anything but the most acute emergencies to Plymouth.

By Monday evening her blood pressure was up to 160 over 120, and her heart rate was 120. He sat with Sara for an hour but then he was called out to yet another flu victim and didn't see her again until the following morning.

That night, a man appeared in the bedroom doorway. He stood watching her. He had shoulder-length hair, rain-drenched and glossy black, with sideburns that reached to his jawbone. He wore an oil-streaked denim jerkin over a biker's leather jacket. His ragged jeans were soaked with rain. There were thick studded leather bands around his wrists and chunky silver rings on his fingers.

He opened her legs.

'Gonna love this, Tchoolip.'

She looked down at her body. From her chest to her belly, her flesh was turning a strange colour. A wine-red rash had begun to spread across her body.

'Gonna see shooting stars. Gonna be all psychedelic . . .'

The heat was suffocating. She sat up and vomited blood down herself.

She could hear horses' hooves coming softly up the muddy track.

Somewhere, the snicker of a horse.

*

Tim found her in the morning, flat out on the bed, almost naked, the duvet on the floor. She was lying in blood and vomit. Her upper body was covered with a deep red rash. The arterioles – the smaller blood vessels – were haemorrhaging. Blood had been leaking from her ears, her nose, her eye sockets. She was making faint, delirious, murmuring sounds.

He ran downstairs and called the West Cornwall hospital to warn them he was bringing her in now.

He went back upstairs and wrapped her in the duvet. With the blood vessels constricted, the circulation was gradually dropping. He picked up her hand. Her fingers were already turning black.

It was early evening. Clare and Roger had finished dinner. Alex was in the drawing room, watching television. Lynn was upstairs with the twins. Tim called in on his way home. He had spoken on the phone to the medical registrar at the West Cornwall hospital. Sara's condition was no worse and no better. Her temperature was 106, but they had stopped the haemorrhaging. She was in isolation, attached to a heart monitor but breathing without a ventilator.

'Do they have any idea what it is?' asked Clare.

'Not yet. They're running every possible test.'

'But is it infectious, this thing?' said Roger, more worried about the children than Sara.

'Impossible to say. It could be an opportunistic infection, catching her when her immune system's worn down by flu. Or it could be something toxic that she's been ingesting – maybe from the well water.'

'Such as?'

'All kinds of toxins can drain down to the valley with the rainfall. Agricultural chemicals get dumped, insecticides leak into streams. Organic phosphates cause heavy sweating, fatigue, lethargy. DDT and chlordane cause hallucinations and delirium. And there's contaminated waste in the old mine shafts at Wheal Bran.'

'But they haven't mined at Wheal Bran for a hundred years or more,' said Clare.

'That's partly the problem,' Tim replied. 'Mineral waste in

the abandoned shafts takes decades to work through to the streams and rivers.'

'Well, do they know what they're doing over there?' asked Roger, and jabbed a thumb in the vague direction of Penzance.

'They're very good but they haven't got all the facilities they need. They'll move her to the Royal Cornwall as soon as her condition stabilizes.'

'How do you rate her chances?' said Roger.

Tim made a vague gesture. 'When I found her this morning, I didn't have much hope. But they've managed to dilate the arterioles, which has brought the blood pressure and the heart rate down, and checked the haemorrhaging. Her circulation's a little better. But they couldn't save her fingers. They had to amputate the top joints.'

Clare put her hands to her ears and turned away, sickened.

'Is she conscious?' asked Roger.

'When she's not asleep she's delirious.'

'We're going away for Easter,' said Clare. 'Should we cancel it?'

'Why?' said Tim. 'You're not going abroad, are you?'

'Only to my parents at Lyme.'

'No, you go. Nothing you can do to help her.' Tim turned to Roger. 'Are you going too?'

Roger shook his head. 'Not with this.' He tapped on his plaster cast with his knuckles. 'Can't get it in the bloody car.'

Clare followed Tim outside and accompanied him across the yard. 'The last time we talked about her,' she said, 'you thought her problems were all in her mind.'

It was a fine mild night. Tim walked unhurriedly and glanced up at the stars.

'I still think they are, to some extent.'

The truth was, he didn't know what to think. He felt threatened, thwarted, pushed back on the defensive. The basic tenets of scientific method were like a framework for him, around which he structured his approach to medicine. But something was reaching out and shaking that framework, shaking it to the very rivets.

'Did she show you that chapter in the Reverend Lanarth's diaries about farmer Thomas Doriel in 1797?'

Tim said no, without thinking, but then remembered. 'Oh,

yes. A scruffy old book. Why do you ask?'

'It just struck me, the coincidence. The disease he talked about, that burned the throat and caused bleeding.'

'That was probably ergot poisoning,' said Tim. 'They called it the burning disease. It's practically unheard of in this country today.'

'I'm only saying it struck me, the coincidence.'

They came to the front of the house where Tim's Rover was parked.

Clare said, 'She told me about the papers that she found torn up and burnt in the Rayburn. Some sort of journal that Bryan was writing.'

Tim nodded. 'I saw the remains.'

'This obsession he had with Beryan ... You know she found a Beryan in the parish records?'

'Yes, she told me.'

'And she thinks Bryan was looking through the parish records too.'

Tim leaned against the car, resting his elbows on the roof. It was already damp with dew. He looked out across the moonlit downs that spread east across the valley towards Nancledra.

'What else did she tell you?' he asked.

'That she'd erased all her computer files.'

Tim's face creased up. 'She *what*?'

'All her computer disks. Her thesis, everything. She thinks that something is trying to stop her finding out the truth.'

'The truth about what?'

'About Beryan. She thinks there's something there, in the house, that's doing this.'

'You see, I told you,' said Tim. 'I should have insisted she saw a local psychiatrist, not waited to see this man in Plymouth.'

'But Bryan told you there was something there at Crowjy, didn't he?'

'He was hallucinating. He saw terrible things.'

'While you were away in London, she went to the Devon records office in Exeter. She was trying to find links between the Doriels at Trevow, the Doriels in Devon, and the Doriels that Roger's descended from.'

'What the hell *for*?' said Tim, exasperated. 'What did she

think she was playing at? She should have been at home in bed.'

'The next day, she called me and asked me to go and see her. She was quite agitated about something. She wanted to go through her notes with me. Something to do with the 18th April.'

'This coming 18th? Saturday, you mean? Her birthday?'

'No, no, she was talking about something historical. Kadan Doriel's wife and children, she mentioned. I didn't quite understand. She was beginning to gabble. Something about a cycle. And a gap in the cycle. And Bryan was on to it, as well, she said.'

'It all keeps coming back to bloody Bryan,' said Tim. 'He's the cause of all this guilt, and this silly Beryan business. I'm glad he's not alive now, because he and I would have such a God almighty row.'

'But doesn't it ever occur to you to wonder,' said Clare, just a little exasperated herself, '*why* Bryan was so obsessed with Beryan? She obviously wasn't a fantasy, Sara's proved that. And Vera Roscarrock told you there was something unpleasant at Crowjy.'

'Vera's a religious nutcase.'

'You see, this is what upsets Sara. Any time anyone mentions this, you say they're drunk or mad.'

'Vera's a crackpot. She thinks she's got arthritis because God's punishing her. I've offered her a referral for hip replacement but she doesn't want it because she thinks pain is God's way of purifying her for heaven. Can you credit it?'

'Because she's very religious doesn't mean she's mad.'

'I can't believe we're having this conversation, Clare,' he said, getting irritated. 'I'm a doctor. I practise medicine. I work from a rational basis. I can't bugger around worrying about old widows' babble and superstitious claptrap.'

'It's not *all* claptrap.'

'Oh, come *off* it. Not you too? I thought I could count on you, at least.'

'You just told me that Sara had lost the tops of her fingers.'

'There was no circulation to the extremities. They were gangrenous.'

'So what was Bryan? A prophet?'

'What are you talking about?'

'On Saturday afternoon, I went to a preview for the art auctions in Truro this week. I saw one of Bryan's paintings there. It was a picture of a menhir in a wood. The lower half was stone, the upper half was woman. And the woman was unmistakably Sara.'

'What of it? Bryan was in love with her – or so she says. She broke his heart, or so she says. He wrote about her coming from a womb of stone.'

'In this painting,' said Clare, 'the tips of her fingers had been cut off.'

Tim took a moment to absorb that. 'How do you mean?' He looked uneasy.

'There was a hole in the middle of this stone – like the stone she told us about on Bodmin Moor, and like the stone in the woods. Her hands were lying flat on either side of this hole. The fingers were splayed and bleeding. The top joint of each finger was missing. And blood was trickling down the stone.'

Tim was remembering another picture like it – one of the two where Bryan had used Lynn as a model; the one in which she was peeling an apple and had cut off the top joints of her fingers.

'This painting at the preview,' Clare added, 'was dated 1988. And it was called *Beryan*.'

Tim had been troubled by so many coincidences these past few months: the case of the Dutch girl with her strange skin condition; the welts that had appeared on Sara's back; the bleeding on New Year's Eve; Vera's account of the barn fire and the death of Ethan Pierce; the sudden death of Clare's dog in the pool. He had managed to keep fending them off, pushing them aside into a dark corner where he didn't have to think about them, where they didn't complicate normality, mess up the existing complexities of everyday life. But now there was no room left in the dark corners. They were filling up, and the inexplicables and the coincidences were spilling out all over the place.

'Clare,' he said wearily, 'I'm carrying about as much as I can carry right now. Sara's fighting for her life. I can't give you all the answers. I'm not sure I can even give you *any* answers. But talking about this kind of thing isn't going to help.'

He took out his keys and climbed into the car.
He lowered the window as he started the car.
'When are you off to Dorset?'
'Good Friday.'
'Well, I'll call you as soon as there's any improvement.'

He stopped at the barn-cottage on his way home. He still had Sara's door keys. There was a dreadful smell in the house. He threw open the windows and wedged open the front and back doors.

He walked slowly round the house and took a look at all the mess. There was enough soiled laundry scattered around to fill the washing machine three or four times over. The bedlinen and the mattress were so fouled they were past redemption; they would have to go to the council dump or be burnt.

The decomposing remains of an abandoned meal lay on the kitchen table, turning furry with mould. He took a bin liner from the broom closet and threw the whole lot, crockery and all, into the bag in case the health inspectors wanted to analyse samples from the kitchen. He added the contents of the bread bin, the vegetable rack, the fruit bowl, and anything else that would rot. He left the contents of the fridge and the freezer for the time being.

He fed Charlie. Clare had offered to look after her at Trevow, but she'd run away the last time, so he was going to take her back to his house.

He went into the sitting room and looked down at the telephone. There were five messages waiting on the answering machine. He played them back. Two were from the estate agents in Hayle. One was from Southwest Electricity. Another was from Richard McCormack's secretary in Plymouth.

The final message was from a man who said: 'Mrs Carhays? This is Brother Stephen at Stokeland Abbey. I have some information on John Doriel, if you'd like to call me, thank you.'

Tim walked through to the studio, tore a sheet from one of her notebooks and scribbled a reminder for himself to call the estate agents, the power engineers, and Richard McCormack.

He sat down at her work table and looked dispiritedly at the blank computer screen. He thought about all the work she had put into her thesis. He thought back to last spring, their first afternoon here together, their trip to the Minack, their summer walks on the moors, their weekend sailing trips, Florida, everything. For the first time, it began to cave in on top of him. He wondered what he would do if she died. He had a GP's way of distancing himself emotionally from the dead and the dying. He had never lost anyone he was very close to. He glanced over the small piles of books and plastic-covered files that were laid out across the table in front of him. He flipped open one of the files – thesis research, Xerox copies, scribbled notes.

All this work. Probably for nothing.

He flipped open another file and found several loose pages of notes and jottings, and a number of photocopies. He moved the file closer and studied a single sheet of A3 paper on which Sara had drawn a large circle.

In the centre of the circle she had written: *Beryan. 20.4.1794.*

Lines radiated out from the centre like the spokes of a wheel. Where each spoke touched the outer circle she had made a note of some event – most frequently a death – together with a date.

Working his way clockwise around the circle, from a position of about two o'clock, Tim read:

Kadan's family died, 21.4.1827.

John died, 26.4.1860.

Trevow (fire) 18.4.1893.

Ethan died, 18.4.26.

Adrian's father died, 19.4.26.

Adrian found dead, 20.4.59.

Cattle deaths, Trevow, April/May 59.

At the top of the circle Sara had written simply: *18.4.1992.* Just the date. Nothing else.

That was this coming Saturday. Easter weekend.

He looked through the photocopies. They were all from old newspaper reports: a fire at Trevow in April 1893; the death of Ethan Pierce in a barn fire at Nansgever in April 1926; the death of George Doriel in Tollford, Devon, April 1926; Ministry of Agriculture inspectors quarantine Trevow farm, cattle disease, May 1959.

Tim read that last article right through. Cattle were haemorrhaging, bleeding from the mouth, the nostrils, the eyes, the ears, the rectum. They took up to forty-eight hours to die from the onset of symptoms.

He remembered what Clare had said about the cattle disease in bygone times. He got up from the table and went back into the sitting room. He searched the bookshelves and found the Edwardian reprint that had no covers. He glanced through the table of contents:

Chapter eighteen: starvation and potato blight; corn shortages; murrain and poverty in the Nansgever valley . . .

He turned to chapter eighteen. January 1797. He read aloud:
'"... Cattle are dying for lack of feed or are sick with the murrain. I have witnessed the pitiful sight of oxen in their death throes, blood flowing from mouth and nostrils, their eyes wide with terror and suffering. Not five miles hence, in the Nansgever valley, the Doriel family, yeoman farmers at Trevow for generations, have lost their oxen, goats and every living thing to this disease. Thomas Doriel, who lost a wife and child to the ague, and now his livestock, has sold his home and land to pay his debts, and his sons are gone away to seek such living as they may.

'"I have heard them call this terrible affliction the Burning Disease, for it so burns the throat and lungs and does afflict man and beast alike. There is fear of this disease throughout the parish and foolish rumours of sorcery and ill-wishing. For in such parts of West Penwith they have little commerce with persons from outside their parish, and for all that they are hard-working and careful with their meagre wages, they are an ill-educated and superstitious lot."'

He sat up in bed that night, with Charlie for company, and read through every document in the white plastic file. The last photocopy had been taken from the *Cornish Guardian*, Thursday 27th April 1961: MYSTERY CHILD AT MOOR BLAZE.

His eyes skimmed the whole article and then returned to the second paragraph.

She was discovered by John Argall of Lower Garrow Farm, and his son Keith, who set out in their Land Rover to investigate the fire in a derelict shepherd's cottage not far from Brown Willy at about ten o'clock on the night of Tuesday 18th April. The girl is thought to be about two years old . . .

He looked down at the photo of the little girl, and the caption:

DO YOU KNOW THIS CHILD?

18th April 1961. Two years old. So she was born about April 1959, at about the time that Adrian Doriel was found in a Plymouth cellar, his back a mess of welts. And about the time that the cattle disease was striking Trevow.

He thought of the strange criss-cross contusions on Sara's back.

Thoughts kept swimming round in his head – random half-connected thoughts, colliding, breaking up, re-forming, coincidences, echoes, reflections in disturbed water, pieces of a jigsaw puzzle.

He looked through her notes a second time. *Brother Stephen* caught his eye, written twice, on a sheet of paper torn from a shorthand notebook. And *Stokeland Abbey*. And a phone number. And *John D* ringed twice in blue ballpoint. With *Mon or Tues?* beside it. And, lower down: *1860. April 26*.

April 26 . . .

They had to be coincidence, these events. She was being selective, *trying* to find things, every thirty-three years. Pure chance.

He telephoned Stokeland Abbey the following morning after surgery. He asked to speak to Brother Stephen. After a long silence, Brother Stephen came on the line.

'You telephoned Sara Carhays recently,' said Tim, 'and left a message on her answering machine.'

'Ah, yes . . . She was going to call me.'

'I'm afraid she can't do that. She's been taken ill and she's in hospital.'

Brother Stephen expressed his regrets.

'My name's Tim Hendra. I'm her GP. I'm also a close friend and I'm looking after her house while she's away. I wondered if there's any message I can pass on.'

'Well, she was enquiring about a penitent who lived here at the abbey in Victorian times,' Brother Stephen replied. 'I was wondering ... Is she making a family enquiry? Is she related somehow to this man?'

'No,' said Tim, wondering what exactly Sara had told him. 'She's a history student. She's writing a doctoral thesis.'

'It's just that if she were family,' said Brother Stephen, 'it might have been distressing for her. Perhaps you could tell her that there *is* a recorded death of a penitent here by the name of John Doriel. He died on 26 April 1860, age unknown. There's also something about him in the archives that a historian might find interesting. I can't send her photocopies, we don't have facilities, but she could come here and look at the archive herself if she wishes.'

'I'll pass that message on.'

'Visitors are allowed on Saturday afternoons only. Perhaps you would be kind enough to tell her that as well?'

'I will,' said Tim. 'She'll be very grateful for your help.' He added as an afterthought, 'Purely out of curiosity ... Do you happen to know the *cause* of death?'

'According to the archive,' Brother Stephen replied, 'he was burned in a fire. He died of his injuries about a week later.'

THE PENITENT

Sara was walking across a desert. A wide endless desert. Sand dunes stretched to the horizon, like a range of hills. The sand was soft and hot. Her feet were sinking in deeper with every step. She was out of breath. Her throat was like a dried-up river bed. The sun was baking her alive.

She was on a glacier, brilliant white.

She was wallowing in a tropical swamp.

She was walking barefoot through a canyon, the remorseless burning sun reflected off a solid sea of grey dust.

She was an eagle flying. Giants threw quoits.

'I'm Mickey the Rings,' said the biker, and showed her his ringed talons: silver rings, jewelled rings, skull rings with ruby eyes, coiled serpents, a wolf's head.

She saw Annie Carkeet, kneeling at the pool, splashing water over her face.

She saw the girl with the goat bells and the Aztec bag. The sun had melted her chocolate and left finger smears on her book of poems.

She saw Senara, sweating in death.

She was floundering in hot volcanic mud.

It was daylight. Someone was moving around. Through half-open eyes she saw a moving shape; it was like looking through a window with rain cascading down the glass. The shape came to the side of the bed.

He said softly, 'Are you awake?'

There was sunlight outside. It seemed so bright. She felt as if she had been away somewhere, a long journey, a long night on a slow train. A man in a white coat was sitting on the bed, his body angled round towards her. There were two nurses with him.

He said, 'Sara? Can you hear me?'

She felt empty. She could not move, she was so weak. She

was bones and hollow spaces. She felt as if a thief had stolen the muscles from her body in the night. Her skull was heavy as rock.

'I'm Tony Shipman,' he said. 'The medical registrar.'

She felt frightened and confused. She was in a strange place with strangers. She was trapped, tethered, hooked up to things, plugged in.

'You're in the West Cornwall hospital,' said Shipman. 'In Penzance.'

There were daffodils and tulips on the table beside the bed, and some small brightly wrapped packages.

She looked at the bandages on her hands. She looked at the white coat sitting on the bed. Her eyes crept shut again; she did not have the strength to keep them open.

'You've been here since Tuesday,' said Shipman. 'Do you remember anything?'

Her eyelids flickered partly open. Her face was wet with perspiration.

'Tuesday,' she echoed. Her eyelids drooped and closed again.

'It's Saturday today,' said Shipman. 'It's Easter.'

'Easter.' Her lips were hardly moving.

'It's your birthday.'

Four days had gone by. She remembered nothing.

'We're moving you to Treliske in a day or two,' said Shipman. 'To the Royal Cornwall. You'll be more comfortable there.'

'Tell Clare . . .' she whispered. But she could not remember what, or why. Breath failed her.

'Clare will come and see you soon,' said Shipman soothingly. 'Just rest. You're doing well. You're doing fine.'

'Got to tell Clare . . .'. She was beginning to drift back to sleep.

'Just rest. Won't be long. Soon have you back to normal.'

Lynn awoke just after half past seven on Easter Saturday. Roger was still asleep beside her. She slipped out of bed, put on her bathrobe and crept out of the bedroom, closing the door. She woke Louisa, took her to the bathroom, washed her face and took her downstairs. They had breakfast together. Just after nine o'clock, she took a cup of coffee upstairs to Roger. He was awake but sleepy and crumpled. She put the coffee down on his bedside table. He reached out and tried to pull her down onto the bed.

'What are you up so early for?' he grumbled.

'Early?' she scoffed. 'Half the morning's gone. I've got a little girl to look after, and two horses to feed and muck out.'

She drew back the curtains. The sun was struggling to break through a bank of smoky grey cloud. Roger turned his eyes away from the light. 'You're getting as bad as Clare,' he muttered.

She blew him a mocking kiss, walked out and closed the door. She was about to cross the landing to go back to her room when she thought she heard a sound from the guest bedroom, next to Clare and Roger's room. It was very faint and it lasted barely a few seconds, but it sounded like a child whimpering. She wondered if one of the cats was trapped in there. She opened the door and looked inside. There was not a sound. Nothing moved. She looked under the bed. But there was no cat. She wondered what it was that she'd heard. She looked around the room. She stared at the painting that Clare had hung in here – Bryan's painting, the one that had been in the drawing room, the menhir with the hole in it, sticking out of the dark pool, the one that kept reminding Clare of Bosun's death. Now Lynn noticed something strange about the painting that she had never seen before: there was blood coming from the hole in the menhir. It was flowing down the stone and over the surface of the dark pool. She wondered why she had not noticed it until now. It was suddenly so striking. The whole surface of the pond was blood red.

Clare was helping her mother clear away after breakfast. The children were loitering, waiting for someone to make decisions. Jo wanted to go swimming.

'It's not swimming weather,' said Clare. 'It's too cold. There's a strong wind off the Channel.'

'We can still go to the beach,' said Alex.

'I'm busy this afternoon. Maybe Granny and Grandpa will take you.'

'Why, where are *you* going?' asked her mother, as if she had no right to venture off alone.

'St Melyn.'

Ben said: 'Can I come too?'

'No, darling. You'll only get bored. There's nothing there.'

'Then what are you going for?' said Alex.

'She's got a toyboy,' said Jo mischievously.

'Ho-ho,' said Clare. 'We wish.'

'I want to go with you,' Ben persisted, tugging at the belt of her trousers. 'Pleeease ... Don't wanna go to the beach, it's too *cooold*.'

'Don't whine,' said Clare, and brushed his hands away.

'What's in St Melyn?' Alex persisted.

'It's where Kadan Doriel and his family were buried.'

'Is he one of Roger's lot?' her mother asked. She didn't much care for Roger's lot. She thought they were rather common.

'Kadan's father,' Clare explained, 'was the last Doriel to farm at Trevow, two hundred years ago. We think there might be a connection between them and Roger's family.'

'I thought Roger's lot were Indian?' said her mother.

'His great-grandfather, Edwin Foster Doriel, was in the Navy,' said Clare. 'He just happened to be born in Calcutta, we don't know why. We don't know anything about Edwin's father.'

'Probably a stoker,' her mother murmured.

Tim was working that morning. He was at the surgery as usual from eight thirty to ten thirty. He was planning to have an early lunch and play golf that afternoon, but it was gone two by the time he had finished his house calls. He was driving home from St Ives, listening to the car radio. Rain was forecast for late afternoon. He was wondering whether to scrap his golfing plans and put in a few hours' work in the garden instead.

He drove through the village of Lelant, past the turn-off to Hayle, and approached the large roundabout where the Hayle and St Ives roads joined the main A30, London–Land's End road. Usually, he would take the westbound exit off the roundabout, towards Penzance, and cut inland at the village of Crowlas. Instead, on an impulse – or perhaps he had been thinking about this for days – he turned east for Bodmin and the Devon border.

An hour later, he was turning off the A30 at Launceston and taking the road north for Barnstaple and Stokeland.

There was a high stone wall around the cemetery, and a pair of wrought-iron gates at the entrance.

Clare opened one of the gates and stepped inside. The cemetery sprawled across ten acres or so, shaded by sweet-smelling cedars, larch and hemlock. The grass needed cutting and the paths needed weeding.

She was searching for over two hours. She was wishing she had brought Ben after all; she could have used those sharp young eyes.

She found Kadan's grave first.

Kadan James Doriel. Died 5 July 1828. Aged fifty-three years. That was all it said.

Not far away, she found the other stone. It was furred over with emerald green moss and the engraved names were difficult to read:

> Jayne Doriel
> David Doriel
> Eliza Doriel
> Beloved wife and children of Kadan
> Taken by fire this 18th day
> April 1827

April 18. That was what Sara was so agitated about.

What did she mean, a kind of cycle?

She noticed one last inscription, along the bottom of the stone, almost lost beneath the red clay in which it was buried. She brushed away the earth. It was a Biblical reference: Exodus 21 xxv.

Stokeland Abbey was six miles from Barnstaple. There were no signposts. Tim had to ask at a local pub. He followed a byway just outside the village of Bratton Fleming, deeper into Exmoor country, until he came to a post by the side of the road that marked a SITE OF HISTORIC INTEREST. Here, a track forked away from the road, wide enough for motor vehicles, and, judging from the tyre marks in the dirt, well used. A wooden sign in the hedgerow said: VEHICULAR ACCESS TO ST EYOT'S ONLY. He drove slowly along the track for half a mile or so, until the public footpath parted company with the track at right angles. Straight ahead there was a gateway and a cattle grid. The gate was wide open. Another painted sign, white on black, read:

> BROTHERHOOD OF ST EYOT
> PRIVATE ROAD
> PLEASE DRIVE SLOWLY

Beyond the cattle grid he found himself inside a fenced estate, passing through skimpy woodlands. The woodlands gradually thinned out and became a tidy plantation of shrubs and small trees, which in turn gave way to a garden of rose beds and herbaceous borders and patches of neatly trimmed lawn. He could see vegetable allotments and orchards. And beyond that, open fields, cows and goats.

The driveway terminated at a wide gravel parking area. There were several cars parked, also a flat-bed truck with 'North Devon Farmers' on the cab door, and a plumber's van. Tim pulled up in front of a high brick wall, got out of the car and approached a pair of black wrought-iron gates. One was closed, the other was ajar. He walked on through and along a broad gravel path that passed across the front of the monastery.

It was an elegant brick building on four floors, whose age he could not guess at; possibly late Elizabethan. It looked like a school or a university college from the front. Half-way along, a gated archway beneath the first floor led through to a paved courtyard. He stopped and peered through the bars of the gate. There was no one about.

A monk came along the path towards him, trundling a heavy wooden wheelbarrow. Tim asked him where visitors were supposed to go. The monk directed him through the courtyard, to the public entrance. Tim thanked him, pushed open the barred gate and walked across the paved yard. The public entrance led into a reception area. A notice asked visitors to ring the bell.

Tim shook the small brass handbell and an elderly monk in a charcoal grey habit appeared. Tim said he had come to see Brother Stephen to enquire about an entry in the archives. He gave his name and mentioned Sara's name as well. The elderly monk went off in search of Brother Stephen.

Ten minutes or so passed, and then a young monk – no more than thirty or so – entered the reception hall.

'Doctor Hendra?'

'Brother Stephen?'

They shook hands.

'Miss Carhays is going to be in hospital for some time,' Tim explained. 'I wondered if I might be allowed to see the passage in the archives that you were going to show her? Then I could take some notes and pass them on to her.'

He was presented with the visitors' book and asked to sign it. Then Brother Stephen led him along stone-floored passageways, beneath arches, and through the monastery library. They came to a stop beside a narrow oak door in an ante-room adjacent to the library. Brother Stephen tried various large keys in the lock.

'How old is this building?' Tim asked.

'About three hundred and fifty years. The original abbey was Norman. It was destroyed during the Reformation. The ruins are quite near by, on the other side of the cemetery.'

'Was John Doriel actually buried here?'

'Yes. But I doubt if you'd find his grave. Most penitents requested that their graves should remain unmarked.'

'Why was that?'

'Penitents came here in search of peace. Many, one imagines, were deeply troubled souls. But whatever unhappiness they experienced in the life they left behind, it was the life hereafter they were more concerned with. They attached no importance to being remembered here on earth.'

He unlocked the door. It was pitch dark beyond. He fumbled along the wall inside and switched on a light. Tim followed him down a spiral stone staircase to the undercroft.

'I take it,' said Tim, 'you don't have penitents any more?'

'Not since the middle of the last century. The practice was open to abuse, as you can imagine.' Brother Stephen smiled. 'People trying to evade the secular law.'

'But they came here for life, didn't they?'

'Well, life in a monastery on Exmoor, even in the old days, was preferable to being hanged or given twenty years' transportation. And, besides, there was nothing to stop people leaving if they really wanted to.'

'Were they asked *why* they were penitent? Why they wanted sanctuary?'

'They were questioned when they came here, but only to try to establish that they were sincere. Their personal details were never recorded. Penitents left their past lives behind them. Any who came here with money or personal possessions gave everything to the abbey. They were left with nothing that tied them to the outside world.'

They were now in the undercroft. It was like the crypt of a cathedral. The air was thick with the pervasive odour of heating oil. Brother Stephen unlocked the door to the cellar storeroom where the archives were stored along with the surplus book collection that the library shelves could no longer hold. They stepped inside. There were parallel rows of bookshelves running the full width of the cellar, in addition to the shelves that lined the walls from floor to ceiling. There were inverted half-moon windows along the exterior-facing wall at ground level which let in a little daylight; but it was too dark to read by. He switched on the lights. They were few and far between.

The archives were in large volumes, some of them the size of lectern Bibles. The older volumes had been bound in leather by the monks. They were covered in dust; some had not been touched in decades by the look of them. Brother Stephen took down the volume for 1860 and carried it to a table beneath one of the unshaded lightbulbs. He turned the thick flaky pages until he came to the month of April. The paper had yellowed and the ink had faded to a soft brown but the immaculate copperplate writing was still legible.

He turned the pages for April 1860 until he came to the 26th day. At the end of several pages devoted to rain damage to the vegetable crop and some poor trading in the matter of three horses, he indicated one isolated sentence:

> John Doriel, Penitent, passed from us this night into God's mercy after eight days of torment.

'If you turn back to the 19th,' he explained, 'you'll find it starts there, and there are two entries during the course of his suffering, and then you'll find a lot more in the days *after* his death.'

'Thank you,' said Tim. He sat down at the table.

'I shall be in the library upstairs if you need help,' said Brother Stephen. 'I'm afraid visitors are asked to leave by five o'clock, so ...' He plucked back the sleeve of his habit and looked at his wristwatch. 'There's only half an hour left. I'm sorry.'

Tim smiled. 'Medical students are used to writing quick notes.'

Towards the end of the archive entry for 19 April 1860, Tim found:

> John Doriel, Penitent, suffered injury this night past, when a quantity of naphtha for the lamps was spilled and somewise lighted, burning him and causing him great suffering. He is tended by Brother Michael.

Five days later, on 24 April, Tim found:

> JD, Penitent, lies grievous sick with fever and his suffering cannot be much more prolonged.

There was no mention of him again until his death was noted on the 26th:

> John Doriel, Penitent, passed from us this night into God's mercy after eight days of torment.

Two days later, on 28 April, the archivist recorded:

> Brother Michael did this day solemnly bear witness to the Abbot and Fathers in council, that he did attend upon John D., Penitent, at his death and that John did, upon this Seventh day, beg the Lord's mercy, and being sick with fever of his burns and near to death, did profess that he approached his Judgement with monstrous evil upon his conscience.
>
> He did impart much more to Brother Michael, but they were the ramblings of a fevered mind and naught could be clearly heard, save but a few words wherein he called upon the Lord. The interment of the body has been stayed

by the Abbot so that he may enquire further into the circumstance whereby J.D. met his death.

Two days later, on 30 April, the archivist recorded:

George Knights, Penitent, solemnly bears witness to the Fathers in council that his penitent brother in Christ, John D., did many months past speak to him of great wickedness that bore heavily upon his conscience and that he unburdened himself to G. who can recollect neither names nor dates but solemnly believes the following to be a just account of J.'s confession.

J. spoke of his boyhood on his father's farm in a distant place whose name G. cannot recall, knowing only that he has never heard the name before or since.

There was a maid employed there, in the farmer's house and about the farm, a poor creature, who could neither read nor write, and yet cunning in her knowledge of herbs and simple physick.

J. was familiar with this maid in his early years, as he was with all so employed about the farm. J. developed a true affection for her and, when he was fifteen years, he was led into temptation by her.

She conceived a child by him, and when her condition was revealed, and she being unmarried, J.'s father questioned her as to the father of her child. She named John.

His father, a cholerick man, then inquired of J. if this was true and if he could deny what she had confessed. J., being afraid of his father's wrath, said that she did bewitch him with her cunning, and came to him in the night and lay with him as he slept.

His father and brothers spoke harshly with this maid, and fearing sorcery, imprisoned her in a cellar, stripped her of her clothing, and searched her body for a witch's teat by which she might give suckle to familiars. Finding none, they shaved the hair from her head, but found none there either.

No such mark being found upon her, the farmer and his sons did scourge her with rods to make her confess her sorcery. The maid pleaded she was guiltless and begged mercy. But J.'s brothers did return to her by night, and while that she was imprisoned, abused this poor creature in a way that is wrong both by God's law and by nature. And in such manner that she suffered great pain and loss of blood and did lose her unborn child.

Weak and ailing, she was taken to her own dwelling, where she was pitched down and left to starve or fend as best she might.

Not many weeks thence, J.'s young sister, a sweet child, took sick with fever and began to waste away. Wise persons of the parish proclaimed she was ill-wished. No physick known to man could stop her fever or prevent her wasting quite away. She died at length, babbling in her madness, burning with ague and spitting dark blood.

In their grief, and fearing she was ill-wished, J.'s father and brothers came secretly to the hovel where the maid dwelt and inflicted great suffering upon her to make her confess her sorcery. They dragged her from her home and pitched her in a pond to see whether she might float or sink, that being the true test of a witch.

The poor creature did float. Whereon the farmer and his sons lighted the straw on the floor of her home and threw on faggots from the hearth. And when the straw was well alight, the wretched creature was pushed inside the burning hovel and hurled upon the flames. Sick and weak from the loss of her child, and near drowned, she struggled to escape the flames. But the farmer and his sons drove her back with pitchforks, and kept watch until her piteous screams had quite ceased.

The people who lived thereabouts believed the burning was a just act of God. For many believed she was a child of the Devil who had endowed her with dreadful powers.

The farmer's oxen, sheep and goats began to weaken and fall sick with murrain and to waste away. Each time the farmer replaced a beast, the sickness would claim two, so that within a short time he was ruined by borrowing and had lost his farm and lands to his creditors.

Naught but tragedy pursued him and his sons thereafter. J.'s mother was taken by fever, his father died in gaol, a debtor, and J.'s own wife was taken in childbirth. One brother lost his wife and children all, when fire consumed their home. The other went to sea and took ship for the East Indies.

J. came here to Stokeland, destroyed in spirit and tormented by guilt, to atone through prayer and labour. And yet for all the goodness shewed him here and his yearning to expiate his guilt, he has not until this time dared speak of his torment to any living soul.

Here ended the account of George Knights, Penitent.

There was no further mention of John Doriel in the archives until 2 May, six days after his death. Tim found one last entry:

The Abbot and Fathers in council have determined that, John D., Penitent, was of such advanced years that no reliance should be placed upon the confession alleged by George K. It cannot now be ascertained if any such events took place at all. It is not known where in England he was born and spent his childhood. He was past his eightieth year and of unsound mind. He was taciturn of nature and no one else did hear him speak of it. Yet if there were substance to his terrible confession, it is unlikely there could be found alive any person who might now attest to it.

The Fathers in council have ruled further that it cannot justly be determined whether John died by act of God or at his own hand. He should not, therefore, be denied the rites of Christian burial.

Clare was alone in her father's study. It was early evening. The children were watching television with their grandparents. She had an oppressive feeling hanging over her, like a shadow that was just behind her and that vanished every time she looked around.

She was haunted by the words on the grave of Kadan's wife and children: *Taken by fire this 18th day*.

She was thinking about the Biblical reference along the bottom of the gravestone.

Exodus 21.

She took down a copy of the Bible from her father's bookcase.

She turned to Exodus 21. God's judgements to Moses. An eye for an eye, a tooth for a tooth.

At verse 25, she read:

Burning for burning, wound for wound, stripe for stripe.

Louisa was standing in the old rumpus room, next to the hole in the wall that led into the barn. She was looking up at the ceiling, where a funny red blob the size of a plate was suffusing the white plaster.

In the room above – the guest room next to Clare and Roger's bedroom – something was dripping off the bottom edge of Bryan's painting. It was oozing silently from the hole in the menhir onto the surface of the pond which had begun to overflow and trickle down the picture frame and down the wall in several thin, blood-red streams.

THE BURNING

It was early evening. Tim found Keith Argall's farm at Lower Garrow and drove as far up the track as he could, until mud and granite made it impassable for cars. From that point on he walked along the track, towards the misty hump of Brown Willy in the distance.

He came to the ruin. It was smaller than he'd imagined. How could anyone have lived in a place like this? So small, so isolated, so bleak, with nothing but sheep for company.

He saw the menhir, about a hundred yards away across open moorland. He tramped through the mud and grass to take a closer look. It was tall, almost twice his height, and very like the fallen stone in the woods behind Crowjy. He touched it. He put his hand into the hole and felt the smoothness of the stone.

Sara was neither quite asleep nor quite awake. She sensed a shadow moving across the floor and felt it like cold breath across her face. She could sense a hand reaching out to touch her, could feel it caressing her, reaching inside her, feeling the smoothness of her flesh . . .

A nurse looked in on her at a quarter past seven. Sara was asleep – the same semi-delirious sleep she had been drifting in and out of all day. But she was improving all the time. She was off the heart monitor now.

There was an hour or more of daylight left but it had clouded over outside and the lights were on in her room, but dimmed. The Venetian blinds were lowered to keep out the brighter lights from the corridor, and nosy prying eyes. The birthday cards and presents sat unopened on the bedside table.

The nurse fitted a fresh bag of saline solution onto the intravenous drip stand. Sara muttered something in her feverish half-sleep. The nurse made entries on the chart, and left her in peace.

*

Sara's mind was adrift, like a small boat in the middle of a still lake. She could feel something drawing her away, drawing her like a strong arm on the bank of the lake, pulling on a rope, towing her slowly towards the shore.

There was danger somewhere. She felt threatened.

Her eyes began to open, little by little, flicker by flicker.

There was something she had to do ... Something she'd left behind ...

She could hear voices, drifting in on the wind, far away. One voice she knew from somewhere.

She opened her eyes fully now.

She was meant to *be* somewhere.

She pushed herself up onto her elbows. And then upright. She struggled to get out of bed. She was tethered by tubes, strung like a puppet. She felt a flutter of panic. They had tied her down. She was a prisoner. There was danger, something terrible was going to happen, and they were tying her down. She tugged at the tubes and pulled them free from her body. She pushed herself up off the bed and stood upright, swaying ... Giddy, dizzy, falling ... She put a hand out to steady herself. So hot in here. She moved towards the door, lurching like a drunk.

She opened the door and looked up and down the corridor. Where was she? *Have to find her, have to warn them ...*

She shuffled along the corridor, past the women's wards and patients eating their evening meals, visitors gathered round on plastic chairs. No one looked twice at her. She tottered past the wards and bathrooms, barefoot, in her hospital nightdress, her face deathly white and glossy with sweat. She walked as if she had suffered a stroke and was trying to recover the use of her legs. Her gaze was fixed on something in the distance.

At the end of the corridor she came to a door. On the door the words: NURSING STAFF ONLY. Above the door in red: EMERGENCY EXIT. She pushed at the door and found herself in a small square room with two washbasins and some steel lockers along the wall. She saw a green raincoat hanging from a peg, and a matching floppy rain hat. She could not remember leaving her coat in here. She could not remember having a green coat. But she was cold and she had to be somewhere, she had to do something, had to warn them ...

She put on the floppy hat and the green coat. She struggled with the belt. She couldn't get hold of it, it kept sliding out of her grasp. She looked at her hands and noticed they were bandaged. What had they done to her hands?

She looked down and saw shoes beneath a bench. She couldn't remember leaving any shoes here. She put them on. They felt tight and uncomfortable. She walked towards the fire exit. She slumped against the crash bar and her stumbling weight pushed the door open. She stepped outside onto an iron staircase, descended unsteadily to a yard at the rear of the hospital, and walked out onto the street.

It was drizzling with rain. She wandered up St Clare Street, past the council estate, wondering where she was, trying to remember where she was supposed to be. Passers-by looked at her as if she were drunk. She came to a roundabout where the main road bypassed Penzance on the way to Land's End. She stumbled across the road, oblivious of cars swerving and hooting.

On the other side of the bypass, she came to the village of Heamoor. Her head began to ache. Lucid moments were starting to flicker through her mind, like shooting stars across a dark winter sky, there for just a second and then gone from sight. Her mind was like a radio that was just off-station but picking up stray signals. The name Boskinnow came back to her. And Crowjy. And Clare ... *Clare* ... That name came to her like a lifeline thrown from somewhere in the outer darkness. She tried to grasp it and hold on: Clare ... Have to warn her ... Have to be there ...

Her mind was a fog of confusion. Everything around her looked alien and forbidding. This was not Boskinnow, this was not Crowjy. They had moved her, they had brought her to this grim grey place.

She stopped in front of an elderly woman walking along the main street.

'Where am I?' she mumbled. 'What place is this?'

'This is Heamoor, my love.' The woman was troubled by Sara's sickly appearance. 'Where are you tryen to get to?'

Sara looked up and down the street, trying to remember. What *were* those names?

'Where's home to, my love?' said the elderly woman, a little slower and louder, as if Sara were deaf.

Sara reached deep into the swamp of her mind.

'Boskinnow,' she remembered. 'Crowjy. Clare . . .'

'Boskinnow?' The elderly woman looked worried. 'You'm nowhere near. That's out Nancledra way. You can catch a bus from Gulval. That's about th'only thing I can suggest. Turn right at the crossroads here . . .' She indicated the junction fifty yards ahead. 'And keep walken. That'll bring you out past Gulval village, on the St Ives road. You can get a bus to Nancledra but I don't think they go through Boskinnow this time of night.'

Sara looked as if she had not even registered what the woman was saying, but she turned and lurched away towards the crossroads.

'You sure you'm all right, my love?' the woman called after her. 'You don't look too well to me.'

But Sara walked on.

They were facing each other across the kitchen table, mirroring each other, elbows on the table, both hands holding a wine glass. Lynn had made a casserole for dinner. It was about the only thing she could cook that did not come out of a tin or a packet or the freezer. Roger had just finished a second helping but was still hungry.

'Any more?' he said.

She shook her head and sipped her wine.

'Not even a scraping?'

She shook her head.

'Not even a lick?'

She felt his toe nudging up the inside of her calf.

'Depends . . . Whether you're a good boy or not.'

The telephone began to ring.

'I'm an invalid. I need special attention.'

The telephone went on ringing. They sat watching each other, as if it were a game to see who would blink or smile first.

'Are you going to answer that?' asked Lynn.

'It's only my wife. Checking up on me.'

'She wants to be sure you're getting plenty of bed rest.'

'Tell her we're working on it.'

Lynn reached for the phone.

'You dare me . . . ?'

Clare was listening to the ringing tone. She was alone in the kitchen. The children were in the sitting room, watching television with their grandparents. No one was answering at Trevow. She clicked her tongue impatiently and wandered restlessly around the kitchen, as far as the telephone cord would permit. Her mother came in and rinsed out a couple of tea cups.

'Can't you leave them alone for ten minutes?' It was beginning to get on her nerves. 'What's wrong with you? You're on holiday.'

Roger picked up at the other end.

'It's me,' said Clare.

'We guessed,' he said.

'How are things?'

'Oh, pretty much as they were when you rang this morning.' There was a note of dull sarcasm in his voice. 'What have you lot been up to?'

'Nothing madly exciting. The kids went to the beach and froze. I fiddle-faddled around. Buried lots of chocolate for the Easter egg hunt tomorrow. How's Louisa?'

'Fast asleep. Lynn took her out this afternoon.'

'Has she been asking where I am?'

'Hasn't mentioned you all day, matter of fact. I don't think she's noticed you're not here.'

There was something casually spiteful about the way he said these things.

'No trouble getting her off to sleep?'

'Not really. Lynn wore her out this afternoon.'

'While you were doing what?'

'Watching rugby league. What else?'

'Ask a stupid question. And what are you doing tonight?'

'We've just eaten. Lynn made a casserole. I suppose we'll end up watching telly. For a change.'

He was being sarcastic again. Clare couldn't think of much else to say. She was not even sure why she'd bothered calling in the first place, except to know that Louisa was all right.

After she had rung off, her mother said, 'You're like an old mother hen. You've got to learn to let go, you know.'

'I don't like leaving her,' Clare replied.

She felt no easier in her mind for making that call. She couldn't explain it. It was just a bad feeling, intuition.

'I never left Alex or the twins when they were so small,' she said. 'Roger's so useless. Children are like toys to him. Everything's like a toy to him. And he's so bad-tempered with that broken leg.'

'Well, the girl's there, isn't she? Liz, whatever she's called? I thought you said she was good with Louisa.'

'She is. But that's not the point.'

'Then what *is* the point?'

'She's my child, for heaven's sake,' Clare snapped. 'I want her with me.'

'Well, all right, dear . . .' Her mother looked taken aback.

Clare moved to the sink and poured some water in the kettle to make herself some coffee.

'I'm sorry. I'm just . . . I don't know. A bit wound up.'

'You're only here till Monday. It's hardly a wrench, surely? And we're only three hours' drive away, it's not as if we live abroad.'

Clare stood with her arms folded, watching the electric kettle come to the boil. Her mother was right; in fact, it was less than three hours – a *lot* less, the speed she drove, and at this time on a Saturday night.

She came to an abrupt decision. She switched off the kettle and walked out of the kitchen. Her mother watched her, perplexed, and went back to the sitting room.

'I don't know what's got into that girl,' she muttered to Clare's father, as she sat down again to watch the television.

'What girl?' He turned to look blankly at Jo.

'What did I do?' asked Jo, looking equally blank, and turned to her grandmother.

'Not you dear,' her grandmother replied. 'Your mother.'

They heard Clare's footfall on the ceiling above. She came down a few minutes later and put her head round the sitting-room door.

'I'm off,' she announced. 'I'll be back tomorrow morning.'

Her parents turned to stare at her.

'*Off?*' said her mother. 'What do you mean you're off? Off where?'

'Home,' said Clare. 'I'm going back to Trevow.'

Now the twins took notice. It took that much to get their eyes away from the television. Only Alex did not seem to have heard.

'Why are you going home?' asked Jo.

'Whatever are you thinking of?' said her father.

'I'm going to fetch Louisa,' said Clare. 'I'll be back here in time for lunch.' She pointed a warning finger at the children. 'No nonsense from you while I'm gone. You do as you're told.' She blew them a kiss. 'See you tomorrow.'

'You can't go home at this time of night ...' her mother called after her.

But Clare was already half-way to the front door.

'She's never been right since the baby was born,' her father grunted. 'I said she was too old.'

'Oh, don't be so stupid,' his wife muttered irritably. And hurried out of the room after Clare.

Alex seemed to notice that something had happened and enquired, without looking round from the television, 'What's wrong with Mum? Why's she gone home?'

'Hormones,' said his grandfather.

'What does hormones mean?' asked Ben.

'Nothing you or I have to worry about, lad.'

Clare's mother caught up with her outside, just as she was getting into the car. 'Have you taken all leave of your senses?'

'On the contrary,' said Clare. 'I'm very much in touch with my senses. That's why I'm going home. Louisa needs me.'

'But you've just talked to Roger! And everything's fine – perfectly perfectly fine.'

'Well, this doesn't *feel* fine,' said Clare, putting her hand on her belly.

Her mother was looking scandalized, as if Clare had gone out of her mind.

'What are you talking about? You're not pregnant *again*?'

Clare started the car. 'Intuition, Ma,' she replied. 'That's what I'm talking about.'

Her mother was lost for words. 'But it's Easter Sunday,' she pleaded, when all else failed. 'You're driving me to Mass.'

'Well, if you ask God nicely, I'm sure He'll understand,' said Clare, shooting an ironic glance at the stars. 'Suffer little children to come unto me . . . So on, so forth.'

The doctor on duty was standing just inside the room, gazing at Sara's empty bed.
'When did anyone last check on her?'
The ward sister said, 'An hour ago.'
'You've searched this floor?'
'Everywhere.'
'All right, alert security. Alert every ward and department. Search the hospital from top to bottom. She can't be far away, she hasn't got the strength.'

Sara was stumbling and tottering along the winding lane between the villages of Heamoor and Gulval. It was almost dark now. She had pains above her eyes – sharp searing pains – and the ends of her fingers were starting to ache. She had no idea how long she'd been walking, or any idea where this road was leading. She would know what she was looking for as soon as she saw it.

There were no more houses now. It was just a country lane. A few cars passed by. It grew dark. Night came in. She came to a junction where another lane angled off to the left. It led to the hamlets of Carfury and Mulfra, and eventually out to Gurnard's Head on the west coast. But her legs would go no further. She clutched at her chest, desperate for breath, and pressed the heel of her palm to her forehead, trying to push away the migraine pain. She swayed. Her vision fogged. She struggled on a few small, shuffled steps and then her knees began to buckle.

She heard Lynn saying, *'You'm in a braave ole figary 'ere, my git lover.'*

Her body slewed to a crazy angle, she reached out to Lynn for support but clutched at thin air and dropped in a heap in the road.

Lynn was locking up the stables.

She walked back across the yard in the almost dark. The

wind was blowing from the west. It smelt clean and salty. It would be a fine day tomorrow.

She came to the Tudor barn. Roger had left the door open wide to air the place, to get rid of the stench of wood preservatives that a specialist firm had been spraying everywhere. She stepped inside the barn and closed the door, bolted it, turned the mortice lock and went back through the old rumpus room and across the hall.

Roger was in the kitchen. He pointed to a gift-wrapped package on the table.

'That's your Easter egg,' he said.

She considered it. It didn't look much like an egg – if it was, it was a terribly flat one. She picked up the gift-wrapped package and felt it. It was very light and soft but slightly lumpy in small places.

'Hope it fits,' he said.

'Is this what I think it is?' She could guess exactly what it was. She could feel the suspenders.

He was grinning boyishly. 'Not very original, am I?'

'I think,' she said, 'I shall have to find you a grubby white mac.'

She went upstairs to the guest room that had become *her* room these last few weeks. She opened the gift-wrapped package.

Black satin basque; almost cupless. She couldn't help smiling. Oh, so predictable, Roger. Totally impractical, very uncomfortable, and probably the wrong size.

She opened it out. Some more bits and pieces fell out. Stockings and panties to go with it too.

She wondered, as she pulled off her sweatshirt, whether he had ever persuaded Clare to squeeze into things like this. As she shucked off her jeans, she felt something weighty in the pocket. She pulled out two keys ... The keys to the stable and the keys to the barn door.

She tossed them onto the dressing table; she wouldn't be needing those before morning.

A farmer in a Volvo estate was driving along the Gulval–Heamoor road on his way home to Carnaquidden Downs at around half past eight. He was approaching the turn-off for

Mulfra, when he saw a woman in the middle of the road. He thought at first she had been run over. She was trying to get to her feet. He pulled up, switched on his hazard lights and climbed out.

'Don't try to get up, my love . . .'

She mumbled something incoherent.

'You stay down thear now. We'll get an ambulance here djreckly.'

But she took no notice. She struggled to her feet. 'Waiting . . .' she muttered. 'Tell Clare . . . Warn them . . .'

She held on to his arm and pulled herself to her feet. She stumbled towards his car to prop herself up. He opened the nearside door.

'You sit here a moment,' said the farmer. 'Collect yourself. Are you hurt? What happened?'

She sank down onto the passenger seat, sideways on, her feet on the road. She started mumbling about the 18th. And cycles. But he could make neither head nor tail of it. He wondered if she was drunk but he could smell no alcohol. Her eyes were half closed. He could see the sweat on her face, glistening in the glow of the car's interior light. There was an unpleasant smell coming off her, a sour unwashed smell. He had come across a girl in this state before – one of a bunch of drug addicts who lived near St Ives. There were a lot of them about there these days.

He noticed her bandaged hands, her grazed knees. Her raincoat and floppy green hat were wet through.

'Where are you trying to get to?' he said. She did not respond. He shook her very gently. 'Where's home to, my dear?'

'Crowjy . . .' she said, slurring the word so that he began to think she *was* drunk, after all. 'Crowjy . . .'

She looked as if she were talking in her sleep. He could scarcely make it out. He thought she said Kerrowe-something. Kerrowe was not far away. There was Kerrowe near Gurnard's Head, and Higher Kerrowe just north of Mulfra Quoit. This road would take her to both.

'I can drop you off at Carnaquidden,' he said. 'Far as I go, I'm late as 'tez. Now come on, let's get you in.'

He helped her lift her feet up off the road. 'Now swing your legs in . . . That's it, proper job.'

He shut the door, came round to the driver's side and climbed in. Her head fell back against the headrest. Her eyes closed and she drifted back into stupor. The farmer drove on.

'How did you hurt your hands, 'en?' he asked.

She started muttering, gibbering, just burble to his ears.

He glanced at her but it was too dark to make her out. She gibbered on and on. It sounded as if she were talking to herself.

'I can't understand a word you're saying, my love,' he said. 'You might just as well save your breath.'

But she took no notice. She did not seem to hear him.

About two miles along the road, he pulled up.

'This is Carnaquidden, where I turn off.'

She was still mumbling to herself. She made no move to get out.

He got out of the car, came round to her side and opened the door.

'This is Carnaquidden, my flower,' he said. 'Out you get now. Far as I go. It edden far from here.'

She tried to get out but was held back by the seat-belt. He leaned across her, released the belt and stepped back to help her out. She looked ahead at the ribbon of hilly road illuminated by the car's lights.

'Know where you are now? You keep going straight as your nose for Kerrowe, about one mile. Then you'm home and dry. You get yourself a good night's sleep, and you'll be right as rain in the morning.'

She lurched away up the road, like a drunken sailor. She said neither goodbye nor thank you. He watched her for a few moments, just to make sure that she stayed on her feet. When she had walked beyond the reach of his headlights, he climbed back into the car and took the right turn that led up to Boscully Farm.

Roger was in the kitchen. The bathroom was just above. He could hear Lynn's radio and the sound of the water tumbling into the tub as she topped up the hot water.

He was picturing her, lying back in Clare's huge Victorian tub, playing the madame. She would be helping herself to the array of fragrant oils and balmy extracts that Clare was given every birthday and Christmas; making a cocktail of them, splashes of this, squirts of that, wallowing in sweet-smelling foam. For fifteen minutes she would be a movie star, a gangster's moll. She would come out with a shine on her skin – just slightly oily – smelling deliciously of strawberries and lemons and honey.

He took a bottle of champagne from the fridge and a tub of chocolate fudge ice cream from the freezer, and put them in the ice bucket. *She* would have to carry that upstairs; he couldn't manage that on crutches.

Eighty miles away, Clare was crossing Dunheved Bridge into Cornwall, on an almost empty road, approaching Launceston.

Sara had come to a T-junction. The road ahead led out to the coast at Treen, near Gurnard's Head. To the left of her sat Mulfra Hill, a humpy black silhouette in the moonlight. To the right of her, a lane branched off and curved around Carnaquidden Downs, winding southwards around the foot of Trevow Hill towards Boskinnow.

A little way along that lane, a large bonfire was blazing in the field. People were dancing round the flames. Sara stopped to watch. Her heart beat faster with excitement. She was a child at a circus, she was laughing, she was breathless. The night shimmered with the fiery heat. She saw Lynn across the flames, a satyr dancing in her eyes, the gleam of malice.

Farmer Argall stood beside her and said: 'Burnen like fury. The heat was too much, we couldn't get near. It made some braave old roaring noise – the fire, the wind and all. We didn't see no one at first. Then thear you were, a liddel tiny thing, stood thear looken at us, like you want to say, Hello, booys, what are'ee doan 'ere? You had your thumb in your mouth. I thought, Dear Christ, she'll roast alive.'

She saw Bryan and Tim. Bryan bloated and purple with wine.

He said, 'My sister comes to me at night. She wants to destroy me. She and her.'

Tiny sister. Born in a womb of stone.

She moved on along the road, past the bonfire. Rebecca was waddling towards her, busy busy, through the valley.

'I know where you live.' Her voice of dry twigs. 'I've seen 'ee thear many times. I've been seeing you thear all my life long.'

Timeless evil. Firechild.

She passed the hippie girlchild with her Aztec bag. She passed Vera, creaking to chapel. She passed Alan Penberthy, the chimney sweep. He carried Clare across his shoulder, fireman's lift. She saw Louisa, six or seven years old, practising the piano. Mirages in the night, dissolving, new mirages forming, images melting into images, dreams and memories, fading in, fading out, overlapping.

She looked up at another black hump of hill in the near distance. Something about its dark shape was familiar – the silhouette of rocks piled high on top. The eagle's claws. Quoits and giants.

She was looking at Carn Ewyn.

She came to the lower slopes of Trevow Hill. She looked up at the huddle of farm buildings on the southeastern slopes. She saw a light in the house. She remembered now ... She knew this place ...

She stopped still in the middle of the road, shuddering with cold and swaying with dizziness.

What in the name of God was she here for?

She stepped off the road and stumbled onto the footpath that curved up the side of the hill. But the path grew narrower and petered out, and left her struggling through thick heather and gorse. She was trying to walk towards the lights on the hill but she could not see where she was walking. The moon had been smothered by low cloud and she could feel the cold clutch of misty rain coming down around her like a shroud. She was stumbling, tripping, slithering towards the light. She slipped and fell into the gorse and mud.

It had been like this before ... in her dreaming.

She remembered it suddenly with perfect clarity. She had dreamt it – the night after her first visit to Trevow. She had dreamt all this; this slithering, this fine drizzle falling, this sharp gorse tearing at her bare legs, this slithering through mud, these clouds low and heavy across the moors, now swallowing up the moon, these dark shapes of farm buildings on the hillside. She had heard a sad, despairing cry ring out across the moors ... A strange, wailing cry. A cry of distress. Like nothing she had ever heard before, a cry of anguish, of deep inner pain, like the cry of a broken heart, a cry of the most desolate despair.

For just that moment, she was entirely lucid. Her mind was like a radio on a spacecraft adrift in a remote constellation, a radio that momentarily hits a wavelength, picks up a signal from a far-off civilization.

She and her ...

There is no she and her. She is me. And I am her. There is only one.

At that second she felt the agony of knowing what had to happen, and knowing that she was not here to stop it ... She was here to *do* it.

It was predestined, her coming here. The fusing of body and soul, of her and her, she and she. Nothing could stop them. No one could come between them. They were together again.

I am her body. And she is my soul.

Timeless evil. A tiny organism afloat in the deaf, uncaring silence of eternity.

Did you know that, Bryan? Did you get so far? Was I there at nights, tormenting you? I don't remember. Did I hold the plastic tight around your throat? And did I destroy your journal? I have no memory. I am timeless ... Out of a womb of stone ...

She felt that lucid moment, those few vivid seconds of total self-knowledge, melt away like a snowflake in the heat of her delirium. She saw Bryan's wet spaniel eyes look up at her with hopeless longing.

It was the last glimmer of clear light in her mind as the coffin-lid of her own dementia began to close.

Sweet Jesus, help me ...

She fell onto the wet heather and wailed to the blind empty sky; one long curling scream of utter despair.

To Clare, fifty miles away on Bodmin Moor, it curled and soared like a sad and beautiful bird and faded slowly away to nothing.

Perhaps it was imagination. Perhaps it was the wind. Perhaps it was just the shriek of car tyres on a freak patch of wet road surface.

Roger was lying on the bed, naked except for the white log of plaster that extended almost from his hip to his toes. He slipped a Miles Davis tape into the radio-cassette player on Clare's side of the bed. Muted brass crept out into the room. He lit up one of Lynn's pre-rolled spliffs and took a long deep toke.

He heard Lynn tap on the door. She said, 'Are you ready?'
'Got the bubbly and the ice cream?'
'Right here.'
'Hang on . . .'
He adjusted himself so he was sitting comfortably, his back against the wall.
'Okay . . . Show-time. Easter parade. Stun me.'
The bedroom door swung open and Lynn presented herself with a flourish.
'Can you dig it?' she said, with a wiggle.
She was wearing a candy pink candlewick dressing gown that Clare's mother had left behind at Christmas.
'Oh, bollocks.' Roger snorted and blew her a raspberry. 'Get it off.'
She threw off the candlewick dressing gown, presented herself a second time and sprang onto the bed with one leap.
'Easter bunny!'
'Oh, wow wow wow . . .' Roger's face lit up like a boy with a new train set. 'Come to me, little rabbit . . .'

Sara was standing outside in the barnyard, her feet caked with mud, her legs scratched by the gorse. She stumbled towards the glass-sided storm porch, the scullery door. She peered in. She wiped the wet glass with her bandaged hands. They were hurting now.

It was dark in the kitchen. There was a light in the hallway beyond. She opened the porch door and stepped inside, into the scullery and the kitchen, into warmth and savoury smells.

Where was she? Nothing was familiar. Nothing was right.

She moved across the kitchen, into the hallway, shuffling like a punch-drunk boxer, into the drawing room. She crossed to the fireplace and looked down into the hearth. The fire was still alive but it was little more than a red glow amidst the ashes and a few smoking embers.

There was no light in the room, only the light from the hallway. She looked around for a candle but could not see a single one. There was a newspaper lying on the arm of a chair. She picked it up and rolled it lengthways to make a torch. She put the tip of it into the glowing embers of the fire. It began to smoke. A blue-yellow flame curled around the outer edges. She held it up and looked around the room. The flames from the burning paper threw dancing shadows across the ceiling.

She moved towards the window. And put the torch to the curtains.

Upstairs, a champagne cork popped, Miles Davis trumpeted softly on the radio-cassette and a haze of marijuana smoke hovered lazily above the bed.

All the way home from Stokeland, Tim's mind was churning over what he had read in the abbey archives: the cellar, the scourging, the shaving of her head, the rape, the miscarriage of her child, the pool they almost drowned her in ... Too many terrible coincidences.

Yet there had to be a way of rationalizing it.

Had Bryan been there to the abbey and read the archive too? Had he written about those things, and had Sara read what he'd written? Had he put those ideas into her head?

But the bleeding was real ... And the welts on her back ...

He thought, too, of how Clare's dog had died in that pool. Heart failure. Shock.

And the fuses blowing.

He got back to Nansgever just before eight o'clock. He telephoned the hospital and spoke to the ward sister. Sara's temperature was down a little, her blood pressure was dropping, she was off the heart monitor. There was a new mood of optimism there; they felt they were getting on top of the situation.

He tried to shake off his dark mood. He tried to convince himself that this could all be explained; that she was mentally ill and under Bryan's influence. First, they would cure her fever, make her well again. Then they would tackle her psychological problems. One step at a time.

He fed Charlie and cooked a meal for himself. He watched the news and weather on television but he could not keep his mind on it.

The telephone rang just after ten o'clock. It was Tony Shipman, the medical registrar at West Cornwall.

He said, 'We've lost Sara Carhays.'

Tim thought he meant that she had just died. He was so stunned he couldn't speak for a moment.

'Tim?' said Shipman.

'What happened? She was doing so well . . .'

'She is – or she *was*. But she's walked out. Some time between seven-fifteen and eight-fifteen this evening.'

'What do you mean she *walked*? She was semi-delirious.'

'We don't know what happened. The police are out looking for her. She can't have gone far, she's extremely weak, probably got no idea what she's doing or where she's going. Does she have friends in Penzance, do you know?'

'Let me make a couple of calls,' said Tim. 'I'll get back to you.'

He rang off and tapped out Clare and Roger's number at Trevow.

The sofas and the armchairs were burning now. Sara pulled down the burning curtains so they set light to the rugs on the floor. The smoke was making her cough, so she opened the windows to let in fresh air. The breeze bustled in and harried the flames.

She could hear an extraordinary sound. A warbling sound. Like a bird. She stopped and listened. It was like no bird she had ever heard before. It went on and on and on. She looked around in astonishment. It was coming from a strange green box. She shuffled over to it and looked down.

The phone was ringing upstairs as well; the cordless phone on Roger's bedside table, beeping shrilly through the jazz music.

Lynn was on all fours, her breasts above Roger's face, tantalizing him with ice cream smeared over her nipples just a centimetre or so above his lips, always just out of range of his tongue tip.

The phone was getting on her nerves.

'I think you should answer that,' she murmured.

'You answer it,' he said, and pulled her closer.

'Could be your wife.'

'Tell her I mustn't talk with my mouth full.'

But then the phone stopped ringing.

Tim was getting impatient.

Come on, come on . . . Where the bloody hell are you?

He wondered if the whole family had gone to Dorset, after all. He was about to ring off and drive up to Trevow to see for himself, when someone picked up.

'Roger?'

There was no answer.

'Hello?' Nothing. 'Roger?'

Total silence.

'Lynn? Hello? Anyone there?'

There was. He could hear breathing. But more than breathing . . . It sounded like someone gasping for breath.

'Lynn? That you? Are you all right?'

No answer.

'Who *is* that?' he shouted.

She had picked up the funny green box. It had stopped chirping like a bird. Now it was making angry squawking noises. The voice sounded familiar. Why was he shouting?

She was beginning to choke on the smoke. Her eyes were watering.

'Who *is* that?' he demanded.

Why was he angry? Who was she? Who was the voice?

Different worlds, different realities began to collide in her mind.

'I don't know,' she whispered, confused and choking.

'Sara . . .?'

Sara? She knew that name from somewhere.

'I don't know.' Waves of confusion broke over her. 'I don't understand . . .'

'Sara!' he shouted.

The smoke was too much for her. She covered her face. The funny green chirping/squawking thing slipped out of her bandaged hands and fell to the floor and smashed. She fumbled her way blindly out of the drawing room, away from the smoke and the heat. She blundered across the hallway and into the kitchen, eyes streaming.

There was a loud clatter from the other end.

'Sara!' Tim shouted.

But the line had gone dead.

He got another dialling tone and pressed the recall button.

It could not possibly have been her, surely? How could she have got from Penzance to Trevow? She had no clothes, no money.

All he was getting now was the engaged signal. He dialled again – and again and again, but there was no ringing tone.

He gave up trying and called the hospital. Tony Shipman was somewhere in the building but no one seemed to know where. They were paging him but he was not responding. They left him hanging on. No one came back to him. No one told him what was going on. He decided he could wait no longer. He rang off, grabbed his medical bag and car keys and ran out of the house.

His car was in the garage but the up-and-over door was still open. He tossed his bag onto the passenger seat, started the car, backed out into the lane and accelerated down to the junction with the valley road. He sped on past Vera Roscarrock's house and through the bends towards Boskinnow.

As he came onto the straight stretch by the track that led up to Crowjy, something flew out of the dark at him, out of nowhere ... He did not see what it was. It hit the windscreen like a giant fist, one hell of a bang, shocked the life out of him. The windscreen shattered from one side to the other, a wall of frost in front of his eyes. He stamped on the brakes. The car slewed to a halt on the drizzle-damp road surface and ended up sideways-on across the road. The engine stalled.

He jumped out, wondering what he had hit. It came straight out of the night, hit the windscreen dead centre. He took a flashlamp from the boot and shone it back down the road, but there was nothing there – no dead or injured creature lying on the road. He shone the light over the front of the car, over the radiator grille and across the bonnet. Something had struck it with such force and yet there was no blood or feathers anywhere, and not a dent or a scratch on the bodywork.

He got back into the car, smashed a hole through the frosted windshield and tried to restart the engine. He turned the ignition key but nothing happened. He tried the windscreen wipers, the indicators, the horn ... Nothing was working. The electrics were dead.

He did not know whether to run back to the house and phone for help, or hoof it to Trevow through Piskey Woods. Trevow was probably nearer, and he had the flashlamp to light his way. He pushed the car off the road, onto the wide turning space at the start of the track. He grabbed his medical bag and jogged up the track, past Crowjy, dark and empty, and along the path towards the woods.

As he was running past Sara's back garden, he tripped and fell sprawling. It was like being tap-tackled from behind. He fell heavily, face first, onto the stony path and turned his ankle as he went down. He got to his feet. His ankle was so painful it was as much as he could do to stand upright. He wondered what he had tripped on. He looked round for the flashlamp. He found it a few feet away. It had hit Sara's garden wall. The light had gone out. He tried the switch but the lamp was dead.

He hobbled on into the woods, took the path by the stream, and disappeared into the pitch dark.

She lit a fire in the kitchen; lit newspapers that she found in the alcove beside the Aga, and added the bed linen and the clothes that she found in the laundry baskets in the scullery. As the kitchen table and chairs began to burn she went out to the hall. The fire was already creeping out of the drawing room. She lit more newspapers and scattered them around, under the furniture and inside the junk-filled store cupboard beneath the stairs. She took a freshly lit torch of newspaper and started up the staircase.

She stopped for breath half-way up. She could hear music from somewhere – harsh, brassy music.

She came to the top of the stairs and looked around. The music was coming from behind the closed door. She looked down the passage. It all looked familiar yet strange ... Nothing was quite as it was supposed to be.

She went into the nearest bedroom and dropped the burning newspaper onto the bed. She picked up a girl's nightdress that lay draped across a chair and dangled it in the flames. The nightdress caught light. With the nightdress she set light to the curtains and the sheets of brightly coloured paper that were stuck to the walls.

Jo's posters. Rock stars. One poster fell off the wall.

Sara picked up the burning paper and took it into the room next door. She let light to the bedding and the curtains.

At the far end of the passage, she found a pale night-light burning on a side table. And an infant sleeping in a cot.

At that instant, a memory of another life, another time, flashed through her mind. Past and present smashed together in her mind, images flared, showers of sparks in her head, vivid fragments of light.

A tall woman with lovely honey-blonde hair said, *Louisa was a miracle.*

A pretty black-haired woman said, *How did Roger feel about her?*

Thought he was cock of the walk, my dear. Ever so chuffed with himself. Can't think why.

He had the easy part.

Oh-ho. And how.

The infant opened her eyes and looked at Sara, and her face expressed no thought, no feeling, anything. Sara backed away from the cot, apprehension turning to fear, turning to horror. Something was terribly wrong, horribly out of control.

Oh, God Jesus, help me ...

She backed out of the room and stumbled along the smoke-filled passage. She heard the child cry out. She started back down the staircase. She felt dizzy and sick. She gripped the banister rail and almost toppled over. The smoke filled her lungs. Something was burning her ... The coat she was wearing, the green raincoat, it was on fire. She fumbled with the belt and the buttons with her stumpy bandaged fingers. She pulled the coat off and let it drop to the hall floor. The nightdress had caught light too. She pulled it over her head and the floppy hat fell off. She flung the burning nightdress aside. She stood naked in the hallway. So unbearably hot, so hard to breathe.

Upstairs, the child was beginning to cry.

The atmosphere in the bedroom was so thick with marijuana smoke, they had not noticed the smoke that was creeping under the bedroom door.

Lynn was astride Roger's groin and gently impaling herself, when Louisa began to cry out.

'*Lyyyynn . . .*' she heard, from along the passage.

Long pause. And then the same again. But louder. And longer.

'Oh, not now, Lou,' Lyn moaned. 'Please . . .'

'Leave her,' Roger murmured. 'She'll go back to sleep.'

But Louisa went on calling.

'I'll have to go to her,' said Lynn.

'No no, leave her, leave her,' Roger protested.

'She'll only get up and come looking. She'll find I'm not in bed and come in here.'

She eased herself off his body and clambered off the bed. It was only as she reached for her bathrobe that she noticed how smoky it was.

'Pwfff . . .' She waved her hands across her face. 'Worse than the Tinners' Arms on darts night.'

She opened the bedroom door and a bank of dense grey smoke came bundling into the room, enveloping her, sending her falling back in shock.

'Oh, Christ!' she screamed. 'We're on fire!'

She could see the flames licking up around the stairwell.

'Get Lou!' Roger shouted, reaching across the bedside table for the phone. 'Grab Lou and get out! Any way you can.'

Lynn snatched a breath and ran down the passage to Louisa's room.

Roger picked up the phone but there was no tone. He tried again and again, but the line was dead. He threw the phone aside and reached for his crutches.

Lynn ran into Louisa's room, pulled back the bedclothes, picked her up and snatched the quilt off the bed to keep her warm.

'It's okay, don't be frightened,' she said. 'Something's caught fire, and it looks very frightening but it's not really, and we're just going to wait outside while Daddy makes it right . . .'

She hurried back along the passage with Louisa and stopped at the top of the landing. She looked down and felt sick with terror. The whole staircase was burning and the hallway below.

Roger appeared in the bedroom doorway, naked, on his crutches.

'Just go!' he bellowed. 'Go on, before it gets worse!'

Lynn started down the stairs, slowly at first and then moving faster. She stepped on a corner of the quilt that was trailing from her other arm, stumbled and nearly fell head first with Louisa in her arms. She put a hand on the banister rail to steady herself but the paint was already melting. Her hand slipped and touched burning timber. She squealed with pain.

'This phone's dead!' Roger shouted behind her. 'Get Loulou out, then try the phones downstairs!'

Lynn carried Louisa into the kitchen to try and get out by the scullery door, but the kitchen was already ablaze and there was no way through. She turned to the front door but the flames had spread from the drawing room and cut off that side of the hallway.

'I can't get out!' she screamed up to Roger. 'We're trapped!'

'The barn!' he bawled down. 'Through the barn!'

Lynn fumbled her way through the smoke, clutching Louisa tight to her body, and into the old rumpus room, where the air was much clearer, and through the hole in the wall. She felt for the light switch on the wall but couldn't find it. She gave up searching and moved quickly through the dark towards the new barn door that opened out onto the yard.

She put Louisa down and tried the handle. It was locked. *Shit* . . . She remembered, she'd locked it herself, the last thing she did before she went up to bath. She'd put the key in her pocket with the stables keys, and had left them upstairs when she undressed. But there was a spare in the kitchen, on the dresser . . .

'I've got to go back and get the key, my love,' she said to Louisa. 'You stay right here and don't move. I'll be straight back.'

She hurried back through the hole in the wall. The fire was already beginning to creep into the rumpus room. It had now taken such a hold in the hallway itself that the staircase was impassable. She couldn't see the top landing because of the smoke. She shouted up the stairs to Roger but could hear nothing above the roar and crackle of the fire. At least there were windows up there. Even with a broken leg, he could jump if he had to. She turned round to enter the kitchen and found someone standing right behind her. She leapt back in shock.

'What in the name of God—'

Sara was standing in the middle of the hall. She was naked, her body the colour of lard, her legs streaked with mud, her flesh running with sweat. She was staring at Lynn, swaying like a plant in the wind, her mouth agape.

'What are you doing here!' Lynn screamed, and tried to push past her to get to the kitchen. But Sara grabbed her, wrapped her arms round her, and started gibbering. 'Senara, Senara . . .'

'Get off me!' Lynn screamed, and began to panic. 'Get out, for Christ's sake! We're burnen down!'

She shoved Sara away but Sara grabbed hold of Lynn's short satin robe to stop herself falling. The fabric tore, Lynn was pulled off balance, and the two women stumbled to the floor. Lynn screamed and rolled backwards to get away from Sara's pawing, bandaged hands, but her robe touched the flames and flared up. She yelped and tried to pull the thing off, but Sara was tugging at her, still babbling dementedly.

Lynn swatted her away with a backhand swipe that hit Sara in the mouth. She threw off the burning robe, but now the satin basque was alight. She tried desperately to unclip it but it was too tight. She smelt her own flesh burning and cried out for Roger, but her lungs were choking on the smoke. Sara came at her again, like a zombie, blood trickling down the side of her mouth. She pushed Lynn backwards into the blazing panels beneath the staircase. They shattered like panes of glass, and Lynn fell tumbling back into the closet behind, amidst all the burning junk that was stored inside.

Upstairs, Roger could hear her screaming. He had abandoned his crutches and was trying to roll a fire extinguisher from the back of the landing, around to the front, to jet the water down the stairs. As he looked down and yelled to Lynn, he saw Sara for the first time. She was tottering around the hallway, pointing towards the closet beneath the stairs and wailing something incoherent.

Roger started down the staircase, just two steps, and dragged the extinguisher down with him, hit the plunger and aimed the hose down the stairs. But he lost his grip on it, and the extinguisher slipped out of his hands and overbalanced, rolling down a couple of steps and then crashing clean through the burning timber. It plunged down into the closet below, bringing down a cascade of flaming timber behind it.

Roger looked down and could see Lynn kicking frantically to free herself, her face buried now beneath burning timber.

'Lynn!' he roared. 'Lynn!' And tried desperately to find some way to get down and rescue her. But there was no way through – the whole middle section of the staircase had fallen in, and the few treads that were still intact were blazing furiously.

There was a second extinguisher at the far end of the passage, by Louisa's room. He hobbled down the passage, dragged the extinguisher back to the landing, aimed the jet towards the gaping hole in the staircase and kept spraying until it was empty. But it was a waste of time. He couldn't even see down there now because of the smoke, and he was driven back by the relentless blasting heat. Lynn was no longer screaming. She was no longer even moving.

His only way out was through one of the bedroom windows. He retreated into Alex's room and stumbled through the smoke to the window. It was a casement window, about two feet square on each side of a central divide. The wall was over two feet thick and there was a wide ledge. He tried sitting on the ledge and easing his good leg through first and then pulling himself out backwards, but that didn't work. He tried lifting his plastered leg onto the ledge instead but he was not tall and didn't have the flexibility in his hip joint. He managed to get the heel of the plaster cast onto the very edge of the ledge, but it slipped straight off and threw him off balance. He fell backwards, cracking his head on the corner of a central-heating radiator, and slumped to the floor unconscious.

Downstairs, Sara wandered blindly through the smoke, choking, eyes streaming, drawn towards the sound of a child crying. She stumbled across the old rumpus room where the fire had now spread. Flames were licking around the gap in the wall that led into the barn. The new door frame that Roger had installed was already burning.

Louisa was still waiting by the locked barn door, terrified out of her wits and crying out for Lynn. She saw a figure, completely naked, silhouetted in the opening, against the light of the flames.

Sara saw the child. Fragmented images flashed and flickered through her mind. Memories of a stone ruin on the moor, blazing heat against her back. She moved towards the child, picked her up in her arms and tottered across the barn to escape the ever-thickening smoke.

Clare was driving through Boskinnow at much the same time that Tim was limping through Piskey Woods. As she came out of the village and onto the flat stretch of road that curved around Boskinnow Downs, she came within sight of Trevow. From that angle she could see the front of the house, the whole east face. She looked and saw the flicker of fire behind the windows. For a moment she thought it was a trick of the light – the flames from the log fire reflected off the white walls and ceiling. But she could see the same effect through Roger's study window ... And through the two hallway windows on either side of the front door. It was no trick of the light.

She cried out to Louisa, as if the child could hear her from so far away, and drove hard around the downs and up the track to Trevow. The flames had already cracked the glass in the windows and were leaping and jostling towards the night sky. The wind was blowing from the west, pushing the heat and smoke in her direction. She could see there was no way in through the front of the house. She jumped out of the car and ran round to the yard.

Now her panic turned to horror as she saw the full extent of the fire, blazing through every window along the west face, and no one here, no one outside in the yard, no sign of Louisa, Lynn or Roger. She screamed their names, screamed her head off. But if anyone was answering, then the roar of the fire was drowning it out.

Where in God's name *were* they? They couldn't have gone anywhere, Lynn didn't drive. And besides, the pickup was still here. If they were inside, why weren't they trying to get *out*?

She ran across the yard, into Roger's workshop and flipped the light switch. The ladders were stowed against the side wall. They were stuck behind a pile of cement bags, fifty kilos each, stacked six feet high.

She heaved each bag of cement to the edge of the pile and pushed it off, let it fall to the ground, until she had shifted enough bags to pull the ladders free from the side wall. There was a wooden extension ladder that was too heavy for her to lift, but there was a lighter aluminium set too. She dragged it out of the shed and lugged it across the yard to the southern end of the house, beneath the children's bathroom window. She raised the ladder to the perpendicular, pushed up one extension and let it drop onto the bathroom window ledge.

She climbed up. One of the two windows was partly open. She reached inside, released the window and swung it open as far as it would go. She entered head first, crawling over the sill and dropping clumsily onto the bathroom floor on her hands. Flames were already eating through from the drawing room beneath.

She opened the bathroom door. The fire hit her with a terrible roar. She was driven back by the force of the heat. The smoke was so thick she could not even see the landing at the top of the staircase. All she could see were flames, like medieval torches flickering through fog. She held her breath and crossed the passage into Louisa's room.

Her heart stopped with dread: Louisa's bed was empty. She stepped back into the passage. Shielding her face with one arm, she kicked open the burning door into the guest room that Lynn was using. But that was empty too.

She looked inside Alex's room and saw a body on the floor. The smoke was so dense and her eyes were watering so much that she had no idea who it was until she knelt down and felt the plaster cast. She shook Roger and shouted at him, but he did not respond. She grabbed his feet and tried to drag him across the floor, but he was so heavy and she was choking on smoke. She pulled him out as far as the passage but then the smoke overcame her. She dropped his feet, sank to her knees and tried to crawl back to the bathroom for air.

*

Tim was approaching the end of the woods. His sprained ankle was slithering around in thick mud, making every step more painful than the last. He came to the stream and the one-plank bridge that led across to the footpath that curved round the side of the hill. He had to stop for a moment to catch his breath. Now he was directly downwind of a fresh westerly and he could smell the smoke – thick, billowing smoke. He limped on up the hillside. He could see the flames lighting the dark sky even before Trevow came into sight. He saw headlights approaching up the track from the Mulfra road; a car and a van, locals perhaps who had seen the fire and were coming to help.

Now the house came into view and he saw Clare's Espace glitteringly lit by the glow of the flames. He wondered why her car was here when she was supposed to be in Dorset with the children. If she was here, why hadn't she answered the phone when he rang? Dreadful fears began to enter his mind. He limped around the side of the house and into the yard. The light was on in Roger's workshop but there was no one there. He bellowed across the yard – for Roger, for Clare, for Lynn – but all he could hear was the raging of the fire. He saw the ladder perched against the wall and began to clamber up. As he did so, two men came running into the yard. One of them shouted up to him:

'People trapped en thear, ezzer?'

Tim knew the voice. It was the local chimney sweep, Alan Penberthy.

'Don't know!' he bawled back. 'Could be five of 'em here but there's no one around!'

'Someone called the fire brigade?' the other man shouted.

'Don't know! Call 'em anyway! And an ambulance!'

Tim struggled through the bathroom window and dropped onto the floor. He took a lungful of air from the open window and struggled through to the passage beyond. He saw Clare, a few yards away, on her knees, clutching her throat. Roger was lying on the floor behind her. Tim knelt down, draped Clare's arm around his shoulder, and half carried, half dragged her, back to the bathroom. Alan Penberthy had climbed the ladder and was standing outside the window.

'God knows how we're going to get her down,' Tim shouted. 'This floor's not going to hold much longer!'

'You get her out,' Penberthy shouted back. 'I'll get her down.'

'She can't climb, she's almost unconscious.'

'Get her out feet first,' said Penberthy, 'and I'll get her down!'

Tim was not going to argue. Penberthy had a strong back and was up and down from roofs every day. He pulled a small chest of drawers a foot or so out from the window, sat Clare on it, picked up her legs, pushed her feet through the window and helped her onto the ledge. She cracked her head as she tried to duck under the window frame.

'Over my shoulder!' said Penberthy. 'Let yourself go, I've got good hold of 'ee here . . .'

He took her over his shoulder like a meat porter with a side of beef.

Tim took another lungful of fresh air and went back into the passage. But there was nothing more he could do for Roger. The flames had surged around his body and were swallowing him up. Tim took one last agonizing look and retreated to the bathroom. The burning floorboards were already beginning to fall in beneath his weight.

Sara sat shivering on the cellar floor. She was leaning back against the granite wall, holding Louisa and rocking her slowly from side to side, murmuring an old Cornish cradle song that came back to her from long ago. Flames teetered at the top of the stairs and began to spill down. The smoke was getting thicker, the air was running out in the cellar. Louisa was coughing and wheezing, her eyes were streaming.

Sara struggled to her feet, holding Louisa in her arms and moved to the small window that looked out onto the hillside. There had been a door here once but Louisa's careful father had sealed it up for safety. He had blocked it up with hedging stone, leaving just one small window, which he protected with two vertical iron bars, like a prison cell. He had left a tin of paint on the ledge, black paint for the iron bars. Sara picked it up in her bandaged hands and hit the glass with it, broke the pane, and knocked away the jagged glass from around the edges. She put her face to the empty window space and breathed in the delicious salty wind gusting in from the ocean.

She picked up Louisa, set her on the window ledge, and pushed her small body through the bars. Louisa stood tottering on the edge like a drunken toy.

Sara fell back against the wall. All her strength had gone, her legs could no longer hold her. She slid slowly down the wall and collapsed on the concrete floor. She looked up the small flight of stairs to where the fire was spilling down from above in all its savage glory. Come to take her, come to free her spirit from this sick redundant flesh. She wanted to open her arms to it, to welcome it. But her eyes were closing . . . So tired, so very very tired . . .

Louisa stood outside on the window ledge and peered back in through the broken window to where the lady with no hair had fallen down and gone to sleep.

Outside, Alan Penberthy reached the bottom of the ladder. Clare slid off his shoulder and sank to the ground, gulping in lungfuls of air. Penberthy slumped forwards, hands on knees, exhausted by the effort.

Tim clambered out onto the ladder and began to climb down. He slithered down the last six feet or so of ladder, landed badly on his sprained ankle and rolled over on the ground.

Clare was shrieking, 'Louisa! Where in God's name is Louisa?'

Penberthy was trying in vain to open the barn door. He rammed it with his shoulder but his vast bulk made no impression.

Clare was shouting, 'Smash it! Smash it!' But her lungs were scorched and her voice was giving out.

Penberthy hurried to the workshop while Clare ran out of the yard and around to the front of the house. The flashing blue lights of fire engines were approaching along the Mulfra road. She jumped into the Espace, started up and drove into the yard just as Penberthy emerged from the workshop with a sledge hammer. He lumbered back to the barn and began to take huge swings at the door locks.

Clare turned the Espace round and lined up the rear with

the barn door. Penberthy had not seen her and the Espace's engine was inaudible above the roar of the fire. Tim scarcely had time to push him out of the way as Clare floored the throttle and reversed the Espace like a battering ram into the barn door. It struck it at an angle, smashing the door right back off its hinges. Clare palmed the gearstick into first and pulled forwards. Buckled steel disengaged itself from the granite with a painful screeching sound.

The first of the two fire pumps was turning into the yard.

Tim rushed forwards to get inside the barn but the heat sent him staggering back. The fire inside sucked in the fresh oxygen and flared up with all the more fury. Clare jumped down from the Espace and ran to the open doorway. She tried to get inside. She could feel the heat clawing the flesh from her face, she could smell it burning her hair and her clothes. Penberthy pulled her back as a brigade sub-officer came running over from the first fire engine.

'Anyone in there?' he shouted.

'Two adults,' Tim replied, 'and one child.'

'My child!' Clare screeched. 'Get my child!'

The sub-officer turned and shouted to the two firefighters who were pulling on breathing apparatus. The other firefighters were running out hoses. The second pump had pulled up outside the yard.

'Where's the child?' the sub-officer shouted to Tim.

'We don't know!' Tim pointed to the ladder against the wall. 'We got in but all we found was one adult and he's ...' He didn't finish. 'That whole wing's an inferno!'

They could hear the ceilings breaking up, and burning furniture crashing down inside. Two firefighters came thumping across the yard in breathing apparatus.

'Get in there!' Clare implored them. 'Find her! Find her!'

The firefighters moved into the barn entrance, but at that moment the upper floor began falling in and the sub-officer pulled them back. Overwhelmed by despair, Clare ran to the doorway and would have waded straight into the thick of it, had Tim not grabbed her and restrained her with the help of the sub-officer. She fought them, bucking and kicking to break free, until the strength had drained out of her. She sank into

Tim's arms, buried her face against his chest and broke down with wild, shuddering grief.

Firefighters from the first pump were already hosing water onto the west face of the house. The crew from the second pump were fighting the blaze from the other side.

They were all so preoccupied that no one saw the child at first. No one noticed where she came from, but suddenly she was there, beside the barn, bathed in gold by the fire's reflected light, and standing so close to it that she looked as if she might catch light herself.

Clare moved towards her, strangely slowly, as if she had stumbled on a miracle

Louisa was not crying. She did not seem at all afraid. She was just standing, watching them, wearing only her nightdress.

She looked at them as if they were just ordinary strangers passing on an ordinary day. Her eyes were large and open wide. She sucked on the tip of one thumb.

Tim was staring at her, thinking of that photograph in the *Cornish Guardian*, 27th April 1961, and the caption underneath:

DO YOU KNOW THIS CHILD?

LOUISA

Clare and Louisa stayed with Tim that night.

Louisa was the only one who slept. She slept in Clare's arms. She seemed unaffected by it all. Unsettlingly so. Distant, even, as if she had been drugged.

In the morning Tim telephoned Clare's father in Dorset. She didn't have the strength to make the call.

Easter Sunday was warm and sunny. A perversely beautiful day.

Fire investigation officers picked through the burnt-out ruins. They went through every square inch of the house and barn. They found only two bodies. One was Roger's – though they could only tell by the remains of the plaster cast on his leg. The other was female.

Clare identified the serpent pendant that was still hanging from a chain around the neck. The body was formally identified, later, from her dental records.

The Fire investigation team found no other human remains anywhere in the house or barn.

Ron Vincent from Hayle was leading police enquiries. He asked Louisa how she got out of the cellar window, for she was far too small to reach it by herself.

All she could say was: Lady-no-clothes. Lady-no-clothes.

He asked her what happened to lady-no-clothes.

She stood outside the broken window and pointed down into the cellar, to the wall where lady-no-clothes had lain down and gone to sleep.

'But where did she *go*, darling?' Vincent pressed her. 'Because she's not here now.'

Louisa shook her puzzled head, as if he were talking a foreign language.

*

They sat in Tim's kitchen. Tim told Vincent about what he had read in the archives at Stokeland Abbey; the alleged confession by John Doriel.

There was everything and nothing in Vincent's facial expression. There was disbelief, there was suspicion, even accusation, perhaps a smirk of contempt.

'What are you asking me to believe?' he said finally.

'Not asking you to believe anything,' Tim replied shortly. 'I'm just telling you what I read. You can go to Stokeland and read it for yourself.'

'I might just do that,' Vincent murmured. 'Did she read it?'

'Sara? No.' Tim added as an afterthought, 'Her brother may have done. He may even have told her about it. We've no way of knowing.'

Vincent glanced over his shoulder, as if he could actually see the bedroom where Clare was trying to sleep.

'Does *she* know about this?'

'Not yet, no. I haven't told her.'

'Well, do me a favour and keep it that way for the time being.'

'She knows quite a lot about this already. I think she should be told.'

'I don't think that's a good idea,' said Vincent. 'Not until I've looked into it all.'

'Well, you do as you please,' said Tim. 'But she's a personal friend of mine, and I intend to tell her.'

Vincent contemplated the kitchen table, and scratched at something with a thumbnail, as if there might have been a small clue written there, just beneath the surface.

'Did you know that Roger Doriel was shagging the au pair?'

'What makes you think that?'

'It was about half past nine when the fire broke out. Why was he naked when his body was found? Why was there a bottle of champagne beside his bed, in a bucket, with two glasses? And why was the girl's wristwatch on the bedside table?'

'How do you know it was hers?'

'Her mother identified it for me.'

Vincent looked just a little smug.

'Have you told Clare about this?'

'Not yet, no.'

Tim could see exactly where this was leading.

'Do you have to?'

Vincent gave him a long steady look. 'Not necessarily.'

'What am I supposed to read into that?'

'Read what you like into it,' said Vincent. 'The choice is yours.'

Sara Carhays was never found. Or any trace of her.

Crowjy is empty. An estate agent's board leans at a drunken angle at the bottom of the track by the valley road. Squatters and vandals break in from time to time but no one in the valley bothers to disturb them any more.

Tim Hendra has left the valley. He married again and now lives in Australia. He still keeps in touch with Clare ... But merely a card at Christmas, a few words.

He still feels responsible in some way, and probably always will.

Clare and the children live in Shropshire now, in a part of England that has no memories or associations for them.

The girls have coped better than the boys. Jo is like her mother, anyway, a natural survivor. But Ben is withdrawn. And Alex is growing into a difficult and temperamental youth.

Clare will not let herself think about the so-called cycle, about the next time, about what could happen in 2025. Alex and Ben will be approaching middle age. She has shut her mind to it all, has convinced herself that whatever was there, has gone for ever now, that whatever happened is all over.

Louisa seems the least affected by it all. She was so young. She does not even remember Trevow. Yet sometimes, she sits at the piano and picks out a tune that no one has taught her; a lullaby, an old Cornish cradle song that hardly anyone remembers any more.

She has grown into a happy child. She has a lot of friends, but one very special friend that no one knows about; a *secret* friend, who only comes to her at night.

They cuddle together in the blackness. Her friend feels soft and smooth. Her skin smells faintly of lemons. And her breath is cold, so cold. As cold as space. As cold as eternity.